April 2015

Emma,

Than

The Coolest Way to Kill Yourself

Thank you for being one of the cool ones. Please read with an open mind and an open heart.

**by
Nicholas Tanek**

Sincerely,

outskirtspress
DENVER, COLORADO

Nicholas Tanek

WARNING: This book contains strong sexual content, drug use, violence, and extreme adult situations.

This is a work of fiction. The events and characters described herein are imaginary and are not intended to refer to specific places or living persons. The opinions expressed in this manuscript are solely the opinions of the author and do not represent the opinions or thoughts of the publisher. The author has represented and warranted full ownership and/or legal right to publish all the materials in this book.

The Coolest Way To Kill Yourself
All Rights Reserved.
Copyright © 2014 Nicholas Tanek
v3.0 r1.0

www.thecoolestway.com

Cover Image by Melissa Blair

This book may not be reproduced, transmitted, or stored in whole or in part by any means, including graphic, electronic, or mechanical without the express written consent of the publisher except in the case of brief quotations embodied in critical articles and reviews.

Outskirts Press, Inc.
http://www.outskirtspress.com

ISBN: 978-1-4787-0187-3

Outskirts Press and the "OP" logo are trademarks belonging to Outskirts Press, Inc.

PRINTED IN THE UNITED STATES OF AMERICA

For D.

FOREWORD FROM ARIANNA ASTUNI

Most people chalk their past loves and lovers up as "a mistake that happened that I don't want to repeat." Most carry forward, with them, the bad things that they must watch out for, avoid, never fall into again. Loves become like wars fought, a battle field ripe with pain and suppressed memories. Eventually we all run to hide in Canada. Not Nicholas Tanek.

Without pretense or affectation, Nicholas celebrates the mine field of his love. Nicholas embraces, both spiritually and physically, every woman who has ever come into his life. He analyzes, celebrates and above all, loves them for every ounce of joy and pain they bring to his life. He knows that each and every relationship, no matter how short or long, has made him who he is today.

He writes from the eyes of a realist who was once a romantic. Once a romantic always a romantic, but once a realist with a romantic bent, you become someone who sees exactly what is in front of you and loves her despite of it or because of it.

We follow Nicholas through the cockiness of young love, to his first deep puppy love, to secret love, to marriage, and finally to the purest love of all, the hardest love of all, the love that finds you down and out with nothing to offer and it pulls you up on faith alone. For Nicholas, this love could only be ephemeral; a perfect girl whose time in his life is limited immediately by a malevolent illness. Without the normal societal worries or fears, Nicholas throws caution to the wind, and lives 100% in the moment with this broken woman who gives him the love he finally deserves. She makes him whole even as she fades away.

And still there is no anger or pity. Just the story and the empowering understanding that at the end of the day all we have is love- the love we accept and the love we give. Nicholas Tanek understands this and so he is already a success in life. Nicholas Tanek knows this and he offers it up to us in this gem of a book, no bells and whistles, "I dare you to read it," gift.

We can take this ride with Nicholas. We can laugh and cry and get angry. But one question will remain on your lips as you read. Who will be lucky enough to be loved by him next?

FOREWORD FROM MELISSA BLAIR

This morning, I woke up thinking about Lynn. I thought of how special and how wonderful her book is. I think it's pretty close to perfect, about as perfect as a work that embraces imperfection can be. I am not sure how many books there are which can so effectively and repeatedly make you laugh, make you cry, make you cringe, make you ache, and turn you on. Leave it to you to add that one last element to set it apart from the rest.

All of those nights that you read to me over the phone, I was mesmerized. I was drawn in, and I fell in love with these messed up characters as they fumbled through life. I have mourned a loss that was not mine. That is the power of your words. The entire spectrum of emotion is woven throughout this story, from love to loss, from happiness to bitterness, from arrogance to humiliation, and everything in between. At its core, this is a love story about second chances – not just romantic love, but love between friends, and love within families. As you sat down and wrote your very first sentences, I am sure you had no intention of writing something of such depth. I think that somewhere along the way, the tale took on a life of its own and you were just along for the ride, getting it all down as best as you could and hoping to do right by her. I think that you did.

Last night, it was hard for me to get through the last chapters as I wiped my eyes and stopped to blow my nose over and over again. I can barely imagine how difficult it was for you to write it. I'm so proud of you, for what you've done, for where you've been and how you came out of it, and the strength you've shown since she's been gone. A lesser man would have taken an easier road, given in to self-pity and addiction. It takes strength to pull yourself back and settle in to pour out several hundred pages about your mistakes, tell the tale honestly, and create something beautiful. That's the power of love. True love is constructive, not destructive. I think that when you truly love someone, it makes you want to be a better person.

No one wants to be defined by their mistakes. The true measure of character is what someone takes away from their far-from-finest moments. Knowing where someone has been, and seeing where they are in spite of it – that should be the focus. It is more than simply choosing to look past their flaws. It is being able to see what is more important, and in that way being able to accept their mistakes, not just ignore them. The lessons you've learned are worth sharing, and I'm thankful I have been able to share in them with you. I know that some people would not be able to understand that, but that is their problem, not yours. Let them hate you. Be who you are. It's the coolest way.

ACT ONE

The letters on a typewriter or keyboard can be overwhelming for a man who wants to write for the love of his life. Still, I am going to tell her story. Twenty-six letters can create an infinite amount of meaningful words at the tip of the fingers. If you have lost someone you loved, close this book and write about them now. The more time passes, the more the memory fades.

It is 2012, and Hurricane Sandy has devastated New Jersey. I am a 37 year old man sitting in my parents' basement, writing about a woman I loved. Right now, we do not have power, but we have a generator. I am using precious fuel, which is needed to heat our house and keep our food from spoiling, to power my laptop so that I can write these words.

Let's start at the beginning. In the early 90's, when I was 16 years old, I went to my first illegal underground rave in New York City. I took ecstasy and stayed out at the party until 6 AM. I got dropped off at my home, stumbled into my bedroom, and crashed. Luckily, all I had to do was press play on the CD player's remote control. The 20-minute-long song, "A Huge Ever Growing and Pulsating Brain that Rules from the Center of the Ultraworld" by The Orb, was the perfect song for my come down.

Eleven AM rolled around and my mother woke me up and said, "Nicholas, there are three women here for you."

I looked like crap. I felt like crap. I am so thankful that I did not smell like crap, but I am sure I did not smell refreshing. I was strung out from a night of partying. The walls of my small bedroom were covered with rave flyers and posters of bands like My Bloody Valentine, Happy Mondays, Sonic Youth, The Stone Roses, The Jesus & Mary Chain, Pixies, and The Orb.

Three beautiful women entered my room and sat Indian style on my cluttered bedroom floor. I sat up on my bed, Indian style. I do not know why but I thought it was the proper thing to do. In the back of my strung out mind, I had an image of myself as some kind of teenage drug guru. Basically, these young ladies wanted to get high. When I was 16 years old, I was known for writing, getting laid, and getting high. I was the guy that many people thought had marijuana. Sometimes, strangers knocked on my parents' door looking for me to see if I had any weed. (Note to young people who want to get high: Do not do that!!!)

Rita was a young, beautiful Hungarian goddess with a sexy accent like Nico, who sang with The Velvet Underground. I would have loved to have some kind of relationship with her, sexual or otherwise. The issue was that everyone knew that I was trying to court a young lady named Zia, who was Rita's best friend. Rita probably never thought of me in that way, anyway. That morning, she was my connection to these other women whom she brought over to my house. Basically, two women from Spotswood, NJ wanted to get high and Rita suggested that I may have some weed.

One of these women was blonde-haired, blue-eyed, Tiffany. All through her life, she had been told that she was beautiful by many men. Still, she was so insecure that she threw herself at guys to get attention.

As I looked up, a young lady sat in front of me who was extraordinary compared to these other two beautiful women. She sat on my floor wearing a Goth/hippie dress. She had straight, black hair in a Chelsea cut, and these sensual, exotic green eyes. From the floor, she looked up at my young, hung-over face. The way she looked at me made me feel adored. Her gaze made me feel cool. I could not take my eyes off of her.

Rita introduced me, "This is Nicholas."

"Good morning, ladies," I said with an overtired tone, even though I loved the fact that there were three ladies sitting on my floor. With a desperate attempt to look cute, I said, "I have a wild guess why you came to see me on a Saturday morning at 8 AM."

"It's 11:30," Rita responded. "Are you okay? You look like you had quite a night."

"I went to my first rave last night under the Whitestone Bridge in New York. It was a much different experience than the hardcore punk shows in Middlesex," I said with a smile. After a slight pause, I said, "Let me guess why you are here. You want something to smoke?"

"Yes," Rita said. "This is Tiffany."

I looked at the other young lady with the Chelsea haircut and said, "And who are you?"

The girl with the green eyes looked up at me and smiled with a slight blush in her cheeks. She said, "I'm Lynn."

As I slightly rocked in my bed, I said, "It is a pleasure to meet you, Lynn. I am Nicholas."

Lynn laughed, "I know. We were just introduced." She smiled an adorable smile and asked, "So, you like The Smiths? I see the poster of 'The Queen Is Dead' behind you. I love Morrissey."

"Yes, I love The Smiths. I also like The Jesus & Mary Chain, My Bloody Valentine, The Stone Roses. The list goes on and on," I said, without losing eye contact. I tried to flirt with her through looks and smiles as we spoke. "Hey, we should talk. Let me give you my number." I took a pen and a Storm Rave flyer, wrote down my phone number, and handed it to Lynn. "We should talk about music… and other stuff." Although I wished that I said something clever and charming, I figured that less was more.

"Cool," Lynn said.

Rita interjected, "Hey, Nick. Do you have any?"

"I will give you what I have left. It's not much," I said as I reached for the box of an old VCR game. Under the game in the box, I pulled out my stash of weed. The plastic sandwich bag only had about a dime bag worth inside. "Here, you can have it."

"We can pay you," Lynn said. "Seriously, we'll give you something for it."

"Hey, don't worry about it," I replied with a smile. "I'm a sixteen year old who woke up to three beautiful ladies in my bedroom. I think I did alright. I could not ask for more."

The three girls laughed as Rita took the bag from me. They got up off the floor and began to walk out of the room.

"Lynn, call me," I said, "I'm serious. Call me. I would love to talk with you."

With a shy smile and flushed face, Lynn responded, "I will. It was nice meeting you, Nicholas."

I closed my eyes and smiled. Attempting to be gracious, I said, "Oh, the pleasure was mine. Any friend of Rita's is my friend, too."

The three young ladies got into Lynn's Toyota Celica, happy that they took the 45 minute long ride from Spotswood to Edison and actually scored.

Immediately, Tiffany commanded Lynn, "Hey, give me his phone number."

"No," Lynn said. "Why? He gave it to me."

"Well, you're not going to need it," Tiffany said. "You're going away to college. Plus, he's a good weed connection."

"Tiff, you always do this," Lynn sighed. "When Frank gave me his phone number, you made me give it to you. Now, you are with him. You are actually dating Frank right now. Nicholas gave his phone number to me. I want to call him."

After rolling her eyes, Tiffany said, "Whatever."

Lynn did not want to fight with her friend, but was frustrated that Tiffany always went after the guys who were remotely interested in Lynn. With initially nothing in common but The Smiths, marijuana, and a Hungarian female friend, Lynn was interested in me and I was interested in her. I remember listening to "Phone" by The House of Love and wondering if she would call. Soon, the wondering evolved into a wish that came true.

THE COOLEST WAY TO KILL YOURSELF

Love is suicide. Maybe I am being pretentious, but think about it. If you truly give yourself to someone, you leave the life you had behind. Sometimes, love can be like not caring about anything else but that other person. You do not care what anyone says. You do not care about the consequences. Like a suicidal person on a cliff, you just jump. Love is a feeling that is worth dying for.

As a teenager and young adult, I was responsible for actions that I am not proud of. An unconventional relationship saved me. It was not religion. It was a woman. A woman saved me. This is a very unconventional love story dedicated to a woman who loved me.

Before I continue our story, let me give you an idea of who I am. I was born in August of 1975 in Rahway, New Jersey. In many ways, I feel like a kid in a man's body. My wavy brown hair is just long enough that it falls into my eyes but short enough to look professional. Some people think it is annoying, but Lynn loved my hair. I'm of average build, and I have been told I have a decent sized cock. I do all right.

I have always loved women; I am truly in awe of them. Sexually, I am a typical male and I admit it. I constantly think about sex. When I see a woman walk by, I cannot help but to look. My mind races. I think about how beautiful she is, no matter her appearance. I try to see the beauty in her… and I usually do. There is always something beautiful in every woman. I love the female body in all its forms. Most importantly, I love the heart and mind of the female. Men… seriously, we are just animals. Females are human beings.

I am a post-modern romantic. When I was in elementary school, I wanted to fall in love when most boys my age were throwing gum in a girl's hair. As a teenage boy, I became obsessed with women, sex, and writing. I edited and published an independent student-run newspaper called "The Weekly Zoom." On the last day of middle school, my so-called staff of writers and I circulated a filthy, uncensored issue filled with profanity and humorous sexual situations. A janitor found a copy of "The Weekly Zoom" and turned it in to the high school. At the start of my freshman school year, we all got called into the office, certain that we were in trouble. Ultimately, we were not punished because of freedom of speech. I made a deal with God that I would not masturbate for one whole month if my parents did not find out that I got in trouble in school. I had my calendar marked, and could not wait for that month to be over.

My parents are moral and intelligent people; they are good providers and have always been very loving. I was terrified of disappointing them. Dear parents, if you are reading this, prepare to be extremely disappointed in your son. I was never scared of getting beaten or getting grounded. My parents never hit me. I was simply scared of shame. Obviously, I have changed.

I grew up in a middle class family in Edison, NJ. I was somewhat spoiled. My parents gave me opportunities that many people did not have. I put them through hell. Maybe I am not smart enough and maybe I should have known better, but I followed my heart. I was raised Catholic, though I do not believe in or support organized religion.

I started out as a skater boy into East Coast punk rock. I listened to The Dead Milkmen, The Dead Kennedys, Sonic Youth, Violent Femmes, and other music not on commercial radio. I got interested in a show called "120 Minutes" on MTV and found a whole new culture of music. Music is a force that has changed things in my life and affected my decisions. The music embraced eccentricity, and I was eccentric. I eventually began listening to and loving everything from My Bloody Valentine, The Jesus & Mary Chain, The Stone Roses, Happy Mondays, The The, The Smiths, Galaxie 500, The Velvet Underground, Pixies, The Cure, etc. A whole world opened up to me. All of a sudden, I loved a world made of music, art, and film. People like Irvine Welsh, J.D. Salinger, Allen Ginsberg, Hunter S. Thompson, Jean-Michel

THE COOLEST WAY TO KILL YOURSELF

Basquiat, and Andy Warhol were more important to me than professional athletes or movie stars. The very early 90's were an amazing time for unique minds. The jocks were not cool. The alternative was cool. It was a beautiful time to be an individual. I am so incredibly happy that I was not afraid to be unique.

When I began writing this story, I felt overwhelmed, not sure of where or how to begin. As memories replayed in my mind, I began writing them down. I found my rhythm. I began thinking of these excerpts from my life as drops in an ocean. The story begins with the first drop: our first date.

CLUMSY AND ROMANTIC

Lynn called me a couple of days after we met. Instantly, we felt that we had a connection with each other. We talked music, literature, drugs, and sex. One time, while we were talking on the phone, she was taking one of those dumb teen magazine quizzes that determined if you were a prude or a slut. I told her the truth. I was 16 and had sex with several girls. She only had sex one time, and it was far from romantic. Lynn was the kind of girl who never thought she was pretty enough or girly enough. She was taken advantage of by an older guy named Jake, who she had a crush on.

We made a date for Friday night. Me… being an idiot… made no plans but for us to get high, share some witty banter, and hook up. During that time, I was a horny teenager but I was not expecting actual sex. I was hoping for it, but I was realistic and a gentleman.

She had just graduated from high school and was going away to a college in Trenton in a few months. Since I was 16, I did not have a car. She pulled up in her silver late 80's Toyota Celica. I felt so cool that a woman was picking me up and driving me around. Then, I realized, "Shit. I don't have any plans." With a bag full of weed, a little pipe, some gum to make my breath nice, condoms, and 40 bucks in my wallet, I jumped into her car and she drove me away. I made her a mix-tape. I tried to make a stoned out, psychedelic, noisy romance mix. It was filled with songs from Close Lobsters, The Stone Roses, The Smiths, My Bloody Valentine, Psychic TV, Slowdive, The House of Love, and Robyn Hitchcock. The mix was made with the intention that she would listen to it throughout the summer.

We drove to the skate park across the street from my high school. As we sat on top of the half-pipe ramp and smoked some very potent marijuana, I felt like I was in a psychedelic John Hughes film. It was "Some Kind Of Wonderful" meets "Sixteen Candles" meets anything by Hunter S. Thompson. We started to hear noise from other aspects of the park. She was a little scared, but this was my home turf. I took her hands and we climbed down. Without much warning, we walked into a huge party in the park. I had no idea that this was going on, but I went with it.

We talked and mingled. There was a variety of ages and types of people. Since there were too many people, the cops eventually showed up. The entire crowd scattered. Everyone was running away in a frenzy, and the police were chasing after them. I put my arm around Lynn's shoulder and we casually walked away, looking like people who were not guilty. We made it out to the suburban street and walked along the sidewalk. I took my bag of weed and stashed it under someone's BMW. We walked along trying to find Lynn's car. A couple of streets down, a squad car approached us. I put my arm around her waist and pulled her towards me. As the police car came closer, I leaned over and kissed her under the streetlamp. The police car pulled up next to us. We continued the kiss. The passenger window of the police cruiser rolled down as I kept kissing her. I wondered how long we could do this before he interrupted. Her body felt as though she melted in my arms as she gently pulled me towards her. Still, I needed to be smooth. So, I stopped and pulled my face away from hers while looking directly into her eyes. I turned my head towards the policeman, giving him a look like, "Come on, I'm trying to have a romantic moment here." This was our first kiss.

The policeman said, "Excuse me, sir? Ma'am? Were you in the park?"

"No, officer," I said. "I'm just walking my girlfriend home."

"Where does she live?" he asked.

"All the way on New Dover Road. It's a beautiful night and we wanted to walk," I said. I gave her another kiss. Even though we were stoned, we hoped that we just looked happy, not drunk or high. Even if we did, the romantic in the police officer kept him from causing us trouble.

"Okay," he said. "Be careful. There are many crazies out tonight." He drove away. We tried not to smile too hard.

"Girlfriend?" she said. Lynn smiled at me and laughed slightly.

We walked a couple of blocks and found her car. Then, we drove around listening to The House of Love and The Stone Roses while we looked for the place I stashed my weed. Finally, we found it. The night was winding down, so I took her to a place I called "Meet The Pro." It was part of a golf course near my house. "Meet The Pro" was a hidden putting green section surrounded by trees. It was always quiet and off to the side of the golf course. Usually, I went there to be alone, smoke weed, read, or write poetry. There was a bench and painted on the bench were the words: "Meet The Pro." I did not get the double meaning until years later.

My 16 year old hands danced over her clothed 18 year old body. If I was not kissing her lips, I worshipped her pale neck with my mouth. There was an instant connection, but I could also tell that she was nervous. From our previous conversations, I knew that she had some issues with boys in the past.

Let me tell you about Jake, the first of many men who messed this woman's mind up. Jake looked a little like Morrissey, from The Smiths. Personally, I do not like sideburns, but the guy was handsome and Lynn loved The Smiths. Jake was a part of the New Jersey hardcore/punk scene. He was dating someone, but he knew that Lynn was infatuated with him. So, he would constantly sneak off and try to have sex with Lynn. He liked the idea of an affair. Lynn felt like the girl who could only get the guy in secret. She hated herself for that, but she felt that was all she could get. One night, at a party, they snuck away and ended up in a bedroom. Lynn felt swept away while Jake just wanted someone to have sex with. After the foreplay, he ended up on top of her. Her panties were on the floor and his pants were around his ankles. She wanted romance but he just wanted to be inside her. She was a virgin and the whole action began to physically hurt.

After many moans, heavy breathing, and sweat, she asked him to stop. He did not even think of stopping.

"Please. Jake, stop," she moaned. Jake just continued. Lynn started to cry and dug her nails into his skin.

"Stop! Jake, stop!" she cried.

"Just let me cum and pretend I am enjoying this," he moaned.

After Jake was finished, he just put his jeans on and left. Lynn was scarred for life. This was a young man who she had a crush on. He was the so-called cool guy who would not let people know that he liked or even did anything sexual with someone like Lynn. The sad aspect was that Lynn was actually pretty, intelligent, loving, and thought she was in love with this man. In reality, she was just another addition to the list of women he had sex with.

In the past, I have been in situations where I knew I had the upper hand. I knew that the woman wanted me and I could have done anything I wanted. Even in this situation, I never took a woman against her will. I want to be with someone who wants me. I want to make her feel beautiful.

A rapist is the lowest kind of man. After this incident, Lynn did not trust men. I did not blame her.

At the golf course, Lynn and I continued to kiss each other.

She let me know that she wanted to take things slow.

"It's cool," I said. "I love just hanging out with you… talking and kissing."

Lynn said, "That's cool. That's cool of you."

"Hey, I would never want to make you feel uncomfortable. I do want you, but only if you want me."

"I do want you," Lynn said. "I'm… I've been through so many things and I want to take it slow."

"Hey, I'm cool," I said. "Tonight was a little bit wild, huh?"

We both laughed as we got up off the bench and walked to her car. She drove me home and we had the longest goodnight kiss that I could remember.

THE CONTACT LENS WARNING

I met Lynn right around the time when I found my confidence in who I was. When I was 15, I was head over heels in love with a girl named Carmen. Three days after she broke up with me, I slept with another woman. Carmen was shocked and jealous. That changed everything. It was then that I realized that when a woman wants to have sex with you, sometimes, that makes other women want you. From then on, I had the upper hand.

Carmen and I got back together, but circumstances led to severe emotional issues for her. Our relationship ended when she was sent away to a school for troubled youth.

I sit here and look back on the insanity of some of my past relationships and become more introspective every single day. Believe me; it affects the way I deal with people in the present sense. I am kinder. I am more patient. I am humble. I am more open-minded.

When I was 16, I was dating different women, though I suppose that they are "girls" at that age. At that time, I was completely smitten with a woman named Zia. I will get back to that later.

I think of the incident I call "The Contact Lens Warning." Because of all the emotional turbulence that I had to deal with towards the end of my relationship with Carmen, I was looking forward to being with a woman who was a little more stable. Quickly, I learned that no teenage girl is stable. I'm not saying teenage boys are stable, either. Even my parents would constantly twist the metaphorical knife with comments like, "You need a normal girlfriend." Sometimes, they would flat out ask me, "Is she crazy?" I was hopeful that I would not hear those comments about Lynn.

Remember those beautiful green eyes Lynn had when I first met her in my bedroom? Those were contact lenses. Her real eyes were hazel-brown. Now that I think of her eyes, her natural eye color was much more beautiful.

One of the very first times we started hanging out, I took Lynn and her Polish friend Magda into the woods to smoke weed. In 1992, smoking weed was not as socially acceptable as it is now in 2012. We were in the woods behind the skate park and somehow, someway, one of Lynn's green contact lenses slid out of her eye and it was lost. She immediately went into a state of panic. She was crying and shaking. Magda was constantly telling her to relax.

"Calm down," I said. "We will find it. Don't worry."

She cried, "But they're so expensive and we're in the woods! We…"

"Seriously, take a breath!" I said with my hands on her shoulders.

The contact lens was on her shoulder. I picked it up with my finger and gave it to her as if we were exchanging eyelashes for luck.

Right then and there, I was taken back. Her anxiety instantly reminded me of Carmen. My mind started to race with the fear that I would have to go through being with an overly emotional girlfriend all over again. My last girlfriend, Carmen, stole credit cards and stole more than $1500 in cash from her best friend's father. My friends and I almost took the blame for it. She nearly got us arrested multiple times. At one point, she ran away from home. Carmen perpetuated actions that helped me drive my parents insane with worry. Once, Carmen tried to stab me, and she threatened to commit suicide. As I tried to calm Lynn down in the woods that day, I thought that I may have a different kind of Carmen in my life. Would Lynn be more troublesome?

As I write about this many years later, I look back at Carmen with a great fondness. Carmen fixed her life up and now is an upstanding member of society. I am proud of her. She is working in the creative arts industry in New York City. She actually made out better than I did. She's doing what I should be doing.

Emotional women are magnificently and uniquely mind-blowing. They are usually exceptional and imaginative lovers. They are wonderful at conversation. They are open-minded. They are kinky. Right then, I knew that being with Lynn was going to be a wild ride.

OUR FIRST TIME

I was a horny teenager. I still constantly think about sex. To be honest, I was attracted to Lynn but she was not classically "pretty." Sometimes, I had to dig deeper to see the attraction. I am so glad that I had a metaphorical shovel. She began growing her black Chelsea cut to a longer and more feminine look. I liked to think of her as a brown-haired Nico from The Velvet Underground or like Belinda Butcher from My Bloody Valentine. As a teenage male, I was ridiculous in every way. The hormones were raging. My ego was out of control. Though my intentions were noble, Lynn was nervous.

Since I was disgusted when I heard stories of young teenage boys begging for sex, I always tried to keep my cool and not be too obvious or forward about sex. Although I did not want to pressure her in any way, my 16 year old hormones were very adamant about wanting to make love to Lynn. My physical affection was constant and I tried to compliment her on everything from her poetry to the real color of her eyes.

After every one of our many evenings together, we would talk on the phone before we went to sleep. One evening, we had a very affectionate phone conversation. She said, "Tonight was wonderful. This whole summer has been wonderful. It's like we are in a classic post-modern romantic movie."

"I am loving it," I replied. "I love hanging out with you. I love talking with you. I feel like we have known each other for a very long time."

"You know what?" Lynn said, "I think that I am ready."

"What do you mean ready?" I asked, knowing exactly what she meant. I wanted her to say the words.

As she tried to be quiet and not wake up anyone in her parents' house, Lynn said, "You know exactly what I mean. This whole time, what Jake did messed everything up for me. I felt like I could not trust any guy. I feel that I can trust you. I don't think you would do something like Jake did."

"Oh, I would never," I replied. "Come on…"

"I know," Lynn said. "I just feel that I am ready. I think it is cool that you did not pressure me or make it a big thing. Even though I am going away to college after the summer is over, I am glad you did not guilt me into it. I am glad you let me come to this realization on my own terms."

"Okay, alright. It's cool." I asked, "So when do you want to do what you think you are ready for?"

After a slight laugh, Lynn said, "That's for you to find out."

One summer evening in 1992, we went to a party in New Brunswick at one of her friend's houses. We almost did not leave each other's side the entire evening. Of course, we drank and smoked pot, but we were not completely out of our minds. Neither of us mentioned what we were "ready for." We made jokes and flirted with each other.

After Lynn finished a cigarette outside, she found me in a hallway, threw her arms around me, and kissed me. In a dark hallway, a wild party was going on around us and people were passing us by. The voices of the partygoers and the music seemed to fade away as we embraced and kissed each other. She held my hand and we walked into a bedroom. One bedroom was filled with coats. The second bedroom was for an infant. Since three is the magic number, the third bedroom we found was a guest bedroom. There was a made up double bed in the middle of the room and the moonlight shone through the venetian blinds. I locked the door behind me and we began to take our clothes off as we kissed. We tried to hold each other while taking off each other's clothes. Soon, we fell onto the bed and had a renewed feeling of romance that was not limited by clothes.

We made love. I do not mean we just had sex. We truly made love. We looked into each other's eyes as the splintered light from the blinds fell on us. At that moment, we felt a special sexual connection. Sure, it was young and simple-minded. It was irresponsible. It was two people who wanted to turn each other on. It was two people who wanted each other. All of this happened in a maelstrom of naïve emotion.

We left the bedroom to rejoin the party, and we could tell in the eyes of some people that they knew what we had done.

My best friend, Kevin, looked at me and said, "Hey, something is different about you two. Did you two do what I think you did?" All I did was smile and close my eyes, using shyness to brag.

A whirlwind started in both of our lives. From that moment on, we were inseparable for the rest of the summer. Privacy was something that we looked for like junkies looking to score. Backseats of cars and bedrooms in houses that people were not in became our sanctuary. We could not keep our hands off of each other. Among our friends, Lynn and I were considered a couple. We tried not to think about the imminent parting we would have to endure. While we knew we would have to say farewell to each other one day, we knew we had the summer to be together.

WHEN LYNN MET CARMEN

My relationship with Carmen ended after an abortion, a stolen credit card spree, and her being committed. Although I broke her heart (after she broke mine), I will always have a special place in my heart for this woman. She was beautiful, with full lips and big gorgeous eyes. She was a cool young Argentinian lady. After the mental issues and our break up, she started a new life. However, old habits did not die.

Every once in a while, Carmen would call me and our conversations walked that tightrope between comfortable and uncomfortable. During one of these phone conversations, I told her that I was going out with a new girlfriend who was going to college in the fall.

In an immediate change in topic, Carmen asked, "You still smoke pot?"

"Of course I do," I replied. "It's been dry in central Jersey for a little while."

Carmen stated, "I cannot smoke these days, but I have a way to get you some."

"You are selling weed now?" I asked as I rolled my eyes.

"No, you asshole!" Carmen said, "I can get you a plant."

"A plant?" I asked.

"Yes, a plant." Carmen continued, "I was at a very boring dinner and I noticed a huge marijuana plant on this guy's backyard deck. It's just sitting there between two ferns."

"Okay," I replied very slowly. "What are you getting at?"

"We can take it," Carmen said. "Maybe, we can make some money."

"I don't have a car, and you don't have one either right now."

Carmen asked, "What about this new girlfriend of yours, Lynn?"

"Is this what this is about?" I asked. "What are you scamming?"

"Look, I'm bored," Carmen whined. "I can't smoke. I can't drink. I can't run those crazy scams anymore. This will get you some money. Plus, I can get out of the house for a while, meet your new girlfriend, have a little fun."

I asked, "You really want to do this?"

"Yea," Carmen answered.

"Lynn's on her way here anyway," I said. "I'll see if she wants to do it."

"You have to run it by her, do you? You need her permission? She has power over you like that?" Carmen's laughter was condescending.

"Shut up," I replied with a mutual laugh. "Trust me. I have the upper hand in this one."

When Lynn came by, I did not give her an option of choosing not to drive us. Basically, I said, "Come on, we have to pick up Kevin and Carmen."

"Carmen?" Lynn asked. "Do you mean your ex-girlfriend, Carmen?"

"Yup!"

After picking up Kevin at his house, Lynn drove us to Carmen's house in Metuchen. As soon as we pulled up, I knew that this was an awkward situation but I felt cool that I was keeping my cool. I

THE COOLEST WAY TO KILL YOURSELF

acted like it was normal to have my current girlfriend and my ex-girlfriend in the same car to steal a marijuana plant from a yuppie's backyard. To me, it was just a typical day. Carmen looked stunning. The months of therapy and being clean made her seem to have a glow. Carmen and Lynn greeted each other with civility. Everyone acted very mature even though we were about to do something very immature.

Lynn stopped at a convenience store to get cigarettes. Kevin, who was wearing a Charlatans UK shirt that just had the word "Weirdo" on it, got out of the car to buy a drink, leaving me alone in the car with Carmen.

Immediately, I asked Carmen, "So, what do you think?"

"She's prettier than me," Carmen said.

"Don't say that," I replied. "Lynn saw pictures of you and she said that you were prettier than her. Anyway, you know I think you are beautiful." I did not say those words to be nice or to try and keep her in love with me. I said those words because I meant them.

"She's nice," Carmen said. "I like her. I do."

"You know what's funny?" I asked.

"What?"

I said, "Most ex-girlfriends meet the new girlfriend of their ex at a party or a social event. Sometimes, all three of them bump into each other on the street. You're meeting my new girlfriend while we are on a minor heist."

The mission started as soon as Lynn and Kevin came back to the car laughing. Kevin climbed into the car and said, "Show us the way!" I did not pay attention to where we drove to because I was finding songs on a mix-tape I made for Lynn.

"You made Lynn a mix-tape?" Carmen asked. "Lynn, he makes good mix-tapes."

"Yes, he does," Lynn agreed.

The two young ladies talked as if they were friends. They had similar tastes in music and liked the same kind of art. They complimented each other on the clothes they were wearing and talked about buying expensive clothes by Betsy Johnson and Patricia Fields for very little money.

Carmen eventually directed us to the condominium complex and we parked down the street from the actual condo. Without hesitation, Kevin got out of the silver Toyota and said, "Let's do this! Carmen, we need you, girl. We need your slickness."

Lynn asked, "Wait. You are just going to go on this person's backyard deck in broad daylight? What if they are home?"

Kevin replied, "So what? Keep the car running. What is he going to do? Is he going to call the cops and tell them that someone stole his gigantic and very much illegal marijuana plant that he is growing on his backyard deck?"

Carmen got out of the car, ready for action. When it came to being a thief, she was like a Bond girl. She was focused and determined. Suddenly, I had memories of the stolen credit cards she used to buy us thousands of dollars of merchandise. Half the songs on the mix-tape we were listening to were from CDs she stole for me. Sometimes, because she had personal information like the social security number and address from the person's wallet, she actually got on the phone with the credit card company. She would curse them out and persuade them to extend the credit limit. She would probably never admit it, but stealing that plant was probably the most risky fun she'd had in a while. As Kevin and Carmen quietly walked to the backyard deck, I was reminded about a story I wrote about Carmen and I being a con artist couple. This time, Kevin and Carmen were the team of crooks.

As Lynn and I sat in the car, engine running, the obvious topic was brought up in conversation. "I like her," Lynn said. "I thought I would be jealous and feel awkward, but she's really cool. She's very pretty, too. She's prettier than me. I can see what you saw in her."

"She said the same thing about you… being pretty, and cool," I replied. "Anyway, you know that I think you are beautiful."

Carmen led the way with a graceful stealth as Kevin followed whispering funny comments. Trying not to laugh, Carmen whispered, "There it is!" Kevin started to walk up the back stairs, when Carmen stopped him.

"This is me," she said, and walked up herself.

Carmen saw the gigantic marijuana plant sitting there between two ferns. Slowly, she walked up the stairs of the deck up to the plant. She placed one hand at the root. Before she could grab the plastic pot, she heard a voice yell, "Hey!" Carmen and Kevin looked behind them and saw an elderly man looking at them. Carmen looked at the man as her grip on the root of the plant tightened. With a massive yank, Carmen tried to rip the plant from the pot but the roots and dirt just moved the pot around. Dragging the pot on the deck, the dirt began to loosen and she freed the plant from the pot. Carmen looked at Kevin and they immediately ran away.

Lynn and I were listening to the album "Pure Guava" by Ween on her tape deck. Suddenly, we saw Carmen running down a front lawn with a huge marijuana plant in her hand while Kevin ran behind her. The gigantic branches from the top of the plant kept on smacking Kevin in his face. Immediately, I opened the door and moved the front seat up. Both of them quickly got in the car with the plant. Adrenaline was high as Lynn sped away from the condominium complex. The green leaves of the plant blocked the rear window and brushed against Carmen's and Kevin's faces. With the precision of DJ Premier sampling records, I effortlessly changed tapes. As we laughed and came down from our adrenaline high, we listened to "Loose Fit" by Happy Mondays. We pulled into a parking lot of some corporate office park and put the plant in the trunk.

Even though Lynn and Carmen got along, everyone (including Carmen) assumed that Carmen would be dropped off. We stopped to get some food at some fast food place and laughed about what just happened. Kevin loved to act out what happened and retell the story. Lynn, Carmen, Kevin, and I laughed as equals. Most people in our situation would have been uncomfortable, but there was a certain playful criminal charm to the situation. I gave Carmen some cash and purchased her food. When we dropped Carmen off at her house, Carmen kissed me on the cheek goodbye.

"Lynn!" Carmen said, "I think you are great. It was a pleasure meeting you."

"You, too!" Lynn said. "I think you are really cool."

Carmen smiled and waved goodbye. As she walked up those steps, I could not help but watch her legs and her hips. Memories of Carmen and me raced through my head while I sat in the passenger's seat, right next to Lynn.

"Dude!" Kevin said from the backseat. "Carmen looks better. She's acting better. She's not all crazy anymore."

I laughed and replied, "Kevin, Carmen just took us somewhere to steal someone's gigantic marijuana plant from their deck in their backyard. Besides that, I think you are right. She benefited from the therapy."

"I cannot wait till we dry it out so we can sell it and smoke it," Kevin said as we drove away.

Once again, the surreal feeling overcame me. Memories of being in Carmen's house and walking down this street would not leave my mind. Still, there I was with my new girlfriend leaving Carmen's house with a huge plant of cannabis in the trunk of my girlfriend's car.

LAUGH AT LYNN TIME

I was not always very nice to Lynn, and I regret that. I always knew that I had the upper hand in the relationship, and would constantly remind her of this fact. Lynn was known for talking... a lot. There were sometimes when I would just tune out and come back in the conversation without her realizing.

One day, I was on the phone with her and she was telling me this story of which I have absolutely no recollection. Kevin, Ryan, Jamal, Kendrick, and Tim just walked into my bedroom without warning or invitation. The front door of my house must have been left unlocked because my parents would never have let those hooligans inside. I wanted to get off the phone with Lynn and go hang out and get stoned with the crew. She just kept on telling her story. Ryan showed me this gigantic ounce of marijuana. As soon as he opened the bag, the smell permeated the tiny bedroom. Kevin made the smoke weed signal, taking his thumb and pointer finger to his lips. Ryan just shoved the bag in my nose.

"Nigga, let's go! We got izm from Brick City!" Jamal said. His shirt had a marijuana leaf on the front. I was so thankful that my parents were not home. These guys were loud as they danced around laughing with their huge bag of weed.

Kevin asked, "Is Lynn still talking?"

Lynn was still talking. I passed the phone to Kevin and put a finger over my lips, signaling for them to be quiet. Then, I got my jacket and my Airwalk sneakers. Kevin passed the phone to Tim, who listened to Lynn go on about… something. Tim then passed the phone to Jamal, who had to cover his mouth because of his snickering. Then, Jamal passed the phone off to the other psychopath, Ryan. I saw the urge in his face to say something horribly offensive. I looked at Kevin and he saw my worry and motioned for the phone. Ryan gave the phone to Kevin. Instead of passing the phone to me, he passed it to Tim for one more round. This telephone cipher of making fun of Lynn babbling went on two more times. Each time Ryan got the phone, I was worried that he was going to say something belligerent, but at the same time, I thought it was funny. Each time, Kevin quickly got the phone from him. Finally, he gave me the phone and I heard Lynn's voice talking through the receiver. As I put the phone to my ear, there was a pause in her story.

Keeping my composure, I said, "That's crazy."

She said, "Isn't it!?" Then, she immediately began talking more about this story of which I was oblivious to the content. I politely told her that I had to hang up because my friends arrived. All of us laughed, completely at her expense.

In a teasing manner, I told her later what I had done and she was not happy. I remember her punching me in the arm. I deserved it.

THE GROOVIEST DAY IN THE WORLD

Acid is a drug that is guaranteed to create nonsensical cinematic memories. One beautiful sunny summer day in the early nineties, we all told our parents that we were going to Point Pleasant beach. Lynn came to Edison from Spotswood and picked me up. We picked up our friend Julie and then, we picked up Kevin from his mother's house on Stephenville Parkway. Dressed like someone going anywhere but the beach, he walked out holding a bathroom towel and got into Lynn's silver Toyota Celica. We literally drove down the street to a kid's house, John, who was Kevin's friend. We were totally using him for his house because we needed a place to trip out for several hours. We dosed and hung out while tripping our faces off.

Lynn found a kitchen timer shaped like an orange. As she played with the timer, the subject of all conversations returned to the orange timer. John thought it was funny to exploit our absurdity and poured himself a glass of orange juice.

"Ooh, just like my orange!" Lynn said, "Orange juice. May I have a sip?"

In a very creepy way which was typical of John's nature, John said, "I can give you some, but you'll have to molest me first."

Lynn replied for everyone to hear, "I do not want to molest anyone. I just want a sip." While this was not funny or clever to typical sober people, the people in the house who were on LSD thought this was hilarious. All day we kept on saying, "I do not want to molest anyone. I just want a sip." It was the answer to every question asked by anybody. Without logic or meaning, we embraced absurdity.

Now, when you are tripping on acid, doing mundane tasks in public becomes a plan. In your head, you have to plan things out and set yourself up for interaction with other human beings. So you think, "Okay. Okay… I have money. That's good to have money. It's not the 'be all end all' of everything, but it's good that I have some money in my wallet. Money actually really messed things up for many people. People steal it. Countries are destroyed because of the concept of money. Wait! Concentrate! We are just going to the mall!"

So, the four of us on LSD ventured out to Menlo Park Mall listening Happy Mondays, Psychic TV, Spacemen 3, The Stone Roses, and My Bloody Valentine.

We were four teenagers in the early 90's tripping on acid, going to the mall with no intention of buying anything. We went from store to store, laughing and playing with the items. Lynn carried her orange with her. Every time the timer went off, Lynn yelled, "It's time for my orange!" To this day, I have no idea what that means. We purchased these weird bookmarks from The Nature Store. I do not know why The Nature Store was selling plastic bookmarks with kaleidoscopic psychedelic designs on them. We called them psychedelic money. Kevin and I came up with an idea for a film called "Psychedelic Pimps" and the tagline was, "Psychedelic Pimps want their psychedelic money and they pimp out psychedelic hoes." We all knew it was magnificently stupid, but stupidity did not matter.

When you are tripping on acid with like-minded people, you

are in on a secret that the rest of the world does not know. Growing up in the 90's, all aspects of past generations blended together. We were also wacky funsters, like a 90's version of Ken Kesey and The Merry Pranksters. So, we were living in a 90's version of a 60's psychedelic novel. Now, this secret that we had was that we were on a major psychedelic and psychotropic high. Legally, I guess we were psychotic. We were laughing at laughing. Lynn was walking around with the orange kitchen timer. Throughout the day, she repeated, "It's time for my orange!" People around us could probably tell we were high. Dear reader, do not try to understand why we were laughing hysterically. All four of us had the comic timing for witty banter. On LSD, it's absurdist witty banter. The best kind of laugh we had were the consistent jokes that we repetitiously wove in throughout the day. That joke was the secret. The joke was this: Every time we were alone as a group (especially when we closed a door), we would break out dancing and someone would make the wah-wah wakka-wakka 60's/70's psychedelic dance guitar sound. It was the grooviest day in the world.

    Why did I write about this? What does this contribute to the story? What rhymes with orange? It's LSD, does it matter?

A QUICK TALE OF THE SPOTSWOOD FIFTY FOOTER BRIDGE

BDSM and femdom are an important part of this drop, and the whole book. Sex has always been a very powerful and important force in my life. Kinky sex is essential.

Femdom is when the woman takes complete sexual control. My introduction to female dominance was Kim. When I was 13 years old, I met a very sexy and crazy girl in a record store called Vintage Vinyl in NJ. With a Bauhaus t-shirt, black eyeliner and dyed black hair, she was the post-punk rock girl who would probably grow up to be a dominatrix. Kim was a 16 year old woman who just wanted to use me as a play thing. She knew it would have a crazy effect on me and the fact that she could pervert my young mind turned her on. During one summer, she would steal her father's Jaguar and pick me up in the middle of the night. I would sneak out and she would drive me back to her house. Her mother had passed away and her nihilist father was always traveling. I only met her father twice. Every time, he looked at me like I was just another one of her playthings. He seemed to know that Kim was a survivor. He knew that she was in control and I was not someone that would be a threat to her. He was right. Kim always told me what to do and I would obey without question.

Kim taught me what kinky was. Maybe I was too young. Maybe I was naïve. I was her play thing and I loved it. There was no hope of a relationship, monogamy, or commitment. I did not know it then, but that was freeing. She would tie me up to her bed and just enjoy me. She would tease me. She loved the sexual power she had over me and I loved that someone wanted to have sexual power over me. She owned me.

She once told me, "Nicholas, you are a good looking young man. I am going to teach you. You can get laid. Be yourself and be sexy. You will get laid. Go out there and get it. You are constantly horny. Women want to be wanted. In your case, show them how much they turn you on. Women love turning a sexy guy on. Be that guy. Think of me as your sexual boot camp. You will be shipped out soon, private."

After Kim, most girls I was with wanted me to initiate sex or initiate a situation where we could be together. I longed for the feelings of being teased and owned by a woman.

Let's get back to the story.

The Fifty Footer is a railway bridge in Spotswood that is 50 feet above water. The train rarely comes, so many teenagers would hang out on it and drink, smoke, or do whatever.

One evening, after I went down on Lynn while we were on the Fifty Footer, she decided to be kinky and take control. She was 17 and I was 16. I constantly hinted about BDSM and femdom before I truly understood those terms. I would constantly talk about kinky sex and fetishes. Looking back, I guess I thought it was cool to be different. Lynn had a sexual mind, but at that time, she was not ready. During that time, she wanted to be swept off her feet. That night, she decided to try being dominant. The moon shone blue over us as we irresponsibly embraced on a train bridge that was fifty feet above a cold river. We rolled around on the wood in between the train tracks. She took her little pink bra off but kept her Jesus & Mary Chain t-shirt on. She laid me down on the train tracks and used her tiny pink bra to tie my wrists together, then tied what was left of the bra to one of the wooden planks. She unzipped my jeans and slid them down my waist.

What if a train came? What if she could not untie me? Even though I could have probably just ripped that little pink bra at any second, I wanted to give in to the fantasy. She was trying so hard. Then, it happened. I gave in to the fantasy. She went down on me. I came inside her mouth while my hands were tied to a train bridge that was 50 foot in the air. My hands came undone, but it was the thought and energy that counted. I sat myself up and she saw how the bra was untied from the tracks, but still around my wrists.

Everything is relative. Later in life, we both thought this was her pathetic attempt at being dominant. Now, I realize this is the kind of thing that does not happen to most people. As I wrote this drop, I realized how incredible this was. Just when we had caught our breath, we heard the train whistle and we immediately stumbled off the bridge. At that time, I wanted more. I had experienced kinkier things before. I should have appreciated the moment. What seemed like a failed attempt to be kinky, was actually one of the kinkiest things I had experienced at that age. She was just not packaged in garter belts, stockings, and a corset. I realized just how crazy we were. Two teenage lovers could have been splattered by a train that night, and all they would have found was a tiny pink bra tied to two wooden railway planks.

TWO COUPLES IN A ROOM TRIPPING ON ACID WITH ONE MIX-TAPE

Lynn and I were a couple and we became very close friends with Tiffany and Frank. If you remember, Tiffany was there with Lynn when we all first met. She was extremely promiscuous and constantly cheated on Frank. One of the people she cheated with was my best friend Kevin. All five of us were supposed to take LSD together, but Tiffany and Lynn knew that Kevin and Frank should not drop acid together, especially while Tiffany was there. We had just come back from the Jersey shore and dosed. We thought that we had Lynn's house to ourselves, but little did we know that her very straight-edged sister was there. So Lynn, Tiffany, Frank, and I were stuck in Lynn's little room with only a mix-tape that I made especially for Lynn.

In the 90's, a mix-tape was an art form. The pause button and the fade in and fade out were essential. I had a Yamaha receiver, Onkyo equalizer, and Sony dual tape deck. The mix consisted of "A Prophecy" and "In Spite Of These Times" by Close Lobsters, "Don't Stop" by The Stone Roses, "Come In Alone" by My Bloody Valentine, "Pigeonhole (the secret track)" by The New Fast Automatic Daffodils, "The Last Song" by Trisomie 21, and more.

(If by some bizarre turn of events I get famous, these mix-tapes may be worth money someday.) This one I made for Lynn was special in many ways. Each song was carefully chosen and put in a specific order. I even inserted vocal samples from other bands between the songs. Psychic TV had some song called "Loose Nut" which had the sample where someone said, "A thing or two I know about the chief of police makes him my slave!" I do not know where it is from or what it even referred to, but we kept on saying it over and over again. We listened to that mix-tape with a psychotic psychedelic repetitiousness. As Lynn wrote poetry, everyone else broke into hilarious side conversations.

I wrote a poem and showed it to everybody but Lynn. She got frustrated and finally ripped the poem out of one of our hands. The poem I wrote was titled, "A Poem That Lynn Will Never Read."

The poem is as follows:

> *This is a poem that Lynn cannot and should not read.*
> *If you have this poem, do not show it to Lynn.*
> *If she asks, tell her that this poem does not exist.*
> *Tell her this poem is not about her.*
> *Tell her this poem is beautiful.*

She read the poem and growled. Then, she said, "I cannot be mad at you!"

Since Lynn's sister had been outside tanning, she was walking around the house in a bikini. All four of us were in the room and did not want to even venture outside of that bedroom. We were constantly giggling. Frank mentioned something about Lynn's sister being in a bikini. I smiled and laughed. Lynn immediately caught on. She always felt like she was in her sister's shadow. Lynn started shaking. "You want to have sex with my sister!" she said.

I immediately went into "make sure she does not freak out"

mode. I held her face, looked her in the eyes and said, "Lynn. I love you. You are tripping on acid. Keep your cool. I love you."

"But..."

"No. Say it... say it. Tell me that I love you."

"You love me," she said.

"Yes," I said. "I love you."

She smiled at me and quickly kissed me. At that moment, the groovy hidden interlude track from The New Fast Automatic Daffodils began playing on the mix-tape. We all started dancing. The bedroom door was open just a crack and I saw Lynn's sister walk past and peek inside. Everyone else was oblivious. I saw her look in, confused at first, then very dismissive. I smiled at her, half wicked, half drugged up, psychedelic innocence. She saw four teenagers dancing on acid in a small bedroom and laughing at an inside joke that did not make any sense.

ANOTHER TALE OF RECKLESS SEXUAL BEHAVIOR

Romance and danger are intertwined. The danger makes the romance sexier. I once tried to write a story about a woman and man who were sexually aroused by near death experiences. I was going to call it "Suicide Kings" or "Dancing All The Way to the Grave."

Our romance was only supposed to have lasted one summer. When senior year started and Lynn went away to college, we were no longer monogamous. We still talked and were sexual, but there was no commitment.

Happy Mondays, Coil, My Bloody Valentine, The Vaselines, Television Personalities, Blur, Primal Scream and The Stone Roses consistently blasted on mix-tapes in my Walkman. While most of the world was listening to "Nevermind" by Nirvana, I was more into the romantic psychedelic music from Europe. I will admit, Nirvana did help open the world up to new and different music.

I walked down the halls of my high school, flirting with the female students, feeling like a drugged up god. I was going to parties, taking ecstasy, and having sex with women whose names I did not know. I did everything from rolling around the Garden State

THE COOLEST WAY TO KILL YOURSELF

Arts Center lawn with a woman to going down on a woman in the one-person bathroom in the club, The Limelight, in Manhattan. At the time, I was egotistical and actually getting somewhat popular. In the early 90's, individualism and eccentricity were praised. The feeling of doing whatever I wanted and embracing hedonism was the coolest way to live for me.

The ride into Manhattan was a ritual that I always appreciated. The lights of the city looked like an ocean that I wanted to dive into. Every evening we drove in, those lights welcomed me as my mind raced with endless moments that would become memories.

Raves meant that Lynn and I kept seeing each other. Every weekend, Lynn and I would go to a club called NASA on Fridays. NASA was a gathering of New York City ravers that took place inside a venue called The Shelter, right near The Holland Tunnel. We were regulars who were always on the guest list. Our Saturdays were reserved for actual illegal underground parties. New York had more of a techno & trance scene when it came to the underground parties. Jay Dee's "Plastic Dreams" was a NASA theme song for many people. Moby, Lady Miss Kier, and DJ Dimitry from Dee-Lite regularly attended. Dee-Lite recorded "Dewdrops in the Garden" around that time. The artists were approachable and cool to hang out with.

Many mornings, teenagers and young adults would stumble out of a club or rave completely whacked out of their minds on a myriad of drugs. When that sun hits, the glamorous or cool image you had under those psychedelic lights changed into a shambolic and disoriented state. The girls' make-up was always smeared and their faces looked worn out. Every pimple was pronounced and almost throbbing on their faces. Eyes were bloodshot and the pupils were dilated. The psychedelic glamorous evening gave way to the morning reality.

One morning after a wild night of ecstasy and dancing at NASA during a blizzard, we had to make our journey home. This was not the first time we drove back home in a blizzard while coming down off ecstasy. Lynn was driving, I was in the front seat, and Kevin and Tiffany were in the back. The blinding snow fell on top of us and the Pulaski Skyway. I am a music fascist. When I want to hear a song, I want to hear that song right then and there. I put a tape in her tape deck and I wanted to hear the right song. "Don't Stop" by The Stone Roses is a poignant, psychedelic song with magical sound and wonderful sentiments. I was fast forwarding and rewinding the mix-tape I made. Kevin and Tiffany started making out in the back seat. All caution was tossed to the wind and Lynn drove through a blizzard.

As we drove on the snow-covered Pulaski skyway, all hell broke loose. As soon as Kevin got Tiffany's jeans down around her knees, the silver Toyota Celica began to slide as Lynn lost control and we started to spin. The sound of the tires screeching and the snow crumbling echoed. Another car that was speeding behind us passed us and missed us by inches. Lynn's car did a complete 360 degree turn. As soon as we straightened out, "Don't Stop" by The Stone Roses started on the tape player. I lifted myself up and sat back, like nothing abnormal or scary had happened. I looked over at Lynn and she was frozen with shock. Her thin arms were shaking and her hands were clamped at the 10 and 2 o'clock position on the steering wheel. Her cute little eyes were wider than I had ever seen. She was right at the point where she was about to start hyperventilating. I slowly reached over to her and brushed her thin, black hair out of her eyes and pushed it behind her ear.

"Are you okay?" I asked.

She was silent for a while, but then she shouted, "Holy shit! We just did a 360 and we all could have died!"

"We are safe," I said. "We are lucky. We are together."

After that drive home, Lynn and I had that non-showered, "we stayed up all night" sex. We had been candy-flipping (ecstasy and LSD) in a New York City club all night long. We were both sweaty and dirty, but it did not matter. After we had sex, we fell into each other's arms and fell asleep. This sleep was deeper than a typical sleep. Not only was it an "after sex" sleep, it was also a "we were up all night doing drugs in the city" sleep.

That morning we got word that Lynn's friend, Donna, got into a horrible accident during that same blizzard, and ended up in the hospital. After a couple of days had passed and the abundant piles of snow began melting, we drove down to Trenton to see Donna in the hospital. Immediately, we saw how lucky we were because we did not get into an accident. While Kevin was pleasing Tiffany, I was trying to find a song on a tape, and all four of us were high on very strong illegal drugs. During that same blizzard, Donna and her friend had totaled her car and sustained injuries after leaving the same club. Donna had scratches and bruises all over her body, and multiple sprains. We talked with her and comforted her. We told her how we dodged that metaphorical bullet on the Pulaski Skyway when our car did that 360 spin.

After we left Donna in her bed, I drove Lynn home. I finally had my driver's license, and I drove a beige Dodge Caravan. It was a long trip home and the main roads were cleared of snow, but also very wet. Lynn and I started to talk about sex. Once we began to talk about sex, there was a time where we knew something sexual would happen. We would just look at each other, and simultaneously crack a smile. I was driving northbound on Route 1 in South Jersey. She moved my right armrest up, knelt down, and unzipped my jeans. She reached her hand into my jeans and found my half-hard cock under my boxer shorts. I was driving and trying to keep the van moving inside the straight lines of the highway. I could hear the tires on the wet pavement. A seductive danger was in the air. As I drove down Route 1, I actually looked around to see if people in the other cars could see what was going on. Then, I thought to myself "Just drive safe…. Just drive safe…. Just drive safe… and enjoy it."

We stopped at a red light and a woman in a Volkswagen Cabriolet pulled up next to me. I could hear Lynn's saliva and her lips. I looked over to the other car and this blonde Jersey woman looked at me. I gave a shy smile, making eye contact and then slowly looked away. I peeked at her again and she was still looking at me. Did she know? Could she see? Probably not... but it was happening. The light turned green and I drove forward. Lynn started to move faster and suck harder. I could not believe that this was happening while I was driving. I had had many blow jobs already at the age of 17, but no one's safety was ever at stake. There were green lights as far as the eye could see. I felt my body shake. I came inside her mouth as I moaned and breathed heavy. After I was done, I realized that I was going 70 miles per hour on a wet highway.

After I left Lynn's house, I drove home. The highway was desolate in the evening hours. At a mall in Menlo Park, I had to cross Route 1 by pulling off into a jug handle. A convertible pulled up next to me as I waited at the red light. There was a bearded man in a very expensive red Porsche that was in the left turn lane. I was going straight to cross the usually busy highway. I looked over and I saw a man with his head back and his eyes wide open. He turned his head to look at me and I immediately had the thought in my head, "What the hell is with this guy?" I saw a blonde woman's head come up from the passenger's seat. The man smiled at me. The light was still red. The woman's head went back down and he pushed the gas pedal hard. He sped straight across Route 1 and a fast-moving car smashed into his expensive red automobile while a woman had him in her mouth. His car spun 360 degrees. The crashing of the metal and shattering of the windows echoed throughout the winter midnight. Shocked and scared, I was frozen. Everyone got out of their cars. I asked if they were hurt and they said, "No." I saw another car pull over and stop, so I felt alright to leave, since they had help. As I drove away, I wondered why he had the top of his convertible down in such cold weather.

Thinking back, Lynn and I were extremely stupid and magnificently lucky. We felt like we were these horny people who could be sexual and dangerous while the world around us was in chaos. It was almost like a scene in an action film where the star has fire, bullets, and violence all around him, but he walks calm, cool and unhurt. We felt invincible.

As I drove further away from the scene of the accident, I thought to myself, "Learn how to get a blowjob while driving, dickhead."

UNECSTATIC ON E

Lynn was pro-life while I was pro-choice. I believe that a woman's choice is hers. Lynn actually had a bumper sticker on her wall that said, "God Is Pro-Life." Dear reader, things change with time. So, take inventory.

When I was 15 years old, before I met Lynn, I experienced my first serious relationship. Carmen and I had been deeply in love. At first, she broke my heart by going on a date with one of my oldest friends behind my back. At the time, I was very clingy and overly emotional. The tables soon turned when I had a one night stand with a different woman immediately afterwards. Carmen wanted me back. After we began a sexual relationship, we became pregnant, and decided to have an abortion because we were so young. Having no money to pay for the procedure, Carmen stole credit cards, purchased jewelry from various malls and shops, and pawned it at a jewelry exchange. Due to the intense emotional drama of a teenager having to get an abortion, Carmen had a severe mental breakdown. She became a kleptomaniac who even stole from me, my family, and her own family.

Eventually, I fell under the pressure from my family to break up with Carmen. She did not take it well. After a suicide attempt and more insane behavior, she eventually was sent to a high school for emotionally disturbed children. Throughout the years, I have often thought of what our child would have been like. At the time of writing, I am 37 years old and the child would now be 22 years old. Carmen has grown into a completely different woman. I see photos of her on Facebook and see how happy she is with her married life and successful career. Although we rarely talk, my feelings of love for her remain with a complicated purity. Carmen truly is a completely different book, but our experience of having an abortion haunts me even while I write this sentence.

When I was 17, Lynn and I thought we were pregnant. Like any other Friday night, we went to NASA, but this Friday was not typical. We took ecstasy, danced and laughed, but there was that feeling of worry. We had been doing drugs all along. We had no money. We could not have a baby. I was always very much pro-choice, and she was actually thinking of compromising her stance because of the situation.

Kevin could sense our worry. We were not our usual happy-go-lucky selves. We told him about our situation and he said, "Guys! Don't worry! I have money! I will pay for it if you need it." Although money was an issue, it was not the complete issue. The heavy questions were asked: "Could we raise a family? Could we get married? Will I love this woman for the rest of my life?" Maybe Kevin just wanted to keep the party going. Maybe, he truly cared. Either way, he proved to be a friend.

In the chill out room, Lynn sat down next to me while deep trance music was being played by DJ DB. My mind was racing with worry. Even the drug ecstasy could not displace my sadness.

"Hey, I have something to tell you," Lynn said.

I looked up at her. "Yes? What's that?"

"I just got my period while I was dancing. We thought we were pregnant and I got my period while dancing on ecstasy at NASA. I never thought that I would ever utter a sentence like that."

I put my arm around her. As music played and the crowd surrounding us had fun, we sat there with a sad sense of relief.

SHE'S LOST CONTROL

As my senior year of high school progressed, I could not stop thinking of and talking with Zia. She was a beautiful, exotic, sought-after young Russian Jewish woman. Her parents did not want her to date anyone who was not Jewish, but I was persistent. Her beauty was on autopilot. Lynn was attractive, but she never felt attractive, nor did she have Zia's confidence.

Zia was also cold and detached; imagine Ayn Rand, though a painter instead of a writer. Still, her beauty amazed me the first time I laid eyes on her during freshman year. I was in love with her for four years and she was never with a man. I wanted to be her first. Outwardly, Zia had this sweet bimbo quality, though she was actually very intelligent. She had sparkling green eyes, dyed red hair, voluptuous breasts and curvy hips. Her elegant beauty made heads turn every time she walked into the room. Her foreign culture enhanced her sensuality. Basically, I yearned for Zia, and she played with me, acting like I was not good enough. I practically followed her like a puppy dog and was incredibly jealous of all the guys who tried to get with her.

Lynn hated Zia. Sometimes she would say, "I want to hit her with my car, get out of my car, and then hit her with my fists. Hit her pretty little face!"

My friends told me that I deserved better than Lynn. My

family thought I should be with someone who did not do drugs or do anything wild. Even though I initiated a majority of the wild times, they blamed the people I hung out with regardless if I tried to take responsibility and tell them everything was my fault. My whole life was ahead of me, and there was pressure to be with someone beautiful, successful, intelligent, popular, and cool. At the time, only part of me realized that connection and trust is the foundation of love and romance. Still, there I was, caught up in what everyone else thought. It is ironic that I prided myself on my individuality, yet I let everyone else influence me.

One evening, Lynn, Kevin, Amanda and I went to visit a friend named Jeff in Carteret, NJ. Jeff was Kevin's childhood friend. We were basically using him for a safe place to hang out and get free weed.

Lynn and I were arguing on and off all day. We got incredibly high and listened to psychedelic songs like "Teenage Lightning" by Coil. Lynn fell into a mental zone when she heard "Don't Ask Why" by My Bloody Valentine. At first, we were in a beautiful and fun moment of marijuana-induced wit and laughter. Then, we started to bicker.

Jeff and Kevin had just dropped acid. They were both trying to hook up with Amanda. Amanda was a Goth girl with extremely low self-esteem who was a cutter. Kevin was getting Amanda's clothes off. Very willingly, she let him take off everything but her black panties and her bra. As a good friend of Jeff, he actually motioned to him to participate. They were about to have a threesome right before all hell broke loose.

Completely stoned, I told Lynn, "I don't want to be with you anymore. Seriously, I'm in love with Zia." If I had been sober, I would have been much gentler with my approach. "I mean that I don't think we should even hang out anymore. I can't be with Zia and hang out with you."

She started to shake with a mixture of anger and fear. "You act like you're the star of your own movie! All I wanted was a small part!"

"I can't help how I feel!" I exclaimed.

Shaking, she paced around the dark basement room. If she was sober, she would not have been so physically animated. She started to throw pillows at me. She paced back and forth, yelling profanity at me one minute and crying the next. She was truly in a mental state of insanity. Jeff's parents started to get agitated upstairs. We could hear their footsteps and voices during the extremely short pauses between Lynn's crying and yelling. Kevin and Jeff were just looking at each other in shock.

"I cannot fucking believe you!" she screamed.

"Lynn, calm down!"

"Fuck you! Why!? Why don't you love me?" she cried. Hitting me in the chest, she cried, "Why!?"

Jeff looked terrified, like a bunny trapped where two carnivores were battling for territory. He quietly mumbled, "Um, can you calm down please?" Amanda put her clothes back on.

Kevin tried to move in and said, "Look, Lynn. You have to calm down. We have to get out of here." He gave us our jackets. Lynn quickly put hers on and stomped up the stairs. She was our ride home. One rule everyone should abide by: Do not break up with your girlfriend when she's your ride home.

Kevin and I both looked at each other and simultaneously said, "Shit!" We ran after her. Kevin spit out his acid tab. In a rage, Lynn got into her car. Jeff was also angry. He was tripping and he wanted Kevin to be tripping, too. He also had just lost the opportunity to be in a threesome. That would make any 17 year old guy angry.

"I just lost my trip!" Jeff said in frustration.

Amanda, Kevin and I jumped into the car, worried for our lives. Since we were high, the worry quickly faded to the back of our minds. Lynn turned the key in the ignition and drove off right

THE COOLEST WAY TO KILL YOURSELF

as I closed the passenger's side door. Kevin and Amanda immediately started taking their clothes off. I could hear the saliva as their lips smacked against each other. I tried not to focus on Lynn's crying. Lynn sped down a suburban road with a 25 mile an hour speed limit, easily doing about 55 miles per hour. I glanced behind me and saw that Kevin had his face in between Amanda's legs. I turned my head quickly and saw a blur as I suddenly heard and felt a jolting crash. Lynn had hit an open door of a parked car and just continued to drive. Kevin's head popped up from under Amanda's dress. Just so you know, that was the third time in my life that I had been in some kind of car accident where Kevin either had his fingers or his tongue inside of a woman while in the backseat.

"What the hell did you do!?" I yelled.

"Oh my God, Lynn!" Amanda exclaimed. "You hit a car!" Kevin tried to go back down on her but she pushed his head away. "You took the door off the car!"

"I don't know!" Lynn screamed in panic. "What the fuck did I do? What do I do? What do I do!?"

"Pull over! Calm down," I begged.

We got to Inman Avenue in Woodbridge when we were pulled over by the police. Kevin had LSD in his system. We had all been drinking and smoked an abundant amount of marijuana. The cop walked over to the car and shone the flashlight inside.

Lynn was sobbing. "Please officer! I'm sorry. I did not know what to do! I panicked! I'm so sorry!" Maybe it was the drugs, but everything went by very quickly. Now that I think about it, I cannot even remember if he had pulled her over for speeding, or if it was actually because of the parked car she hit. He wrote a ticket and a report and let us go.

We went back to my parents' house and quickly went into my bedroom. Lynn was crying and we had this uneasy energy which led to a loud, panic-stricken argument, very late at night. My parents woke up and asked what was going on. Lynn called her parents. Immediately, her father drove to my house as she began to argue with her mother over the phone. When Lynn's father arrived at my house, she did the walk of shame down the driveway.

Lynn's father, who is normally a very gentle and kind man, yelled, "Get in the car!" He had every right to yell at her. She was crying her eyes out as she climbed into her own car, and her father followed her home.

The next day, we found out that Lynn actually took the entire door off of a parked pick-up truck. She had to go to court, plead guilty, and pay for the damages. Once again, our passion, anger, and our stupidity of drug use could have killed us or someone else. In the circle of friends, the story became a legendary tale of teenage insanity. I am so surprised no one was taken off to jail.

I have done many selfish and stupid things in my life. Breaking up a relationship in this way was one of the many idiotic actions that I have done. Every action has a reaction. The next day, I talked to Kevin and he told me that he did not have a good night. Taking acid, getting in a car accident while performing cunnilingus, and almost getting arrested does not make for a good acid trip; memorable, but not necessarily good. He spent the rest of the night alone in his room, crying while listening to Slowdive.

THE MOMENT

By this time in my life, I was deep into the New York City rave scene, and had a reputation for having sex with women, but more dangerously, doing drugs. However, I was a decent student who actually did pay attention in class… most of the time. I had just finished taking a pre-calculus quiz. Since I finished the pre-calculus test early, I decided to use the bathroom. As I walked down the hall, I worried a little about the physics test that I was going to take a couple of periods later that day. When I walked into the boy's room, I immediately smelled marijuana. I looked around and did not see anyone in the bathroom. The stalls were open and empty.

"Oh shit!" I said out loud to myself. "I have to get the hell out of here!" I immediately walked out and went back to class. I still had to urinate.

When I was sitting in class, a security guard came to the door. Clyde was this gigantic security guard who looked like Michael Duncan Clark from the film "The Green Mile." He took me down to the office. There was another kid there who was crying his eyes out. His eyes were bloodshot red. We both were accused of smoking weed in the boy's bathroom. Now, I've done some crazy actions in the past. I have been high while I was in school. I came to the first day of my senior year drunk on St. Ides. I have taken acid and tripped the whole day thinking about "Music" by The New Fast Automatic Daffodils. I understood that I had a reputation, but I was not stupid enough to smoke weed in a high school bathroom.

The nurse was brought in to check both of us out. She looked me right in the eyes and said, "You're sober, honey."

That was not good enough for the vice principal. They called my father, who worked from home, and he came down to the school. Now, my mother used guilt to discipline me, but I was terrified of my father. His yelling could make the windows shake. Even though I was innocent, I was guilty in their eyes. Still, because I was known for being one to get wild with the illegal substances, the school wanted a drug test.

In rave culture, many times popular logos were tweaked. For example, a friend of mine made a shirt that had the Dunkin Donuts logo changed to "Fuckin' Donuts." It was funny. (Dunkin' Donuts actually sent the guy a cease & desist letter.) Many rave flyers would have the logo of a package of EZ-Widers, but it said "NASA." Every product you could think of was lampooned from Evian Water to Bazooka gum.

The vice principal left his office and came back in and said, "Can I see your shirt?" My shirt bore the Slush Puppy logo and on the cup, it said, "Fug Tup." Being accused of smoking weed in a high school bathroom wearing a shirt that said "Fug Tup" did not help plead my innocence.

The school demanded a drug test, so I went down to the local medical center. Feeling like a dirt bag, I sat in the waiting room next to my parents as they angrily flipped through magazines. Eventually, I was called in, and finally, I got to urinate.

It was Friday night and there was a very cool party in Edison that I wanted to attend. I was 17 years old and I was not allowed to go. I sat alone in my room listening to "Yes Please" by the Happy Mondays.

Saturday was a different tale. Lynn picked me up and we went to the Evolution Vibe Tribe rave in Queens. Donna, Lynn and I took pure MDMA. I was trying to act cool, but my mind was going crazy with worry. The day before I took the drug test, I took bong hits with Kevin. I knew that I was going to test positive for marijuana and who knew what else. I had an awful feeling of dread, like it was my last night of freedom before going to some kind of suburban prison. Lynn and Donna sensed my worry. They sat me down, one woman on each side of me. Their arms were around me. The ecstasy kicked in with an elegant intensity. Our arms just felt like they melted into each other's bodies. We put our heads together in the center. This was not sexual, but it was real. Our respect and admiration for each other danced together in what felt like a blissful, out-of-body experience. We all peaked together, holding each other.

"Do you feel this moment?" I asked, in complete awe of the beautiful act of friendship.

"I feel this moment. This is an absolutely incredible moment," Lynn said.

Donna said, "I fucking love this moment!"

My dear reader, I know we were high. Just because we were completely out of our minds on illegal psychotropic drugs does not mean our emotions were void. Each one of us took something out of that moment. We were each different people. It was not just consciousness change through drugs, it was also consciousness change through love and friendship.

The New York City Fire Department shut the illegal warehouse party down. Dante, one of the leaders and DJs of The Evolution Vibe Tribe looked absolutely devastated. I called out, "Dante! You did a wonderful thing tonight! This was an absolute classic party."

As the weekend closed, and Monday came around, I felt a sense of impending doom. I would not only be in trouble with my parents, but I could get expelled or suspended. Lynn made everything normal for me over the weekend. Taking E in Queens was my norm. She took my mind off the stress with sex and late night phone conversations. Our conversations were dances of a post-modern suburban romance. We were no longer boyfriend and girlfriend, but our friendship was still there, a strong connection beneath the layers of sex and drugs. There was a special level of trust between us, and I knew that I could depend on her. I could cry in front of her. I could be a disgrace in front of her. At the time, I did not appreciate that.

On Monday morning, my mother woke me up and told me, "Nicholas, we got the results." I did not even ask. I knew they were going to label me as guilty. I knew I would be positive for illegal drugs. I knew I would get in trouble in school and would have to live in a house where I was considered a horrible son.

My mother said, "The test came back negative for everything."

I could not believe the news. I wanted to say, "What? Are you sure?" but I stopped myself. So, I just said, "See! I told you."

KLASS TRIP

Lynn and I loved writing and we ran in the circles of young, creative writers. That may sound cool, but it really was just groups of teenagers who acted like they were poets and novelists. What is worse than a pretentious poet? Is there any other kind of poet?

I went to something called Arts High School. I had to audition and I made the cut. Once a week for 3 years, I was taken out of my high school and went to a special program that promoted creative writing. It was a wonderful and inspirational time. In the school, there were actors, dancers, painters, and more. I made new friends and learned about the artist lifestyle. This led to me getting published in some very minor anthologies. Some of the girls liked me, too. I loved it. Many of the poems and stories I wrote were not written well, but the subject matter was unique. I wrote about heroin in the suburbs, cunnilingus, and romantic evenings. It was the John Hughes film quality that many of the girls seemed to like. I thought of myself as a young poet, but I truly tried hard to not be considered pretentious. Instead of being a young teenage poet who just destroyed everyone else's writing with harsh comments, I tried to embrace their creativity and had a genuinely positive attitude. I always tried to have wit in my criticism, which I think made me easy to be around.

The other students seemed to like me, and I loved being around creative people.

Lynn felt that her writing was never worthy of publication. She was in the situation that I was in with music. I absolutely love music and would love to be a unique, importantly creative and innovative musician, but I am not a talented musician. I cannot do what Kevin Shields (My Bloody Valentine), John Squire (The Stone Roses), Lou Reed (The Velvet Underground), or Jimmy Page (Led Zeppelin), does with a guitar. I cannot produce music like Brian Eno or Martin Hannet. I can appreciate and enjoy their art. Lynn felt that although she could not write like Oscar Wilde, J.D. Salinger, Allen Ginsberg, or Hunter S. Thompson, she could enjoy their work and be a part of the group of people who loved their work.

There was a young Filipino man in the rave scene named Ernesto who came from an upper-class family. He was a down-to-earth guy who I knew would go far in life. He probably was considered a nerd in school, but he was considered a genuinely decent and intelligent person in the scene. We had long talks about films, writing, art, and drugs. He wanted to start a magazine for rave culture. At that time, "Project X" was the only New York City magazine that represented New York night life culture. In Ernesto's magazine, there were articles about handling yourself when you were going to take ecstasy, advertisements for psychedelic party lighting companies, music reviews, and a new poetry section. Lynn and I both submitted poems to the magazine. One of her good friends, Donna, also submitted a poem. My poem was about Zia. I wrote it to the melody of "3rd Generation Liquid Song" by The House of Love. It was a collage of cool sounding phrases mixed with emotions of love and adoration for Zia.

THE COOLEST WAY TO KILL YOURSELF

"Poem for the Liquid Girl"

"Drop a grain of doubt from celestial purity,
The soul in the eyes and the angel in hands.
Our time of dreaming will last in thought forever,
And the earth is within you,
And the walls crumble down,
You cover up your eyes.
And a life in a thought,
Breathes heavily though the day.
Your eyes will be closed.
Clean air and red hair are in front of a light blue sky.
There is such perfection in the back of your neck.
Your arms never seem to reach out with faith.
There are perils in wisdom and cruelty in lips.
The moral hands so still.
The liquid flows too quick.
You cannot see clearly.
And the clouds form shapes
And the sun peeks through
Your eyes will be dry.
The laugh of your mouth and the wonder of your thinking
Puzzles the ego and drains the confidence.
The look for the future and the interest in others
Is a simple acceptance to a jigsaw of words.
With the days that last
And a moment which fades,
Your eyes will be burned.
But clouds drift on
And substance fades away.
I'll never be blind."

NICHOLAS TANEK

In the early 90's, we were at a rave called "Essence" in Long Island, NY. It was a huge party with more than a thousand people. The boxes of Ernesto's magazine arrived with his entrance and we all crowded around them. We felt as if we were musicians and our debut album was in our hands for the first time. Each of us got copies and we flipped through the pages. Somehow, I found my published poem as soon as I opened up the magazine. I had my own page and an illustration. Lynn's friend, Donna, had half a page with her poem about thrift store rave culture fashion. Lynn turned every single page, looking for her poem. After she went through the entire magazine, she started over and flipped each page, searching for her poem. There was a horrible poem called "Shake Your Fat Ass" by Anonymous. They could have published her poem instead of a very juvenile rant about shaking your dancing ass. As soon as Lynn realized that she did not get published, she immediately started to cry. I tried to console her. I hugged her but she pushed me away.

One of her other friends, named Potato Chip, tried to tell her, "It's only a little magazine! It's just a zine!" The point was that she felt that her creativity, her work, was not good enough to be published, even in a tiny zine. She felt that the work of her friends was better than what she created.

When I tried again to console her, she said, "I'm upset because most importantly, you wrote something for Zia! Your work, which I fucking love, is for Zia! No one is ever going to write something for me. No one! Why can't I be the one someone loves and writes something for? I mean nothing. I mean, what you wrote was beautiful, but it was for Zia! Why can't anyone write something good, something beautiful, for me?"

Now, my timing is off. Maybe, it's too late. I sit here, writing this in my parents' basement in 2012. As I began writing, I slowly began to change. I have become obsessed with telling this story. I have to finish it. All day at work, it's all I can think about. It's all

THE COOLEST WAY TO KILL YOURSELF

I talk about. I sometimes talk to my friend, Melissa, from North Plainfield. She's much younger than I am, and has led a completely different life. I find myself amazed as I read excerpts to her. I realize that even though I have not travelled the world or made a fortune, I lived a very full life and felt love in that life, and that is what is important. My trusted friend, I am writing this for the girl who felt that no one would ever write something for her.

THE HEROIN INTRODUCTION

Many of the artists and musicians whom I appreciated had been heroin addicts. Such artists include Spacemen 3, Spiritualized, Primal Scream, The Velvet Underground, The Brian Jonestown Massacre, Television Personalities, and Jean-Michel Basquiat. I had a fascination with heroin. Maybe I thought it would make me a better writer. Maybe I was just looking for a beautiful high. I was 17 years old the very first time I did heroin. I went from being a happy, stoned out, post-psychedelic suburban teenager who wanted to be a writer to a dark-minded young adult who entered a world of gritty desperation.

Edison is a large town in New Jersey. Most of the town is a mixture of middle-class white, Asian, Black, and Indian people. Only 10 minutes away, there is an impoverished city called Plainfield. Being dumb suburban white kids, we would venture over there to either a place called The Hill or an apartment complex we called The Bricks. In the 90's, they would sell drugs right in front of everyone. Sometimes, there were Black middle school kids selling it. They could smell the fear of the rich, spoiled white kids. A quick flash of a gun and the money could be stolen. Although I was one of those young, dumb, naïve kids, I soon became friendly with some of the dealers. Eventually, I ended up playing the card game Spades with them. I was not scared of being mugged or shot, and I think they respected that.

The first time I tried heroin, the cellophane bag had a stamp that said, "9 ½ Plus Up." That name was actually synonymous with Christopher Columbus Housing Projects in Paterson, NJ. That first time I tried it, I could not drive my minivan. My friend Ian drove me and our friends around. After I sniffed some of the brown powder in the bag with a little cut straw we called a "clicker," a warm wave slowly and calmly flowed through my body. I started to see double. I touched my face and my skin felt so amazingly soft. The color of my flesh faded as if I did not have blood in my veins. I looked in the mirror and thought my skin looked translucent. The first thought in my mind was "I am going to die." Immediately, I actually felt a comfort in those words. We stopped at the library and I vomited right on the brick wall. I continuously vomited that evening.

I ran into a friend of mine named Dave and I told him what I did.

He told me, "Wow. Nicholas, that's not you. You are usually outgoing and lively. This is different. This is not you." Little did he know how much it would become me.

The problem with Plainfield was that it was expensive. Most bags were $15. I had a friend named Cindy who went to my high school and was very popular in the Edison drug scene. She was my first connection to getting good dope.

Lynn and I had to get tickets in New York City for an event called Maskarave. Cindy and Kevin came along so we could make a stop in Spanish Harlem. Cindy always said, "I'm Black. There's always a better chance that we won't get robbed if you are with me. Let me handle it." We totally believed her at the time. Later, I found out she did that because she wanted to get her hands on the fatter bags. Being white middle class, I was scared of, yet fascinated with, ghetto culture. The acceptance of different races and cultures as it is today seemed like it was still only just beginning back then. As I write this, Barak Obama is the first Black president of the United States. In the 90's, that concept seemed impossible.

We stopped and got bags of "Good O" while listening to the song, "Oodles of O's" by De La Soul. I doubt they were rapping about selling dope, but we let the song mean that for us.

Lynn did not do heroin that night; in fact, she was very much against it. She was definitely exposed to the culture though. She only wanted to smoke weed, drink, and do LSD or ecstasy. Because she had a very addictive personality, she was scared of the hard drug lifestyle and the temptations involved with it. She constantly smoked cigarettes, and wanted sex as often as possible. When she liked something, she wanted it often.

At the time, I was not addicted to heroin. I was just trying it every once in a while, as I was that happy-go-lucky guy who liked psychedelic drugs and loved being one of the people who contributed to the good time at the party. Soon, many of my friends stopped going to raves or going to the city. Instead, they were making runs to Plainfield, Newark, or Harlem. Then, they would hide in their rooms together and either smoke cocaine or get doped up on heroin. A dark cloud was forming over central Jersey.

AN EARLY 90'S NEW YEARS EVE

Regardless of race, creed, culture, or location, New Year's Eve is always a memorable evening. By this time, I had a job parking cars at a country club in Westfield, NJ. I had to fill in for one of the parking valets and got paid double the usual rate. We had tickets to a New Year's Eve party at the Limelight in New York City. Lynn and Donna went to my house to pick me up. I had to stay late at work, until after midnight. Any man with a sense of romance knows that you want to kiss someone at midnight. I missed that chance. When midnight came and the ball dropped, Lynn and Donna sat in the family room watching it on television with my parents, while I was opening doors for wealthy Jewish golfers. I rushed home as soon as I could. When I came home, I could tell that Donna was angry because she wanted to be on the dance floor in New York City's Limelight at the magical time. Instead, she was hanging out with my parents. Donna was wearing a very large red fuzzy hat that looked like it was from Alice in Wonderland. Previously, I had told Lynn to go without me, but she wanted to wait. That always meant something to me.

We rushed to Manhattan in her silver Toyota Celica listening to "Dewdrops in the Garden" by Dee-Lite. Although the New

York City skyline still held that magical ocean of lights, I felt the waves were getting choppy. As soon as we got to the Limelight, we saw a huge crowd. The fire marshal broke the party up because there were too many people. Fifth Avenue was filled with hundreds of teenagers and mid-20's hipster douches that were peaking on ecstasy.

Someone shouted, "Party is moving to Caffeine!"

We just scored several tabs of E and decided to go to Caffeine in Long Island. We took the long drive there and arrived before most people showed up. It was so early that the DJs did not arrive yet. Since it was an emergency back-up party, someone had just put on an album to play. When we walked in, they were playing an album by The Orb.

A bad trip is a mind-splintering and spirit-shattering experience. Someone once told me that every time you take acid, you are legally insane. From the beginning, the vibe was creepy, awkward, and scary. These leftover party-goers dropped acid and E in glamorous Manhattan, and then they were thrown into a cool, but not glamorous, club in Long Island. The vibe was instantly negative. We tried to stay positive, but every room we went to, the vibe was just off. We even went outside into this bus where people would hang out.

Someone said the most horrible words you can say if you are tripping: "We will all have a bad trip." I do not remember if it was Lynn, Donna, or me. We tried so hard not to go into this psychedelic downward spiral into mental agony. Conversation after conversation, someone stopped the flow and said, "We're having a bad trip." We all said it at different times. We were all guilty of making a tense situation worse. Then, I noticed that we all used the term "we," not "I." That made the difference.

The ride home was an emotional nightmare because we thought that the car would crash or break down. At the time, my best friend Kevin started to do heroin more and did not come out to the city anymore. I was worried about him. The E that was on the New York streets was cut with heroin more and more. Since I knew that I had this unhealthy fascination with heroin, I was terrified. My mind was racing. I saw how I would mess my life up and I felt like I could not stop it even if I tried. It was going to happen. I knew I was out of control and I was horrified of myself.

All three of us crashed at Lynn's house. Her parents were always away at the Poconos for the weekend. Donna just wanted to hang out. We did not want her there. Lynn and I were crying softly, vulnerable and holding each other. She told me all of her worries.

"You are going to leave me! You are going to completely leave me for Zia! You are going to leave me for someone prettier, someone cooler! You are beautiful and you are going to want to be with someone beautiful! I'm going to end up alone because I'm ugly and too emotional!" Lynn wailed.

"I am a failure!" I said. "I'm a shallow asshole but I truly want to be a good person! I disappointed everyone who loves me! My parents do not deserve to have such a horrible son!"

Donna cried, "I am no one! I am insignificant because no one loves me!"

Lynn and I had the kind of sex that people have when it is the only thing they can do to feel better. We were terrified of the oncoming day and days to come.

Eventually, Lynn and I fell asleep in each other's arms. When I woke up, I saw Donna sleeping on the floor at the edge of our bed. Had she been there the whole time? When we woke up, we were all normal again, but weathered. Ctrl-Alt-Delete. It was like someone hit the reset button on our emotional state. Disheveled, dirty, and mentally burnt, we all went our separate ways that morning, but with an understanding.

At the time, we were foolish and reckless. We took those drugs because we wanted a fun, interesting, and psychedelic experience.

NICHOLAS TANEK

We knew the risks. Looking back, we shared a beautiful vulnerability. As teenagers, vulnerability is not cool. Vulnerability is ugly. Everyone loves a confident and beautiful person. Crying makes people not want to be around you. When someone honestly wants to comfort you when you are crying, that person loves you. When both of you can cry together, you love each other.

LYNN'S PARTY

One week, I went on a family vacation to California. While I was gone, Kevin brought a bunch of the younger pot-smoking crew from high school to a party at Lynn's house. The crew was unofficially called "The Grundles."

When I came home, I knew something was different. I knew that Kevin, my best friend since 6th grade, had a secret. I flat out asked him, "Did something happen with you and Lynn at that party?"

He lied and said, "No."

At that time, I did not know for certain what was going on. Later, Kevin and Lynn told me about a phone conversation they had.

"Lynn," Kevin pleaded. "He's my best friend. Don't tell him!"

Lynn said, "I think it's alright. We don't have to lie."

Kevin responded, "I bragged about it to The Grundles. He's going to find out."

"It's okay," she said. "He probably does not care. He's too obsessed with Zia and his other sluts."

Kevin pleaded, "Seriously, he's my best friend. I'm not scared of him or anything, but he cannot find out. I never lie to the guy, but I did this time. I told him nothing happened. It was like he just knew."

Lynn responded with that matter-of-fact voice, "That's funny. Nicholas is like that. He's a sexual Sherlock Holmes. Kevin, listen to me. It does not matter anyway. Nicholas and I are not together. He gets with other women. He's not in love with me. I have accepted that. "

A couple of days passed and I felt like I was a sort of lie detection puppet master. I started talking on the phone with Lynn a little more than usual, but for the wrong reasons. My friends were hiding something from me and I wanted to know about it. I almost did not care what it was they were hiding. The fact that they were hiding something was driving me crazy.

One evening, Lynn and I were lightly flirting and I navigated the conversation to the party that occurred when I was in California.

"Come on," I said. "What happened?"

"What do you mean?" Lynn asked.

"I know my friends. You know how I feel. What is up? Did you have sex with Kevin?"

"No!" she said with complete honesty and a little disgust.

"What happened?" I repeated, knowing that my tone of voice and my upper hand in the relationship would cajole her to tell me anything.

"Well…"

"What happened? Come on, you know my stance. We're not together. You know that Zia and I are getting closer. Tell me."

"Yes, something happened."

"What was it?"

"Well…" she began in that confessional tone. "You know that I had a party in my parents' house. Kevin knew I was upset because of you. Look, let me get this out. You broke up with me. I was upset. He kept on telling me to forget you and move on. Eventually, we ended up in the car while the party was going on."

"Just tell me what happened," I coaxed, unable to keep the

exasperation from my tone.

"I blew him."

"You blew him?"

"Yes."

"You put your mouth on his penis and sucked on it?"

"Shut up."

"Did you like it?"

"It was a blow job."

"I know," I said. "Did you enjoy it?"

"It was like a typical 'I'm getting back at my ex even though he probably will not care and I'm mad that he doesn't care and I feel foolish for doing it' blow job."

"Oh, one of those? Just curious, is his dick bigger than mine?"

"No," she laughed. "It's smaller."

I laughed and then asked, "Is there anything else you are hiding from me?"

"Wait. You're not upset?" she asked.

"I'm upset that you guys hid it from me." I deadpanned, "If you guys had a good time, that's cool. I'm not jealous. If you are going to suck on a cock, do it because you enjoy it and you want to give that man pleasure. Don't give a revenge blowjob. That's just sad. Next time you truly wish to suck on a cock, give me a call."

"You were in California!" Lynn said.

I replied, "So, you have to give a blowjob every week?" I laughed and continued, "So, when I am not around, any penis will do?"

"No! That's not what I meant!" Lynn exclaimed. "I was upset! I don't know. I was upset about you hanging out with Zia so much, but still seeing me every once in a while. You know Zia and those other women don't do for you what I can."

"I was joking." I said, "Hey, I'm cool with it. Just don't hide it from me."

"So, you are really not mad?" she asked as if I should have been.

"I'm kind of pissed that you would hide it from me." I said,

"As soon as I got my first phone call when I got back, I knew that someone was lying to hide something. Both of you did a magnificently terrible job of even attempting to lie about it. As someone who has lied quite a bit, I think I will take your membership card away from the liars' club. Hey, we are not together in a monogamous relationship. It would be unfair of me to be mad at you or him. Tell me the truth, though. Did you really just give Kevin a blowjob because you were upset with me?"

She exhaled loudly. "Yes!"

"Lynn!" I said, "You are excellent at giving blowjobs. You are probably the best woman…"

"Probably!?" she asked with anger.

"Okay," I responded. "The best. There are erections yearning for your mouth all over New Jersey. Is that better? Men would give you money for them, they're that good."

"Well, now that you put it that way…"

"Seriously!" I exclaimed. "Oral sex is an art form! Do you know how many men would kill for a couple of minutes of your lips?"

"Now you jest, you fucker! Stop being vulgar," she said.

"Lynn, just be open and honest about stuff dealing with sex. When it comes to me, I am open-minded and I try to be open with the women I am with."

"All your fucking women!!!" Lynn started to get agitated and said, "Nicholas, you know that sex is an emotional act, don't you? Sex is not just about you cumming or me having an orgasm. It goes deeper than that."

I snickered and responded, "That's from someone who gave an angry blowjob to my best friend to try to get back at me in some way."

"Oh!" she said. "See the effect? See the effect it has on people?"

"Was his penis that much smaller than mine?" I asked with a half-mocking tone, just to see if it would make her laugh.

She laughed and I almost heard her eyes close over the phone.

She said, "It was a pity blowjob."

We laughed and continued our post-relationship conversation.

Next time I was around Kevin, I addressed the situation in a very lackadaisical manner. We were smoking blunts at the court, laughing at something absurd. I had to leave to go to Zia's place. On my way to my car, keys in hand, I said, "Kevin, I know Lynn gave you a blow job."

"What!? Wait, what the fuck?!?" he exclaimed.

"Yes. Dude, just tell me the truth next time. Be upfront about it." I added, "She also told me that you're not packing that much down there."

"Oh, dude," he said. "Fuck you!"

"Bro, I love you," I stated with a confident smile. "We'll be alright. Everything is cool."

Sometimes, I could be such an asshole.

A QUICK TALE ABOUT TIFFANY

Several weeks later, Lynn had another party in her parents' house. I arrived very egotistical, knowing that she wanted me to be there for her. She actually told me that she wanted me to know that she was popular, too. Lynn wanted me to know that there were people who wanted to be around her and her friends.

Dear reader, do you remember the blonde woman who was with Lynn when we first met? While I was drunk, the blonde, freckled, weed-buying Tiffany told me that I had to talk with her. She pushed me into the bathroom and closed the door behind her. Throwing her arms over my shoulders, she said, "Look…. Lynn sucked Kevin's dick." Honestly, I wanted nothing to do with Tiffany. She was drunk. I could have been a creep and totally have gotten laid. I'm horny and consumed with sex but I'm not a creep. Lynn and I were not monogamous at that time, but I knew that it would break Lynn's heart if I debased myself to be with Tiffany when Lynn was willing and waiting for me the whole time. I turned Tiffany away. As horny as I get (and I get horny), Tiffany was not worth it.

"Hey, I'm not interested." I responded, "You are pretty and all, but I'm just not into it right now. I'm flattered though. Thank you."

THE COOLEST WAY TO KILL YOURSELF

That evening, Lynn and I made love. Afterwards, Lynn wrapped her arms around me and she said, "Thank you."

"Why are you thanking me?" I asked her.

"You did not disappoint me," Lynn said. "You are someone who did not disappoint me. Every man I was ever with was susceptible to Tiffany because she was easy. You actually did not have sex with her. Tiffany told me. She said that she wanted to be with you and I know that we are not together so I told her that it was okay. Then, of course, I asked her what happened afterwards. She said that she tried get with you. You know me… I got it out of her."

"Of course, baby," I said.

"Seriously, Nicholas." Lynn said, "I thought it was very cool of you. I know that you blatantly love Zia and she's stringing you along. I'm dealing with that, but I thought it was cool you did not act like a typical male. I love the fact that you turned Tiffany down."

We cleaned up, but not well enough. When her parents came home, they found a ripped-open condom wrapper on the floor. They were livid. Lynn did not want her parents to hate me. For some reason, Lynn blamed her friend Donna, her rave friend from college. It would have been much more believable for her to blame Tiffany, the blonde girl from Spotswood who cheated on every boyfriend and tried to have sex with many guys she met.

"COCAINE SEX IS FAST AND EFFECTIVE"
- *Renegade Soundwave*

Around this time in my life, I was living on Hamilton Street in New Brunswick but still going to school in Edison. I basically used my friend's apartment as a place to crash, where I did not have to worry about the hassle of my parents. I needed the freedom to find pleasure, and they disapproved of my hedonistic ways. They should not see such debauchery (so I wrote a book about it instead).

New Brunswick was always in the shadow of New York City, but it still offered the crazy pleasures of any urban setting. Sometimes, that pleasure was cocaine. My friends began to indulge in cocaine, and one friend gave me a little bag of it. I was terrified to do it, but of course I did.

I had some left and it was a school night. Lynn called me up and asked me to meet her on Route 1 in North Brunswick. She drove up from her college in Trenton and I met her in my Dodge Caravan. We had a pretty grounded conversation. She told me that she did not want to be a problem or be a crazy ex-girlfriend, but she loved me and wanted me in her life.

Unfortunately, my mind was on cocaine.

THE COOLEST WAY TO KILL YOURSELF

"Do you want to do some coke?" I asked.

"Okay," she said with a naïve acceptance. She told me that she had tried cocaine already, so I did not feel guilty. When you are a teenager in drug culture, many people say they have tried drugs that they only dreamed of ingesting. I never wanted to be someone who introduced someone to drugs. I only wanted to give drugs to people who were already experienced.

I pulled over into a condominium complex and found a dark place to park. I took the little plastic Ziploc bag filled with two abundant lines' worth of cocaine. I had a clicker. Using a Beastie Boys "Paul's Boutique" album case and my driver's license, I split up two lines. I felt like I was in a crazy 80's film. I sniffed my line first. Without hesitation, she sniffed her line afterwards. We lifted our heads and looked at each other. A wave of euphoria pumped through our veins. Our arms just wrapped around each other's bodies as we began to kiss with a fierce hunger.

"Backseat," one of us said.

We climbed into the back seat. We could not get our clothes off fast enough. I pulled off her jeans and panties and had barely begun to go down on her when she pushed me away so that she could unbuckle my pants. She started going down on me, but I grabbed the back of her head by the hair and pulled her away, laying her down on her back. As I got on top of her, she looked me in the eyes with a frantic, yet satisfied, smile. I made love to her like the world was ending around us. It felt like there were explosions outside the car and panic in the streets. Society collapsed and it was complete anarchy. The world was over. It was Armageddon but we needed to have sex. I thrusted myself inside her like my life depended on it. She wrapped her naked legs around my waist as she moaned and grabbed my hair.

"I'm cumming!" she screamed at the top of her lungs. I could not stop. I felt her vaginal walls constrict and her juices flooded the upholstery. Then, I felt it. I felt this amazing feeling in my body. I could not control myself. Then, it happened. We both screamed in wonderful ecstasy at the same time. Our limp bodies fell on each other and we soon noticed lights being turned on in the condos around us.

"We have to get out of here," she said. We put our pants on in a rush and got into the front seats. I turned the van on and we drove back to where Lynn had parked. I parked next to her car, and we stopped for a quick breather. We were covered in sweat and our hair was incredibly messy. We looked in the visor mirrors and made this half-assed attempt to fix ourselves up. She got her purse and things together.

She kissed me quickly on the lips and said, "Nicholas, do you know that is the only time I ever had an orgasm during actual sex? Usually, it is from you going down on me. Think about that. The first time I ever had an orgasm during actual penetration was with you in the backseat of your van in a parking lot." She smiled and got out of my car and into hers. I sat there for a couple of minutes. I waited for her to leave before I left because it was the gentlemanly thing to do. I thought that she may have needed my help if her car did not start. She drove away and I heard "Gravitate to Me" by The The coming from her car. I was out of breath, out of time, and out of ideas. I was in a state of sexual euphoric come-down. As I turned my car on, the Roxy Music cover version of "Sea Breezes" by Siouxsie and The Banshees blasted out of the speakers. It was the end of the song when the drums just roll over and over. This amazing feeling of sex without boundaries, but with chemicals, shattered every conception of love and sex that I had.

There was cocaine involved, but we were two people who had feelings for each other. Was there something deeper? There is lust and there is passion. The two meet, but they are different. I tried to make the distinction between a sexual drug high and a true romantic experience.

BEEP!

One day, the Edison crew of wannabe suburban gangsters piled into my van and we drove to Plainfield to score some weed. I was making a left from Tingley Lane onto Inman Avenue, when a drunk driver hit my van and we did a 360 degree spin. What is it about 360 degree car accidents and my life? The back hatch opened up and Kevin shot out of the Dodge Caravan like a cannonball. We were all taken to the hospital in ambulances. My parents actually came to the scene. For some reason, my father listens to police scanners. Do not ask me why. He appeared when they were loading us into the ambulances.

I lost my mode of transportation. At that time, Zia was actually driving out of her way to pick me up and take me back and forth to school every day. My connection with Zia was getting stronger every time I hung out with her. I used to cut study hall and hang out with her in the darkroom in the art wing of my high school while she developed photographs. I was quickly preoccupied with Zia.

Lynn had become a friend who I could get high and have sex with every once in a while. The last couple of weekends, I got rides to NASA from either Kevin or a friend of mine named Aaron. One weekend, when I was not home, Lynn wanted to talk to me and was extremely emotional. I had one of those old answering machines that used a cassette tape. I walked into my bedroom the morning after a night of beautiful debauchery and found the entire side of the tape completely full. I pressed rewind and it felt like it took forever for it to get to the beginning. I heard the whirring of the tape rewinding and left the room. I came back and thought to myself, "What the hell?" The tape just kept rewinding. I could not believe she filled the whole cassette. While I waited, I went to my compact discs and found a Close Lobsters song that I wanted to hear. As I found the right track, the tape was still rewinding. As soon as the song by Close Lobsters started, I heard the buzzing of the tape stop. I looked at the machine with a wicked smile on my face, knowing that it had been Lynn who filled the tape. I almost resisted pressing play, but I had to.

"Hey, Nicholas. This is Lynn. Just checking in and seeing what you are doing tonight. Call me back."

BEEP!

"Hey, Nicholas. This is Lynn. You still haven't told me if you were coming with me to NASA this Friday. Janice and Donna cannot go for some reason. I would like it if you would come with me."

BEEP!

"Hey, Nicholas. This is Lynn again. Regarding that last message… I hope you know that we are just going as friends. I don't expect anything or… you know. Anyway, call me back."

BEEP!

"Nick. Where are you? It's still early. It's not like you to leave for the night yet. Call me back."

BEEP!

"Nick. Lynn again. I don't mean to clog up your answering machine, but I want to talk with you."

BEEP!

"Seriously, Nicholas. What the fuck?"

BEEP!

"You think you are so cool. You think that you are just God's gift to women. You think that your cock is the be all and end all of everything. Fuck you. I hope you know that I can get other guys. You are not the only guy out there who can fuck me or wants to fuck me!"

BEEP!

"Look… I'm sorry. I got a little mad. You know me. I get a little emotional at times."

BEEP!

"Why!?!?! Why the hell do you not love me!?!? We read the same books! We listen to the same music! We like the same films! We have the same interests! We both love drugs and the rave scene! We both love sex! We both love sex with each other! So, why? Why? Tell me why!"

BEEP!

"You are with that bitch, Zia. Aren't you? She's going to break your heart. That's what you want. Go. Go fuck and prosper. Just remember me when you are heartbroken and remember that there was a woman named Lynn who loved you!"

BEEP!

"Fuck."

BEEP!

"Look, Nicholas. I'm sorry for being like this. I truly love and appreciate our friendship. I do not want to be another crazy ex-girlfriend like Carmen was. Ouch! I just burned myself with a cigarette!"

BEEP!

"Seriously, Nick! You love fucking me! I love fucking you! What the hell is wrong with you? Hey, I will have this crazy open relationship where we just have sex. I love you that much… you beautiful fucking asshole motherfucker! I will do that for you. I do not want that, but I'll do that."

BEEP!

"You know what? Forget that last message. I deserve better than that. I am a beautiful and smart woman! You should feel lucky you have me."

BEEP!

"Seriously, Nicholas. I may do something horrible tonight. Please call me."

BEEP!

"Ugh!" *Click.*

BEEP!

"I'm serious!"

BEEP!

"I honestly do not know what I will do tonight."

BEEP!

"Of course he's not answering…" *Sound of sniffling. Click.*

BEEP!

"Look, Nicholas. Ignore those previous messages." *Rustling of paper.* "Shit! Now I am out of cigarettes! Fuck me with a Morrissey CD! Ugh!"

BEEP!

"I'm so sorry! Nicholas, I love you. You know that. I know we are not going to be together. I do not want to be that girl. I'm not crazy, but you have to admit that… I love you. I'm sorry. You do not deserve this. You don't need this. You were upfront about your feelings. It's just… really difficult for me."

BEEP!

"Nicholas, I have already reached the point of no return. I have embarrassed myself on tape. I told you so many times how frustratingly in love I am with you. Now, I am at a point where the truth is the only thing I can say. I am sorry for this. I'm sure you will make fun of it. I know I'm crazy but I am honest in my emotions. I am going to feel like the biggest loser if I go to NASA alone. You are my friend. I will treat you as a friend and not act like you're my boyfriend or lover. Let me put it this way. I would truly like and appreciate your company on the ride to NASA this Friday. Please let me know. I will only ask you about this when I speak to you ag-" Her words were cut off as the tape ran out.

As soon as the answering machine tape reached its end, I immediately called her to see if she killed herself. The phone kept ringing, and I thought she had done something horrible.

"Hello?" she answered.

I sighed with relief. "Are you okay?"

"I'm a little mixed up," she said.

"You left these crazy messages on my answering machine!" I exclaimed.

"Will you go with me to NASA this weekend?" she asked.

I paused. I felt like I was being coerced, and I just breathed into the phone.

"Don't just breathe. Please just tell me," she said.

"Yes," I said. "If you drive me to NASA this Friday, I will go with you."

The beauty of the New York City underground rave scene was that every kind of person was usually welcomed, tolerated, or glorified. Just walking through the event on the first lap took an hour. In between greeting the people I knew, I would look at the people around me. DJs were either glorified or completely ignored. The funny thing about the music was the snobbery. One week a vinyl record was pressed and played, the next week people would say that it was "old." The drug dealers made money and walked through the dance floor and the chill out room like The Pied Piper. The promoters gave you a glossy flyer that you would either hang up on your wall or throw away. There was always the person who did not understand the scene and was angry that alcohol was not being served. There was the silly raver wearing a pacifier around his neck and Vicks Vapor Rub on his face while dancing frantically in front of the speaker. Without fail, at any given time, someone was in a bathroom stall puking. You could always spot someone freaking out on their psychedelic drug trip. Some people were experiencing what people called a "K Hole," which meant they took too much Special K (aka Ketamine). Other people could be seen freaking out on LSD. The true grimy street people smoked angel dust and would punch you because it would make them laugh. The heroin addicts would nod off in the corner. They would lean over but somehow, they would never completely fall. The cocaine fiends would be talking a mile a minute as they pointed at each other, thinking that they were philosophizing about truly important and sophisticated issues. Sometimes, I would see the slutty girl who just wanted to sleep with someone. She would be right next to a frumpy girl, trying to make herself look better. Despite all of the strung out people, the scene did not look like a ghetto crack house. The scene was a hip New York experience. People wore expensive and flamboyant clothes as they pontificated about art, film, music, and youth. Fashion wise, I was more the baggy pants and unique shirt type who always attempted to look hip and handsome. The scene was like Renaissance Florence on psychedelic drugs.

One type of raver who always made me laugh to myself was what I called The Muppet Baby Raver. For some reason, many young men and women went through a phase of regression, to the point where they appeared to be a bunch of toddlers attending a psychedelic play date.

"Hey, Poppy!" a female in overalls and pigtails said as she sucked on a lollipop.

"Oh, hey Dawny!" the male raver said, dancing around, doing this ridiculous movement with his arms in front of him. He would stare at the visual trails his arms made as they moved.

"Do you want to play in the chill out room?" the female asked, Vicks Vapor Rub all over her face. "Potato Chip and Mr. Clever will be there as DJ DB and Mr. Kleen spin a new set. We could play and laugh and dance! Maybe we can play games and there will not be any mean people there."

"Sure, Dawny!" the male raver said, continuing to dance. "I think Mr. Kleen has candy!"

"Candy!?" the female raver exclaimed, jumping up and down with her eyes bulging out of her skull. They giggled like a bunch of weird characters in a depraved children's television show.

"What the hell am I seeing?" I asked myself. In a drug-induced high, Lynn and I just watched and listened. We broke out in laughter and said at the same time, "Muppet Baby Ravers!" We wondered how the hell we ended up even being around those people. Then, we looked at each other and realized that we were no better. We had been out of our minds on drugs many times. We probably acted even dumber, weirder, and sillier than them at some point in our lives. I took her hand and walked to the dance floor. "Plastic Dreams" by Jay Dee started and the crowd cheered. The dance floor was packed and the lighting by Scotto was impeccably psychedelic.

All of the sudden I heard someone say, "I love this song!" I turned around and saw a grown man, who sold ecstasy and went by the name of Potato Chip, dancing. He actually had a necklace made that had a potato chip at the end of it. I immediately thought to myself, "What the hell kind of world am I in?" Then, I felt the rhythms and the E kicked in. The lights created a psychedelic effect of fun and hedonism.

"I'm so happy, but also sad," Lynn said.

"Why?"

"You're getting a new car this week," she said. "What is going to happen next week?"

Lynn and I looked at each other and we instantly moved closer together. We held hands as we looked into each other's eyes. Suddenly, we stopped dancing. Everyone around danced as if the world ended tomorrow. Our arms embraced each other and pulled our bodies closer together. We had a passionate kiss on the dance floor in the middle of a couple of hundred people dancing while tripping on ecstasy. For one small moment, we felt like we could stop as the rest of the world went on. I remember that kiss. Her kiss was the kiss of a woman who felt as if she would never kiss me again.

PLEASE JUST FUCK ME

Manchester, England was an essential element to the birth of rave culture. Although Chicago house music, which the Americans ignored, was given a re-birth in underground night clubs throughout Europe, Manchester had a long and rich history of influencing music and popular culture. The list goes on and it includes the following: The Hacienda (a club), Happy Mondays, The Stone Roses, Joy Division, New Order, The Fall, and tons of the drug ecstasy. Sure, there was the urban element and crime element, too. There was rock music and dancing. The late 80's and early 90's was a true mixture of white culture and black culture. We were just "24 Hour Party People." I remember waking up in apartments with the floor covered with bodies that were sleeping after being up for 24 hours straight.

The next weekend, NASA sponsored a Manchester music night and I scored this gigantic blue capsule of pure MDMA from the UK. At around 4 in the morning, they started playing "Fool's Gold" by The Stone Roses, "Loaded" and "Come Together" by Primal Scream, and "Step On" by Happy Mondays. Not all of the music was from Manchester, but the intended vibe was achieved. In the film "24 Hour Party People," Tony Wilson's character summed it up perfectly when he quoted Wordsworth: "*Bliss it was in that dawn to be alive, but to be young was very heaven.*"

Lynn and I danced on a dance floor that had a fraction of the people they usually had. The E was magnificent. I felt loose, comfortable and loving. We sat down in the "chill out room" and talked. We talked just as friends. We talked about music. We talked about NASA and how it had changed. All of the party goers seemed younger. Although it was comfortable, I could see the sad feeling behind her eyes. When I know someone is emotional and trying to hide their feelings, I tend to bring it up in the conversation but I try to do it with delicacy.

"Lynn," I said. "We're having fun. I am glad we remained friends. I am thankful that I know that you and I are friends."

She smiled at me as she exhaled her cigarette smoke. "I know. I knew that you would come around."

We looked into each other's eyes and smiled. There was this sadness and longing in her eyes that I absolutely loved. I loved the fact that she wanted me and loved me with such purity. I had to be true to my heart, though. During the week, Zia and I were getting closer. I did not want to hurt Lynn, or lie to her.

We shared a very innocent kiss and quickly pulled away from each other. We sat back with huge smiles on our faces looking out to the beautiful and psychedelic dance floor. It was not the most popular or most crowded, but we both loved this music. The DJ switched styles and moved the crossfader to "Plastic Dreams" by Jay Dee. As soon as the DJ put on the song, people energetically flooded the floor. We looked at each other again and smiled. Without one word, we nodded to each other and walked out into the crowd together.

Potato Chip danced in the background and yelled, "I love this song!"

The next morning, I crashed at her house. I thought it was safe because we were not having sex anymore and I thought that it would not be emotional. We stumbled into the empty house. "Crash on the bed," she said. "I have some stuff to do."

THE COOLEST WAY TO KILL YOURSELF

I fell onto the bed and closed my eyes. I fell into a deep sleep, but I soon woke up with her on top of me. She was unzipping my baggy black pants. I was strung out and not erect. She started to suck and stroke me, but my head was killing me.

"Lynn, my head is killing me. Please, don't," I said. She stopped and let out a disappointed sigh. I fell back to sleep, and woke up with her straddling me. My head was pounding. Normally, I would not have turned her away, but I felt like my brain actually hurt, like it was pulsating and hitting the inside of my skull.

"Seriously, Lynn," I said. "I cannot now!" She got off of me. I closed my eyes, and then I heard my pants unzip again. Immediately, I got up and grabbed my bag. I walked to the front door and she ran after me. She literally jumped in front of the door.

"Don't leave!" she yelled with an insane look in her eye. Her body was shaking. "If you leave, I will fucking kill myself!" I grabbed her shoulders and moved her in front of a closet that had doors made of those thin wooden slats. The doors bent a little bit and she lost her balance. Furious, she pushed me against the wall. As soon as I hit the wall, I hit my head and slid down to the floor. I was shocked. I could not believe this was happening. The next thing I saw was her get up and run to the kitchen. I slowly got up and tried to open the door, but it was locked. I felt a little dizzy as my hand went for the lock.

"You do not fucking leave!" she screamed as she ran towards me with a large kitchen knife. Again, she got in between me and the front door. She was pointing the knife at me with her irrational, non-blinking eyes. Her head was furiously shaking, as was her hand, which was pointing a rather large knife.

I said in a rather faithless tone, "Oh, you're going to stab me?"
She just looked at me, crying, with all rational thought gone.
"Stab me then! If you truly loved me like you said, you would not be holding a knife to me!" I slowly moved towards her and reached for the knife. I grabbed her wrist and she dropped the

knife. I heard the metal bounce off the floor tiles.

    She started throwing punches at my chest yelling, "I hate you! I fucking love you! Why do you do this to me?!?!"

    I grabbed my backpack and turned around. I ran through the kitchen and into the family room. I went to the screen door and quickly grabbed the pole of wood that was in the track so the door could not be opened. I fumbled to try to get it out for a second or two, but finally got it. I heard her coming. In complete fear and panic, I slid the door open and ran out onto the backyard deck. The sun hit my eyes. I felt like a vampire coming out of a house at dawn.

    With a backpack in my hands, I ran from the backyard to my new silver Mercury Sable. I fumbled with my keys like a victim in a horror film. When I finally got the driver's side door open, I threw my backpack onto the passenger's seat, plopped my strung out body into the driver's seat, and turned the car on.

    Suddenly, she was there. She was in-between the car door and me. It was like she was dropped from the sky. Panicking, I started to drive away without closing my car door, and suddenly I realized that I was driving down her street while she stood on the rocker panels on my car.

    "Please! Please! Please!" she begged. "We can just go back inside. Please just come back inside. I can do better! Please, just fuck me! Or, we don't have to! Just please don't leave! I'm sorry I tried to stab you!"

    I stopped the car and tried to get her to let go, but she was gripping too tight. Eventually, she let go. As soon as her feet were not inside my car and she was not grabbing onto the car, I drove away. I looked in the rearview and saw that she was not hurt. Ironically, "Soopaman Luva" by Redman was playing in the tape deck.

    My mind was racing. "Holy shit!" I said to myself. Of course, my ego took over. This woman tried to stab me, then ran out and hung from my moving automobile while begging for me to have sex with her. Then, on the ride home, the reality set in. This was an emotionally unstable woman who was high on drugs. Why did I let my mindset of open relationships have this effect on her? The sex was "casual" for me, but it meant something much more to her. Even though I was honest about my emotions with her, she was hurt. I was not trying to hurt her. I could not believe that another woman tried to stab me. It was like Carmen all over again.

When I got home, I heard several messages from her. I was so worried, but I could not have stayed there. She had pulled a knife on me. I called her up, and when she answered the phone, I could hear the sniffling of her nose.

"Look, Lynn," I said, "I know you're in a bad way right now, and I want to make sure you are alright. Promise me you won't do anything."

She yelled, "I'm sorry! I'm sorry! I'm sorry!"

"I know," I sighed. "My head is pounding and I have to go to sleep. Just promise me you won't do anything."

She continued, "I'm sorry!"

"I know, I know," I said. "Just promise me."

"Yes," she said, "I promise."

I crashed onto my bed and fell asleep. She kept calling and leaving messages. Then, she called the outside home line. I told my parents to ignore it. I could not talk to her. I did not know where to begin.

Throughout the day, I had to help my father with yard work. I was standing in the shed, staring at a few dried leaves that were on the floor. The veins in the leaves always looked psychedelic to me. My father caught me staring at them in a post-drugged up daze.

My father called, "That girl, Lynn is here for you." I was on the side of the house and looked out to the front. There Lynn was, standing at the end of the driveway with a look of fear and shame in her eyes. She was wearing the same outfit, and I could see her body trembling. She had driven 45 minutes from Spotswood to

Edison. I walked down to her with an angry swagger.

"What the hell are you doing here?" I asked. "I cannot talk to you now."

She started talking incredibly fast, her tone pleading. "I needed to talk with you! I need to apologize. I don't want you to hate me."

"I don't hate you!" I said. "You have to go. Look, we will talk later."

"You hate me!"

"I don't hate you, but this morning was insane behavior! Go home. Please!" She got in the car and drove away. I walked up the driveway and into the backyard. Then, I let out an exasperated sigh.

"Wow!" my father said, "She really likes you."

"Yeah. She really does. You have no idea."

FIRST RIDE ON THE D TRAIN

An epidemic of angel dust swept the Edison drug underground in the spring/summer of 1993. Jamal was a regular in our cypher and a solid drug connection. At first it was weed, but it quickly moved to angel dust. He knew this Black suburban couple who got their hands on it first. All of the high school kids who smoked pot started smoking dust.

The first time I smoked angel dust was at a place we called "The Court." Tim and Ryan had a full basketball court in their backyard that was surrounded by trees. A typical afternoon included going to the court to smoke blunts in the cypher (a circle of people smoking). Soon, the cypher became very popular. There was always free weed there. Kevin, Tim, and Ryan would sometimes play basketball, but it was really just a place to smoke and hang out. Jamal arrived at the court with a yellow bag with a stamp that said "Crazy Eddie." The bag consisted of this crystalline substance on mint leaves dipped in formaldehyde. Even though we were outside, I could smell the chemical odor as soon as the small bag was opened. The cigar was broken open and the tobacco was dumped out. The weed was put in. Then, he sprinkled the dust on the weed.

"You only need one or two hits!" Jamal warned. "I'm serious! Only take one or two hits! You white niggas will go crazy."

I took three hits and I was transported into another world. It was unlike any high I had ever felt in my life. Redman's debut cassette was playing in the background. I was on a psychedelic supernova that made me feel invincible. I was hooked in a parallel dimension infinitely evolving and destroying itself.

For that whole spring and summer, Kevin and I smoked tons of "Posse" and "Crazy Eddie." We would go on skateboards and rollerblades and skate through condominium complexes. We would go to New Brunswick and climb up the buildings' stairs to the roof. Then, we would run and jump from rooftop to rooftop. Sometimes, we would just destroy stuff on the street. One time, we had little bits of logs and we set them on fire and played soccer with the flaming logs. While most people have a healthy fear of the grim reaper, we wanted to hang out with Death and see what records he listened to.

Dust also makes you incredibly mean and arrogant. Kevin and I went on a double date with a Depeche Mode-obsessed college girl and her snobby Asian Goth friend. They usually would make fun of everyone, but they could not win against the dust brothers. All night, we made fun of them hard. The Depeche Mode girl was attractive and loved the same alternative music I liked, too. I had spent my whole high school life thinking she was cool and attractive. That night, Kevin and I spewed insult after insult at her. We were making fun of their pretentious behavior while acting superior to them. We went and saw the Johnny Depp film called "Benny & Joon." Till this day, if I see it on TV, I want to do what Elvis did to his televisions and shoot them. Twenty years later, Kevin thinks that we were with two different women that night. That may reflect that he does not remember now, when in reality, he did not remember then.

Soon, the craziness came to an end when the supplier began

THE COOLEST WAY TO KILL YOURSELF

to run out. I started to get a tolerance. Sometimes, we would go to Harlem and buy from the kids we called "dust bunnies." Dust bunnies were 12 year old Black kids on the corner who would smoke straight dust blunts and throw loaded automatic pistols at each other from across the street. They would laugh when bullets sometimes hit windows and nearby buildings. Miraculously, no one died. PCP made me end up in shady places, but it made me feel invincible. Eventually, even Harlem did not have Phencyclidine. I do not believe in God, but I would say that it was a blessing that I could not get my hands on angel dust anymore that summer.

THE REAL BREAK UP

Although Lynn and I had broken up, we were still going to raves together. Basically, that meant that we would stay up all night in New York City taking ecstasy, dancing, and socializing. We would come home smelling like illegal underground parties and looking like we were just gloriously raped by Dionysius. Our relationship had a wonderful yet depraved level of comfort. After the knife incident, we stopped having sex but we remained friends.

I decided to throw a massive party at my friend's place in New Brunswick. Lynn knew about the party and she knew that I wanted Zia there. Lynn always felt nerdy and ugly, and she knew that my mind was not on her.

Before the party, she told me, "I'm going to look so hot and sexy that you are not even going to pay attention to Zia." She really put effort in. Her post-Chelsea hair cut had a Bettie Page look. She had on a black skirt that slightly belled and a very tight striped shirt that accentuated her small breasts. Lynn was never the glamorous, need to look beautiful type. Unfortunately, her attempt did not work. I still wanted Zia and was amazed how beautiful Zia looked without effort.

That night, I had a friend of mine bring turntables and speakers. This was at a time when having turntables and a good sound system in a high school/college house party was considered somewhat unique and impressive. Looking back, I have to admit that it felt cool. I was making things happen. People looked up to me as a party person, who knew cool people. I had people from the New York City rave scene in a basement in New Brunswick, NJ.

Zia lied to her father about where she was sleeping that night. Because I had put directions on my answering machine's outgoing announcement, her father was able to find her. He ended up coming to a New Brunswick party filled with wasted teenagers and college kids. People were smoking weed in the streets. I stood outside and watched Zia get into her father's car.

Lynn found me outside, and we had one of those brutally honest, very long post-relationship talks. While we were emotional, the conversation had a calm, melancholy feel because we were resigned to the fact that our affair was over.

"Lynn, I love you," I said. "I have been trying so hard and I have loved Zia for so long, even before I ever knew you. I do not want to hurt you. I do not want to lead you on. I love talking with you. I love being with you. Still, I truly want to give this a chance. I am in love with Zia. I always was in love with her. I cannot deny that. It would be cruel to continue being with you. It would be cruel to you. It would drive you crazy and it would also mess things up with her. I know you do not want to hear details, but I feel like I am getting somewhere with her. I love you, but I am in love with her. I am sorry, but I cannot help the way that I feel."

We hugged and she cried into my chest. I am a very emotional person, so tears were in my eyes, too. I am not afraid to cry in front of anyone.

I had crossed the line and finally committed. Even though I got Zia in trouble that night, and I was in the doghouse with her father, for some reason, I thought being cute and cool would make everything okay and keep everyone happy. Making everyone happy is impossible. Only now do I realize that I had learned a very important lesson. That lesson was not learned until much later in this tale, but trust me, it's important. The last thing I remember about that evening is both of us sitting on the curb while a 90's central NJ indie/rave/punk version of a Caligula's mansion party was going on behind us.

SUPER ASSHOLE

I was about to graduate from high school. I had a yearbook of collected signatures and stories of all of the wonderful, weird, and wild people I grew up with in both high school and the rave scene. My adult life was waiting for me and I wanted to take a break before I caught up to it.

In all honesty, my life was spinning out of control. I was lost in the world of angel dust, and I was so fragile and upset that Zia and I may not work out. I left a woman who loved me for a woman I loved. I finally made love to Zia and wanted to be monogamous. Unfortunately, she would constantly pull away from commitment.

I got a ride to a rave club in Long Island called Caffeine. Remember my ex-girlfriend, Carmen, the suicidal kleptomaniac who eventually got the professional help that she needed… and also helped us steal a marijuana plant? Lynn and Carmen became good friends through the scene. According to Lynn, they talked about me quite often. Somehow, they ended up being my ride home from Long Island. I smoked straight dust blunts that night. As word got around, people started to follow me around like I was the Pied Piper of PCP.

Carmen whispered in my ear, "Some of these people are using you for your angel dust connection."

Being on angel dust is almost impossible to describe. At first, it's a little like being instantly high on marijuana, but you get the confidence and paranoia of cocaine exponentially amplified. The psychedelic aspects wash over you as much as the power. Not only do you not care about anything or anyone, but you feel as if you could do anything you want without repercussions. On top of that psychosis, it magnifies the egotistical aspect of being on cocaine and mutates you like a person who got bit by a psychedelic radioactive spider. The drug morphs you into invincible Super Asshole.

This was the situation: Super Asshole was in the back seat of the car while his ex-girlfriends (whose hearts he had broken in the past) were in the front. Carmen was driving and Lynn was in the passenger seat.

"Both of you want to fuck me," I said. "Come on, admit it." I may have been right. I may have been wrong. Either way, I was being an asshole.

Lynn and Carmen had a strong friendship and connection already. They did not say it out loud, but they were basically thinking, "He wants to get his heart broken… let him."

Right then and there, a wave of sadness came over me. "You Can't Always Get What You Want" by The Rolling Stones came on the mix-tape that I made them put in. Actually, it was not a mix-tape. It was the album "Yes… Please" by Happy Mondays and the Rolling Stones song was tacked on to fill the side of the cassette. The mixture of the Happy Mondays album and The Rolling Stones song triggered something inside me. As I listened to the Rolling Stones, I knew my heart would be broken by Zia. Maybe it would not be immediately, but I knew it would happen. I slowly repeated the chorus out loud.

If you do not know the song, the narrator goes to a wedding reception and sees the woman who he once loved and still loved. His life has spun out of control with drugs and the woman who had once loved him has moved on. I imagined being in the scene. I saw myself at some party, seeing her with someone else. At that moment, I severely and almost hypnotically spiraled into a state of depression. Lynn and Carmen noticed and began to question what was happening to me. They saw that I could experience the heartache I caused them. In the back of my mind, I knew that was true. I no longer felt better than them. Any sense of entitlement was gone. I was terrified that I would feel my heart break like they did.

"I'm sorry I hurt both of you," I whispered. Till this day, I do not know if they heard me.

Lynn and Carmen let me crash for a little while in Carmen's apartment in New Brunswick. After a very slow shower, I picked up my belongings and left. Without any conversation, I hugged both of them goodbye and walked out of the apartment. Their sympathy and wisdom from that situation was something that I still cherish to this very day.

I decided to love. I decided to love even though someone may break my heart. I would rather feel my heart break than be someone who had never loved anyone enough to have the honor of feeling heartache. I need passion in my life. That is why I loved sex and drugs. Most importantly, I loved the connection I have with a woman who loves me.

These two wonderful women, Lynn and Carmen, comforted me and sent me back out into the world. I was tired. I was weary. I looked horrible. I felt worse. I was coming down from many serious drugs and my life was in shambles. As I walked outside, anticipating the sunlight that would hit me in the face, I remembered the come down from that evening. I remembered them giving me water to drink, a pillow to lay my head, and they stroked my hair as they covered me with a blanket. I almost did not want to leave, but I had to. These two women once loved me and I was going off to love some other woman. I had to go off on another one of my adventures. The love of these two women gave me strength. I finally began to understand that a person is strong because of the people who love them.

NICHOLAS TANEK

I drove off listening to "The Last Song" by Trisomie 21. At first, I just loved the emotion and the bass line of the song, but the lyrics had an emotional meaning for me. Even though I was coming down from hard drugs, I was so happy that I found a connection. I found love. These two women helped and nurtured me; they openly and honestly loved me and I had been foolish enough to let myself lose them. I did not know it then, but a beautiful and sensual part of me opened up. I did not know what to do or how to do it, but I wanted to create. I wanted to love. I wanted to hold Zia in my arms even though I knew it would break my heart. Even if my actions led to my own heartbreak, I would be a better lover to the next woman.

EPILOGUE

I loved Lynn and I broke her heart. I thought I deserved someone prettier, someone cooler, someone... better. I was so wrong.

Hard drugs changed the rave scene for all of us. Potato Chip died from a mixture of cocaine and heroin. At his funeral, more than 20 ravers started playing techno music and dancing in front of his mourning family. Although I did not know him well, Michael Alig became a notorious murderer when he killed Angel from the Limelight. The crowds became much younger and the regular people I knew began to feel awkward. Even though the atmosphere was trippy, many of us felt it was time to grow up. The party was over but the drug use remained. The joyous dancing and socializing changed to a dirty and dangerous dependency.

My whole life was ahead of me. The plan was to get an education, have fun, have wild affairs, get high, and feel complete. I was going to be a famous writer, author, auteur, musician, actor, director.... I ended up being a beautiful fool.

ACT TWO

My father always told me, "The only constant in life is change." Life went on... so it goes.

After high school graduation, Zia and I had this majestic and romantic summer. We were inseparable, artistic, and sexual. Now, it was not the kinky sex I wanted, but it was with Zia. She was beautiful, intelligent, exotic, and looked great on my arm. In the fall, I was going to a university in Wayne, NJ and she was going to college in the Bronx. We went on to college in long-distance-relationship mode.

I chose a school in North Jersey specifically because it was close (but not too close) to New York City. I wanted danger, but I wanted to save my parents some money by going to a school in New Jersey. I was a spoiled white boy with the opportunity to learn about the fire but not get burned. Burned was exactly what I got.

Lynn and I truly parted ways. Lynn was still at college in Trenton and was trying to stay sober. Carmen and Lynn became incredibly close friends, but then had a huge falling out. Lynn also had a falling out with Donna. The fight between Donna and Lynn was so petty that Donna actually called Lynn's mother and told her that the condom wrapper they found in their house was from Lynn and me.

I continued to be hedonistic, which led to a downward spiral of self-indulgence. I was walking that ridiculous tightrope between being a complete drug addict and an upstanding member of society.

BAGS OF DREAMS

Scoring dope is for the obsessive compulsive person. As an addict, I started searching for the precious moments. The sex on heroin was so majestic that I wanted that experience back. Even if I just passed out with the woman I did dope with, the high was so amazing that we thought we had an ethereal experience, as if an angel reached out and made love to us.

Anticipation was everything. Some people actually enjoy the danger of copping, but I was more obsessed with scoring and actually holding the dope in my hand. Whether it was on the street or someone I knew in a parking lot, the waiting drove me crazy. Always late and never with the amount I wanted, I found myself going on scavenger hunts for heroin. From Newark to Paterson to Plainfield, I found myself spending hours sitting in my car. When I was not listening to hip-hop, my music playlist consisted only of Spiritualized and Spacemen 3. I always put on "Laid Back In the Sun" by Spiritualized while I drove up the Garden State Parkway.

Typically, when not at the hot spot in Paterson, the transaction would be with someone I considered a connection. I would pull into a parking lot and wait. There was one dealer I had who was always on a motorcycle. He was known as W.B.S. When I asked him what W.B.S. meant, he said, "W.B.S. stands for White Boy Slappa! You can call me 'Dub' for short."

THE COOLEST WAY TO KILL YOURSELF

"Okay," I replied. "You know, you may get more white customers if you just went by 'Dub.'"

"That's a good idea, my nigga. I'll think about that," White Boy Slappa said as he gave me a clip of 10 glassine bags wrapped in a small rubber band. The film, "The French Connection," inspired me to put the bags in the rocker panels of my car. There are a myriad of hiding placing in an automobile.

First thing I did was look to see if there was anyone suspicious around. Any passerby or stranger could be a cop. I would drive away obeying every traffic law. I usually drove home listening to "Medication" by Spiritualized. I had my fix, my beautiful moment in a cellophane bag.

As soon as I put the dope in the spoon and added water, the ritual began. The candle was lit and the cotton was picked from the cotton swab. I was out of control but I knew that I could not just stop. Someone or something was going to have to stop me.

I put all of my emotion and time into a chemical while other people were adding to their list of accomplishments. People who used to be my friends were starting companies, families, and being productive, creative members of society. Eventually, getting high was not as fun or magical anymore. What had started out as something cool soon became something I was ashamed of.

My dance with the Goddess of Dreams was coming to an end. The song was ending, but I always wanted an encore. In some fast food restaurant in Newark, I looked in the mirror. When it comes to drug use, a good long look in the mirror is the ultimate intervention. I felt ugly. I felt unsexy. I was a failure. I was everything I never wanted to be.

As I looked at myself dead in the eyes, I said the following words aloud: "I am better than this."

After I hid everything that could get me in any trouble, I walked out of the bathroom and into my car. I wanted to throw all the drugs away, but there were two reasons why I could not do that. First of all, there were customers who were relying on what I scored. Most important, the second reason was that I needed it. I needed to be stopped but I did not know how. I would soon find out.

Heroin became the dominating force in my life, my writing, and thought process. While at college in Wayne, being familiar with ghetto culture, I stumbled on Christopher Columbus Projects in Paterson. My first year in college, I met a young man named Anton who loved drugs and the band Ween. Women loved Anton. We became friends quickly and became drug brothers even quicker. We smoked weed constantly. We drank every night. Every Monday, we smoked angel dust. My major was getting high and my minor was cunnilingus.

One day, he was very upset because he got into an argument with his teenage girlfriend, Miranda. He knocked on my dorm room door and as soon as I opened the door he said, "Let's go find something to get us high." I gave a wicked smile and grabbed my ghetto jacket. A "ghetto jacket" is a piece of clothing that a white kid wears to make sure he does not look like a typical white boy in the ghetto. In this case, it was a black hoodie. We drove his ridiculous Toyota, which was falling apart, into Paterson. I saw the project development in the distance.

"Go that way!" I said as pointed to two white dilapidated apartment complex towers. We pulled the car into this parking circle of Christopher Columbus Housing Development. As soon as we pulled up, 20 Black and Hispanic men and children surrounded both sides of the car.

In his naïve way, Anton asked, "Do you have weed?"

One black man who was missing his teeth showed me a glassine bag and said, "9 ½ Plus Up."

"What is..?" Anton asked.

"Get it!" I said. We gave the guy 20 dollars. Some kid tried to grab the cash from my hand and the older toothless man punched

THE COOLEST WAY TO KILL YOURSELF

the kid in the nose. The bags fell in my lap and as I rolled up the window, some of the kid's blood hit the glass.

"Go!" I said. Then, Anton sped his way out of the Christopher Columbus projects.

We went back to the dorm and sniffed up the dope. We got incredibly high and ended up vomiting all night. Now, my dear friend, once again… please do not judge. We act stupid when we are young. Sometimes, young people just act stupid.

As time passed, that housing project became legendary. During sophomore year, the crazy times continued. That is for another book. I had my own show on the school radio station. I broadcasted myself snorting lines of dope. I would not tell people what I was doing, but those CDs had brown and white powder stains on the jewel cases. Eventually, the heroin copping got out of control. The spot got very hot.

One Thursday, Anton and I went to Christopher Columbus Housing Projects to get some bags. I had $75 cash. We pulled in the parking circle and no one was there. So, we drove away, but we noticed a car following us. Feeling defeated, we went to The Salvation Army to look at thrift store clothing. We stopped by the radio station, but the only thing we could think of was getting bags of dope. Once again, I realized that this was not about having fun or getting high anymore. This was about not being sick. After an hour, we ventured back into the projects. We pulled in the parking circle again but no one rushed our car. There was one little black kid who looked like Chi Ali with a black Fat Goose puffy jacket.

"Where is everyone?" I asked.

"Cops rushed us! Muthafuckers straight up racist."

"Five."

Cash and goods were exchanged and the kid said, "Peace nigga!" We drove away with the relief that we had scored. At a stoplight, two cops opened our car doors and put guns to our heads. At first, we thought we were getting carjacked, but we were getting arrested. I almost pissed my pants.

"Give me the pieces!" the Black cop said, with the Glock to my head.

"We do not have guns!" I yelled.

"The drugs, you fucking white motherfucker!" he screamed.

I did not have a choice. I gave him our 5 bags of "9 ½ Plus Up." They pulled us out in the middle of the street, handcuffed us, and brought us into the police station. Even though I had done my share of dumb illegal activity, we were scared white boys and they knew it. One Puerto Rican cop kept on yelling at us, "Fucking white boys!!!"

To make a long story short, I went to court and I was terrified. I got bailed out and arraigned. With my own money, I paid for a lawyer. I was going out with Zia and seeing her on the weekends. Zia stood by me and supported me. She did not do anything to help me, but she did not leave me. We both loved getting high, but we both realized that not being able to get heroin was a blessing.

A change was necessary. Through the grapevine, I heard Lynn was in Narcotics Anonymous. I always kept her number written down somewhere. I remember thinking of her while listening to "The Other Side" by Gil Scott-Heron. I went through my clothes, my desk, my boxes, and then I found a yellow post-it note. As soon I saw those digits on that yellow piece of salvation, I called her.

She knew it was me as soon as she heard my voice.

"Nicholas?" she said. "Is that you?"

"I fucked up." I immediately started crying. "I'm a fucking drug addict. I need help."

"Nicholas," Lynn said, "I can help you. You are in Wayne or Paterson, right? I can find a place you can meet with people. Just fucking go. I've been there. I've been at rock bottom. I will help you, but you must go yourself."

I felt helpless. I felt weak. I felt uncool. I felt unattractive in the eyes of the woman who had worshiped me and was heartbroken because I left her. I broke this woman's heart and she was helping me. After a bunch of shuffling of papers, she found an address of some church. I felt so vulnerable and embarrassed when I cried to her on the phone. Before then, I felt that I always had the upper hand in the relationship, even when we were not in a "relationship." Now, she saw me as someone with a weakness. Still, she wanted to care for me. That's the sign of a loving woman.

I went to a meeting that was in a church in Wayne. As soon as I walked in, I saw a group of people who my parents would instantly think were dirt bags. There was a shaky 30-year-old woman who looked 45 and was missing one of her front teeth. She said, "I used to smoke crack." These were people who once reached bottom and wanted help.

I was disgusted. I was a white boy who came from a very moral family. My family did have an elitist mentality, and I was no longer one of the elite. The meeting took a strange and unorthodox turn into religion. I was completely turned off. According to most people in Narcotics Anonymous, religion is not supposed to have anything to do with the meetings. Well, I went to one where they asked people to get on their knees and pray. I am not religious. I actually hate religion and think that more blood is shed in the name of God than in the name of money. I think it's disgusting. Still, I had no God in the first place and now I had no salvation. I could not find salvation in rehabilitation. I had to suffer. I went home for the weekend and locked myself in my room and went through a hardcore heroin withdrawal. I was lying on the bathtub floor, taking 3 hour long showers, constantly changing the temperature because the water was either too hot or too cold.

Eventually, I got a lawyer and went to court. I was scared straight. The judge gave me a "Conditional Discharge." All I had to do was probation, and not do drugs. Due to the Pre-trial Intervention program, or "P.T.I," because I was a first-time offender, it was eventually expunged. My parents never found out…

unless they are reading this now. (Hey Mom and Dad, I love you. It is what it is.)

My probation officer was very motherly. She was this older Black woman who was very sympathetic but could spot a lie from a mile away. She sized me up instantly. She was overworked and dealt with hardcore criminals. I was just some suburban white kid who liked getting high. I never gave her any trouble and she was very compassionate. I thought she was wonderful. She transferred my case to Metuchen. I took one drug test and passed.

I had to call her on the first business day of every month.

She would ask, "Nicholas, did you do drugs this month?"

"No," I said.

"Are you planning to do drugs?"

"No."

"Have you gotten arrested since I spoke to you last?" she asked.

"No."

"Good. There's no hope in dope," she would say, and hang up.

After one year, I secretly went to court to end my probation. They went through the pageantry of the court room and just asked me 3 questions.

"Have you been arrested since your initial arrest?" the lawyer asked.

"No," I responded.

"Have you done drugs since you got arrested?" the lawyer asked, as though asking those questions was wasting his and everyone else's time.

"No," I responded.

"Are you planning on purchasing illegal drugs or consuming illegal drugs in the future?" the lawyer asked.

"No," I responded, shocked that the question needed to be asked. Would there be someone sitting where I was sitting who would say a different answer?

The judge ruled that my probation was over. The whole

courtroom acted as if it was just another act of annoying bureaucracy. They were "going through the motions" so they could go to lunch. I felt that they all knew that most of these drug laws and that the whole court system was a farce. They all knew that it was all about money. I felt that I got arrested to make the Paterson police look like they were doing their jobs so the mayor could look like he was doing his job. Then, the police and the mayor's office could get more funding to do whatever they wanted to do. I may sound like some liberal cynic, but that little rant was overheard from a prosecutor in the courthouse men's restroom. I agree with him.

    I drove my white Toyota Celica back home to Edison. I was free. I told Kevin that everything worked out and he took out his bong. We listened to Spiritualized and smoked pot. It had been so long since I smoked pot, and I savored the high like a sex addict who had not had so much as oral sex in years. The film "Forrest Gump" with Tom Hanks happened to be on. The female lead, played by Robin Wright Penn, passed away from irresponsible living. For the first time since the arrest, I cried. I literally sat on the floor Indian style, crying, watching a film while I was stoned out of my mind. Don't judge. Many people connected with this film. By no means do I think it is one of the classic films in the history of cinema, but at that moment, at that time, the emotional poignancy touched me.

    "Can You Get to That" by Funkadelic was playing on repeat and I realized that I had to get my life together. I could not even begin to imagine the long road of internal struggle that I had ahead of me. I thought to myself, "At least, I have a good music collection."

THE END OF ZIA

Zia and I had a classic relationship. From a schoolboy crush, a true romance was formed. I was the first person she ever made love with. I loved making love to her. I had dreams of being inside her, holding her, feeling her, kissing her, and worshipping her. I wrote poems about sleeping next to her. We became very sexual, but not kinky. We were two young adults who just loved making love to each other. It was pure, honest, and wonderful. She was beautiful and wanted by other men, but she was with me. Still, she was very much aloof. I found it frustrating, yet charming. She loved painting, butterflies, and music.

Her mother passed away when she was nine years old. She had always been told that her mother died from cancer, but later found out that she hanged herself. I will never forget that I was out with my criminally-obsessed friends when she discovered the truth. I should have rushed to her to comfort her, but I did not because there was this drug deal that I set up. It's no real excuse, but I wanted to buy her a ring with the money. We were together the next day, but I think I ruined everything because of my actions. She always told me that I would never be able to marry her because I was not Jewish. At that point, I felt like a nihilist.

Our sex life was still strong, but very vanilla. She did not understand my lingerie fetish. Lingerie has always been an essential part of my life. When I was a child and given a JC Penney catalog to pick out what I wanted for Christmas, I would always look at the lingerie section. I would wonder what those things were, attaching the stockings to that belt. Women in lingerie drive me insane to this very day.

When I was going through puberty, I used to read the Cable Guide to see what Showtime would be playing on Saturday evenings around 11 PM. The films were not Red Shoe Diaries or cheap cable TV soft-core porn. The films were foreign erotica like the films of Tinto Brass. The films were poorly dubbed with a grainy film quality and had subtitles. They usually had castles, wine, and outwardly lustful characters. Most importantly, they had women in corsets, garter belts, thigh high stockings, and endless film frames of silk.

Other films and books like "Sid & Nancy" and "The Story of O" introduced me to the BDSM world. As I became more confident with women, the kinky side of me would always come out in conversations. I have been with quite a few women and think some aspect of BDSM wove into even my most vanilla sexual relationships. While "The Story of O" was about dominating a female, "Sid & Nancy" had two perverse scenes where a dominatrix owned a man who was hanging from the ceiling in chains. These two scenes stirred something inside me. When I could not sleep, I would imagine being in that situation. I would dream of a woman owning me in a sexual sense. I still acted as myself, but when we did anything sexual, I hoped she would use my sexual nature and my insanely strong libido to drive me into a frenzy. A mixture of this and lingerie was a dangerous and profound combination. As a teenager in the 90's, all the women I knew wanted to be swept off their feet. Most of the women I knew wanted a man to be a dominant and masculine force in their romantic life.

Lingerie became my new heroin. Now, as I write, there are stockings and garter belts in a basket in very close proximity to me. Kim, the young woman I had my first sexual relationship with, loved to use sex to drive me crazy and used lingerie to play with her power. Carmen bought expensive corsets and thigh-high stockings with stolen credit cards. It was a dream come true. Still, most teenage girls do not have extensive lingerie collections. When we were young, Lynn had severe body image issues. She was very thin and had small breasts. The typical guy would think that she was "cute," not magazine-cover beautiful. During the 90's, I would always ask her to wear lingerie and she would just say, "That stuff is pretty, but wearing it would make me just feel stupid." Although we could talk and be more open than many other couples, that was a major turn off for me.

I would constantly tell Zia how I would love to be with her while she wore a garter belt and thigh high stockings. One weekend, I drove to her dorm to pick her up. She had purchased a garter belt and stockings, and had them on when I arrived. I wanted her right then and there. I could not keep my hands off of her. I would just run my hands up and down her legs. I worshiped the part where the black nylon ended on her thigh and the creamy white skin was exposed, only to be partially obscured by the strap of the garters. While I tried to make love to her, she ignored my advances, slowly putting more clothing on to go out for our evening in New York City. I do not know if she wanted to tease me or was just getting ready. She could have been a sexual genius at such a young age, but I honestly do not think she was that sexually in tune with fetishes. Still, even when she was not wearing lingerie, I could not keep my hands off of her. We went out to dinner and saw a film at the Angelika Theater in Manhattan. I remember thinking of her beautiful stocking-clad legs all evening. Concentration was an impossibility.

When we finally got back to her dorm room, we made love on the top bunk bed. I worshiped her legs and kissed every inch of those stockings and garters. I tried to make the whole love making

THE COOLEST WAY TO KILL YOURSELF

session last a long time. For me, it seemed like hours, but I was being delusional. The whole sexual experience probably took less than 5 minutes. I made love to her, constantly looking down at her legs with her thigh-high stockings and her garters. I was drunk with desire and reached orgasm incredibly quickly. Then, I collapsed next to her.

"That's it?" she asked. "I don't understand the big thing about your obsession with garter belts, stockings, and lingerie."

She looked gloriously sexy. I was embarrassed to say how beautiful the moment was to me. Now, I know women who consider it an honor when they make men reach orgasm quickly. (Dear reader, trust me, I usually do not... but we will get into that later.) In hindsight, she did not realize the power she had by teasing me. At eighteen years old, I was still very immature when it came to sex. Though I was kinky in mind, I was still trying to be cool. At that moment, I felt that she did not get it. If she did not understand the fetish, she could not enjoy the power. If she did not enjoy the power, she would not continue the kinky behavior. If she did not continue kinky behavior, we would never work out and neither of us would ever be satisfied. Being in love with a beautiful woman is a gift and a curse.

We continued to have a very wonderful and loving sex life throughout our relationship. We even made several sex tapes. Zia was like a conquest to me. I had wanted her for years, and so had other men. I was the one who not only took her virginity, but we had a relationship. I loved her so much, but it was that young, naïve love. It was not the love of two people who will sacrifice everything for each other, and I knew that. We were never going to get married. I would never have her father's approval. I continued to use heroin with and without her, though I made sure to never go to dope spots in the ghetto. I was going through the days of the relationship, just accepting the time that I was blessed to have with her. I knew it would end, and I think she did, too. I was just happy to still love her, to touch her, and to stay in her life. I was desperate, heartbroken, and still in the relationship. We did not argue. We were just somewhat numb. Still, we would have sex often. I would only see her on the weekends, and I feared that if we did not have sex each weekend we were together, all of my predictions would come true. It was almost like a sexual OCD. I have no doubt that she would have let me have sex with her just to make me happy.

The end of the relationship was approaching. I began to prepare for the moment. I broke out my metaphorical black book and started talking to women I knew. I find it curious that no one asked me why I did not do a grand gesture to keep Zia. I would have done something grand, but she kept telling me that we could never be married and have a family because her father did not want her to marry someone who was not Jewish or Russian. I did not want marriage, with her, or anyone. I just wanted to be with her. That was a simple way of thinking.

She would say things to me that were so obvious. "When we are both married to other people, we'll have an affair with each other."

In my mind, I thought, *I would always make love to you better than your husband would. Whenever you are disappointed in him, you will think of how I go down on you.* My actual reply to her was, "If I marry someone, I will be faithful to them."

She would smile and let out a little laugh.

I felt the heartache coming, but in the back of my mind, I hoped that I would find love again.

When your girlfriend goes on vacation without you, that is an obvious warning sign. Zia went on a camping trip with a male friend, Richard. I was not obsessed with it, though. I was talking with other women because I knew our relationship was ending. I pretended that I did not care when, of course, I did. In retrospect, I did that because I knew that even a grand gesture would not change anything between us.

My family took me out for my birthday and Zia could not make it because she was running late from the so-called camping trip with Richard and friends. As I sat at in the restaurant, disappointed, heartbroken, and annoyed, my friend Susan showed up to have dinner with us. I was so thankful for her. It was a moment that I knew that there were "other fish in the sea." There were other women worth loving. Most important, I felt that someone could love me. Susan and I never worked out as a long-term couple. We had this understanding, and a sexual relationship. As I write this, I wonder where she ended up in life, and wish her well.

Zia wanted to end the relationship and I pretended that it did not break my heart. She wanted one final evening that we actually planned. We had her parents' house to ourselves. We truly had an amazing time making love to each other, perhaps because we knew that we would not make love to each other again. We had the lights off and candles burning. We were playing the "Lazer Guided Melodies" album by Spiritualized. She wore her sexiest dress and I wanted her to keep it on while we made love. It was silky, short, black and it belled out on the bottom. I laid her down and went down on her. As I held my hands on her hips, I wanted to have her in my arms forever. I started getting teary-eyed and so did she. I made love to her several times that evening. Afterwards, we held each other in bed and quietly cried.

I did not fight for her, because I felt that this was what she wanted. Inside, I was angry that I gave her everything of my heart and spirit. I felt that she took it and left with it. In a way, I was insulted. Still, I was so deeply in love with her. For four years, I had tried so hard to be with her. I finally made love with her after finals senior year. We had a long distance relationship for years. We did drugs together; went out to parties together. We were admired by other couples. I felt like my pride, ignorance, and addiction made it fall apart.

I drove home playing "The Last Song" by Trisomie 21. The

looping bass line and the words made me cry one of those melancholic, silent cries. The kind when you just stare blankly ahead and the tears just run down your face.

Weeks passed by and I got a call at work. "Nicholas," Zia said, crying.

"Zia?" I asked. "What's wrong?"

She wept, "I'm pregnant!"

Immediately, I left my cubicle and walked to an empty conference room in the office. I asked if she was okay and if she needed anything. Then, I asked the most important question, "Is it mine?"

"No."

"It's Richard's?"

"Yes."

As I comforted her, we started talking more on the phone. She was a college student and so was Richard. They had no money and they were not able to provide the child with a life that that child needed. Their lives as they knew them would be over. She decided to get an abortion.

After the procedure took place, we met one more time. I loved seeing her again. She told me that Richard was actually very mad at her for having the abortion, and made her feel horrible about the choice she had made. As I have said, I firmly believe in the woman's right to choose. Having been through it with Carmen, I knew that the whole situation was devastating. I was furious with Richard for making her feel guilty in any way, even if it was just for a second. I could have exploited the situation, but I am not the kind of person to take advantage. I just held her and let her cry in my arms.

We parted ways, and at the time of writing, had not spoken in years. When Carmen and I had gone through the agony of getting an abortion, I knew the child would have been mine. When Zia said that the child was not mine, I believed her, because that was what I wanted to believe. Throughout the years, I thought of my relationship with Zia. Every once in a while, I thought the child may have been mine. Although I am completely pro-choice and I would still have respected her decision, it breaks my heart to think that the baby may have been mine.

As I sat in my basement writing on election night 2012, I decided to send Zia an email:

> Zia,
> I have an important question. Right now, I am in the 2nd act of the novel. As you know, you are someone who was important to me and Lynn (for different reasons). I'm writing about "our last night" (which I always thought was cool of us)... Sad... beautiful, but just really cool and romantic. I'm trying not to write too much about it because this is about Lynn.
> I knew that seeing me and seeing Richard overlapped. I'm over it. It was a long time ago. I certainly did my share of things in my past. I remember you got pregnant shortly afterwards.
> What I want and need to know is this... Was there any chance at all that the child could have been mine?
> Like I wrote, I know this is painful. I am not trying to hurt or upset you in any way, shape or form. I do not want to bring this up, but it's important for me and it's important for the novel. Losing children through abortion, miscarriages, or through custody plays many, many roles in this story. More than you know.
> I am asking you this with respect. I am writing this from memory, so I am reaching out to you, Carmen, Rita, Lianna, and anyone else that was even involved in Lynn's life in any way.
> Please consider what I'm going through. Yes, I am reliving many wonderful moments, but I am also reliving all of

the problems, pain, and loss that I felt by writing this. Please be sympathetic.
   Nicholas

The next morning I woke up and checked my email account and found the following reply from Zia:

So to be honest I can't say for sure who could have been the father... Yes, things did overlap and that part is fuzzy because we kept getting together several times after ending it. I think it was Richard's because of timing but I can't be certain. I am not that kind of person so I do feel badly about that. When we were together, I wasn't with other people through college. Ironically enough I got pregnant with my daughter around that same week a year later... Sorry that I don't have a clear answer for you...
   Z.

STINKIN THINKIN

Unlike me, Lynn found salvation in Narcotics Anonymous. She became sober and traded one addiction for another. She became addicted to N.A. meetings. The whole culture became essential to her life. She became a born again rehab addict. While I was having sex with women and starting to get back into drugs, Lynn was going to meetings on a daily basis and helping others to organize them.

While she became very popular, there was a man who was approximately 10 years older than her who would suddenly show up at the meetings she attended. He was good looking, and he was infatuated with her. She did not think that someone handsome like him would want someone like her. His name was Ron, and Lynn began to welcome his flirtatious advances.

Both Ron and Lynn were at a vulnerable and emotional point in their lives. For the first time in a very long time, someone was passionate about her. Ron had a wild and complicated past. As a kid, he was molested by one of his family members and then sent to a camp in an attempt to stop his bisexual tendencies. Although he never finished college, he seemed somewhat well-read and educated enough. She did not like some of the bands he liked, but they shared a love of all kinds of music. He was once in a blues/rock fusion band, and they got signed to a major label. They blew their advance on drugs and the lead singer/songwriter overdosed. The rock and roll dream did not come true. That was how Ron ended up in Narcotics Anonymous. At first, Lynn thought she was settling, but she began to truly fall in love with him.

Rehab is an emotional time for anyone who is honestly in recovery. At that time, Lynn and Ron were two people who genuinely wanted to become healthy human beings. Ron's persistence made Lynn feel special. He wrote songs for her and drove her to meetings. When he asked her out on an official date, Lynn accepted.

Lynn's entire social life revolved around Narcotics Anonymous. She could not hang out with her old friends since most of them still smoked and drank. Lynn and Ron became a well-known couple in the New Jersey Narcotics Anonymous scene. They went to dry parties, dances, meetings and other events. From camping trips to fishing trips, they were a couple that was considered an inspiration to others.

They eventually got married at a hall in Edison, NJ. The venue was not the most high-end place, but it was local. In the past, I've been to sweet sixteen parties there. Before the ceremony, Lynn stood in her wedding dress, looking at the cigarette machine. A memory from years before played in her mind, of the time I stashed a bag of weed for her at that very location. She thought to herself, "*I can't believe that I'm getting married at a place I did a weed deal.*" She told me that a million thoughts raced through her head. As a recovering addict, she did not want to think back on the years of drug abuse with nostalgia and longing. Even though the subject of drugs initiated the thoughts of me and our crazy teenage years, she missed me.

Dear reader, please keep in mind that this is what Lynn told me after the fact. Any story I write, where I am not present, is a story that Lynn told me. She told me that at that moment, as she stared at the vending machine, she almost did not want to marry

Ron. With a deep breath, she walked back inside and went on with the wedding.

Lynn and Ron were sober and on the so-called "right" track. Narcotics Anonymous got her off drugs and connected her with a husband. Lynn started a jewelry making business and had booths at various flea markets. She urged Ron to go back to school and take some computer classes. The future was in front of them and they finally felt as if happiness and normalcy were within their grasp.

THE COOLEST WAY TO GIVE A MUSIC ROLL CALL

As always, music consumed me. Hip-hop became a part of my life. I constantly listened to Artifacts, Organized Konfusion, Gangstarr, Wu-Tang Clan, Pharcyde, Del The Funkie Homosapien, and Digable Planets. As I sold drugs and did drug runs, I always listened to hip-hop. Since I am somewhat obsessive compulsive, I would always listen to "Beats, Rhymes, & Life" by A Tribe Called Quest (even though my favorite Tribe album is "The Low End Theory"). When I finally got my packs or clips, I would listen to the "War Zone" LP by Black Moon. When I was not listening to that, I would be creative and think of a book I wanted to write titled Papa Jia, which was about white suburban young adults in New Jersey selling heroin and going back and forth from Plainfield. I still listened to non-hip-hop music like Felt, Denim, Spiritualized, Spacemen 3, Massive Attack, Momus, James, Pulp, Primal Scream, Trisomie 21, The Wolfgang Press, Close Lobsters and others.

I began to write reviews of albums and started my own website. CDs and vinyl were expensive. I loved getting free music in the mail. I started to feel creative. I could not write fast enough. I learned about new artists from every genre. These artists included PAS/CAL, Boyskout, Elbow, The Music Lovers, Five Deez, Lone Catalysts, Atmosphere, MF Doom, The K's, El-P, C Rayz Walz, Vast Aire, Toog, Sebastian Schuller, The Telescopes, Geniuser (The Wolfgang Press), The Beatifics, Ballboy, Black Box Recorder, Coldcut, The Lavender Pill Mob, The Lovetones, Lem, Astronautalis, The Mountaineers, Dudley Perkins, My Favorite, Roger, Slum Village, and Juggaknots.

I ended up interviewing artists whose music I loved. In the indie rock world, I interviewed Shawn Ryder, Toog, The Telescopes, The Razorcuts, Severed Heads, Scarlet's Well, Momus, and more.

In the hip-hop world, my interviews gained the most attention. I interviewed Baatin from Slum Village (the J Dilla-led group), Kool G Rap, Sadat X (from jail), Lord Jamar, Slug from Atmosphere, Camp Lo, Common, Erykah Badu, Cormega, C Ray Walz, Cee-Lo Green, Edo. G, Freddie Foxx, Guru from Gangstarr, J-Zone, Killah Priest, Inspectah Deck, Lyrics Born, Mr. Complex, MF Grimm, Dead Prez, Prince Po (from Organized Konfusion), Sticky Fingaz (from Onyx), Tame-One (of Artifacts), and Butterfly aka Ishmael (Digable Planets & Cherrywine).

I am still very proud of what I wrote and what I published. During that time, I realized that I should have been a journalist. In high school, I earned an effortless "A" in my journalism class. Maybe, I am a fool. At that time, I was a drug addict. What made everything cooler was that I did not do it for money. I did it for art. I only wrote about music and film that I loved and appreciated. In other words, if you were a musician and I wrote about you, that meant that I appreciated your work enough to write about it. I live by the same code.

I still love getting free music and film… (Hint, hint.)

THE NEW JERSEY HUSTLE

I continued to do drugs as I balanced a full time job with being a full time student at Rutgers University. I remember shooting up in a private bathroom on Douglas Campus right before a final. It was an essay final, which I passed with ease, even though I nodded out between sentences. I transferred to the pharmacy program with less than noble intentions. I went from being a writer to a scientist and I wanted access to pharmaceutical drugs so that I could make my own drug concoctions. The idea was absolutely insane and magnificently fatuous. After I finally realized working as a pharmacist would kill me, I changed my major back to English and eventually graduated. I had to find a way to continue my habit and make money.

New Jersey is in the shadows of Philadelphia and Manhattan. We are the wild and weird sibling of the Tri-State family, always kind of the outcast. Regardless of race, class or location, I am sure that drugs can be found in any city in New Jersey. You just have to know where to look. Much of central NJ consists of middle class suburbanites ranging from White, Asian, Indian, Filipino, Hispanic, and Black. North Edison is mainly upper middle class while South Edison is mainly lower middle class. I lived near a busy street. One side of that busy street was all white families, while the other side of the 40 mile-an-hour road had Black,

Spanish, and Filipino families.

Many of the suburban white boys emulated thugged-out hip-hop culture. Although I maintained my indie rock skater image, I was a suburban gangster for a stint, but I did it to sell drugs. The best drugs came from people who had connections. These connections I knew came from ghetto areas. I was one of those connections between Plainfield and Edison.

Rich in a forgotten history, Plainfield had become a haven for drug addicts and thugged out hip-hop kids from Edison. If you wanted weed, you could go to what we called "The Hill." That weed spot was a one-way street where you had to drive up a large hill and everyone from 10 year old kids to old men would surround your car. One time, Kevin purchased a dime bag with a roach in it. For heroin, you had to go to a place called "The Bricks." This was a dangerous place because there was one way in and only one way out. "The Bricks" was a single story housing complex that drug dealers took over. If they did not know you, you got robbed. Once you got robbed, then they would sell to you.

Now, I could have gone to New York or even Newark, but I had enough with copping and scoring with people I did not know. Plus, I did not want to get arrested again. Through some friends, I had met a beautiful blonde woman named Nancy. She was struggling with her addiction and became a dancer at a strip club. Sexually, we had some fun. She was a sweet woman with a wonderful heart. Years later, I actually attended her wedding. I remember that she wore a very sexy white corset. I digress. I warned you about my affinity for lingerie.

Nancy introduced me to Monisha, a rather large black woman from Plainfield. Monisha was very hesitant to meet me, but I had cash in hand. She only sold to dealers, in quantity, so I acted like I was a dealer. The truth was that I was getting bags for my friends. We met in a parking lot in South Plainfield off of Oak Tree Road and Park Avenue. As soon as I got inside her car, I noticed that she was listening to Faith Evans. Music always connects people, so I used music to try to connect with her.

"Faith Evans?" I asked. "Is she still married to Biggie?"

"Who knows?" she said. "What do you want?"

"I want quantity," I said, handing her $300 cash. "These people in Central Jersey have to go to New York or Philly or even Newark. If they go that way, they have to pay $15 or $20 for each bag. These are young adults with trust funds and rich parents. I'm going to tell it like it is. Can I do that?"

"You're talking, ain't you?" she said, acting as if I was just wasting her time.

"I'm white," I said. "I'm a white middle class man. I'm not racist. I love all races, but we can use racism to our advantage, and make money. These white people see you coming from Plainfield and meeting their precious white children at Inman Grove Center or in some Oak Tree Road parking lot, and they get suspicious. Let me show you that you can trust me. Then, start me on consignment. You'll never have to step in Edison again unless you want to."

Monisha dropped bagged-up clips of dope in my lap. With a dead look in her eyes, she said, "If you fuck with me, I will kill you." Then, she sat there silently while listening to a neo-soul R&B song about love. "Well?" she asked. I smiled and got out of the car.

The excitement in my life went up a notch. I went from a stoned out raver kid to a suit & tie man with a respectable corporate job. The only difference between me and the other working stiffs was that I was selling bags of dope. Eventually, I would get consignment of a pack. A pack was a collection of 5 clips, and a clip consists of 10 bags of heroin. They were small glassine bags that were made of wax paper and held heroin in a brown granular form. Usually, there was a stamp on the bag. Stamps had names like "Good O," "Poison," and "Superfly." My own stamp was "Endorphin Bath."

We were getting a reputation and our quality spread through word of mouth. To re-up on the cocaine, Monisha would travel to

THE COOLEST WAY TO KILL YOURSELF

Atlanta, GA. She would drop hints that she knew someone who knew someone in BMF (Black Mafia Family). She may have been bragging or lying. During that time, I thought it was odd that a record label sent me a Bleu DaVinci CD to review because he was part of BMF Entertainment. I think Monisha would get a kilo of coke for only $20,000 and it would last our crew a long time because we had to break it up into $30 bags. For heroin, she had to go straight to New York City. The cocaine run to Atlanta took a day or two, but she always took a long time when she did a heroin run. Monisha knew some people in the drug dealing world. Out of our small crew, she was the one who was making the real money. She did not want to be too flashy. She wanted to make enough money to live a comfortable life with her children.

After someone did a home invasion and robbed her family, Monisha gave me a 9mm pistol. I never used it and found it impossible to hide. If I had ever needed it, I would have had to dig through all the stuff in my car. In my younger days, my father taught me how to handle guns. I was not scared of the gun itself, I was scared of the law and the penalties of gun possession. After several nerve-wracking days of driving around with an illegal handgun in my car, I decided to give it back to her.

The monster in me had to feed and New Jersey was my feeding ground. As I entered parties, people would just follow me. People could just see it in my walk. As I socialized, I would drop hints, using words like "opiates," "dope," "Newark," "Plainfield," and the phrase, "We cannot talk about that here." Couples approached me at parties. I was just sniffing the brownish white powder and felt that I could control myself. One bump to any female and she would beg her boyfriend to buy her a couple of bags. After the three of us came out of the bathroom, the girl would approach me and give me her number. There were many times where the woman came on to me while her boyfriend or husband was in the other room. In my mind, I knew that she only wanted me because she wanted drugs, but my sexual appetite did not care. My personal soundtrack changed from emotionally poignant indie music to more of a gritty hip-hop edge. If I had a soul, it was not around.

At first, I just thought I was living a double life, making enough money to continue getting high. Weeks turned into months and months turned to years. Eventually, I had some people actually selling bags of dope for me. I was making a solid $1000/week profit, but I was sniffing or shooting up half of my profits. On "The 10 Crack Commandments," The Notorious B.I.G rapped the cardinal rule that has been said since the beginning of drug dealing: "Don't get high on your own supply." The sentiment sounds corny or trite, but it is true. My profits began to dwindle as my high was only being maintained. I could not get the dope and cocaine in my blood stream fast enough. Originally, I thought it was cool to be involved in heroin and the drug dealing scene. I very quickly became what I hated. I became an addict and a dealer.

My life changed dramatically as I lost control using heroin. I was shooting it up in my arms via the muscle, not the vein. I was selling just enough to make enough money to get high. I was a mess.

A change was needed in my life. Drugs were not filling the hole inside me. Casual sex was not filling the emptiness inside of me. Although I met women and I treated them right, there was a shallow feeling inside of me. Sex was sex, but I yearned for that hunger and passion. The drugs and the lifestyle had numbed me. My family was disappointed in me. My career consisted of maintaining appearances and working just hard enough so I did not get fired, so that I could sell drugs and get high without becoming a broke junkie. Without passion or an inspirational muse, I just continued to hustle throughout the suburbs of central New Jersey.

THE UNCOOLEST WAY TO KILL YOURSELF

Every addict needs money to feed their habit and I was no different. I ended up cleaning out my bank account, but still maintained a job. I was sick and penniless. Monisha would definitely hurt me if she knew. I was desperate and my parents were starting to notice. Once, when my father was in the shower, I snuck into his room and took some money from his wallet. That day, when I came home from work, my parents and my brother were waiting for me. I had just purchased five bags and eagerly wanted to shoot them up.

The intervention began instantly. Everyone ganged up on me. I deserved it. My own mother was so mad that she said she wanted to choke me. My brother completely joined in. He yelled at me, "See what you are doing to your mother!?!" I wanted to call him out right then and there on some of his own past actions. I should have.

They were not sending me off to rehab. I did not know if it was because of the money or the embarrassment. I was banished to my basement bedroom for the evening.

I did not want to live anymore. Usually, five bags would have lasted me throughout the day, then I would get a couple more later that night. I shot all five bags that evening with the hope to nod out and never wake up. It was not working. I found a pharmaceutical grade bottle of liquid Percocet that I had scored through my connections. I drank the entire bottle, and ended up throwing up all evening. I passed out on my bed crying, my pillowcase covered with the red Percocet liquid which drooled from my mouth.

The next morning, my mother woke me up and said, "You're going to work today. I cannot trust you alone in my house." After my parents went to work, I eventually got up, looked, and found my father's gun. It was a revolver with a lock on it, but I found the key. I sat in his chair, the one that he is probably sitting in as I write these words. I could not decide if I should put the gun in my mouth, under my chin, or at my temple. I kept on silently crying and moving the positions of the gun. I felt weak. I felt like I was not a man.

Crazy thoughts raced through my mind:
"I never asked to be born."
"Every time I wake up I wish I was dead!"
"I will never find out how The Sopranos ends."
"The world would be better without me!"
"I am a burden to everyone I love!"
"I'll never have extremely kinky sex!"
"I fuck up at everything I do!"
"I broke the hearts of several women!"
"I lost Zia! I lost my Zia!"
"I am a fucking failure!"

I took a deep breath, put the gun in my mouth, and pointed the barrel up to the roof of my mouth so I knew the bullet would go into my brain. I was about to pull the trigger and then I had this realization. Every single human being on this planet is a fuck-up in some kind of way. Then, I thought how horrible it would be for my parents to come home from work and find their son lying dead from a self-inflicted gunshot to the head. My father would find his son in his suburban throne, his easy chair. My mother, who carried me in her uterus, gave birth to me, and constantly told me she loved me, would be devastated. Regardless of her anger with me, her life would be absolutely shattered. These people loved me and I betrayed them. I felt selfish. I felt like a spoiled brat. I was.

Slowly, I stood up out of my father's chair with the revolver in my hand. I blankly stared at the wall of family pictures. These pictures included me as a child with a bad haircut, making an igloo with my brother, my family at Point Pleasant beach, and professionally done family portraits. I took the deepest breath I ever took in my life. I slowly put my father's gun away and locked it up. I shaved, took a shower, ironed my clothes, and went to work.

My ordeal with heroin was far from over, but I knew I had to defeat my addiction somehow, someway. I knew I would do it someday… because of that day.

METHADONE BLUES

Methadone saved my life and slowly killed me at the same time. When I was poor, I saved my money up to get on the program. I started out on 30 mg. I still used for a while, and eventually my dose got raised up to 90 mg. At that time, New Jersey would not allow patients, who they called "clients," to be on more than 100mg. Nowadays, I hear some people are on 200 mg. They nod out in the middle of paying their bill. One guy urinated all over himself because he nodded out giving a urine sample. The culture of methadone has a unique sadness.

Before I ended my love affair with the goddess of dreams, I had to be pushed through the system. The first moment of shame was signing up. Making up a lie to take off work to sign up was better than being a dope fiend sitting at my desk. When I signed up, I was a disheveled Caucasian American guy in a suit and tie. At that point, I did not care. I felt no sense of entitlement anymore. I felt shame more than anything. Surrounded by trash of every race and class, I waited in a barely sterile waiting room.

At first, I had to take blood and urine tests which included a complete STD panel. Since I was careful when it came to using protection, and I had never shared a needle, I was not worried. But then, I began to see people leave the testing room in tears. Initially, I thought it was people overreacting or joking. Soon, I realized

THE COOLEST WAY TO KILL YOURSELF

that these people were cursed with some kind of biological problem which stemmed from sex or drugs. It occurred to me that they had probably thought they were healthy, too. As I walked into the examining room, I saw the whole kit laid out on the table, what seemed to be an endless amount of syringes, cotton, alcohol swabs, and vials. The nurse told me to look away, but I looked directly at the needle being stuck in my arm, wondering what answers it held. I could not look away.

The wait was one week and I did not tell anybody. Who could I talk to? Although I absolutely loved and respected the members of my family, I refused to burden them anymore with my worries. Throughout the week, I constantly noticed calendars. When I went to the clinic, News 12 was on in the lobby, always saying the date and time. Every single time I walked into any room, it seemed some kind of calendar was in front of me, reminding me of the weeklong countdown: 7 days, 6 days, 5 days… and so on.

The phone rang and someone from the Perth Amboy clinic asked me to come for a visit. A visit? I did not want to visit. I wanted to know if I had AIDS, hepatitis, herpes, or whatever. Although my lifestyle was irresponsible, I made sure to use condoms, and never shared needles. Still, there was that tiny chance. As I sat in the waiting room, I played a little game in my mind. I looked at the guy with a tattoo on his face and thought, "Oh, he's dead." Then, I thought that I was being prejudiced just because of the tattoo. The young lady sitting next to me started coughing. Immediately, I thought, "She's dead." Then, I wondered what they were thinking about me.

"Nicholas?" the nurse called. "Will you come with us?" I stood up and walked into the back room. As soon as the door opened, I saw a woman walk out with watery eyes. I thought I was walking to my death sentence.

As I sat down, I saw the nurses and doctors had their typical, lifeless quality. I always thought it was interesting that people who held life and death in their hands were so aloof. I guess being immersed in illness and death day after day, they have to become numb to it or else burn out.

"You're clean," the doctor said. "You have nothing to worry about."

"Really?" I asked in disbelief.

The nurse said, "You are lucky."

The feeling of dread lifted. Instantly, I was reminded that I had recently tried to kill myself. I had been given a second chance. How could I have been so stupid? How could I let myself get into this situation? Right then and there, I decided that this would never happen again. As I walked out of the clinic healthy, it seemed like everyone who passed by me was coughing and sick. With an amazing feeling of gratitude, I walked past all of them and went outside. It seemed like the sky above the methadone clinic was always overcast when I was there, no matter the weather. I even did the dramatic *look where I have been* look as I looked back at the clinic. At that moment, I felt as if I was moving in slow motion as I pressed my car key remote to open the door. As I drove away, I could not have been more thankful for the fact that I was healthy. I tried not to cry, but a tear may have crept out of my eye. As I drove through South Amboy and looked at the desolate state of that part of New Jersey, I had the epiphany that I needed a change. I needed to change myself. I needed to be a better person. I needed to be a sober person. I needed to be a loving and good person because I had this second chance.

The crazy aspect of the methadone clinic was the brutal honesty. The counselors all thought everyone was lying, so there was no choice but to tell the truth. The group meetings, which soon became mandatory, were an event.

Every Saturday morning, I woke up early to be there for the 8 A.M. meeting. For a while, the South Amboy clinic allowed everyone to smoke inside the group room. A room filled with junkies who could smoke was insanely unhealthy. The smoke was so thick that I could barely breathe, let alone see who I was talking to.

Every week, an assorted cast of characters simultaneously entertained and repulsed me. There was an old Black man in a shiny silver suit who would nod out and needed to constantly be woken up. There was a 25 year old pregnant woman who had needed a heart transplant because she caught an infection from a needle she reused for 3 years. She was always showing us her scar from her operation. There was this elderly Italian man who would not stop talking about the Frank Sinatra film called, "The Man with the Golden Arm." There was an ex-gang member who was white but claimed to be a part of the Latin Kings. There was Reggie, a small Black guy who was trying desperately to stay clean, but his prostitute wife would constantly steal dope from johns who she robbed. There was a woman who claimed that she was going to jail because she sold her bottle of methadone to someone and that person died. There was an overweight Italian woman who was obsessed with Scooby Doo and called everyone "Scoob." In a state of numbness, I would listen to them all when they went around the room and told their tales. The various statements that I heard were unreal.

"I don't care if he's my son. I'll kill him if he tries to kill me."

"DYFS thinks that I am a bad mother but my kid has chicken nuggets every day. No one can say I do not feed my kid. Also, he never sees me get high."

"I'm thinking of cutting my clitoris off with scissors."

"All I want is people to believe that I am telling the truth. Just because I nodded off at the wedding and I kept on going to the bathroom does not mean that I am using."

"My daughter found my needles. I told her that I was diabetic and that I have to take insulin."

"It's another day in paradise. It's funny. I went to rehab for smoking pot and people made fun of me. Now, I have a real problem."

"I'm pregnant and I do not know who the father is."

"I keep on waking up in weird places. This morning, I woke up in the memorial park on an old Civil War cannon. My back has been killing me ever since."

"Ever since I got jumped in Florida and beaten with a baseball bat, I piss my pants a little when people talk about baseball games."

"My parents and my son hate me. I constantly think of suicide."

"I constantly think of getting fucked."

"I remember being in the Lower East Side and locked in the room for three hours just for 3 bags of dope."

"Someone stabbed me, and since they covered the knife with dog shit, I got an infection and almost died."

"Nicholas?"

Suddenly, I awoke from the maelstrom of recovering junkie stupor. "Yes?" I asked.

My counselor, Skip, asked, "Do you have anything to add?"

I looked around the room and was disgusted. I was not only disgusted at everyone around me, but I was disgusted that I had something in common with these people. "Do I have anything to say? Yes. Can I be real with all of you for a minute?"

The crowd did their typical hushed acknowledgement.

"We are all pathetic," I said. The crowd started to get upset. "Listen to me! I'm in the same situation. I am just as selfish, stupid, and obsessive about getting high as all of you. I am ashamed of all of you, but in some fucked up way, I understand."

The Black man in the silver suit nodded out and hit his head against the wall. Everyone began laughing. Two counselors came into the group room and helped him out of the room.

Margaret was a woman who was my age. She was typical Jersey shore white trash with a musical taste in hip-hop. "Hey, Nick," she said, "What are you doing after group?"

Joni, the pregnant woman with the scar, interjected, "Margaret is pregnant. She's going to try to fuck you and say you're the father of her child so you can take care of it."

Margaret immediately stood up and stormed out of the room. I looked at Joni and she winked at me.

I stood up in anger and said, "What the fuck!? Therapy worked! I want nothing to do with any one of you." I looked around the room and saw that no one cared at all what I was saying. I said, "If I had bags of dope for all of you right now, you would do them instantly, wouldn't you?" Everyone's faces changed and all attention was on me. "Look, I am trying not to judge, but I do not want to get high anymore. I do not want to be anything like you. Seriously, go to groups! Heroin fucking sucks!"

I walked out of the clinic and no one followed me. I am sure they cursed me out, but it was something that I felt I needed to do. I no longer wanted to be a part of the low-life element that for some dumb reason I thought was cool at one point. Disgusted with myself, I realized that I should have been disgusted long before. I realized that I needed to leave that lifestyle behind me.

LIANNA

I was clean for a short period of time, but the devil on my shoulder was very persuasive. When I picked up again, I did it for money. Monisha had me working on consignment. Without physical violence, she coerced me to move what she had left. I was getting 50 bags for 300 dollars and selling each bag for $15, a profit of $9 per bag, which would have been $450 for the pack. Since I was using, most of the profit was going to Monisha or in my body. I had a young woman named Cristina, who kind of looked like a ghetto version of Beyoncé, do runs for me in order to pick up money. Monisha always told me to keep the money and the drugs separate in case I got caught. This way, the prosecution would have a harder case to prove distribution.

During this time, I was truly heartbroken, although I met women and had sex with them. The women were vapid and they only cared about getting high. They were not concerned with passion. They knew nothing of art, film, literature, or love. They were empty and I was becoming empty, too. The petrifying aspect of this situation was that I felt the emptiness and did not care.

Through my many adventures of dealing with junkies and sex addicts, I met a married woman who considered herself a writer, poet, and eroticist. Her name was Lianna and she had a mysterious, erotic gypsy quality to her. She was a NJ woman who was married to someone wealthy. When I met her, she was in her early-thirties and I was in my mid-twenties. Originally, I met her and her husband at a hotel in New Brunswick through one of her friends, for the purpose of selling her dope. They were in town because they were visiting her family for the holidays. There were four of us in the room, but Lianna and I could not stop talking. We both had that moment when we felt like we had met the person who we had been waiting to meet for so long. When I left, I could not stop thinking of her.

Dear reader, once again, please do not judge me when I say that I am a hedonist. Trust me; this is a tale of redemption. This is a tale of someone who has learned his lesson. This is a tale of someone who loves. "The only constant in life is change." Although I was with several women after Zia, I thought I would never fall in love again. I now know how stupid it is to think this way. Life goes on and so does love.

As time passed, Lianna and I would talk for hours on the phone about eroticism, drugs, past relationships, and current ones. I was so turned on by the fact that she was six years older than me. She could teach me. She was a voluptuous red-head with an erotic, poetic mind. Her husband was also buying bags of dope from me. Lianna and I constantly flirted with each other, even right in front of her husband.

Several days after the attack on the World Trade Center in 2001, an affair began while her husband was away. All week, she was alone in her apartment and constantly asked me to come over. She told me she was scared to be alone, but I did not believe that. In the past, she had lived some extremely arduous times alone on the street. The unique passion in her voice was like an erotic elixir to me. She kept on saying, "I want to see you!"

One evening, I went over her house to watch the cocaine-filled Johnny Depp film titled "Blow." We sat on the couch for most of the movie and I just loved making her want me. I wanted her to make the first move. It started with her hand on my leg. Then, her head gently fell on my shoulder. She played with my hair. I loved it and I was grinning inside, but not in a mocking way. I was genuinely elated. Our heads moved closer together, we looked into each other's eyes and then we just accelerated into each other's arms. We kissed like long distance lovers who just met at the airport. The moment was ferociously beautiful.

"I wanted you so bad, Nicholas!" she said. "I wanted you so much!"

"I wanted you, too," I said in between the kisses.

We went into the bedroom and made love. This was not just sex. This was not just "fucking someone while my husband is not home." Even though we did not plan or say it, we both knew that this was the start of a wild and erotic affair. The night ended with us lying on her bed, naked in each other's arms while a beautifully soft blue moonlight shone on us through the windows. The scene was like something out of an erotic foreign film with a solid budget and excellent production value.

As the months passed, we would do everything we could to see each other. I introduced her to new music by making a mix CD with Massive Attack, The House of Love, John Forte, and Pulp. When she would come to my office to buy bags, sometimes, she would go down on me in the parking deck. Sometimes, I would make her cum when we were parked outside my office. She loved it when I moved the seat back and actually got my face between her legs. It's not easy to give cunnilingus to a woman sitting in the front seat of a Honda Accord. Other times, we would go inside the building and into the stairwell. I put her up against the wall and slid my hand into her opened jeans. I would give her an orgasm with my hand as we kissed. If anyone was approaching, we could hear them because we picked a corner of the square spiral staircase. As a person walked by, I would pretend to console her for a death of a loved one, saying, "She's in a better place now." But my fingers were inside her.

We loved sex and we loved sex with each other. Her love hypnotized me. Even if she did not need heroin, she would make excuses just to come over to my house and see me. She would be with me for hours. I purchased lingerie for her, including a French maid outfit. We would have sex at parties in private rooms of the house. Most of the time, I was the dominant one. She made several attempts to be the dominant one, but I got the feeling that she wanted me to be dominant. Once, she told me she lost a substantial amount of respect for her husband because she used a strap-on dildo on him when they were experimenting with sex.

We were in love. We went on vacations. We went to the movies. I took her to Kevin's wedding. We went to poetry circles. We would write and she loved to edit my work. We would spend hours editing my writing while walking around in circles high on cocaine. I'm sure her husband did not want to know or face the truth, even if he was suspicious. He loved her and just wanted her to be happy. Deep in my heart, I knew she would not leave her husband, but I just wanted to be with her. I never had intentions of marrying her or anyone. I just wanted to be with someone I loved, who loved me. My family accepted the situation and she became welcome. This behavior and hunger for not only sex but each other continued for years.

After I wrote this drop, I sent the rough draft to her and she replied:

> *"It makes me simultaneously nostalgic, aroused and sad. The latter of course for my husband because I would never want to hurt him and I would never do it again, and nostalgic because I remember that pull we had on each other... there was no stopping it or rationalizing, it was like we had no choice. In a world and state of mind filled with drugs and drugs being*

the most important thing in my life, you were the only thing that shone outside of it, piqued my interest, snapped me out of my stupor... it was a beautiful whirlwind.

You have also become a better writer. Of course there are minor edits but I am amazed at how few for a stream of consciousness writing that you say it is... Good job.

-Lianna"

A CHOICE

While I carried on a relationship with a married woman, Lynn was married to Ron. At that point in my life, I thought Lynn had found sober life and love. She was expecting her first child, with a normal life ahead of her. She worked at a policy research company in Princeton. Once she became pregnant, Lynn had an overwhelming doubt in her husband's ability to provide for them. She convinced him to get some technical certifications so he could get work and take over the financial responsibilities once she was no longer working. While he found a job with the same company, he was given a higher salary than she had, though she always did a better job. They bought a house, and their focus was on their future as a family.

The stress of providing for his future family apparently brought Ron's true colors to the surface. He would become frustrated and take out his anger on his pregnant wife.

At the time, AOL Instant Messaging had just become de rigueur. Somehow, Lynn found me through the web and sent me a message while I was at work. She made a reference to what we had called "The Grooviest Day in the World."

"I don't want to molest anyone, I just want an instant message," she wrote. We shared a laugh and went on with our day. Little did I know that Ron found out she instant messaged me, and he was extremely jealous. Apparently, I was the only person from her past she had ever talked about in a romantic tone.

My dear reader, please understand that I am not writing this to feed my ego. Lynn always saw herself as ugly, even though I saw the beauty in her. She told me that she had always looked back at our affair as precious. I did, too, but back then, I was somewhat smug about it. I had honestly thought that I could have done better, and I also thought that she would always love me. I had this horrible attitude that because I broke her heart, she would always want me. Trust me; I know it's an egotistical and arrogant way of thinking. I know. Let's get back to the story…

Fueled by jealousy and anger, Ron slapped her across the face so hard that she fell onto the floor.

He yelled, "Tell me! Tell me you will not talk to Nicholas again!"

"It was just an instant message!"

"I don't fucking care!" he yelled. "You are not allowed to talk to him. Say you will not talk to him!"

"I will not talk to him!" she said.

What began as a pleasant and rewarding romance turned into a picture of abuse. Out of nowhere, Ron would have episodes of violence. In a matter of seconds, Ron would switch from being a kind, loving person to an irate and violent psychopath. Lynn wanted their relationship to work out for her child's sake. She just wanted to start a family, and she believed that she could help this man. He would tell her that he was sorry, and convince her of his love for her. At first, the abuse was not happening that often. She was always able to rationalize staying with him.

During one of her doctor visits, the news hit, and the news hit hard. There was a major problem with the pregnancy. Lynn sat in this cold, fluorescent-lit room while the doctor gave her test results.

"You have a tumor in one of your ovaries. You have ovarian

cancer," the doctor said. "You are going to die if you do not abort this child." Lynn was devastated by the news, torn between fear for her own life and the life of her child.

She felt like she was going insane, and the pregnancy hormones did not help with the emotional turmoil of such a difficult decision. One minute, she thought she was going to die. Then, she thought she would be killing a child. She thought that if she terminated the pregnancy, she would burn in Hell. She asked herself if it was worth it to have an abortion so that she could live. She told me that she had asked herself, "Why is my life worth a child dying?"

After days of pacing, crying, and worrying, she made her decision. She was determined to give birth to her child and that gave her determination to live. Her child was now her life. She was on a mission.

The process began, and she found cancer doctors. As she got second opinions, her belly grew bigger and bigger while she became sicker and sicker. She had to undergo chemotherapy. She lost her hair and felt uglier with each passing day.

Fortunately, the chemotherapy did not affect the baby. A beautiful, healthy little girl was born, and they named her Mia. Lynn was consumed with love for her child. In Mia, she found hope.

Surgery was inevitable. For months, the family worried. While she was having the surgery, the family was together in the waiting room: Ron, Lynn's parents and sister, and the baby. Finally, they were given the news that the surgery was a success. Everyone breathed a sigh of relief. The surgeon and his team had removed a tumor the size of a football, and one of her ovaries.

Lynn survived, and life felt worth living again. After all of the drama, her family life was a new frontier on the horizon. Having beaten the odds by giving birth to a healthy child and surviving cancer, she felt like she could survive any problem. Marriage and family life is not cancer, but it is still very complicated.

A LOVE AFFAIR WITH JEALOUSY

Ron and Lynn had made an agreement when they decided to have a child: Ron would financially support them while Lynn would take care of the baby. There were many days when he would come home late and Lynn would ask him to take care of Mia so that she could have a break. Being a mother is not a 9 to 5 job. There are no breaks or vacation days.

"Ron, please," Lynn said. "Can you just take the baby for 15 minutes?"

Ron always responded with a dead expression, "We made a deal. I work and you take care of the baby." He would walk away and go into the bedroom.

They began a descent into an abyss of apathy and lack of passion. Ron had always liked the fact that Lynn had small breasts and one of his fetishes was cotton underwear. His web browser history had links with phrases like "barely legal." They were all very young-looking women in cotton panties with small breasts.

One evening, Lynn put on her cutest pair of white cotton panties and a white cotton tank top that accentuated her small breasts. She always hated the fact that she had small breasts, but she felt happy that she had found someone who appreciated her.

She told me once that she hated Zia not only because she was pretty and I was smitten with her, but also because she had voluptuous breasts. The song "36D" by The Beautiful South comes to mind. Lynn tried to seduce Ron, and sat on his lap when he was on his computer. He was looking at porn and she felt his erection through his jeans.

"Let's go in the bedroom, B," she said. They called each other "B," short for "Baby."

"Nah," Ron replied. "Let me just jerk off."

Lynn was stunned and literally got on her knees between him and the computer. "I am right here! You have a woman right here! You have my pussy right here. You could fuck me right now. Let me suck your cock while you look at your porn."

"B, stop," Ron said. "Sometimes, a guy just has to jerk off."

The baby began to cry in the other room. Lynn got up and went to check on her, then she went to bed.

Ron finished himself off, then came into the bedroom and just collapsed next to her. Lynn laid there, wanting to be ravaged, or to be the one to ravage him. It's one thing to be sexually obsessive, but she just wanted to be wanted. Lynn knew that there was something wrong, and she was right.

Lynn was someone who always wanted to please her lover, yet jealousy played a major, complicated part in her love life. Her emotions and her erotic thoughts were always charged with jealousy. While she was turned on by her lover being turned on by someone else, she was also infuriated. She began to suspect that Ron was cheating on her.

Lynn started her investigation. She was consumed by the need to find out the truth and prove that she was not crazy. The whole process began with reading his browser history and emails. She guessed his password after three attempts: cottonpanties. Before long, she confirmed what she had suspected. Her husband was cheating on her. When Lynn was pregnant and going through chemotherapy, Ron was having sex with a woman named Jennifer. When Lynn was taking care of their daughter, Ron was spending money on seedy hotel rooms to have sex with this other woman. Lynn found herself consumed with jealousy, hatred, anger, and passion. She had given everything to him, and when she needed him the most, he was with another woman.

The day came to confront him and find out what was really going on. Lynn was suspicious of a woman that Ron worked with, who was married and had kids of her own. Ron confessed.

He said, "I have been fucking Jennifer from work."

Even though she had suspected it, Lynn was shocked and felt like time was stopped. Hearing the truth out loud crushed her. The man she devoted everything to had betrayed her. All the babbling and excuses meant nothing. He was caught. He was done. She won. She had lost. She stayed. She stayed to keep her family intact. She stayed for her daughter. She stayed because she felt that she would not find another man to commit to her like Ron had. She stayed because these were the cards she had been dealt, and she felt that all she could do was play her hand.

The betrayal incited a passion within her that went beyond anger. Jealousy consumed her, and drove her into a state of intense arousal. She would masturbate as she thought of Ron being with other women. Jealousy is a dangerous mistress who will always leave you bruised.

THE END OF LIANNA

I felt so cool for all of the wrong reasons. I was having a torrid affair with a sexy, married woman. Lianna was the type of artistic and passionate woman that I had always wanted to be with. I felt grounded even though she was married. At that time, she did not care what anyone thought.

Rick James said it best: "Cocaine is a hell of a drug." Wow! Lianna did a massive amount of cocaine. Heroin was a back-up instrument in our band of misfits. Lianna started shooting up cocaine intravenously. We became cocaine idiots. If you are an idiot, do not become a cocaine idiot. A cocaine idiot is someone who rapidly falls. A cocaine idiot is someone who feels cool. They feel sexy. Watch the Al Pacino film, "Scarface." Even though it is a remake, this version is important. The film is about someone who is obsessed with power. Tony Montana looks absolutely ridiculous, but cocaine makes this little man think he can do anything.

Lianna and I spent hours together editing reviews for underground artists like Five Deez, Mr. Complex, J-Live, Sebastian Schuller, The Jasmine Minks, My Favorite, and Cherrywine (Butterfly from Digable Planets). We would walk around in circles and edit our work. Although I loved our creative energy, cocaine took over our creativity.

Soon the relationship was focused on cocaine and heroin. We

still had amazing sex. The problem was that it took her so long to find a vein to shoot the cocaine. The more someone shoots drugs in their vein, the harder it becomes to find a vein that will accept the needle. Heroin could be injected in the muscle, but cocaine has to be injected directly into the vein or it is useless. Lianna would come over and would spend an hour and a half to just find a vein.

Buying and using illegal drugs is a gamble. An addict can spend hours getting the money, getting the drugs, and the cocaine may not be strong. Sometimes, it may not be real. Even worse, sometimes, it could be poison. There were times when we got "Cotton Fever." If one little piece of dirt or cotton got in the needle, my body would heat up, my skin would turn bright red, and an intense headache would instantly start. Once, Lianna got an infection in her arm. It blew up to the size of a golf ball. She had to go to the hospital to get it surgically removed. The unhealthy lifestyle of abusing drugs was causing problem after problem for both of us.

I loved Lianna, but I hated what we had become. We were better than what we had become. At that time, that relationship could not have lasted. We were drawn to each other, but she was not going to leave her husband. I could not provide a life for her. She did not have the money to live on her own and we did not have the money to live together. There were also the disappointing times. On one birthday, my whole family and I waited for her at a restaurant. She was two hours late and we eventually had to order our food. I felt so embarrassed. Lianna and I started to argue often. We started to get into those deep, heated arguments. I remember once when I was yelling at her and I said, "You make me think of suicide! Do you realize what you are doing to me!? The way you act sometimes makes me think of taking my own fucking life! That's what you do to me!" We would make love later, but there was this weird and sad sense of desperation. We did love each other, and we wanted what was best for each other, but we could not be a real couple. We both fell into a numbness of drugs and acceptance of the situation.

Life was about to change… for both of us.

"My Dearest Nicholas,

If I can give you nothing else
in this crazy time we have together
endless days, promises or plans
a home, a garden, perhaps a cat…
If I can give you love,
pure and raw, slaved and masterful
pulled from every fiber of my being
so, that at times, I'm standing naked
shaking, in awe, paralyzed from its power, your power
love's power exalted above all else.
If I do nothing else, see nothing more
I will thank God and you
for this feeling and with the synergy of our love.
I will stand at the summit of the highest
mountain and become the wind –
perfectly.
If I die tomorrow
The memory of your skin on mine
Your sweet smell and strong hands
Massaging love
Will send me to heaven with a smile
And I thank – all the answers!
If I can give you nothing else…
I will give you everything that matters
I will love you forever

-Lianna
2003"

ALISON

In the mid-90's, I met a woman named Alison at a 4th of July party in Point Pleasant. I was very emotional and feeling very vulnerable about my relationship with Zia. Alison just got dumped by the young man who she was dating. She was beautiful, and I heard many of the other guys at the party make statements about how attractive she was, though they used crass words to describe her. Several guys remarked that she would be easy because she was vulnerable. They disgusted me. Now, there have been many times in my life I have been a so-called "typical male," but I would never take advantage of a woman who was in that fragile emotional state.

She was visibly heartbroken, teary eyed, and stunned to see her ex-boyfriend walk around the party and flirt with other women. She was still in love with him. That evening I called him an idiot to his face because he had broken up with her. He told me, "She's crazy, man."

Alison and I spent the entire party on the couch talking about relationships. We connected. We were both in love with people and our love for them was unrequited. A bond was formed. I told her she was beautiful. I flirted with her, but I never made a move. I never gave her my phone number, and I never asked for hers. I did make sure no one took advantage of her, but I honestly felt a connection with her. Our connection was one of shared heartbreak.

One day, almost ten years later, there was a message in my inbox on Myspace. When I opened up the web page, I saw her profile. This woman was beautiful and sexy. She looked familiar, but I could not place her. She had dark hair, piercing eyes, and beautiful breasts. She was very feminine. There were many pictures of her at parties and in bars. Alison was a rock & roll girl. Every time I think of her, I think of "Mambo Sun" by T-Rex.

I found a new source of energy. The flirting, the emails, the pictures, and the conversation became a whirlwind romance. Suddenly, the prospect of a real relationship was in my grasp. I could be normal person.

Our first date consisted of getting drinks at a bar in New Brunswick. Then, we went to Best Buy and she suggested that I purchase an insane Japanese horror film called "Audition." I should have known better when Alison picked it out. That movie is not a typical first-date film. We went straight to my house and made love all night long.

Lianna instantly noticed a change in me. My parents noticed the change, too. Suddenly, I did not want to sell drugs. I did not want anything to do with drugs. I wanted to legitimately make money and not have to worry about scoring or collecting debt. A safe, normal, regular life with Alison would make me whole. Alison was my salvation. Sometimes, Lianna would come to my work and give me a blow job or a hand job while I drove my Honda Accord around the streets of Edison. She was holding on to me with sex.

I was in love and very confused. Lianna would not be the main woman in my life anymore. I was honest with Alison about the Lianna situation and Alison spent quite a bit of energy keeping me away from her. At the time, Alison was thinner, younger, and extremely enticing. I loved Lianna, but she was married and we had no future together.

One evening, I was making love to Alison and my mother yelled my name from the top of the stairs.

Alison and I were naked. We were under the sheets and I was going down on her.

"Nicholas!" my mother yelled. "You have an important phone call."

"Take a message!" I called.

"Nicholas! Lianna is coming over!"

I got up and threw the sheets to the side. Alison was furious. I quickly put on a pair of sweat pants and a shirt, then walked out of my basement bedroom. The sweatpants made it blatantly obvious that I had been interrupted during sex. I saw my mother standing at the top of the stairs like an authority figure. She was like the policewoman who directed traffic for the sexually insane people. I left the door open, walked up the stairs and took the phone from her. Immediately, I heard Lianna's voice in my ear.

"Nicholas!" she pleaded. "I will leave him. I will leave him. I want to be with you. I cannot take this! I will leave my whole life behind and I will be with you." I walked back down the stairs. When I heard Alison yell my name from the bedroom, I envisioned her, naked, in my sheets. I went down the hall to the bathroom, and I looked at the sign on the wall. It was just a white background with black capital letters that spelled out, "THINK."

"Lianna," I said. "Do you mean this?"

"Yes, Nicholas!" I could hear her crying and sniffling. "I love you. I will change my life. I will abandon everything for you! I love you! You love me! I'm sorry! I'm sorry! I'm sorry! I love you! I will leave him!"

I almost could not breathe as I stood there in the bathroom. There was a beautiful woman in my bed, waiting for me. That woman was someone I could have a normal life with. On the phone, there was a beautiful woman filled with art, poetry, and eroticism. Lianna was a woman who I could actually share my inner most thoughts with, and she would understand. We also shared something else: drug addiction. I looked up at the sign.

"THINK." I realized that Lianna would never leave her husband. If she did, she would hate me. I wanted to believe her.

"Nicholas," Lianna said. "I'll do it."

I took a long dramatic pause. I remember a tear actually going down my cheek. I inhaled and looked at my bloodshot eyes in the mirror.

"Lianna," I said, "I love you, but it's too late. I'm sorry, but it's too late." Although I secretly loved the fact that I had the upper hand, I was heartbroken. I loved Lianna and I still do. Every single time I think of her, I think how my life may have been different. I could not have provided for her. Were drugs and sex enough? I would love to think that they were, but I was a late 20's NJ suburban drug dealer who lived in his parents' basement. Would she have really done it? Would she have truly left her husband for me? At the time, I do not think she would have. Still, passionate people know passion. I love to think that she would have.

THE RISE OF NICHOLAS AND ALISON

Alison and I were hipster NJ slackers, entering our 30's, who lived with our parents. We rushed into the relationship and stayed at each other's houses when we were not working. I practically lived at her house, and we slept in a tiny bed every night. We were in love. I completely fell for it. I was doing those "romantic" things that I never had done or even wanted to do before. I would bring a bouquet of lilies to her house. Our first Christmas, I even brought lilies for her mother, too. Alison's friends were happy for us. When one of her friends found out that her boyfriend of 14 years was cheating on her, he told her in an email, "I saw Nicholas and Alison so in love and so happy. I wanted that."

I stopped doing drugs, but still had some product to move. On New Year's Eve, she discovered that I had some for that special occasion. She was terrified, but soon became more tempted and interested. Now, I was known for doing drugs and selling drugs in certain circles. I remember Lianna warning me that Alison was just using me for my dope connection. Years before, Alison went to Amsterdam and spent a week in a doped up fog. From what I have been told by many people, the heroin in Amsterdam is a million times more powerful than the dope in New York or New

Jersey. Her interest was piqued and she kept inquiring. Soon, she would come with me on pick-ups and drops. I was not using, but I was making some money on the side while I kept a full-time job. The methadone was working. My life was getting in order and I was in love. When she suggested she wanted to try it again, I begged her not to. Days went by and I finally gave in. When we did heroin together, we literally made love nine times in a single evening, listening to a mix CD I made of romantic songs by Cody ChesnuTT.

In love, Alison and I spent every moment we could together. She made me feel cool. We had constant sex and it bordered on the kinky behavior I loved. Although our relationship was filled with passion, we had different definitions of being in love. There were these moments that made me mentally step back. Alison told everyone that we were going to get married. I did not want to get married, but she constantly brought it up in conversations. Throughout the romance, there was a slight desperation that I should have noticed.

One evening, she was crying and when I asked her what was wrong she said, "I told everyone you were going to propose to me and now, I look like a fool!" I could not afford a diamond ring. I hate diamonds. I do not think some kid on the other side of the world should lose an arm so my wife can have something sparkling on her ring finger. Even if the diamond was acquired by non-violent means, I would not want to buy one. I like jewelry, but I dislike the gaudiness of diamonds and gold. Dear reader, I know you are thinking to yourself that I am a drug dealer and I am greedy. Yes, I was a drug dealer, but I was never violent for money. I was never flashy. I drove an Acura, but it was not brand new. I did not have a need to impress others with my jewelry, car, or money. When not in my suit and tie, I was just a NJ skater kid. I loved Alison, but I was very hesitant about getting married. I just wanted to live a comfortable life with her, and she just wanted the ring.

She would ask, "Do you even want to get married?"

I would say, "Sure. I love you." She had asked me so many times that I had finally given in, but I meant that we would get married sometime in the future. This was enough for her to energize her family to believe that she would live happily ever after. The more marriage came into the conversation and the more I just went along with the idea, she started talking about venues, dresses, music, and maids of honor. I was becoming used to the idea of marriage, but I did not care about the planning.

The night after the 4th of July party at my parents' house, she was extremely quiet and distant. She played that game where I had to ask her what was wrong several times. She made me ask the right amount of times before she finally said, "Again, I told my friends and family that you would propose to me at the 4th of July party. I was so embarrassed that you did not propose."

A complete 30 seconds of an awkward moment was taken up by me not trying to laugh at the absurdity of proposing marriage on Independence Day. Again, I was bewildered by how badly she wanted to marry me. The only things I had to offer were that I was employed, loved to write, and I was in love with her. I would like to think that I was an amazing lover and that had something to do with it.

"Baby, I never said we were going to get married in the very near future," I said as I held her hands.

She wiped the tears from her eyes and said, "I feel like such a fool. I wanted to get married. Don't you want to get married? Don't you love me? I told my parents. I told my family and all my friends on MySpace. I bragged how happy we were. They all thought it was so romantic. I feel like such a fool!"

"No, baby!" I said. "You're not a fool and I do love you. We'll get married. The reality of it is we need money. Weddings cost money. Living on our own costs money. We both made some choices that made us end up in our parents' houses."

"So, we will just be girlfriend and boyfriend and just have sex and live in our parents' houses?" she asked with disgust.

"No," I said as I looked into her crying eyes. "We will get our lives together and live on our own. We're saving money. We are people filled with passion. Many people are robots and do not have the passion that we have. That makes life a little more difficult for us. Sometimes, it sucks, but we have to do it right and not just jump into the formality of marriage. I do want to marry you. You truly want to marry me?"

"Yes!" she said as she wiped her eyes again.

"Seriously, will you be there for me if I need you?" I asked. "I will be there for you. When the pressure is on and I need you, will you be there for me?"

"Yes!" she said.

"Hey, I love you," I said. "I truly love you. I look at you and I feel so magnificently lucky to have such a beautiful woman love me. My heart would be broken if I could not be with you. I want to give you the life and the marriage you want. But I know marriage is not easy. Marriage is about commitment. I do not take it lightly. That is why I have not been married. I want to marry you, but I want to do it right. Seriously, do you love me?"

"Yes," she said. That one word shook me to the core of myself.

"I love you, too," I said with complete honesty. "Let's do this our way."

Alison and I fell into a respectable life. We eventually moved to Plainfield. I purchased a faux diamond ring for her that she picked out. At one point, our cocaine and heroin addiction was getting a little out of control and we had money problems. Eventually, she was on methadone, too. We cleaned up. We both got very respectable jobs with corporations and started saving money again. We got married and had an amazingly romantic honeymoon. I was not writing anymore, but life was looking comfortable and respectable.

THE TICKET

Pay the tickets you receive from the police! Here is the back story for this drop:

When we were moving to our apartment in Plainfield, my vehicle registration expired and I got pulled over exactly one day after. I got a ticket and because I was moving, I lost the ticket and completely forgot about it. Yes, I know that it was stupid of me but that is not the point of this little story. Basically, I forgot to pay the ticket that I got for lack of registration.

Fast forward to Friday night, date night. We were driving to Evelyn's Restaurant in New Brunswick. I was wearing a shirt and tie and Alison wore a dress skirt and top. While driving on Oak Tree Road in one of the Plainfields, lights flashed and the siren echoed. A police car was in back of us.

"Oh my God!" Alison panicked. "The police! Do you have anything on you?"

"We stopped doing drugs," I said. "Do you not remember that?"

"Oh my God!" Alison panicked and was on the verge of hyperventilating. She continued to hyperactively repeat, "Oh my God! Oh my God! Oh my God!"

The policeman walked up to my car and I rolled down the window. "License and registration," the policeman said. I pulled

THE COOLEST WAY TO KILL YOURSELF

my papers out of the glove compartment and handed them to him. "Stay in your vehicle, sir." He walked to his car.

"Oh shit!" I said in astonishment.

"What?" Alison asked. "Tell me!"

"I forgot to pay that ticket," I sighed. "Hey, here is my ATM card." I gave her my pin number, which was her birthday, and made her repeat it.

She chanted, "Oh my God! Oh my God! Oh my God!"

"Hey!" I said. "Be calm, be cool. The worst that is going to happen is that they take me to the station and you take this car and get them the cash. It shouldn't be much more than $100."

She just kept on repeating, "Oh my God! Oh my God! Oh my God!"

"Look, Alison!" I sternly said, "This is an annoying thing, but it's no big deal. I'm not going to prison for forgetting to pay one ticket. Take this pen and write my PIN on your hand." As she wrote the number on her hand, I immediately thought that I was going to change it as soon as this was over.

The policeman walked up to the car and Alison began to breathe heavier. "Would you please step out of the car, sir," the officer said. I stepped out and walked with him to the back of my car. "Would you please put your hands behind your back?" he said.

"Really?" I said. "What did I do?"

"You have an unpaid ticket for lack of registration," the officer said.

"I got that ticket because I failed to renew my registration one day after the expiration date," I said as he put handcuffs on me.

"It's the failure to pay the ticket, sir," he said.

"Are the handcuffs necessary?" I asked.

"I go by the book," he said.

Under my breath, I muttered, "I bet you love saying that," as he led me into the back of his police car. He then walked up to my car and looked inside. My car was an absolute mess. It was filled with papers, CDs, seltzer bottles, concert flyers, and maybe a shirt or two. The officer came back to his car as Alison got in the driver's seat of my car.

The officer drove me to the police department. He told me what would happen. "Your wife is going to follow us to the police station. There is an ATM machine across the street. You will have to sit in a room for a little while and we will get you out soon."

We continued to have a very civil conversation. I was somewhat annoyed because I thought a policeman should be looking for criminals who commit more serious crimes, but I did own up to the fact that I was stupid for not taking the ticket more seriously. There were many times where I planned to call the police station, tell them I lost the ticket and ask how I could pay it, but every time I had that thought I was in the middle of something more urgent like the death of my grandmother or interviewing for a job. Sometimes, it's funny what pops in your head during serious moments.

The policeman walked me out of the car and into the police station. He put me in this little room that was considered a holding cell. There was a metal bench attached to the wall with a glass window. Behind the glass window, there was a desk with a phone. I asked to use the phone and the officer opened the window and gave me the phone to use at my free will. I called Alison's cell phone and she answered, crying.

"Oh my God!" she exclaimed.

"Where are you?" I asked. "Did you get the money?"

"What is your pin number again?" she asked as she cried. I repeated the number multiple times.

"Oh my God!" she yelled. "Fuck! The ATM machine ate your card!"

I was dumbfounded by her panic. "You did not remember the numbers that I made you repeat over and over again? You even wrote them down! Did you write them down wrong? It's your own

THE COOLEST WAY TO KILL YOURSELF

birthday! Just use your own card," I said, and I read her the phone number on the police station phone so that she could call me back.

"Okay," she said. She hung up as a policeman opened up the door and led a very frail Black teenager into the room in handcuffs. The police officer handcuffed him to the metal bench, and then he asked me some questions so that he could fill out his paperwork.

As the police officer walked out, the teenage boy asked, "Can I call my mom?"

"Not yet," the cop said. "Think about what you did and the trouble you are in."

There I was with the phone in my hand, in my dress shirt and tie… in all my whiteness. I looked at the poor kid and felt a deep sympathy for him.

"Whatcha in for, kid?" I asked.

"I'm sick," the boy said as he coughed. "They caught me stealing Robitussin from a pharmacy."

The phone rang and as I picked it up, I heard crying. "What the hell?" I said in complete disdain for her lack of coolness.

"The machine ate my card!" Alison cried.

Bewildered by my wife's lack of self-control, I said "Are you serious? How have you gotten this far in life without going over some hurdles? I cannot believe you cannot work an ATM with my card or your card."

"Hey! You are the one in prison!" she screamed.

"I'm not in prison."

"I'm freaking out!" she said. "You have no idea what it's like!"

"I told you to try and keep your cool and be calm. It's no big deal. I gave you a way to easily fix this. We could have been at Evelyn's by now enjoying their Lebanese food. Call your cousin. He owes us one."

As I hung up the phone, the policeman walked in. The teenager asked, "Can I call my mother?"

I explained, "My wife is freaking out, so that means it may be a bit until she gets the money here. She's not good under pressure."

"Well, let's hope she comes through," the officer said. "You don't want to have to go to jail." The officer pointed to the black kid and said, "As for you, no, you cannot use the phone yet. You have questions to answer and I have reports to write." The officer continued to ask the basic questions of the teenager. Once he was done getting the info from the kid, he walked toward the door.

"Please, officer," the kid said. "I have to call my mother. She will be worried and she can get me out of here."

The officer scoffed and said, "Maybe you should be in here for a little while. We have to finish your intake first." Then, he walked out and slammed the metal door. Looking back, I think that they were probably trying to scare him straight.

I looked at the kid and simply said, "Life is unfair sometimes. Keep your head up. I know you were sick and desperate, but shoplifting can become addictive. Trust me, I know about addiction. The subtle racial tension is messed up though, right?"

The kid shook his head and looked up at me with his sad eyes. "Sometimes, I get the feeling white cops just want to beat the shit out of me. They never do though. But, I always think that they are about to."

"Don't think all cops are bad. There are good ones. Here I am, saying this after I got arrested." The phone rang again and as soon as I picked up, I said, "Hello, this is jail. May I help you?"

"My cousin refused to give me the money," she said.

I was flabbergasted. "After I gave him advice when he got arrested for weed?"

"Yes," Alison said. "My mom is coming by."

As Alison hung up, I had this revelation of sheer disappointment over the woman I married. I know I make dumb mistakes. I own my stupidity. Many of the women who I have been with were always "down" for me. They would lie under oath for me. They would have talked the cops out of arresting us. They would not cry and freak out over a simple thing.

When the door opened and I was free to go, I told the kid to keep his head up. Alison's mother and her boyfriend did not look at me as a criminal. They looked at me as some idiot who let some paperwork fall through the cracks.

"I couldn't believe it!" Alison said. "I was so scared."

Alison's mother said, "Alison, it's no big deal. All you had to do was pay a hundred dollars."

We got into our cars and drove our separate ways. Date night was over. We discussed how I should not have lost the ticket. She was completely correct in her anger towards me and I admitted that. I brought up that she could not handle high pressure situations. I laughed when I used the term "high pressure" because it truly was not high pressure. Guns were not pointed at us. Our lives were not at stake. I was not going to be sent to prison.

"I'm calm under pressure," she scoffed.

We had to drive through Plainfield. We ended up driving on a street where half of the traffic lights were out because the ghetto kids would throw rocks at them. At a light, there was a black man in a plain white T-shirt and baggy jeans who started jogging towards my Acura.

Alison began her mantra, "Oh My God! Oh My God! Oh My God!"

The black guy from the street yelled my name. The man was Monisha's partner, who had the nickname of Duda. As I rolled down the window, Alison yelled, "What the fuck are you doing? Don't roll down the window!"

"Chill! Calm down!" I said. "It's Duda!"

"What are you doing here?" he said as he gave me a pound (i.e. we bumped fists).

"Long night, my man. I must get home," I said.

"Peace, Nigga!" Duda said before I drove away.

"Alison, bad things happen. I need someone who is there for

me when bad things happen," I said.

"I'm sorry!" Alison yelled. "I was a little afraid that you were arrested!"

"It was for a ticket," I said. "I'm sorry this happened. I am sorry we did not get to go out on our date night, but you are not the most conservative person in the world. You have done heroin and cocaine. You have smoked pot. You've been to Amsterdam. You were on methadone. If getting a little more than a hundred dollars out of two legitimate ATM accounts is hard for you, I am now scared. We are clean. I do not sell drugs. We do not use drugs anymore. Still, I need you to be calm and cool under pressure. Can you do that?"

"Let's go home," she pouted.

"You have met Duda many times before," I said. "What the hell was that about?"

"We are in the middle of the Plainfield ghetto and some black guy runs up to our car yelling at us, what do you expect me to do?" she asked.

I sighed for many reasons. "I expect you to keep cool. Let's go home," I said.

My dear reader, you can call me selfish once again. You can call me crazy. You can call me whatever name you want. Please know that I do not care what you think of me. I believe that if someone loves someone else and they become partners in life, those two people should have a connection where they will step up and take care of business. Yes, I should have paid that ticket. My stupid action ruined our evening. I take full responsibility for my actions. It was laziness, apathy, and stupidity that put me in that position. If the roles were reversed, she would have been out within an hour after the arrest. I would have used my own money before I even tried her card. To this day, I think she did not have enough money in her own account to bail me out.

ALL I WANT FOR CHRISTMAS IS YOU IN A FRENCH MAID OUTFIT

Kinky pornography has always been a part of my everyday life. In the past, Alison and I enjoyed some kinky sex, but I wanted more. As I saw it, we had only scraped the surface of my kinky thoughts. I tied her up several times. She claimed to love being degraded and dominated. There were times when I would put a collar around her neck and attach it to a leash. I would pull on the leash while I took her from behind. She would be on her hands and knees and she would scream out, "I'm your fucking slut! Fuck me, please! Fuck your little slut. I love being your little whore." She seemed to like it. I never asked her to say those things, but maybe she just thought it was what I wanted to hear. Looking back, I do not know if it was an act. At that time, early in our relationship, we had the idea that we were like the couple from, "In the Realm of the Senses." Unfortunately, after marriage, the frequency of any kind of sex began to fade. Alison and I reached a point where if she found me looking at porn, she would not only get mad that I was looking at it, but she was angry that I was so unapologetic. I will never, ever apologize for looking at pornography.

Once we got married, the kinkiest we got was her wearing

lingerie. She did not even wear garter belts and stockings. In my mind, that is fetishistic blasphemy. I remember many conversations where I would tell Alison, "I want to be kinky! I love you and I think you are beautiful. I want us to be kinky."

Every year, Alison would ask me two important questions. The first question was, "What do you want for your birthday?"

I would always respond with the same answer. "I just want to see you in lingerie and a French maid outfit."

She would laugh, and say, "No, I'm serious."

I would always reply, "So am I." I would constantly drop hints about how sexy she would look in a French maid outfit, and I constantly mentioned my lingerie fetish.

My birthday was approaching. I often imagined this scene: I come home from work in my suit and tie. I walk into the living room and I am awestruck by the sight of her in a sexy black and white French Maid outfit. The low-cut top shows her beautiful breasts, which are held up by the corset underneath. She has on thigh high stockings and heels. When she bends over and her petticoat lifts up, I can see the garters because the dress is just short enough.

It is not like I would actually make her clean and wait on me. I wanted her to visually tease me and embrace the power she had over me. In my fantasy scenario, I just basked in the glory of her sexual power. I imagined she teased me to the point that I would start begging.

My birthday would eventually arrive. I remember coming home from work and seeing her in sweatpants and my old Dandy Warhols concert t-shirt. I love The Dandy Warhols, but I like women in lingerie better. "Happy birthday, baby!" she said, and gave me a small bag. I looked at the bag and thought that there was no way she could fit a French maid outfit in there. As I opened the gift bag, I saw that the gift was a digital camera. I thanked her, kissed her, and looked at the camera. I thought that the digital camera cost $200. The most inexpensive French maid outfit goes for $15. I realized that she spent $185 dollars to not have sex with me in a fun and kinky way.

Four months later, Christmas would arrive. A month before, she would ask me the second important question. "What do you want for Christmas?"

I would always respond with the same answer. "I just want to see you in lingerie and a French maid outfit."

She would laugh, and say, "No, I'm serious."

I would always reply, "So am I."

On Christmas, I would get excited and envision the same fantasy in my head. In the back of my mind, I was preparing for disappointment, but hopeful. Would Nicholas get his version of Ralph's Red Ryder BB gun from "A Christmas Story"? We always exchanged presents at midnight. My gift was in a huge, thin box. Puzzled but optimistic, I thought that it could be like an entire kinky French maid kit or something. I opened the box and it was a huge Sony 40" plasma HD television set. It truly was an outstanding gift, but I immediately thought to myself that it probably cost $1000 (which was spent from our joint bank account). The most inexpensive French maid outfit goes for $15. I realized that she spent $985 dollars to not have sex with me in a fun and kinky way.

I always thought it was funny that when we got a dog, one of the many outfits Alison bought for Mokey was a French maid outfit. She probably spent more than $15 on it.

Dear reader, do not misinterpret my appreciation and love of this television set. The television is on as I am writing this in my basement office/bedroom. The DVD playing is "The Fetish Films of Bettie Page." Alison would not approve.

In one argument about my want - my need - to have and explore kinky sex, Alison said that she was not comfortable with her body. I told this woman every single day that she was beautiful. My comments were not just "throw away" comments either. I sincerely meant those words. Physically, Alison is a beautiful woman who could have used her sexiness in magnificent ways. I think of that saying: "The saddest thing in life is wasted talent." Alison did not have any talent, but she was a beautiful woman who could be very sexy. The problem was that she truly did not know how to use it. I began to realize that she had just used kinky sex to get some guy she liked to marry her. I told her from the start that I was not like everyone else, and she gave me the impression that she was like me. We had sex on our first date. We had sex constantly until we got married. Once we got married, sex slowed down. Sex never slowed down in any relationship I ever had before in my life. I am not the type of person who begs for sex, unless we are playing a sex game. I wanted someone to want me. More than that, I wanted a woman to be sexually dominant, and to own her sexuality.

Femdom is a fetish that is based on the submission (and to varying degrees, the humiliation) of the male, which means that for the man, it is important to be with a woman who he can trust. So, if we did anything femdom-related, it had to be kept secret. Alison was not someone who could be trusted with that kind of secret. She would have used it against me.

In the beginning, I thought I had committed to a lover who I could trust. I did not want to be with a lover who did not understand sexuality, and got mad if I looked at pornography. Sexually, we were not on the same page anymore. She was not even in the same book.

MOKEY

Another year passed, and I thought we had everything we wanted. We were married and had a future. We had beaten addiction and gotten our lives together, but marriage can be very complicated.

Alison and I found a place in Woodbridge which was closer to work and safer than the area we had been living in. It was a two floor, two bedroom house with a backyard. Every month, we paid twice the amount of money we had paid for the previous apartment. The man who owned the house once tried to force himself on Alison. He was a creepy man who made his own teenage daughter wear provocative outfits. Still, this was a better situation than we had in Plainfield.

Another Christmas was approaching. We decided to get a computer as a joint gift. While I was looking for the larger Mac, Alison kept looking at websites for pet stores. As we hung out with her cousin and his girlfriend, Alison would always bring up the pet store websites. She constantly talked about one specific white and brown Pomeranian-poodle. I did not pay attention. I kept looking at the Internet on my Blackberry and texting friends.

One evening, after helping her cousin move, she pulled into a pet store on Route 22.

"What are we doing here?" I asked. "I just wanted to get home."

"I just want to look at the puppies," she said.

"Wait!" I said as she earned my full attention. "We are not buying a dog."

"We are just looking at the cute puppies," she said.

"We are not buying a dog. We cannot afford it and we need a computer. We both agreed that we were going to get a new computer. We even picked out the Mac."

"We're just going to look," she said.

"No. Promise me that we are not going in there to actually purchase a dog," I demanded.

"Don't be silly," she said.

"I'm being serious," I said. "Promise me."

"Okay, I promise."

"Promise me again," I demanded.

"I promise," she said with a guff.

"Promise me one more time!"

"Okay!" she said. "I promise!"

"That's three times you promised me," I said.

We got out of her beat up SUV and walked into the pet store. I remember that "La Poupee Qui Fait Non" by Cristina had been on the CD player. Little did I know then, but the song fit perfectly for the occasion. As we walked in, Alison immediately walked to one specific dog. The puppy was very fuzzy, mainly white, with a brown spot one of her hips, on the shoulder blade on her other side, and a brown spot that completely circled her left eye.

The sales clerk walked over and greeted us as though he was glad to see Alison again.

"You've been here before!" I accused.

"Well, I like to come by and look at the dogs," she explained.

"That's low and sneaky, even for you," I said.

The sales clerk took the little white and brown Pomeranian-poodle out of the cage and blocked off an aisle so we could play with the dog. As the puppy pranced around, I tried not to get too

THE COOLEST WAY TO KILL YOURSELF

attached. Alison played with the little dog and gushed about how cute she was.

The sales clerk said, "Her parents were named Texas Nae Nae and Texas Chili. She is very curious, so we call her Dora." He paused and then said, "I'll leave you three alone."

"What do you think?" Alison asked with a childlike anticipation in her eyes.

"What do you mean?" I asked.

"Can we get her?" She had a huge smile on her face.

"No," I said.

Alison's gigantic smile turned into a huge frown of disappointment. "Why not?" she asked, astonished.

"Did you not hear me outside? First, we cannot afford a dog," I said. "Second, it's a living creature and you cannot even take care of our guinea pigs, Kamomo and Tinta. When is the last time you cleaned their cage? Third, we both decided that we are getting a computer for Christmas. Finally, you promised. Three times."

She looked at me as if she was about to cry. My eyes started to get watery, too. "I cannot believe how you did this!" I said in a harsh whisper. "You fool me and try to manipulate me so you can have a dog?"

"So, we are not going to get this dog?" she asked as if I just committed the most atrocious act imaginable.

"No," I said. "Come on, babe. Let's go. We'll talk about this later."

"I'll take care of it," she said.

"No, you won't," I plainly stated.

"I'll walk it," she said.

"No, you won't," I plainly stated again.

"I will pay for the veterinary bills," she said.

"No, you won't. You are going to think it's cute and play with it, but you will get bored and be pissed off when you are cleaning up urine and feces off of our carpet."

"I promise," she said.

"You just promised me that you would not try to guilt me into getting a dog, but here we are!" I exclaimed.

She shrugged and walked out of the store, leaving the dog inside the blocked off area. I got the clerk to put the dog back in her cage before I walked out to the SUV. She was silent during the ride home. She was so mad that she angrily turned off "La Poupée Qui Fait Non" by Cristina.

"I hate that fucking song!" she said. I grinned because it is a French disco version of a song about a woman who constantly says, "No." The fact that the song infuriated her gave me a small sense of satisfaction. Personally, I love that song.

At home, she woke me up out of a deep sleep while I was dreaming of women in garter belts and thigh high stockings. "I want that dog!" she said. "If you love me, you would buy that dog."

"What?" I asked, amazed by her insane lack of logic. "My mother is the queen of making me feel guilty and she would laugh at your attempt."

"I'm serious," she said, tears in her eyes. "We are not going to have children. We do not want children, but I want to take care of something. I want that dog. Will you go with me there tomorrow again just one more time?"

"You're going to take care of it?" I asked.

"I promise," she said.

"You're going to walk it?" I asked.

"I promise," she said.

"You are going to pay for the vet and clean up after it?" I asked.

"I promise," she repeated.

"That's three times you promised," I stated. "Okay. I will go with you tomorrow." Then I fell back to sleep.

The next day, I found myself back at that store on Route 22, buying a white and brown pom-poo. The sales clerk cried when he said goodbye to her. We purchased food, toys, and a cage with a bed. We decided to name the dog Mokey. Jim Henson, the creator of "The Muppets," had a show in the 80's called "Fraggle Rock." Mokey was the name of the very sensitive Fraggle, who happened to be a poet. The puppy also looked like a fraggle.

Mokey became loved and well-known in the town of Woodbridge. I constantly took her for walks, and met many people on our travels. Women especially loved to stop and pet Mokey. If you are a man who is looking to meet women, an adorable dog in a town with a varied population helps.

At first, Mokey would urinate and poop all over the house. She was difficult to house-train. I found myself always preparing her food. I found myself walking her during the evenings and during lunch breaks from work. Alison had morning duty. Her one and only job became to wake up in the morning and take her out of her cage and into the backyard. Since she was still being trained, we kept her sleeping in her cage for the first 2 or 3 months.

One Saturday morning, hung over, I woke up to the horrible smell of dog feces. Half asleep, I nudged Alison and said, "Babe, Mokey had an accident in her cage."

Half asleep, Alison responded, "So?"

"So?" I asked. "You have morning duty. My head is killing me. Please clean it up."

"Just let her stay in there," she said. "I will clean it up later."

My eyes began to flutter as I was roused by her neglectful behavior. "Did you really just say that?"

"Yes!" she moaned. "I'll clean it up later! Go back to sleep!"

I sat up and said, "Wake up! That is not only disgusting but how do you treat an animal like that? At first, I was mad that you promised to clean up after her and didn't, but now I am shocked that you were going to leave it there for later. She is going to sleep in her own shit and we are going to smell it."

"Fine!" she said as she got up. "You're overreacting!"

"I'm not yelling," I calmly pointed out, still amazed at her behavior. "I just think it is horrible that you would do that to a living creature. I will help you."

As we both got up out of bed, Mokey whined with anticipation to get out of the crate. Alison said a phrase that stuck with me to this very day. Alison looked at me with tired and hung over eyes. She yelled, "All you care about is that damn dog!" I was dumbfounded.

I unlocked the cage and grabbed Mokey. I walked down the stairs and let her out in the backyard so she could urinate. Then, I picked her up and cleaned her paws as Alison cleaned up the cage. I knew this was an argument that I could not win. She just would not understand.

As I looked at Alison cleaning up dog feces with such anger and hatred, Mokey's clean little paws landed on my leg as she stood up on her hind legs. I looked down at the most adorable face I have ever seen on a dog. She had the saddest yet most loving eyes.

"Hey, buddy! Hey, Mokey!" I said, looking down at her endearing face and her wagging little tail. She just looked at me with this intense gratitude and unconditional love. "Let's get you breakfast and go for a walk. Maybe that girl Leslie, with the shih tzu, will be out," I said as she ran circles around my feet and then, followed me down the stairs.

"Mokey, my friend, this is the start of a beautiful friendship."

EPIPHANY

My dear friend who is reading this, I am so thankful that you made it so far. I sit here writing this and I hope that you read on. Please trust me. There is true redemption in this story. Remember, this story is written for love.

By this time in my life, I had the epiphany that people who are genuine and who are decent at the core are the people I should be around. I have been a criminal, a sex addict, a drug addict, a drug dealer, a horrible boyfriend, and a generally selfish person. Like Malcolm X, I overcame my horrible habits. I felt as if I had been deservedly slapped in the face by everyone I loved, and I had a moment of clarity.

The realization that I had lived my life as a horrible person who only thought about himself hit me hard. I could not live my life that way anymore. I started to look back at my youth. I only cared about what Christmas gift I received. I only cared if my birthday party was the coolest. I looked back at all of the snide comments that I made and how I would embrace the feeling of making others feel uncomfortable. I thought of all of the hearts I had broken. I found myself looking at the mirror while drunk on vodka. I was listening to the "Maggot Brain" album by Funkadelic. I specifically loved the song, "Can You Get to That." I danced alone, drunk. I looked in the mirror and saw my sad, handsome face.

As I looked at my reflection, I told myself, "I am a good person. I am just a good person who did bad things. Deep in my heart, I am a good person."

I laughed at the fact that I was talking to myself. Still, determination overcame me. "I am a good person," I said as I looked into my own eyes. "Continue being a good person. Be good."

I stopped Funkadelic and put on a song by Close Lobsters called "From This Day On." I looked in the mirror and thought to myself, "From this day on… I will be a good person. I will be honest. I will be true. I will go forth with love. From this day on, I will be myself." For a second, I felt sad that I had to actually have a moment like that. About 3 seconds later, I felt grateful that I had that moment.

I thought: From this day on, I will actually try to do the right thing because I am a human being who is fallible. I recognize my selfish behavior. I recognize that I could cause pain in people. So, as long as I am honest and I spread love, I may feel pain but I will love. The fact that I will love and experience love is worth it.

Dark emotions began to set in. The realization of death sunk in my mind and body. I began to think of the experiences I had and the experiences I did not have. I began to ask myself why I did drugs and why I was extremely hedonistic. I decided to not worry about having or being with a stereotypical pretty woman. All I cared about was feeling love in my life. The materialistic life sickened me. Many outwardly beautiful women are horrible and disgusting people at the core of themselves. Many physically unattractive women are magnificently beautiful people. I began to see people as attractive when they were acting in a very honest and loving way.

I was reminded of my brother's opinion of the 4AD band called Pixies when we were on our way to the WFMU Record Fair in the mid 90's. The lead singer of Pixies is overweight, yet the music is amazingly electrifying and unique. I loved to play the song, "Hey" by Pixies on the album "Doolittle."

"I love this song," I said. "It is the best song on the album."

"I don't like the music of The Pixies," my brother said.

"Why?" I asked.

"The lead singer is fat and ugly," he said.

Amazed by the ignorance of the appreciation of true art and beauty, I asked, "What does his weight have to do with the music?"

My brother responded, "He's fat and ugly. I don't like him."

The realization that we were living in a world of appearances struck something deep inside. As I stood in front of the mirror listening to Close Lobsters, I thought of Lynn and how she had always thought she was not pretty. I always loved her quirky and unique style. She accepted who she was and dealt with the fact that she would never be on the cover of a magazine for glamour. I remember thinking how cool she was and how much she liked me as a person. At that moment, I wondered where she was and what she was doing.

My thoughts became darker with every day that passed. I did not care about social networking or my bank account. I did not want drugs. I did want sex, but I did not want boring vanilla sex. I was married, but deep inside, I wanted a connection. I wanted an honest connection and I wanted to be accepted for all of my insane thoughts and I wanted to be with someone who I accepted. I began to realize that I was becoming some kind of robot controlled by money, corporations, and society. I felt that I had to dress a certain way. I had to drive a certain kind of car. I had to make a certain amount of money. I had to be someone who was not me. I had to be who everyone else wanted me to be. I wanted not to care anymore. I wanted to kill the person I had become so that I could be the person who I always wanted to be.

THE LONG FALL OF RON & LYNN

The marriage of Ron and Lynn fell apart faster than Lynn could put it back together. She felt as if Ron was peeling an orange, and she was following behind him, picking up those pieces. Even if she could have managed to put the pieces back together, the orange was going to rot anyway.

The abuse began with laziness and neglect. I have already mentioned that Ron refused to help care for his own child. As a new mother, Lynn was exhausted. She felt like time and space had been obliterated and she had to put entire planets in orbit. Ron would constantly arrive late from work. Whenever Lynn would ask him to take the baby for just one hour, he always refused and would get angry.

As the months passed, the anger and arguments began to escalate. Every couple argues, especially when they are under the strain of being new parents. Regardless of who started the argument, Ron's reactions were not justified. One time, he punched her in the face and she was bleeding from her mouth and nose. Reflexively, she touched her face, but she did not realize at first that she had blood all over her hands. Feeling dizzy, she leaned by the wall and walked to the bathroom to fix herself up. As she walked, she left a thick trail of blood on the wall. The brand new wallpaper was almost ruined. Furious, Ron yelled at her to clean the wall. Lynn told me that she cleaned up her own blood off of her own hallway wall. When her baby began crying because of the yelling, she felt pathetic and helpless.

Lynn had always loved sex but also thought it was an obligation of a wife to sexually please her husband. They'd had many kinds of wild sex throughout their relationship, but the sex became violent. Sometimes, he would just stumble into the bedroom and take her. Sometimes, he would force her to have anal sex. Most of the time, she hated it. Other times, she felt pleasure in the degradation. She hated herself for finding any kind of enjoyment from the situation. Other times, he would be so apologetic and loving and they would make love so poignantly that she felt that sex could almost erase the bruises. Their relationship had a very complicated dynamic.

As time went on and the abusive episodes became more frequent, she kept rationalizing her reasons to stay. She mistakenly thought that a child growing up in a broken home would be more devastating than the current situation. She was not thinking straight and did not realize that her house was already broken. Ultimately, she thought that no one would love her again.

As she tried to raise their child, the slaps and punches to the face continued and became a part of everyday life. Throughout this entire time, she felt like not only a failure as a woman, but a failure as a parent. She could not believe that someone who she loved would treat her this way. She could not believe that someone who she loved would physically hurt her on purpose. Still, she stayed, and after a while the apologies slowly stopped negating the abuse.

One evening, Ron was throwing books and pictures around while screaming at Lynn. I do not know what the argument was about, but he picked up a wiffle ball bat. Lynn was holding her baby in her arms, hiding in the other room. He burst in, grabbed her by the hair, and pulled her back into that same hallway where she once had to scrub her blood off the wall less than a year before. She did not want to fall with her baby, so she walked with him as he pulled her short hair. She held her baby in her arms while he swung the bat back as if he was going to hit her. She immediately turned her back to him, using her body to shield the child in her arms. She tried to run away, but he grabbed her short black hair, which was growing back after chemotherapy. He started wailing on her with the yellow plastic bat. Both she and her baby were sobbing as he hit her back over and over again. When she saw her keys on the table by the front door, she turned around, kneed him in his groin, and ran. With the baby in one arm, she grabbed the keys and ran out of her house without a jacket, without her purse, and without a diaper bag. She got in the car and drove away. A block away, she stopped to put the baby in the car seat, and then she drove to her parents' house. She did not know it until later, but Ron did not run after her.

Lynn's parents have always been very practical, good-hearted people. They are people who I call "infrastructure." They do not create problems. They are the kind of people who help everyone else pick up the pieces. They are not artists and they are not eccentric; they like football and The Discovery Channel. I do not know much about their past, but I do not think they had ever dealt with that kind of insanity before. They welcomed Lynn and her child into their house and told her that she could stay. Of course, they told her to stay and to not go back to Ron.

If you have ever watched a Lifetime TV movie about domestic violence, you know what happens next…

Ron called several times and both Lynn's mother and father protected her by not letting her speak to him. Eventually, the longing of love and the need to make her family whole made her cave in. Most women and men would say that if any man hits a woman, the relationship is completely over. Although I have never hit a woman, I have known many women who have been in abusive relationships. Lynn used to tell me that the mind control and emotional vulnerability is as strong as every battered woman says it is. Make no mistake: A low self-esteem, a broken heart, and a sense of helplessness will make you act in ways you never have before.

Slowly, Ron's phone calls changed. At first, the constant, obsessive calls were angry. Then, he became poetically apologetic. He convinced her that he was heartbroken. The power of his words and persuasion were superbly effective. Ron knew what he was doing. He knew how to convince her. In some insane way, he believed he loved her and was the right man for her. He apologized profusely and told her that he would change. He told her that he would go to counseling and take medication. The conversation continued with a preposterous amount of manipulative layers. He would constantly mention their daughter because he knew how emotional Lynn would get. He would bring up issues of security and stability. He would talk about the meaning of love and his love for their family. He took inventory of everything he did positive to her and she did negative to him. Most importantly, he preyed on the fact that she thought no one would ever love her like he did.

My dear reader, you know as well as I do that this loser was monumentally wrong, but his words hooked inside her spirit and her self-esteem was pushed back into this little pathetic ball that was not useful anymore.

She told her parents that she wanted to go home and she would take her child. They pleaded with her to reconsider. They actually became extremely angry that she even considered going back. Her decision solidified the fact they could never trust Ron, or Lynn, when she was with him. This was the moment that they felt that they had completely lost their daughter. Against all odds, she and her child had survived her battle with ovarian cancer, only to become victims of an abusive relationship that was itself very much like a cancer. Lynn's father tried to talk her out of returning to him. I'm sure her parents even thought of kidnapping the child, but they are rational, law-abiding people. Basically, Lynn fought with them all night. She argued that she was an adult and that Mia was her child. Lynn was correct in her argument, but not her judgment. Lynn felt that no one else would ever love her like Ron did. She felt that she had made her bed and now she had to sleep in that bed with an insane and abusive man who was the father of her daughter. He was the man she had married. He was the man she had vowed to love, for better or for worse.

As I write this, I try to imagine what she thought on the ride home to Ron. I wonder if she saw her baby in the backseat as she looked in the rear view mirror and if she considered going back to the safety of her parents' house. I'm sure she thought other women would hate her decision to return to him. I picture her crying as she thought that everyone, especially other women, would call her weak. She would have been the first person to admit, "Yes! I am weak! I am a weak and emotional person who feels that no one else would love me! I do not want this, but this is what I have created! This is all I have." She told me that there was this one moment of doubt in her driveway, when she seriously considered going back to her parents. She just stared into space and did not even know that her cheeks had tears rolling down them. Emotionally, she pulled herself together. With a feeling of failure, but most of all, fear, she took her child and walked back into her house.

I'LL FOLLOW YOU DOWN

My dear friend who is reading this, I feel it is my responsibility, as a friend, to let you know that this story gets very dark. Some people who may read this are not as open-minded as you and I. Shall we move on without judgment?

As a couple, Lynn and Ron were doomed from the time they said, "I do." Ron let his past catch up with him. He was always an extreme drug addict, but his abuse took on new levels. He began to seek out hard, illegal narcotics. After the baby was born, their new, "normal" life was not satisfying enough. A suburban life with a woman who loved him was not cool enough for Ron. Now, perhaps I am a little biased, but trust me when I tell you that this guy did not care about anything but drugs. When Lynn asked what his proudest moment in life was, he did not talk about any of the moral or decent aspects in his life. He did not talk about the birth of his child or his marriage. He did not mention any of his accomplishments. Ron said that the proudest moment of his life was shooting heroin with someone involved with the band Alice In Chains. Now, as someone who glorified drugs yet overcame heroin addiction, even I think that is the saddest, pathetic, and most tragic way of interpreting pride.

Due to her physical health problems, Lynn was prescribed Oxycontin. Secretly, Ron was taking Lynn's pain medication and getting addicted to Oxycontin, morphine and other opiates. He constantly stole her medication. Her physical pain was so intense that she was in a frenzy, needing something, anything to relieve the pain. Ron used this as an excuse to score heroin.

Heroin became a major part of their lives. Lynn did not want anything to do with drugs. She was an ex goth/punk/NJ hardcore/rave subculture woman who just wanted to find paradise in a normal life. Somehow, they both became involved in drugs again. Lynn just followed him down that path. The money in their bank account dwindled. When Lynn realized that she should not trust her husband, she felt like the situation was too far gone. All three of their lives were in danger. There was an era of complete insanity. There were a million actions going on at the same time. There was some pleasure, but it was mainly anarchy. She used sex to try to keep him happy. Eventually, they could not pay their bills. Medical bills and utility bills were thrown away. It was like a typical montage out of a film where the people get strung out on drugs. Unfortunately, this was real life. No heat and no electricity makes Jack a strung out boy!

They needed a solution before they lost their house to foreclosure. There was one four-letter word that they eventually saw as their only salvation. Lynn tried to make it poetic. "F" stood for the future that they could have. "I" stood for "inferno." "R" stood for "rare," as in, the pictures and beloved memories they would lose. "E" stood for "everything," as in every single aspect of their lives was about to change. Fire destroys everything. Ron thought he had a master plan.

One evening, Lynn woke up with her crying baby in her arms. Without fully understanding what was going on, she looked into Mia's beautiful eyes and felt a moment of peace.

"Get out!" Ron yelled. "I did it!"

Scrambling, Lynn had to collect not only her thoughts but everything she owned. She smelled the smoke first, but when she saw the flames, she was struck by the realization that every memory was burning away. Every single picture was being erased and would be forgotten. There would be no nostalgic moments. There would be no resting her head on her husband's shoulder, saying, "Remember this?" It was all over. There was nothing left. There was absolutely nothing left. Ron burned the entire house down. The pictures were gone. Her clothing was gone. Her past was gone.

Although so many important things had been lost in the fire, the authorities found remnants of drug paraphernalia. While the insurance company put them in a very nice hotel in South Jersey, the police and fire department made sure that DYFS would be very much involved. When child services becomes involved, they stay involved. After investigating Ron and the incident further, the evidence of drug addiction was found. Lynn and Ron were declared unfit parents. Lynn was crushed. She went through agonizing days of worrying that her daughter would be in a foster home. Lynn begged her parents for help, terrified that her daughter would be taken from her. Fortunately, Lynn's parents stepped up and took custody of her daughter.

Lynn was a failure. She felt she had nothing. She was suicidal. Her parents and her family had every right to show their utter disgust and disappointment of her. She did not see any way of fixing the situation. She truly believed that her daughter would not only be better off with her grandparents, but she thought her daughter would be better off without her and her husband.

After the insurance money ran out, Ron and Lynn did not have a place to live. They lived on the streets of Trenton. They would crash at the houses of fellow junkies. The time on the street in the cold mixed with the insanity of constant drug use and lack of money made for a maelstrom of abuse. Ron would constantly hit her in front of people. Several times, both strangers and known drug dealers would step in and beat him right on the sidewalk. He started losing teeth. The uglier Ron became, the more he would say how pretty Lynn was and how she could use her femininity to get money. The desperation became overwhelming for both of them. Still, she stayed by his side.

STICKY FINGERS

The average day consisted of various schemes intertwined with arguments and getting high. If they were not waking up in a shelter, they were staying in the decrepit apartment of someone they knew. Many times, the shelters would only take women and Ron would get mad at her instead of being grateful that his wife had a warm place to sleep.

    The first aspect of a good shoplifter is image. Whenever I intended to shoplift, I wore a dress shirt and tie. I have countless memories of walking into a record store on my lunch break to steal new CDs by a variety of hip-hop artists and indie rock artists. Sometimes, I would have the bottom of my jacket pocket sliced open. I would remove the security tag of the CDs I planned to steal. I would carry 4 but drop the middle 2 CDs in my pocket. They would fall through the pocket and into the lining of my expensive jacket. I was a white middle class professional in a suit and tie. There were countless times when the retail employees would harass some young Black kid who wore hip-hop attire and I would walk right out the door with stolen merchandise in my coat. The key was to always buy something, anything. Even though I spent $12 on one CD, I walked out with 6. I kept 3 CDs because I loved the music and could not afford to buy the albums. I sold the other 3, still in the shrink wrapping. My way of paying the artist was to write very positive reviews of the album.

Lynn was an excellent thief, but she was a compulsive one. Sometimes, when we walked into a pharmacy to legitimately buy a soda or get a prescription, I was amazed at the amount of expensive make up she had when we left. Even I had no idea she was stealing. We would get in the car and I saw eyeliner, nail polish, lip gloss, lipstick, and foundation. Sometimes, she did it for the rush. Often, it was simply out of habit. Shoplifting had just become second-nature.

Back then, Lynn and Ron were living on the street and looking for ways to get money to cop heroin. As I said, Lynn was excellent at shoplifting. She would shoplift DVD box-sets then walk across the street to the pawn shop and sell them. Unfortunately, shoplifting is similar to gambling in a casino. The more you gamble, the house will eventually win. She got caught several times. She became well known to the police and retailers. Soon, she was not even allowed into many stores.

In the mornings, Ron would always say, "B, please. Please. I need some. Can you do what you do?" This meant anything. She was numb with the constant mantra from his mouth, numb to the routine. She did not even know how long this was going on. She did not know what day it was. She did not know what month it was. If it was snowing, she knew it was winter. If it was hot, she knew it was summer. Birthdays and anniversaries were not remembered, not even spoken of. Without jobs or prospects, Lynn had to make money because the sickness of withdrawal was not an option.

Lynn likened her shoplifting to being a con artist. Appearance is the first and most important element. She could not look like a homeless drug addict. The business woman look was always a solid cover. She was lucky enough to get a large knock-off Coach pocketbook. She wore a sexy professional pants suit. Even though she wore pants, she wore stockings underneath. Heels were the key. They were sexy and distracting, and legitimized the disguise. Heels could be taken off quickly if she needed to run. Make-up was the second step. Red lipstick was always applied, but not a slutty red. Eyeliner was essential, but it was important that she looked tasteful. Men are idiots. If any pubescent retail stooge even noticed her, she would lock eyes, flutter her lashes and smile. Then, she would look down as though slightly embarrassed in the poignant moment.

She went from store to store, taking whatever she wanted. Day after day, she stole DVDs, CDs, jewelry, clothes, perfume, and more. When she walked in a store, she was not walking in to look at the merchandise. She was sizing up the security and checking out the cameras. She knew what she could get and where she could get it.

One incident solidified the horrible situation she was in regarding her marriage to Ron. While Ron was going through heroin withdrawal, Lynn had to bear the burden of not only finding money for the drugs, but scoring the drugs herself. As she walked out the door of whatever place they were staying, she knew that something horrible could always happen. On this specific day, she traveled north from Trenton to Princeton. When she told me this story, she told me that she thought of the sign on the Lower Trenton Bridge. The sign says, "What Trenton makes, the world takes."

She looked professional and felt confident. She went to the only mall that she was still allowed to shop in. When I say she was an excellent thief, I am right. The problem is that when you steal from everyone multiple times, you will eventually get found out. That day, she hit every store in the mall in Princeton. After she snatched the merchandise, she hid it in some secret hiding place before moving on to the next store. When she recounted this story, she joked that the merchandise was probably still there.

Lynn walked into the FYE and she was spotted from the beginning. Unfortunately, the high and rush of stealing or working on a con is addictive. The feeling of aborting the con creates a fear of failure. That is why some people steal objects that they do not even want. She looked professional, but if anyone sincerely took the time to take a look at her, if they had looked into her eyes, they would have seen a scared and weak woman yearning for help. She walked around the store and the middle-aged man appeared to suspect that she may not be a customer. The kid who reported to him could not have cared less if she stole from the store.

For CDs and DVDs, retail security has evolved throughout the years. In the early 1990's, they used those bulky plastic anti-theft devices. Then, in the late 90's and early 2000's, there was a time period when they had metallic-looking stickers on the outside of the cases. When they started putting the sensors inside of the cases, Lynn would complain of "female problems" and ask to use the restroom so that she could open the packaging and remove the devices. Now, in 2012, everyone just steals everything off of the Internet.

Those were the days when she would peel the metallic sticker off the case and hope that there was no internal sensor because the discs were worth more in the shrink wrap. She slid 5 seasons of "The Sopranos" into her expensive-looking coat with a slice in the lining. If anyone closely inspected the coat, they would see the stains and the wear and tear. She walked up and purchased a compact disc single. The transaction took place uneventfully. When she walked out through the grey gates that detect the anti-theft sensors, she kept her cool. That second always felt torturous when shoplifting. She walked through the sensors and no alarm sounded. Her heels echoed as she walked to the escalator. Halfway down the escalator, she saw that mall security was starting to gather at the bottom. At first she allowed herself the illusion that they were waiting for someone else, but when they locked eyes, she knew that they waited for her. There was no excuse. There was no mistake. She was guilty. Apparently, they were observing her all day at the mall and she was caught.

She curled her toes and her shoes came off her heels. The escalator was slowly bringing her down to the hell that was her judgment. She moved her feet in the shoes again and those sexy black high heels fell off her feet and onto the silver moving step of the escalator. Once she felt that the heels were off, she lifted her head and realized she was almost at the bottom. In one motion, she grabbed the heels and drew her arm back, like she was a gunslinger of sexy femininity.

"These shoes are stolen from your fucking shitty mall!" she yelled as she threw them at the two security guards. She did not look back as she ran up the escalator that was moving down. She did not know until afterwards that her sexy black heels had landed right in the chest of one of the security guards. Lynn pushed people out of the way as she ran up the escalator. Climbing back to the top felt as if it took an eternity. As soon as she got to the top of the escalator, there was a little boy with chocolate ice cream all over his mouth.

"Hi," the little boy said.

Lynn smiled down at the child's honest face. "Hello," she said, then ran away through Macy's department store. She heard the security guards following. She ran past mannequin after mannequin, wealthy ladies getting makeovers, and men who were buying jewelry for their girlfriends. Then, she saw the exit and ran as fast as she could. Salvation was there. She saw the sunlight and Route 1. She thought that she could get away. Focused on the doors, she bolted past the honest shoppers. A wind rushed against her hair and face as she pushed open the doors. She was free. She did not get what she wanted, but she could get away. She continued to run, but then a brutal force rushed over her like a tidal wave. This was a security guard tsunami. A police woman was there too. She felt concrete on her face and then she heard the *click*. The handcuffs were on and she was caught.

They picked her up off of the concrete as a pair of middle class women walked into Macy's, one complaining to the other that her husband did not make enough money for the party they were going to throw. The police kept her overnight. She could not get in touch with Ron, and there was no one else to call but her father. As though it was not bad enough that her parents already had custody of her daughter, Lynn was overwhelmed with the amount of failure she felt when she made that phone call. When Lynn's father bailed her out, the scene was silent. He drove her to where she was staying. He did not drive her home. Lynn did not have a home. She had a "place to stay." She had a small bag of "things" that she held onto while she lived this horrible and painful life.

Disheveled and completely embarrassed, she repeated two phrases when she got out of the car. She smelled of jail. Her hair looked like she was a mental patient. She felt shame, but she was thankful.

"Dad," she said. "Thank you. I'm sorry. I am so sorry. Dad, thank you. Thank you." Her father is a decent man. Her father is a dependable man. No one would think less of him if he had wept on the way home. I imagine that he stayed strong and waited until she walked to the front door of the place she was staying.

When Lynn walked in, Ron was sleeping.

"Did you get any dope?" he asked as soon as he woke up. He slept through everything and never even asked where she was. "Did you even fucking try to get us dope?"

This was that moment. This was that moment of clarity. This was the time when a woman knew she wanted someone else to fall in love with.

Lynn said with complete honesty, "I got arrested trying to get money so we can get drugs."

"Fuck!" he yelled and threw a piece of clothing. Then, he went back to sleep because it feels better to sleep than to go through withdrawal.

Ron did not ask what happened; he did not ask about her safety. There was no "Baby, are you okay?" He was just mad that Lynn did not get bags of heroin. Once again, Lynn felt like she was in some Lifetime made-for-television film. She knew that her moment of clarity was long overdue. She wanted more, but she felt like it was too late. She had lost her chance at a normal life. She had lost her child, and she felt like her daughter was better off raised by grandparents than the low-lifes that she and her husband had become. The only positive aspect in her life was a transgressive, drugged up guy who loved her. He said he loved her. She loved hearing the words, "I Love You." There was always the thought in the back of her mind that he was saying it just to keep her around, because they had no one else. Lynn felt as if she did not have a choice. Her bed was made. She felt there was only one decision to be made. She knew that at that point in her life, she could only get by or get away. She felt she had nowhere to go, so that left her with one path.

THE STROLL

The day had come and gone that Lynn accepted that she had reached rock bottom, but the truth is that there is no such thing as rock bottom. Everybody can sink lower. She mentally prepared herself for the descent. Lynn put on her tightest and sexiest blue dress and walked out onto what she called "The Stroll." A whole new world opened up, and this was not a loving or glamorous world. This was a world of debasement. Sex was cold and detached. She soon learned the slang and where to stand. There was one block for the new girls. There was another block for the cheap girls. There was a block for gay men and a different block for transsexuals. Since Lynn had all her teeth and did not look like a crack whore, she soon picked up regulars. Some men stopped going to their regular girls to go to Lynn. Now, I know that she was absolutely amazing when it came to oral sex, but this was not the kind of blowjob she wanted to give. Her life was out of control. In her mind, this was punishment for being so selfish and irresponsible by losing custody of her daughter. She felt like she deserved this life.

Throughout the dark times and the horrible men, there were some men who she actually felt that she helped, more than a therapist ever could have. Some men were just lonely, or felt inadequate. Some men had a secret fetish they could not share with their wives. There were men who wanted to wear women's clothing, but felt that their wife or girlfriend would not understand. Lynn truly appreciated the sexuality of the male. She always told me, "Women say men are simple, but they are not. Sure, they are truly controlled by sex, but their sexuality is complicated and every male is different."

Most men simply wanted to ejaculate, but many of them had unique and quirky requests. She told me about a man with an extremely small penis who wore a slutty skirt under his trench coat and wanted to be forced to smoke crack. Another man loved to be verbally insulted. One very kind gentleman would pay her to accompany him to New Hope, PA, where he would buy her clothes and food. These men were perverted, but they were respectful and safe to be around. Unfortunately, she would always have to go back to Ron.

Lynn was a unique type of prostitute, and she became well-known. There was one street in Trenton where the 5 dollar blowjob crack whores stood. Lynn worked the more expensive aspects of the ghetto. She used to work the stroll a block away from the tranny hookers. The other prostitutes would get jealous of her because she had loyal customers.

There were the cross-dressers, femdom fetishists, and some who liked to act as if they were in control. Some men wanted to pretend to rape her even though it was consensual. The man who wanted to be forced to smoke crack liked to watch her masturbate. Sometimes, she was hired by couples. The entire spectrum of perverts was represented. While she did everything she could to stay away from dominant men, she dealt with all men with acceptance.

One evening, she got in the car with someone who looked familiar to her. "So, I never did this before," the man began nervously.

She recognized his voice and realized that he had gone to her high school. "Stop the car!" she said.

"What?" he asked in a panic. "What's wrong?"

"Stop the car right now!" she demanded. The man pulled over

and she got out without saying another word. She felt infinitely embarrassed and prayed that the man did not realize who had been in his car.

Even though most of the men she dealt with were basically harmless, prostitution is dangerous. One evening, Ron was furious because they did not have money and the dope on the streets was weak. Ron sent her out to the stroll. Most of the ladies had been recently picked up by the police on a routine sweep. Also, there was a rumor that someone was killing prostitutes in South Jersey. Police found several bodies spread across the south NJ woods and impoverished areas.

The streets were more quiet than usual. That night, many of the usual johns were not around. She met with several men, but it was only blow jobs in parked cars. The hours passed quickly and Lynn was desperate to get more money. She started to go through the feelings of heroin withdrawal.

Completely alone, she started talking to herself. "I'm out here in my blue dress and no one is around! I'm fucking out here alone. I could get killed and no one would know." As she said those words, she saw her breath in front of her. "Fuck this!" she said. "I'm going home." She started to walk to the shelter, high heels clicking on the concrete. Suddenly, an old Oldsmobile came out of the fog and pulled up next to her.

After the man rolled down the window, she leaned over and asked, "What do you want?"

"I'm looking for a night in a hotel room," the bald man said. He wore glasses and a trench coat. "I want an entire evening with you. I have some dope and coke. Come on, get in."

Lynn looked around and saw no one. "I'm not cheap," she said as she puffed on her cigarette.

The man showed her three hundred dollar bills. "Get in," he said. "We can have some fun."

Lynn was freezing in her blue dress. After she saw the money, she threw her cigarette off the bridge. She got in the car and took the money. The car was warm, but it looked like a car that someone's grandfather would drive. Some kind of horrible country music played on the tape deck.

"Don't you have any other music?" she asked.

"There is no other music in my car," the man said. Suddenly, he pulled off onto a dark, industrial side street. As it became clear that they were leaving town, she became uncomfortable, but going through withdrawal was clouding her judgment. All that she could think about was the cash he had given her, and the drugs that he said he had.

When he pulled off onto a dirt road, into the woods, she blurted out, "Where we going?"

"I told you, we're just going to have some fun."

Fear was finally registering in her brain as she sat up straighter in the passenger seat. The terrible country music and the isolated darkness surrounding the car had her on edge. How had she ended up in some awful slasher film? Was the audience watching the entire time, urging her to ignore the lure of cash and drugs and get out of that car? Were they screaming at her to just yank on the door handle and throw herself from a moving vehicle?

Drugs had put her in horrific situations many times, but she had never before feared for her life. Slowly, she lifted her small, trembling hand and reached for the door handle as the old car bounced its way deeper into the woods. Could she push the heavy door open and get out before he slammed on his brakes? Or should she go along with his game in the hopes that cooperation would keep her alive? She knew she would not be able to fight her way free if he caught her as she tried to run.

She did not get the chance to decide. He hit the brakes, and since she was not wearing a seatbelt, she was thrown forward. Before she could get her bearings, he was on her. The man grabbed her glasses off of her face, broke them, and threw them into the back of the car. As she began to panic, he grabbed her by the neck and pushed her up against the passenger side window.

"Listen to me, you fucking junkie whore," he growled. "I am going to do whatever the fuck I want to you. If you do exactly as I say, I will let you live. Do you understand me?"

Lynn was shaking with fear as she cried. She just let out a weak and pathetic moan.

His thumb pressed into her throat as he pushed her face against the glass. "Do you fucking understand me?!" he yelled.

"Yes!" she cried. "I understand you!"

"Good," he said. "I bet you were thinking that I did it, weren't you? When you reached for that door handle, you were thinking that I could be the guy who the cops think is killing all the whores. Is that what you think?"

Lynn did not answer. She hated what her life had become, but it was her life, and she wanted it. She could not see, and she did not know where she was. She thought she was going to get raped and murdered and left out there among the trees, and she was powerless to stop it.

"I'm not saying I'm that guy," he continued. "But you know that the cops don't really care, don't you? They don't fucking care about some dead whores. Do you want to go back to your shitty life? Are you really going to fight for that?" He laughed at her silence.

When he released his grip on her neck, she remained frozen in place because she did not know what else to do. Seconds later, he pulled out a hunting knife. Lynn told me that she heard the knife scrape against the leather as he pulled it out of the sheath.

"Take off your panties."

Tears streaming down her face, Lynn rolled up her dress and slid her panties down her legs. He held out his free hand, and after she gave him the panties, he said, "I'm keeping these." The panties were thrown over the seat where the glasses had gone. Grabbing her by the hair on the back of her head, he opened his door and

THE COOLEST WAY TO KILL YOURSELF

climbed out of the car, dragging her with him.

"Get on your knees!" he commanded. Lynn did what she was told.

"Unzip my pants," he commanded. Lynn did what she was told.

"Take it out," he commanded. Lynn did what she was told.

"Put it in your mouth," he commanded. Lynn did what she was told.

He held the knife to her neck and said, "You love sucking cock, don't you?"

Lynn was silent. The man slapped her across the face and yelled, "Answer my question!"

She would never tell this disgusting excuse for a man that she loved sucking his cock. She bit down on his penis as she grabbed his wrist so the knife would not cut her. She grabbed his penis with her hand and pulled as hard as she could. The man fell to the leaf-covered ground. As she ran into the woods, she heard the man writhing in agony, and she did not look back.

She could hardly see, but she just kept running as fast as her frail legs could carry her. Without knowing where she was going, she ran in a desperate serpentine path, thinking that if she changed directions he would not be able to find her. All she could see was a dark blur of foliage as she ran through the night, branches hitting her in the face. Eventually, she stopped running, and as she wandered around trying to find her way out of the woods, she thought to herself that the man she had left behind could not have been the killer. He should have known not to let a woman's teeth anywhere near his penis if he wanted to maintain control.

After hours in the forest, she finally got picked up by some NJ policemen in the early morning. She tried to describe the man, but she had the impression that the officers dismissed her as just another prostitute.

When she finally stumbled back into the shelter, Ron was

incensed that she had not been around. She told him what happened, but he just yelled at her for her poor judgment. Fortunately, she had an extra pair of glasses.

Days passed as the stroll wore her down. Lynn had fought for her life that night in the woods, and yet she did not feel her life was worth trying to improve. She accepted her horrible living conditions. She accepted that she was a homeless junkie whore. She became numb and only felt comfortable when high. She felt she did not deserve to be loved and if anyone showed any kindness to her, that love was a gift.

The man who took her down to New Hope never asked Lynn for sex. He only paid her for her company, bought her food, and purchased her new clothes. His wife had died and he just wanted someone to walk with and hold hands. This was a man who Ron hated. Ron became filled with jealousy waiting for her when she was with him.

One evening, she was being driven back from New Hope and she had a feeling of dread. She did not want to go back because she knew Ron would be furious. As she looked at the stars and saw the city of Trenton coming closer, she tried to focus her thoughts on the new clothes in her bag and the delicious food in her stomach.

When the car pulled up in front of the shelter, Ron stomped out the front door. "You cunt whore!" he screamed. A crowd began to gather. When she opened the car door, he grabbed her thin, straight black hair. He pulled her out of the car and onto the street. Lynn fell to the ground and he began to drag her by her hair. Ron backslapped her in the face and she fell onto the pavement, sobbing.

"Please," she begged. "Stop! Please! I'm back now!"

Breathing heavy, he balled up his hand into a fist, pulled his arm back and then, punched her in her face.

Suddenly, a well-built Black man said, "Hey, man! Stop it!"

"Fuck you! Fucking nigger!" Ron shouted. A gasp echoed throughout the crowd of Blacks and Latinos. All of the sudden, someone else stepped up and punched Ron in the side of his face. Then, someone else kicked the back of one his knees. He fell to the ground and hit his face on the dirty concrete. Lynn looked up and saw three Black men kicking Ron. "Get him up!" one of the men shouted. Another man put his arms under Ron's arms and lifted him up.

"Yeah, motherfucking white boy!" the man said as he grabbed Ron's mouth and shoved his fingers inside. The man opened Ron's mouth and spit right inside. "You like to beat on a fucking woman?" He punched him three times dead in his face. Blood was coming out of his nose and mouth. "Keep him up!" the man said.

Another man stepped in front of him and spit on Ron. He punched Ron in the stomach and as Ron's head fell down, the man gave him a swift uppercut. Ron fell limp and the man holding him let him fall to the ground.

One of the men looked at Lynn, who was sitting on the ground in the street, out of breath. He said, "Listen, girl. Walk up those stairs."

Lynn waved and shook her head as if she was going to stay for her husband to take care of him. She tried to utter the words, "Do not hurt him anymore," but the man put his hand over her mouth.

"Listen," the man said. "We're just going to make him repent and then he will crawl back. He deserves this. Go get some sleep." Lynn tried to shake her head again, but the man stopped her. "Walk back upstairs and go to bed. I am deadly serious." Exhausted and confused, she got up and walked up the stairs to the shelter. She heard the kicks and punches land as Ron moaned. She heard spectators exclaiming, "Oh, shit," "Damn," and "That nigga fucked that white boy up!"

She walked through the doorway and the door closed behind her. As she limped to her room with tears rolling down her face, she gave a very subtle grin. Quietly, she said aloud to herself, "You do deserve it, asshole."

THE STAIRWELL

Not many people have respect for a prostitute, or come to a prostitute's aid. Lynn was a prostitute, a thief, a drug addict, and someone who had made poor decisions, but just because a woman is a prostitute, a crime against her is still a crime.

She did not want to go out that evening. Ron wanted bags of dope for that night and the morning. It was almost midnight and he told her to go out to the projects. Reluctantly, she went out to score. Although she ventured to one of the housing projects in Trenton, no one was holding. The Nigerians were her last resort. She was hesitant to deal with them because this specific group of Nigerians in this housing block had a reputation for violence.

She could see her breath in front of her as she walked. The cold air cut right through her jeans, sweater, and raggedy winter coat. From afar, she saw the four of them standing right in front of the steps that led to the boiler room. Suddenly, she stopped in her tracks and turned around, having second thoughts.

A Nigerian man appeared seemingly out of nowhere, catching her by complete surprise. "Lady!" he said. "Are you looking for bags?" He wore typical hip-hop attire of baggy jeans and a puffy winter jacket. The gold chain around his neck caught the light from the street lamp.

"No," she said and tried to walk away.

He stopped her by putting his hand up. "Woman, don't worry," he said, "I have some. I have what you need."

"I'm fine," Lynn said. Immediately, she felt multiple hands grab her hair and her arms. A hand fell over her mouth before she could scream, and the men pulled her across the concrete. Her right sneaker fell off as she screamed and bit into the hand of the stranger who was holding her mouth. They dragged her down the flight of outside stairs that led to the locked boiler room door. She struggled and screamed, but they held her down as they took her dirty, ripped jeans off. One of them took out a box of condoms. They started unbuckling their oversized jeans with one hand while holding her down with the other.

"Shut that whore up!" one said.

"Here!" another man said as he threw condoms to each person.

Lynn cried and yelled, but every sound she made was muffled by a man's hand. Then, she felt it. She felt a man's erection stab into her, violating something sacred. She was a whore. She was in the business of selling sex. Even when johns paid her so that they could pretend to rape her, the act was technically "consensual." Just because she was a prostitute, did not mean that she deserved to be raped by a group of savage men.

The reality set in and she accepted the fact that she was actually being raped. She was being gang raped. The pain and the violation were incomprehensible. She knew this was not going to end anytime soon, and she knew she was powerless to stop them. As she looked up at the stars in the clear, cold sky above her, the moans and laughs of the deplorable men on top of her were almost put on mute until she heard reggae. Out of one of the project windows, she heard a very popular, classic reggae song. The rest of the incident was just a blur. As the four took turns violating her, she gave in and let them take advantage of her body. She was a receptacle.

They stole her money and left her at the bottom of a dirty

outside stairwell with the dead leaves and other trash. After she woke up, she slowly stumbled up the stairs and walked back out to the street. A kind elderly Nigerian man, who saw her with her busted lip and disheveled appearance, came to her aid. This was not someone who was mugged. She was the picture of someone violated.

At the hospital, the nurses and doctors did the necessary procedures. She heard the police laughing at her in the other room. She actually heard a policeman say, "She's a whore. Who cares? You really want to waste time asking her questions?"

The next day, she found her way back to Ron at the homeless shelter. He was furious that she did not score for him. After a half an hour of yelling at her, he eventually listened to her long enough to hear that she was gang raped. Instead of comforting her, he became jealous and smacked her because she was too sexy and everyone knew that she was a whore.

Lynn was just too tired to fight back, let alone argue. She just wanted to lay down and close her eyes. She wanted her old life back. She wanted her baby. She wanted warmth. She wanted love.

THE WALK

Health issues began to dominate Lynn's life. She was living a life where she did not care anymore. She felt that nothing mattered. She lost her daughter. She lost her house. She lost all of her money. She lost the faith she had in marriage. She lost any respect her family had for her. She lost the respect she had for herself.

After a blur of hospital visits and street life, she woke up in a hospital bed and could not move her legs. She wept for an entire day, holding her useless thighs in her hands. She had contracted MRSA, and the doctors told her that she would never walk again. She was confined to a wheelchair. She was considered officially disabled, qualified for Medicare, and placed in a nursing home. Lynn was in a drugged up stupor. The nurses had to lift her out of the bed. Her parents would bring her daughter to visit. Mia was not a baby anymore; she could walk. Lynn was embarrassed to have her child and her parents visit her in a ghetto nursing home.

Ron would come by sometimes and give her bags of dope or pills. Sometimes, she would give him her medication if he asked. Other times, he would steal it. There were times she was in the wheelchair and he would take some of her pills right in front of her. It was not like she was going to get up to stop him.

"I need those!" she would cry.

"You can get more," he would say without remorse.

"The doctors will not fill the script until a certain date," she said helplessly.

"I'll get you some dope," he said. "I can't go through withdrawal tonight." He would kiss her on the cheek and walk out.

In my mind, I picture her sitting in her wheel chair with the strength of someone like my grandmother during her final years. Her hands would tremble as she picked up forks and spoons to eat. When the nurses bathed her, her body would shake and she would slowly bend over as if she had a hunch. Any moment her useless legs would give out, but she tried so incredibly hard not to fall as the Jamaican nurses would stand her up naked.

She also had multiple counseling sessions and group therapy meetings.

One evening, she cried all night in bed because of the pain and the situation she was in. Fed up, a fury boiled inside of her. A serious determination was born. She requested physical therapy. She did her research and found out the government would assist with her decision.

Every day, Lynn was bussed to the hospital down the street. She spent hours doing exercises with the physical therapists. Pablo was the main physical therapist in charge of her case. He began every session by saying, "Hello, Lynn. My name is Pablo and I will do everything I can to make you walk."

At first, it was simply her lying down on a mat and the therapist moving her legs. After what felt like an endless amount of exercise, she would slowly be able to stand with the help of the equipment. Her legs would buckle and sometimes she would fall down on the mat. Every time this happened, she would say, "Let's try again." The nurses and therapists would help her up on the parallel bars. Her arms would shake and tears would come out of her eyes and roll down her cheeks. She was not embarrassed to look helpless anymore. She did not care because she had nothing to lose. She would just thank the therapists. A year passed and she started using a walker. There were little cut tennis balls on the feet of the walker so that she could slide the walker across the linoleum floor. She would tell Ron not to visit her in the nursing home because she wanted to go to physical therapy. He would get mad at her for two reasons. First, he wanted to get some pills from her. Second, he did not feel wanted by her. He was not getting her attention. Sometimes, Lynn would not take his calls. She just wanted to go to physical therapy because it was a haven that gave her hope.

Some say laughter is the best medicine. Every time she fell, Lynn would crack a joke. Eventually, the physical therapists loved her company and stayed past the required shift to help her exercise. She had a bleak and sarcastic humor. She would say slightly humorous things during the most painful and awkward moments.

"Gimpy girl is just speeding across the room, huh?"

"I'm on prednisone. Now, I don't need Botox."

"Don't I look sexy?"

"Did you know I'm trying to walk so I can learn to run away from my husband?"

"One day, we should race each other. It will be like the turtle and the hare."

"You know, I am working this hard just to be able to wrap my legs around a good looking man."

"I am learning how to walk because I know a sexy man with a foot fetish."

"I have a handsome young man who wants to see me in heels."

"I am doing this to walk all over my husband."

Through time, Lynn graduated to using only a cane. At first it was one of those canes with four little legs at the bottom. Eventually, she used a regular cane. Even though she had the freedom to walk, she continued to go to physical therapy.

After many more months, a deep change took place in her.

She felt as if she was at the end of a movie where the protagonist overcomes his or her disability. When she thought of Cuba Gooding, Jr. in the film "Men of Honor," she smiled. Her physical appearance changed. She stood up straight. Her legs and arms did not tremble. Her eyes were brighter and her skin was clear. Most importantly, she was able to hide her pills and not be at the nursing home when she knew Ron would come by. When she had to go to the bathroom in the middle of the night, she would sometimes not use her cane. Eventually, she put her cane in the closet. She had a slight limp and she walked slowly, but she was walking on her own. As someone who had experienced a torturous kind of hell on earth, she felt free. She had survived cancer, an abusive husband, and having been stuck in a wheelchair. She wanted to be a part of her child's life again.

On her last day of physical therapy, she signed the release forms while standing on her own two feet. She hugged the staff as many of them became very teary eyed. She laughed and wiped her own eyes. "You know I love you guys," she said. "Still, I cannot wait to walk out of here." Everyone laughed as she put her pocketbook on her shoulder and walked out the front door. She lit a cigarette and put the lighter in her purse. The nursing home was a little more than a block away. All this time, the shuttle bus would take her there and pick her up. The shuttle bus was waiting for her.

"Lynn," Raul, the shuttle bus driver called. "Looking good, senorita!"

"Hey, Raul," she said to the shuttle bus driver. She took a puff of her cigarette. "I think I am going to walk home today."

Raul smiled. "You got it, girl."

She looked down the dirty Trenton street and slowly made her way down sidewalk. She realized that she had never actually walked down that street before. As she walked, she found beauty that normally would have been overlooked. She noticed the little flowers that grew through the cracks in the concrete. She noticed

THE COOLEST WAY TO KILL YOURSELF

the adorable Latino babies being carried by their mothers. She saw signs of hope in the small, independent shops that she passed.

Recently, Lynn had a very long discussion with her mother about leaving the nursing home and living with her parents and her daughter. Enough time had passed and Lynn's mother welcomed her back but under the condition that Ron would never step foot in the house. Lynn packed her bags and was planning on sneaking out without Ron finding out.

On the day she was about to leave, Ron came by the nursing home. It was as if he had known she planned to leave him. He snuck up on her the minute she locked her paisley covered suitcase. Her father was outside putting the wheelchair, the canes, the books, and the beads she used to make necklaces into the car.

"Where are you going?" Ron asked.

"I have to stay with my parents," she said. "Medicare will not pay for me to live here anymore." She was lying, but was past the point of caring.

"You can live with me," he said.

"In a shelter? No. I need to be around Mia," she stated. It should have come as no surprise that he did not understand that sentiment.

"What about me?" he exclaimed.

"Take care of yourself," Lynn said. "We will still see each other. My parents go to Atlantic City all the time."

"Fine!" he yelled. "You fucking bitch!"

Suddenly, a male Jamaican attendant popped his head in the room. "Are you okay Lynn?" he asked as he stared at Ron.

"I'm fine, Desmond," she said.

"Well, Lynn, even though I will miss you, I am glad to see you go. We're all very proud of you."

"Thank you, Desmond," Lynn said while looking Ron dead in his eyes.

Desmond left and Lynn walked to Ron. They were alone, but

her father would return for her soon. "Ron," Lynn said, "I do love you, but I have to be with Mia. I cannot live on the streets and do drugs."

"What about me!?" Ron said as he cried. "I need you!"

"You'll survive. You always do. You have to stop, though. You have to stop shooting dope. We are going back to Atlantic City next week."

They kissed each other goodbye. Ron was crying like a baby as Lynn's father walked in the room. "It's time to go, Lynn," her father calmly said. Attempting to leave as quickly as she could, Lynn grabbed her suitcase and walked out of the room that once felt like a prison cell. Her husband sat on the bed in the dark. He did not follow her.

THE POETIC BALLET OF VOMIT

The title of this drop is odd, but read on. You are going to have to bear with me on this one. (Author's note: My mother is someone who despises and rarely uses profanity. When she read the rough draft of this drop, she said, "I did not know how fucked up you were.")

"I feel it in the pit of my stomach."

"I feel butterflies in my stomach."

"I know it… I know it in my gut."

The stomach has an emotional significance, but as an organ, it is often not appreciated. We take it for granted, until we are not feeling well. Vomiting is a dreadful feeling. Sometimes, it is devastating, but junkies know how to vomit. There were times when I was with friends, driving around in Manhattan, and vomiting was commonplace. The dope was so powerful that I was at a red light and just opened the door to vomit the falafel I just ate on St. Marks Place. I closed the door and drove away. Yes, I know it's disgusting. It is what it is.

Vomiting in front of someone is a very vulnerable state to be in. You cannot help being ill, but hopefully, you can expect sympathy from your loved ones.

My grandmother had an abusive husband - my grandfather. This may seem like a random tangent, but this story about vulnerability and abuse is not irrelevant. There was a time when my grandmother was in a wheelchair. My grandfather once hit her because she broke a glass. I know how frustrating it is to take care of someone who is sick, but what kind of person hits an 80 year old woman in a wheelchair? My grandfather was so fed up and so frustrated that he hit my grandmother with a broom. Once we found out, the whole family showed up. The EMT called the police, and my grandfather was in real trouble. When asked why he hit a sick woman in a wheelchair, he replied, "I got her a towel to clean up the blood, didn't I?"

Lynn felt like a burden to everyone she knew. She was out of the nursing home, living with her parents and her child, safe in Spotswood. Health-wise, she was not out of the woods yet. Day after day passed as she would sleep on her parents' couch and abuse her Oxycontin prescription. Think of it as a movie montage, where someone is sleeping on a couch in a house in the New Jersey suburbs and everyone else goes about their business at ultra-fast speed. People get up, make breakfast, and get ready for school or work while she just sleeps on the couch in the same clothing for days. She would give her daughter a hug before she went to school, and help her with her homework when she came home. During the day, she just slept and felt ill. There was no watching television. There was no iPod. There was just the salvation and escape of sleep. She only left the couch to go to the bathroom or eat. She only ate when no one was in the house, because she had to run to the bathroom to vomit within 15 minutes of consuming food. She remembered when she lived with Ron and she was extremely ill from the chemotherapy. Instead of caring for her, he refused to help and so she had to clean up her own vomit. He told her that he had emetophobia, which is the fear of vomit and vomiting. Lynn always thought he was lying since he would often vomit from overusing heroin. This made her ashamed to vomit or let anyone know she vomited.

Lynn's stomach situation amplified her deep depression. She felt as if she was a failure as a parent. She had a child, and she wanted that child to be taken care of. Her parents had legal custody and Lynn lived with her parents. She was a failure and the fact that life went on around her was a concept that she could not grasp or accept. She was ashamed, and tried to hide her sickness. Sometimes, she would only let them know about it if she could get some kind of sympathy. Slowly, the frequency of vomiting episodes lessened as her medication was balanced. She began to feel somewhat normal as she found some solace that her old life had officially ended.

Meanwhile, I lived in Woodbridge with Alison and Mokey. Alison and I had settled into married life. There were times when I made some nice money, but life was getting boring for both of us. We worked to pay bills. Sex slowed down. We would go to New Hope and stay at a bed & breakfast. We enjoyed the fruits of our labor, but fell into a rut.

Alison had an extreme anger problem. She would get furious at life's tiniest complications. When she walked in the house and Mokey greeted her, she would yell and scream. We had so many arguments because she did not like the way I styled my hair. She began to hate what I liked. She hated the shows I watched: "Tim & Eric Awesome Show Great Job!" "Ideal," "The IT Crowd," "Aqua Teen Hunger Force," "Perfect Hair Forever," and stand-up comedy. She wanted to watch shows like "Jersey Shore," "Sex & The City," "Keeping Up With The Kardashians," and "The Hills." I still got new and interesting music for free like PAS/CAL, Withered Hand, Sebastian Schuller, and The Lovetones. Whenever I offered to play them or if I asked her what she thought, she would yell at me and say that she wanted to find her own music. Some of the arguments were so intense that several times she took a glass bottle of vodka and threatened to smash it over my head. Many times she would get so furious at me, she would punch me. It was almost like a cartoon. She would come at me and I would just put my hand up, stopping her head while she would just throw her fists at me. She would punch and punch at me but not land one. At first, I begged her to see a therapist about her anger. Soon, I hinted that I would initiate a separation. I suggested that we would still be married, but just take a break to cool off.

When we finally found a psychiatrist, she made an appointment. On her first day, she was running late and could not find the office. She called the psychiatrist and screamed at her. She eventually found the office, and the doctor gave her a prescription. Soon, her episodes of anger slowed down. Eventually, Alison stopped taking the medication and started to reschedule visits. The doctor would comment on how she could not help Alison if she did not take the therapy seriously. Alison would get livid at the psychiatrist she was seeing for anger management, and yell at her. Eventually, she decided not to go anymore.

In 2008, I lost my job because of the devastating recession that hit our economy. As the economy plummeted, there were complete strip malls that became abandoned. Woodbridge, like many towns in New Jersey and across the country, lost many local businesses. When I originally started my job, there were 98 people in the office. When I lost my job, there were 19 left. I remember as I walked out, I saw a sea of empty cubicles and offices. I was terrified that the state of the economy would destroy my life, and the lives of everyone I loved. The atmosphere of fear was engulfing and unavoidable.

Although Alison and I did not do hard drugs anymore, we did drink and smoke pot. Alison loved to smoke weed. The marijuana became so incredibly strong that I was not used to it. I could get magnificently high off of one hit. There were times I got paranoid when I smoked it, but I kept it all in my head and did not have any

THE COOLEST WAY TO KILL YOURSELF

freak out episodes. Alison would constantly smoke weed when she had some. She would wake up in the morning and smoke some before she got out of bed. She began to spend quite a bit of our money on potent weed.

As Alison worked, I stayed home with Mokey and looked for a job. Many times, I found myself looking at kinky porn, going on Fetlife.com, and watching television. I wished that I could do something creative but I did not know where to begin. I used to love to walk Mokey up and down the streets of Woodbridge. I was being lazy, but I did look for work and go on interviews.

As the days passed, I noticed that I would feel this daunting sense of queasiness throughout my entire body. My skin would heat up and my right hand would shake. I began to vomit often. I never tried to hide it from Alison. She saw me run to the bathroom or the kitchen garbage can many times.

One day while Alison was at work, I knew I was in for a horrible day. Even though I was not working, I had to have a sick day. The daunting feeling started in the morning. I was alone in my house with only my dog. I was sitting on my couch while watching a DVR of the Manchester show titled "Ideal" on IFC. I felt the waves of uncertainty, heat, and queasiness increase. I took one look at Mokey's sad eyes and she put her head down. "*Oh, shit!*" I thought to myself. I ran up the stairs to the bathroom. I made it up the 12 steps with four giant leaps as I grabbed the hand railing. I felt it coming. I hoped that the toilet seat was up. I pushed the bathroom door open. As soon as I was in the doorway, the orange vomit shot out of my mouth and landed perfectly in the toilet. I heard it hit the water. Of course, some landed on the seat. Maybe I should not have drunk so much orange juice. My sweatpants and t-shirt were soaked with sweat. My hair was a complete mess and dripping with sweat. I leaned against the molding and took a deep breath. Then, I felt it again. This time I got on my hands and knees in front of the toilet and vomited on and off for three hours.

In between each time, I would lie down on the cold tiled bathroom floor and stare at the ceiling. I noticed the little aspects of the bathroom ceiling that only homeowners see. I thought that there may be water damage. I noticed that there were little cracks in the ceiling. I noticed a little spider web. Then, the feeling would wash over my body again. I was so thankful I had my porcelain buddy to catch my vomit. I gave the toilet a name. I named it, Toilety. I would say, "Thank you Toilety. Thank you for being here for me. You are my friend. Tell me about the people you have met."

After vomiting 14 times over the course of several hours, I collapsed in the vestibule between the bathroom and the two bedrooms with my back on the carpet. I had a whole new ceiling to look at. The shakes began again. Every couple of seconds, I would have these uncontrollable twitches in my arms and legs. Then my shoulders would jerk my upper half of my body up and my legs would jerk upwards. These uncontrollable, seizure-like movements seemed to be the only thing that made me feel better. I felt less nauseous, but I started to breath heavy. My eyes rolled in back of my head and I was blinking incredibly fast. I started drooling. The light on the ceiling was in my eyes and annoyed me to no end but I could not get up. The seizure-like movements increased. I wanted to call an ambulance. I saw my cell phone on the floor but I could not reach it. I started to blink faster and then, I felt nothing.

Hours later, I woke up with something moist on my face. Then, I felt a very small tongue lick my mouth. I opened my eyes and saw Mokey licking me. When she saw that I was awake, she laid down right next to me and snuggled her head into my chest. I laughed, put my arm around her, and petted her. "What the hell just happened?" I said aloud. I looked at my watch and saw that I had been unconscious for 3 hours. I slowly stood up, walked to our bed, and collapsed. The sanctity of the sheets felt like heaven as I drifted back to sleep.

I woke up to Alison yelling at Mokey. She walked upstairs and

THE COOLEST WAY TO KILL YOURSELF

yelled, "What the fuck is wrong with you now?"

"Babe, I threw up 14 times and collapsed on the floor," I moaned. "I'm not well. I'm really not well!"

"Do you need a fucking ambulance?" she said with disdain.

Out of breath even though I was lying in bed, I said, "Let me just rest and see. Please feed Mokey and let her out."

"Fucking ridiculous!" she replied.

"Babe," I said, "I am going to have to see a doctor. Not now, but some time. Seriously, today was a bad, bad day."

"Okay, fine," she said. I could almost hear her sneer as she walked away. I thought to myself, *"What a bitch!"* When she was sick, I made sure she was comfortable. When she was sick, I had sympathy. Who acts like that? What kind of woman did I marry? What kind of person gets mad at someone vomiting? It was not like I drank too much, did heroin, or ate something I knew I should not have. At that moment, I thought of my grandfather hitting my disabled grandmother.

Every health problem became like a dance, as I tried to keep my rhythm and grace in this ballet of illness. When sickness fell on me, I had to do my best to be graceful. Days passed and the episodes of poor health came and went, but the bad days just kept on coming. There were some days when I would just lay in bed and shake. I would watch Discovery Channel documentaries about the end of the world, the Mayan calendar, and 2012. Finally, I decided to seek medical attention.

Since I was on Alison's insurance, I went to my primary care doctor. He gave me some medication. I also discovered that I had sleep apnea and a minor case of narcolepsy. I remembered how I used to fall asleep all the time. Sometimes, I would fall asleep while driving. There were times I literally had to pull over to the side of the road and take a short nap. Other times, I would go to the bathroom stall at work to sleep for five minutes. I would fall asleep in the middle of conversations. I would fall asleep performing cunnilingus. I went to a sleep center and participated in a sleep study. My neurologist said that I also had an acute tremor in my hand because I could not control my hand from shaking. The doctors did not have any true answers. They just gave me medication.

When Easter arrived in 2008, I felt those waves of uncertainty when I was getting dressed to go to my family dinner. I did the dance from my bedroom to the bathroom and vomited with grace. Toilety gulped it all up without any mess. I took some deep breaths, washed my face and continued to get ready. Alison would have loved any excuse not to go to my brother's house and spend Easter Sunday with my family. By this time, I felt like she hated me.

"Are you fucking kidding me?" she said. "Do you want to cancel?"

I looked at the mirror and felt decent enough to go. I never missed an Easter with my family. "No," I said. "I'm okay. Let's go." I heard her guff as she grabbed her purse and car keys. We got in the car and half way down the New Jersey Turnpike, I felt those waves of uncertainty. My body began to heat up and my right leg began to shake. My right hand twitched. I closed my eyes and fell asleep in the passenger's seat. This was not going to be a fun Easter.

As soon as I walked into the door of my brother's beautiful house, my family looked at me as if I was a ghost. I stumbled right to the L-shaped couch, breathing heavy. My brother and my mother surrounded me, asking me questions. I do not remember what they asked. They were worried and confused. Alison just looked incredibly pissed off. I stayed on the couch for a couple of hours.

The laughter and conversation became a musical whirlwind as videogames added to a cacophonic melody. I felt my hands shake faster and my legs twitched harder. Those waves were going to crash on me again. I got up and did the usual dash to the bathroom. I almost tripped over the pink Barbie dune buggy, but my vomit experience prepared me to act like the James Bond or Jason Bourne of being sick. It was like an obstacle course filled with children, appetizers, furniture, and other relatives. I focused on one thing and one thing only. I grabbed the doorknob to the closest bathroom door and felt that it was locked. The downstairs bathroom was occupied. "S*hit!*" I thought to myself. I looked up and immediately sized up the route. I thought to myself *"If I jump over my niece laying on the floor, make a quick left, run up the very long staircase, make a right, I will meet Toilety's cousin Toiletressa."* I did exactly that. I jumped over my niece who was lying on the kitchen floor. What kind of kid lies on a kitchen floor during a family holiday party? I made a quick left and sprinted up the stairs, skipping multiple steps. After I made it up the steps, I darted to the bathroom. The door was closed. I grabbed the doorknob and the door pulled back. My brother-in-law opened the door and looked very surprised. "Whoa!" he said as he walked past me, letting me inside the bathroom. I slammed the door behind me, lifted that seat up, and opened my mouth. As I vomited, I thought to myself, *"Thank you Toiletressa! Thank you for being here so I do not ruin Easter Sunday for my family!"* I collapsed on the porcelain floor and looked up at the ceiling. When I noticed a little crack and a little spider web, I just began laughing. I laughed that crazy kind of laugh that eventually made me cough. From one bathroom floor to another, I became a connoisseur of cobwebs.

I thought that I made a spectacle out of myself even though they did not have to clean a carpet. I thought that someone had to have seen me. I thought, *"Where is my wife? It would be kind of cool if she at least asked if I was okay."*

The rest of my Easter was spent either sitting on the couch, mumbling to my family, or barely standing in the fresh air. I vomited several times and Toiletressa was most accommodating. At this point, I felt I had a better bond with a toilet than I did with my own wife.

NICHOLAS TANEK

Many people pretend that they are sick. Kids fake illness to get out of school. Adults sometimes use a sick voice to call out of work. When you actually vomit in front of people, they see that you are genuinely and uncontrollably ill. Alison was embarrassed, but I am actually glad that I vomited all through Easter Sunday. Not only did my family realize that I was truly ill, but they saw how Alison dealt with my illness. Eventually, the episodes became less frequent due to medicine and proper diet. From visit after visit to doctors or to my pal Toilety, I kept on thinking the following: I spent years taking care of my grandmother and I never hit her. My grandfather hit her with a broom. What would my wife hit me with?

A FAMILIAR VOICE

Facebook is truly a powerful social networking website. By this time, I was working in Edison, but I knew the job would not last. I was disenchanted and just working enough to not get fired. I always kept a Facebook page open on the side while I worked. One day, a little instant message popped up. The word "Hello" was in that little blue box on the lower right hand corner on my monitor. I did not recognize the last name. I clicked on the profile and saw Lynn. I saw that she had a child, and I thought it was weird that I did not see one picture of her husband. While I had reconnected with Alison on Myspace, I reconnected with Lynn on Facebook. I could not believe that it had been almost 15 years since I spoke to Lynn.

We exchanged phone numbers. We had always loved talking to each other. Although we were not romantic, our friendship was rekindled. We were getting older, and we both felt that life was short and love was even shorter. We were honest and poignant. We did reminisce but we ultimately embraced the fact that we had both ended up in lives that we did not expect to live. While Alison looked at me as a cute misfit, a failure who did not have a huge bank account, Lynn saw me as a man who was someone she loved. We told each other our stories.

She told me bits of her sad story. Without the details, she told me about the ovarian cancer and how she was not living with her husband anymore. She told me that she moved in with her parents and her daughter. I was so glad to hear from someone from my past. We were kind, witty, and forgiving to each other. The truth of why she had reached out to me soon came to the surface.

"Nicholas," she said. "I need to ask you a favor."

"Sure," I responded. "What is it?"

"My soon to be ex-husband is a drug addict. We are separated, but I still have to see him sometimes. I had to get hip surgery and the cancer truly messed my body up. I have a prescription for Oxycontin for pain. Please do not be mad at me for asking, but you were always a person who connected to people who have or know someone who could get opiates. I am so sorry, I know I sound pathetic. I am in pain and going through withdrawal."

"He stole your Oxycontin?" I asked.

"Yes, he did. He stole the bottle this past weekend when I went to Atlantic City with my family," she said quickly. "I can even get my mother on the phone to tell you if you have doubts. I hate that I have to ask you this, but if you know anyone…"

"I don't do drugs anymore," I said with a mixture of pride and shame. I was proud that I did not do drugs anymore, but ashamed that I was still thought of as someone who could get drugs.

"Hey, I felt bad reaching out to you because you may have drugs or know someone who has drugs. Look at it this way: I did look forward to hearing your voice. If anyone stirs emotions in me, it would be you. So, I hoped you may be able to help." She may have been just placating or flattering me, but it worked. My mind wandered for a solution and realized that I had one. I had a prescription that I did not finish. I met Lynn's friend Kristen when I went to one of my doctor's appointments. Lynn was too sick to meet me. Afterwards, she profusely thanked me whenever we talked on the phone. I could hear the comfort in her voice and knew that she was no longer in pain and not going through withdrawal. I felt that I was there for a past lover and a dear friend who needed me. Reconciliation is beautiful, especially after many years.

Lynn and her friend Kristen both spoke with me on the phone quite often. We became very honest friends. I would always talk to them when I walked Mokey. They always told me that they loved my brutal wit. They said that they loved how I was both self-deprecating and egotistical at the same time. Of course, I loved how they loved my personality and always mentioned how I should have been a journalist or a writer. I felt as if I was a character to them, this brash, eccentric, intelligent and sexy middle aged man. Although we did not hang out in person, we would have honest and funny conversations. Those two women wanted to talk to me, and I loved talking with them. They balanced each other out. Kristen was very conservative and never did anything wild in her life. Lynn and I shared memories of the wild 90's. Since I am a sex addict, I would mention sex and talk about sex with them often, but I knew that I was married and never cheated on my wife. It felt wonderful to talk with honest people who wanted to talk with me, too.

The friendship with Lynn and Kristen solidified my philosophy that I should only want to be around people who want to be around me. I believe acceptance and tolerance are the key to a meaningful and rewarding life.

KILL YOURSELF OR GET OVER IT

While Alison and I lived in Woodbridge, I felt like I had figuratively killed the person I truly was (but not in a cool way). My wild and creative ways were dying. I was obsessed with providing for Alison. At one point, I started making commission checks of $30,000 on top of my salary. She wanted to have expensive things and live in an elegant house. She wanted to brag to her friends. After we moved to Woodbridge, I gradually stopped writing and became a corporate zombie so that my wife could buy absurdly ugly $500 shoes. I just wanted her to be happy.

After work and on the weekends, all I wanted to do was sit on the couch and watch films. I was a reclusive eccentric who loved to relax and enjoy the fruits of his labor. Alison liked to equate herself to Carrie from "Sex & the City," and her friends were like Carrie's friends. I did not care if she went out with them. When her friends were over, I was very hospitable. I always waited on them, and I contributed to the conversation.

Alison and I became two different people and our life lacked any form of passion. We lost passion for each other. I lost my passion for work. I lost my passion to journalistically and creatively write. Still, I figured since she was my wife, she would stay with

THE COOLEST WAY TO KILL YOURSELF

me, and be there for me like I tried to be there for her.

When the recession happened and I lost my job, our marriage was in turmoil. I was finding work through temp agencies, so there were periods of unemployment when the jobs would end.

My parents sometimes could not stand each other, but their love always overcame any negative feelings. They stayed together for each other and for their children. They were moral, generally decent people. I know I disappointed them. I know I broke their hearts, but I learned from them. I felt that even though I did some horrible things, I was a good and loving person deep inside. Being married kept me honest and drug-free. I have made so many mistakes and I sincerely apologized for the pain I caused them and the pain I caused in others. My parents instilled a sense of goodness and commitment to marriage, which I considered sacred. They represented what I wanted to be in the sense of love and commitment.

Since my father provided for my mother, I felt that I should provide for Alison. We had money saved and I had a decent 401K. Alison's SUV completely broke down. She never had one oil change through the many years that she owned the automobile. I cashed out some of my 401K for her new car and I made a $10,000 down payment. I felt that I was doing my duty to provide for my wife.

As the days passed, we constantly argued or ignored each other. She would go out with her friends and I would stay at home with Mokey. On my walks with Mokey, I would talk to various people of all races and classes. Once, I bumped into Tom Scharpling from The Best Show on WFMU. He probably does not even remember me. I did not mind that Alison was out and did not even care if she cheated on me. I actually believe in open relationships, having learned from my jealousy with Zia. I would not be jealous anymore. As long as Alison came home to me, I was fine.

One night, she sat me down at the end of the bed when I was

getting ready to go to sleep. She said those four words that no one ever wants to hear. "Nicholas," she said. "We have to talk." I felt like I looked up to her in slow motion. "We cannot be together anymore. I do not know what happened, but we cannot be together anymore. We've changed. I cannot do this."

"We're married," I said.

"I know," she replied.

"We are married," I repeated with a flabbergasted anger. "That means something to me. We took vows." My eyes watered as she rambled on about happiness, money, and a general hatred of me.

I put my head down and noticed 3 tear drops on my legs while I sat Indian style on the bed. Once again, I felt like I looked up at her in slow motion. "So, you don't love me anymore?" I asked.

"No," she said sadly, but with a matter of fact tone. "I don't."

I asked, "Are you seeing someone else?"

She looked me in the eye and said, "No." I did not believe her, but at the same time, I really did not care. I never did get jealous of her. I did not care if she was having an affair because I think I was falling out of love with her, too. I did not say it, but that thought made me cry more.

We argued and I cried, but I did not beg her. After everything I had done for her, for us, I was just astonished and hurt. There was a point when I yelled, "I could have been fucking other women this whole time!" I was so upset that I could have been out there meeting women who had similar sexual interests. When our sex life was suffering, I had suggested trying to spice things up by having an open relationship. I did not realize it then, but it was my desire to be kinky that made me not care.

I got up, took a bottle of Svedka, and walked downstairs to take Mokey for a walk. Lynn did not answer her phone, so I called Kristen. Drunk on tears and vodka, I cried on the phone with Kristen for hours. She was extremely sympathetic because she had recently broken up with her husband. The more I drank, the more

I cried. I was so incredibly hurt and angry at Alison. I never wanted to get married in the first place, and she was ultimately the one who decided to leave me. I kept on thinking about the absurdity of how she broke a vow that she practically coerced me to make.

I felt broken. I was living on unemployment with 10% of America, in poor health, and my wife just told me that she was divorcing me. I did think it was funny that I never thought of suicide at that time, given my previous attempt. I had thought about suicide somewhat frequently through the years. As I write this sentence, I realize why suicide never even crossed my mind. At that moment, though I was heartbroken about Alison, I did not think that she was worth the act of ending my life.

WHY DO WOMEN WANT TO STAB ME?

The next evening Alison asked me to move out, but I refused. I argued, "You are the one leaving me! You are the one leaving this marriage. If you want out, then you know where the door is!"

We decided to stay until the lease was up, though I knew that it would be impossible for us to coexist. We stayed in separate rooms. I took care of the dog. There were those deadly silences and those times when one of us could not help but say something scathing. In general, we tried to stay away from each other.

Both of us were drinking vodka one evening when Lynn called. I picked up my Blackberry and left the room. Alison slammed her ass down on the couch with her arms crossed over her Bouncing Souls shirt. I walked up the stairs letting her hear the words, "I'm fine. Thanks for calling. You know how it is when stuff like this happens. It's sad." I could hear Alison mutter to herself before she turned up "The Hills," which she was specifically watching because she knew I hated that show.

As I talked to Lynn, I could not help but to laugh a little harder than usual at her witty jokes about the end of her marriage. I heard footsteps pounding up the stairs. Alison punched the white wooden door, making it fly open and hit the wall.

"Fuck you!" she screamed at the top of her lungs. "Get out!" She started throwing clothing and DVD cases at me. She ran towards me and began hitting me. I saw that she had a huge kitchen knife in her hands. Instead of fearing for my life, when I saw the silver blade, I wondered why women tried to stab me. She did not lunge at me; she just held the knife at the side of her leg with her hand shaking.

I got up off the bed and repeated the phrase, "Calm down! Calm down. Please, calm down."

"Fuck you! I'm calling my cousin to come over here to fucking kill you!" she slurred as she stomped down the stairs.

"For what!?" I screamed, following her. "I didn't do anything to you! I did not leave you. I never cheated on you. I never hit you. My biggest fault is that I like sitting on the couch!"

She went downstairs and frantically searched for her phone. She looked through the books and general mess on the dining room table. She looked near the television, throwing around more of my DVDs. She stomped to the couch and started to lift up the cushions. She found her Blackberry and tried to make a call, but it did not turn on.

"What did you do!?" she sobbed. "What did you do to my phone?"

"What?!" I asked with astonishment.

"What did you do to my phone? You owe me a new phone! You did something to my phone!" she yelled.

"Are you crazy?" I asked. "Why the hell would I do something to your phone?"

She sat there sobbing in her Bouncing Souls t-shirt and my boxer shorts. Why was she wearing my boxer shorts?

"Alison, I did nothing to your phone. You had it last, and you just found it underneath where you were sitting. You probably damaged it when you sat on it."

She gaped at me as though I had just called her fat, then she stood up and walked to the front door.

I got in front of her. "Where are you going? You are in no shape to drive and you're in your underwear. It's 3 o'clock in the morning! Just calm down. Go upstairs and calm down, or I'll go upstairs. Just calm down!"

She took a deep breath and turned around. I moved away from the door. When she started to walk upstairs, I went over to the couch. Suddenly, she turned around and headed for the front door. She stormed out of the house, leaving the door wide open where Mokey could run outside. Quickly, I followed after her, closing the door behind me. I watched her walk away from our house with a murderous anger.

Following after her, I repeated, "Alison! You are in your underwear! You cannot cross St. George Avenue in your underwear! Just come back to the house and calm down. It's not safe! You are not acting rational!"

I ran to pass her and get in front of her. As soon as I blocked her way, she turned around and began walking the other way. I followed behind, but she turned around again and passed me to walk in the direction of her mother's house. Once again I ran up to her. This time, I said, "Look. Let's go back to the house and I will call your mother. It's 3 o'clock in the morning and you are walking around in Woodbridge in your underwear."

She took a deep breath and refused to look at me. I was completely flabbergasted at her loss of control. Finally, we walked back to the house in silence.

We walked in the house and Mokey jumped on Alison's legs. "Get the fuck off me, Mokey!" she screamed. She stomped up the stairs. I heard her curse, "Him and his fucking dog!" I gave a smile of astonishment as I thought to myself that she was the one who wanted the dog in the first place. Then, I heard her yell, "Call my mother!"

She started packing a bag as I dialed my Blackberry. I heard her mother answer and saw Alison standing on top of the stairs.

"Hello?" my mother-in-law said in her tired 3 o'clock in the morning voice.

"Hey, Alison is upset. I think it would be best to come pick her up. She is furious and in no condition to drive. I had to stop her from walking to your house in her underwear. I'm sorry, but can you come get her?"

"Oh, okay," she mumbled and hung up.

Mokey looked terrified. I held her in my arms as I stood waiting. It felt like hours passed before the doorbell rang, but it was only about 10 minutes. I opened the door and my mother-in-law looked concerned, but also had the expression as if she had been through something like this before. Her mother knew Alison's temper.

Her mother looked at Mokey and scratched her adorable little face. Alison's mother said, "Hello Mokey! You're so cute." It was a weird moment when Mokey's innocent cuteness calmed both of us down for one extremely brief second.

When Alison began walking down the stairs, her mother screamed at the top of her lungs, "Come on! Get in the car!"

Instantly, there were tears in Alison's eyes. She cried, "Why are you yelling at me?"

"Get in the car!" Alison's mother yelled. "Let's go!" I watched them leave, then I placed Mokey on the floor and closed the door behind them. I turned around and saw Mokey's brown and white fuzzy face looking up at me.

"I guess it's just you and me, my friend." I walked to the couch and Mokey immediately followed me. She jumped on the couch and sat down right beside me. I picked up the remote control. I looked at Mokey and said, "Don't you hate it how she yells at you every single time she walks in the house? Wait, don't answer that. It was a stupid question... for many reasons." I looked up at the television screen and saw that "The Hills" was still playing. "Ugh," I said. "Words cannot describe how much I hate the television shows she likes." I sat back and changed the show to "The Young Ones."

As I sat alone with Mokey on the couch, I felt as if I was a soldier after the battle had ended. Trust me, I am not equating myself to the men and women who risk their lives for our country. I thought of the opening scene in the film "Saving Private Ryan." After storming the beach at Normandy, the battle is over and they are just looking around at the chaotic damage. I felt that the battle was over. Emotional devastation was the result. But the war was not over.

Then, my thought process changed. "This Is Hardcore" by Pulp began to play in my head. I had been looking down at the floor, and my head began to slowly rise. Although I was loyal to the idea of marriage and my vow, I thought that this could mean a different life for me. Sure, I was becoming broke; I was sick; I was in the process of getting a divorce. When I was not sick, when I had money, when Alison and I were together, the passion of my life had been sucked out by her. I had the thought that maybe I could have that passion in my life again.

I made up my mind that I would give her the courtesy of one more chance, and wait for her choice. We did marry each other and I made a promise, but life is short. I decided that if she truly wanted to break this marriage off, I would follow my heart. I would try to fulfill those fantasies that I had always had. I would embrace the unknown. I knew that I was capable of meeting women. I also knew that, as someone eccentric and obsessed with sex, I am not for everybody, but I love the ones who love me.

To truly implement my philosophy, I decided that I would only be with the ones who love me. I will only love the ones who love me. I will be fulfilled in life, but not because of money, not because of drugs, not because of image, not because of a job, and

THE COOLEST WAY TO KILL YOURSELF

not because of status. I will be fulfilled because of love. The old me would commit a metaphorical suicide and jump off of that cliff into the ocean and rocks below. I thought that all I had to do was follow my heart and follow the people who had love for me regardless of appearance, wealth, or reputation. I would respect the ones who respected me.

I decided to stop caring about what other people thought. I thought it was the coolest way to change. I do not mean "cool" as in "trendy" or "hip," but "cool" as in "the right thing to do." It was about letting others see the genuine goodness in me, and being able to see it in them. People who are obsessed with image are not cool to me. People who are genuine, creative, and loving are cool to me. I felt as if a moment of clarity fell onto me. My mantra was: Be honest, and be loving. I thought it was the ultimately coolest way to kill my old crazy self. I would follow the love and give the love back, even if it killed me.

Sure, I had a couple of drinks in me… I smiled a wicked smile and petted Mokey. I stared out into space and said out loud, "Mokey, my wonderful and adorable fuzzy friend, we have a journey ahead of us. The road can go two ways. We can be where we are and be what everyone else thinks we should be, or we can be like Robert Frost and choose the road less traveled. Because I made a vow, I will see what Alison truly wants with us, but if our marriage is over, the road less traveled awaits us." Mokey jumped up and licked me on my cheek. I sat back and laughed.

"Mokey, love awaits us either way."

A BITTER END

While Alison was not in the house anymore, Mokey and I went on with our everyday lives. By coincidence, I got a job in the same building where Alison worked. I would see her when I got my coffee in the lobby. Although I felt that it was hopeless, I figured that I should at least send an email to her to let her know how I felt while asking what she truly wanted.

Lynn helped me write an email to Alison. At this time of writing, I accept how stupid I acted. I wanted to believe that the person who I married would be there for me. Even after all the craziness, I did not want to give up on our relationship. I felt as if I sacrificed everything for Alison: four years of my life; my 401k; my creative energy. Lynn and I worked on an email because I wanted to know if it was officially over or if there was a chance for reconciliation.

"Baby,

We have been together for a while. We had good times. We had bad times. I know how you feel. I do not want to lose you. As I said before, I accept you for who you are. Please accept me for who I am. I have been loyal, caring, attentive, and most of all... loving. I have quirks, you do too.

THE COOLEST WAY TO KILL YOURSELF

Basically, I want things to work out between us. Remember, it's "us." Both of us have to make things work. Not just me. I know I do many things that you feel "make" you yell at me. There are many times you drive me insane. I just do not express them as much. Maybe, I'm more tolerant. There are many things I cannot stand about you too... but I ACCEPT you for who you are because I love you. When we started, that was part of the foundation of our relationship and our passion. We each accepted the other for who we are... and who we will become. Like I said, I have been good to you. I would like us to stay together... because I truly love you. "

Alison and I spoke on the phone after she got my email. It seemed like the only thing she took away from my email was the line where I said, "There are many things I cannot stand about you." During our phone conversation, she spewed hate at me, criticizing my hair, my clothes, and my taste in music. She claimed that all of our friends and every single member of her family hated me. I felt like Josef K in Kafka's <u>The Trial</u>. As I was on the phone with Alison, I stood up out of my seat and began walking. I walked out the office door, through the hallway, and into the elevator. The entire time, Alison recited this laundry list of things she hated about me. I think she even said, "I hate the way you breathe!" I tuned out and walked out of the office building. I walked across Route 1, which is the urethra of the East Coast, running all the way down to the very tip of the penis-shaped state of Florida. As one insult blurred into the next, I walked to the bank on the other side of Route 1.

"Hold on, please," I said to Alison. I covered the phone and looked at the teller. Handing over my driver's license and my ATM card, I said, "I would like to empty the entire account but leave 3 cents, please."

The teller looked at me with curiosity. She heard Alison

yelling at me through the phone and then gave me an understanding smile. "Yes, sir. Anything you say," she said. She returned with the entire contents of our joint bank account, minus the 3 cents. I loved watching her count the bills. Once the envelope was filled, I paused before taking the money. This was what remained of my cashed out 401K. This was an account that purchased her new car because her old car failed due to her careless lack of maintenance. This was what was left of the money that I invested in us as a couple.

"So, Alison," I said. "You are saying that we are completely over as a couple?"

"Yes," she said.

"Okay," I said. "See you in the next one." I smiled, hung up, and walked out of the bank with every single dollar that was in our account. I felt free. I immediately wanted to call Lynn to tell her the story.

THE MUNCH

Officially single again, I decided to try to make my kinky fantasies become reality. Fetlife is an online social networking website for the fetish community. With a black background in contrast to Facebook's white background, Fetlife is proud to be Facebook's dark and dirty opposite. They embrace pictures of nudity and posts regarding the fetish lifestyle.

Many people on the site are into fetishes that most people are familiar with, like corsets, foot fetish, leather, bondage, dominance, submission, crossdressing, fisting, piercing, sploshing, etc. Out of sheer curiosity, I could not look away from the truly outrageous profiles. There were fetishes I never knew existed and fetishes that I just could not understand. It intrigued me to read about people who were turned on by being punched in the face, scarification, milk enemas, vomit, scat fetish, diaper training, buried alive, burning alive, human toilet, human tampon, recipes with bodily fluid, forniphilia (human furniture), symphorophilia (staging and watching a disaster, such as a fire or car accident), ederacinism (punishing oneself for sexual cravings), mucophilia (sneezing), formicophilia (insects), and more.

Hours could be spent just looking at the profiles and message boards. I saw a beautiful young woman in college post, "I broke up with my faggot boyfriend because he hated punching me in the nose while I masturbate with the blood." One woman's screen name was "YoungDirtySlut666." Did that mean that 1 through 665 were already taken, or was she satanic? For fun, she constantly posted pictures and videos of herself sticking objects inside of her body. Of course, there were also fake profiles and internet trolls, but most of the people on the website were simply looking to explore their sexuality, whether out in the open or in secret. Many of the people on Fetlife are in marriages or committed relationships where they do not feel sexually fulfilled.

I made a profile page and kept mine simple. I wrote that I had a fetish for women in lingerie, and that I had some experience with light bondage and being a dominant male. Even though most of my experience was playing the dominant role in the bedroom, I included that I was looking to explore my submissive side. In a relatively short time, I made several female friends.

An old friend of mine named Bridgette was delighted that I joined. Bridgette was a "brand new" lesbian who was shameless and sexually open. As soon as she heard my marriage was over, she invited me out with her friends. I invited Lynn and Kristen but they did not feel up to the evening. Lynn thought that she was not pretty enough and that she would feel awkward. Even though we had not seen each other in more than 15 years, I told her that she was beautiful. My comments did not make a difference. Several wild nights occurred with Bridgette and her friends. One evening, I actually saved Bridgette's friend from a drunk driver. The car was speeding down the street and I grabbed her and pulled her out of the way. Bridgette was so touched that she emailed Alison and yelled at her in the message. Obviously, Alison was furious.

Fetlife and Bridgette introduced me to several different women. Some were attractive and kinky, but I could not truly connect with any of them. I did not feel that solid honesty I needed in my life. Many of the women who liked femdom were upset if I did not call them or text them back immediately. Many wanted money and gifts from the start. That turned me off to their personality. Some had unattractive bodily features or unattractive personalities. Cassandra was a young Black woman who would get mad at me and hang up on every single phone call. The next day, she would call back as if the argument never happened. Casual sex happened often, but it was not kinky. Neither impressed nor interested, I realized that I was just having sex to make up for the wasted time with Alison. The women felt the same way. Belinda was a woman who knew I liked stockings but she would constantly rip them. Without passion or mental connection, she would call me and say, "I'm bored. I'll come by and fuck you." She would visit me wearing sweat pants and a sweater. She was an attractive girl who did not care if she looked pretty. She put on some stockings and had sex with me as if it was just something to pass the time. As always, we went our separate ways without a care.

Bridgette invited me to a social event called a "munch." While there are both private and public munches, the goal of a munch is to have kinky people get together and meet each other. Some groups are separated by age while others are separated by kink. Once again, I invited Lynn. Once again, Lynn declined. Every time a situation like this would come up, I would tell her, "Come on, Lynn. If I could choose anyone to go to something like this, it would be you. You are the only one I can trust." Lynn was very open minded to the whole concept but her lack of nice clothes, her health, and her responsibility to her daughter made her respectfully decline.

My first munch took place at a restaurant in North Brunswick. I arrived on time but received a text from Bridgette saying that she was running late and that I should go in and introduce myself without her. After pacing around the parking lot in my suit and tie, I cursed Bridgette's name for letting me go alone. Still, I decided to go inside by myself. As I walked into the restaurant I saw a private room in the back. The barstools were filled so I ordered a vodka club and sat down at a small empty table. As soon as I put the glass to my mouth, I saw two old men dressed as Little Bo Peep. They were quite obviously old white men in frilly dresses and petticoats. Some of the other men in the bar laughed to themselves, not purposely loud, but loud enough that it could be heard. After a deep breath, I decided I would walk into the back room.

A third of the people in the restaurant soon gravitated to the back room. Trying to be nonchalant, I tried to blend in with the crowd. There were at least 20 people of varying age, race, and background. There was a middle aged man with glasses who immediately handed me a flyer for a fetish convention. The nervous feeling imploded, and I was clueless as to what to do or say. I decided to introduce myself. I cleared my throat and said, "Hello everybody. I'm Nicholas. This is the very first time I have ever been to one of these gatherings and Bridgette is the person who was supposed to introduce me. She is not here."

"Have a seat!" a chubby elderly woman said. "Any friend of Bridgette is a friend of mine. Does she still go by the name Biannca?"

One of the Little Bo Peeps said, "Welcome, young man."

An older woman wearing all black with glasses and white hair tightly pulled back in a ponytail said in a commanding voice, "Sit." Immediately, I sat down. As the night went on I talked about normal, everyday topics like rent and work, but also discussed things like Fetlife events.

Throughout the evening I heard introductions and side conversations:

"This is Sally. She's an expert in rope. Be careful with her."

"Brian likes to be pimped out, suck on Black cocks and then be blackmailed so his wife does not find out. He'll pay top dollar if you catch him being a male prostitute. He likes it."

"Kate! How is your cuckold husband?"

"My hard drive crashed. I think the computer caught a virus."

"I know this store in New Hope that sells the finest corsets. I heard if you pay an annual membership fee to our group and show them your membership card, you can get a discount."

A young Black man in his mid-20's said, "My boss was going to fire me when he found out I was a pervert, but he knew that I knew that he broke many laws when it came to permits and taxes. I'm alright now!"

An overweight man in a white t-shirt said, "My name is Piggy. Please call me Piggy."

"This is Sandra. She's a sub. She only speaks when her Goddess tells her to." Sandra was a beautiful young woman in professional attire who did not look anyone in the eye.

A very large and sweaty woman was introduced to me by a bubbly young college girl. "This is Mistress Bala. She is into forced feminization."

The bald man who had given me the flyer said, "Yeah, I'm a dom, but I only am with women. You seem as if you don't even know your fetish and you are just figuring stuff out. Just hang out and talk. See what you like. Everyone here has an opened mind."

Suddenly, the man in the Little Bo Peep outfit appeared in front of me and said, "Hello. I'm Stephanie. You know, you should come over and check out my dungeon."

A very sexy dominatrix sat in my seat. She wore a tight PVC black skirt and the boning of the tight corset could be seen beneath her shirt. I did not dare ask her to move, but I did ask for my drink that was sitting on the table. Carefully, I picked my drink up and sat down next to her. I introduced myself. Before I finished speaking, she said, "Listen. You seem nice, but I live this 24/7. I can see it in your eyes. You are not ready yet, darling."

I stuttered, "I was just socializing. This is the first munch that I've been to."

"It does not matter," she said, "I am looking for a live-in who I can dominate 24/7. You are cute, though. Still, you are not there yet. You do not even know if you want to be there yet, do you?"

"Good point," I said. "I'm just interested in kink."

"That's good. Can you consistently wear a butt plug and live in permanent chastity?" My expression must have been telling. "Don't answer that," she said. "Kink is wonderful, but you should know what you want."

I thought for a second and replied, "When it comes to being submissive, does it matter what I want?"

The dominatrix smiled and then let out a very controlled laugh. "Good answer. You have potential, my pet. Trust me, I'm too hardcore for you." With a wink from her black-outlined eye and a smile from her glossy dark red lips, she stood up and walked away. The high heels on the wooden floor could be heard over the surrounding conversations.

A middle-aged man in a suit and tie sat down next to me. "Good evening, friend. My God, you are a young man. What are you doing in the older group?"

I replied, "I'm in my mid-thirties."

"Trust me, young man. You're a kid." The man continued, "You should try the young munch crowd. I can tell. You are young at heart. Do not give up though. I heard a song by a British rock band about helping older people."

"I know that song!" I said with a renewed interest. "That's 'Help the Aged' by Pulp."

"It's bloody brilliant," the man said with his subtle European accent. "You may be like one of these older kinky perverts one day. Sure, it's a little odd. It's a little weird. It's a little strange. When you truly look at the core of it all, it is beautiful. All these people in this room have these elements of themselves that make them feel shame but they come here and feel accepted."

I asked, "Do you like films about kink?"

"Of course I do!" the erudite man said. We discussed films like "The Story of O," "Venus In Furs," "Preaching To The Perverted,"

"Personal Services," "Maitresse," and others. We were just two heterosexual gentlemen who loved women and enjoyed kinky sex with them.

"I overheard what the lovely Mistress said to you. She is correct." The man continued, "May I make a suggestion? Do not be kinky just to be kinky. Are you interested in kink because you think it's cool or are you someone who has thoughts that you are scared to tell anyone else about? I always found it to be fulfilling when both people involved truly love what they do with each other. Do you know what you want?"

After my usual overdramatic pause, I said, "I think I do. I just want to explore."

"Well, explore away! Be adventurous. Be curious. Be kinky with an open mind," the man said. "See, there's a difference. In this world, the man is usually the dominant force in the relationship. It's been that way since the beginning of time. However, it's not always that way. Let's say that you would like to be submissive to a woman. It is one thing to be submissive to a woman every single day but it is another thing to be submissive in the bedroom. More importantly, it is one thing to be submissive to a woman because you get a sexual thrill from it. It is a completely different and beautiful thing to be submissive to a woman because you truly love her. That makes all the difference." The man paused, looked at his watch and said, "Oh, the time!" As the man in the suit stood up, he shook my hand. "I must go. There is a beautiful woman who will be very disappointed in me if I am not there for her when she gets home from work, and I refuse to disappoint her. It was an absolute pleasure conversing with you, Nicholas. I shall look forward to having another conversation with you. You will find your way... because your heart will lead you."

"The pleasure was mine," I said, trying to be very gentleman-like.

As I said my goodbyes and shook everyone's hand, I felt somewhat enlightened as I walked out to the normal bar section of the restaurant. I was not completely enlightened, but I saw the light that I had to follow.

When the outside air hit my face, I immediately thought of Lynn. Together, we would have had a wonderful time that we could have talked about for days. What was I doing? I did not want to be a woman's slave every hour of every day. Although I had an open mind to all types of kinky sex, I wanted to be myself. For me, kink and fetish was a sexual thing. I realized that I did not want to go out in public and have a woman in a collar connected to a leash. Sure, I loved women in lingerie and I loved bondage, but I did not want to experience it 24 hours a day, 7 days a week, for 365 days a year. Although I respected everyone's courage in that restaurant, I was content that I did not live the life that hardcore. At the same time, I did not want to be with someone who would not understand my kinky mind. I paused before I walked to my car, and tried to call Lynn but it went straight to voicemail.

Disappointed that I could not tell her about my evening, I heard the clack of high boot heels on the cement. I saw a young lady in an unzipped sweatshirt, a faded Atmosphere concert t-shirt, and unflattering baggy jeans. She must have been in her mid-twenties.

"Hey," she said. "I think that you were the only younger person in there."

"Yes," I said as I put my Blackberry in my pocket. "I did not see you in there."

"I have not seen you at the other munches. My husband does not know that I go to these things. Are you gay?"

"No," I replied, "I'm coming off of a failed marriage."

As she puffed on her cigarette, she asked, "What's your poison?"

"What?"

"What are you into? You look like a deer in headlights. Is this your first time being at one of these things?"

"Yes," I replied. "I was supposed to meet someone but she never showed."

"Classic. I do that all the time to married men who waste my time on the web. So, what do you like? What is in your crazy perverted mind that led you to this moment?"

With a trying-to-be-charming, purposefully-self-deprecating laugh, I said, "I could not be vanilla anymore. I love women in lingerie. I always was the dominant male and I get turned on when women take control. I cannot force them to take control, though. I'm just trying to find someone to explore that side of myself with."

The young lady smiled as she threw her cigarette on the pavement and extinguished it with the toe of one of her high heeled boots. "Well, I like it when young men I do not know go down on me in public places. I will not suck your cock. You will not fuck me. Don't tell me what your name is. The only reason that I'm even talking to you is because you are slightly attractive and you are not old like the people inside. If you are interested, meet me in the parking lot of the Wal-Mart near the PetSmart on Route 1 South, I'm driving a grey Ford Explorer." She coughed, spit, and lit another cigarette. "I have to get food for my cats." The young lady walked away toward the other side of the parking lot. Completely aghast, I thought I was in a weird film collaboration between Tinto Brass and Werner Herzog.

I thought, *"A dirty slut just asked me to give oral sex to her in a Wal-Mart parking lot."*

Disgusted yet intrigued, I realized that I would pass the Wal-Mart on the way to the NJ Turnpike. The location was near where Lynn and I did cocaine and had sex in my van so many years ago. As I got in my car and drove off, my phone rang. Lynn's half asleep voice welcomed my report from the weird evening. As I relayed the evening's events, she slowly became more awake the more I went into detail. Before I knew it, I had passed the jug handle for the Wal-Mart shopping complex. Soon, I realized that I was much more interested in talking about my evening with Lynn than I was licking a dirty girl's clitoris. It dawned on me... *Of course I am more interested in speaking with Lynn!* Somehow, I caught every single green light as I drove down Route 1 while talking to Lynn on the phone.

> "AND HER LIPS WERE WARM, HER HANDS WERE COLD. I NEVER THOUGHT I'D FEEL THIS OLD ISN'T GREY HAIR JUST THE FIRST LIGHT OF A NEW DAWN"
> - *Withered Hand*

I will never forget the first time I saw Lynn again after all those years. I walked Mokey to the Woodbridge Train Station off of Main Street. I stood at the bottom of the stairs as I heard the rattle of the train. The people slowly made their way down the steps onto the street. I let Mokey's leash loose for a little bit. I wanted Lynn to walk down the steps and just see an adorable white and brown pom-poo waiting for her at the end of the stairs.

"Is that Mokey?" a voice echoed down the staircase. I stepped forward and saw Lynn. A feeling of comfort and acceptance washed over me. We instantly smiled at each other. She looked somewhat disheveled and probably not as pretty as she would have liked to have looked. Still, we embraced. There was that moment where we both realized how lucky we were to have each other in our lives. We were both broken people, but we had each other as true friends.

We walked from the train station to my house. I took another look at her and saw in her face that she had weathered quite a storm in her life. She was not elegant and she wore no make-up. We both had several grey hairs in our scalps. If Alison saw me walking with her, she would have been upset but thought that she was prettier than Lynn. Still, Lynn looked beautiful to me.

We walked into my house and I showed her around. I took out our finest wine glasses and poured both of us drinks. We spent the night talking. I felt so amazingly comfortable being with her. As we sat on the couch, Mokey sat on the back of the couch and looked out the window, as she always did. I played her music she never heard before and she gave me her opinions. I played Withered Hand's "Good News" LP, Keren Ann, Fela Kuti, The Brian Jonestown Massacre, The Dandy Warhols, Pulp, The Good The Bad & The Queen, Moby, Momus, Elbow, PAS/CAL, and "Mother of Pearl" by Roxy Music. We watched shows like "Ideal," "The IT Crowd," "Aqua Teen Hunger Force," "Tim & Eric Awesome Show Great Job!" and some stand-up comedy from Eddie Izzard and Patton Oswalt. Most of all, we talked. We both felt like we were picking up where we left off, as though we were continuing a conversation that had started fifteen years before.

The subject of Ron led her to talk about her dissolving marriage and I deeply related to her situation. At the time, Ron was practically homeless in Atlantic City. Her family did everything they could to keep Lynn away from him. They rarely let him see Mia. Lynn filled me in on the summary of their failed relationship. She told me about the drugs, the cancer, the affair, and how she ended up back with her parents. Everything about the conversation involved the pain and sadness that Ron caused.

"Oh, it's pathetic," she said. "Whenever I stay at Harrah's with my family, he tries to see me. He looks terrible. I swear, if you saw the way he looks now, I would be so embarrassed. He was once a very good-looking man. Now, his hair goes all the way down to his ass and he keeps it in a ponytail. It's all dry, thinning, and stringy. He's missing many teeth, even in the front. He is constantly high. When he gets his check from the government, he spends it all within a week. That's why he took my pills! I can't stand him. I cannot have him around Mia. I know it was my decision to stay with him all those years. He does truly love me, in his own messed up way, but he truly screwed my life up so hard. He always says that he will never divorce me."

"When was the last time you were, you know, with him?" I asked.

"Many months ago," Lynn responded. "It was so sad. We were outside on the beach. It seemed as if there was no one around for miles. For any other couple, it would have been romantic. The moon was shining bright. The crashing of the waves was in the background. There was a delicate breeze. He kept on trying and just would not take his hands off of me."

Quiet tears fell down her face as she stared into space. I gave her a tissue, but she just held it in her hand and let the teardrops slowly slide down her cheek.

Lynn continued, "I remember being disgusted when I felt his hands on my body. I just let him touch me. I just laid back in the sand as he took off my jeans. I looked up at the beautiful stars. When he took out his penis, I stopped him and asked him to wear a condom. He got offended. We started using condoms after I caught him cheating. I insisted he wear a condom. I remember him sighing that he had to put it on. I thought that he should have felt lucky I was even having sex with him. I realized I was having sex with him out of pity. He came almost instantly. It was one of the weakest orgasms a man can have. It was just so… sad. The last time I had sex with Ron was so pathetic and sad."

Lynn looked me in the eyes then dabbed at her eyes with the tissue. She smiled and I smiled at her. I looked into her eyes and saw this pain and sadness inside her. She was so grateful to have me there with her and I was grateful to be there with her, too. Both of us had been through so much before we found each other again. A poignant silence graced this pause. There was no music. There were no car noises from outside. We just looked at each other and smiled.

My mind began to race. We sat there, unable to look away from each other, and then in one quick motion, we wrapped our arms around each other and began kissing frantically. We ended up on the floor, rolling over each other while kissing. Our hands danced over each other's bodies in between the attempts to take off our clothes. We laughed and kissed as our jeans were tossed aside along with our shirts. I laid her down on the couch and went down on her. This was a welcoming body that I had loved before. After her orgasm, she got on her knees and began... She was amazing.

"I have always loved you," she whispered, out of breath.

I laid her down on her back and I went to the drawer to get a condom. After we made love, we were covered in sweat and my hair was falling in front of my face. We both looked at each other and just breathed heavily as we smiled and laughed.

As we put our clothes back on, we did not say anything. We did not have the breath to say anything. We did smile as we repeatedly exchanged glances. I put on the second section of "Mother of Pearl" by Roxy Music.

"I like this song," Lynn said. "I really like this song. Do you know the significance of the singer singing about mother of pearl? I can relate to this."

We took a little nap and then I drove her home. Morning was on its way. We pulled off at Exit 9 and drove down Route 18. When we finally arrived in Spotswood, I put on the second part

THE COOLEST WAY TO KILL YOURSELF

of "Mother of Pearl" by Roxy Music. The closer we came to her home, the quieter we became. The repetition of the groove and the rolling drums mixed in with the crescendo of the uniquely light guitars and various subtle instruments created this wonderful, romantic feeling. The meaning and delivery of Bryan Ferry's lyrics and vocals added to the unique romance.

I pulled the car over to the side of the suburban street. I leaned in to kiss her. I reached over and slid my hand behind her head and gently pulled her towards me. As we kissed, I felt her body melt in my arms. A maelstrom of post-modern romance washed over me. We passionately kissed throughout the rest of the song. When we stopped, we both sat back and took a couple of seconds to embrace that beautiful moment. We smiled at each other and I put the car in drive.

I dropped her off at her house, kissed her once more, and watched her walk to the door. That special poignancy engulfed the atmosphere that dawn. When she quietly opened her front door, she waved goodbye. The smile on my face was proof that I was still a romantic. I drove away and restarted the song "Mother of Pearl" by Roxy Music from the beginning of the second part. The piano gently creates a deep feeling of tenderness. The smile remained on my face the entire ride home. Driving down the New Jersey Turnpike at sunrise is a beautiful sight. At that moment, a feeling of hope washed over me. At that moment, I felt excitement as I welcomed a new beginning. At that moment, I felt very positive feelings about facing a new dawn, a new life, and a new romance.

THE DIVORCE PARTY

When four friends are each experiencing the end of their marriages at the same time, they have an emotional connection. Kristen, Lynn's best friend, was once overweight but now looked beautifully in shape. She had children with a man who then cheated on her. She and Lynn had felt awkward and fed up. They decided to start living their lives and following their desires.

Lynn was constantly arguing with Ron over the phone. When I walked into the room when she was having a phone conversation with him, I heard her say, "It's over! You pushed me too far. You are unhealthy for our daughter and me!" She realized more and more that she did not love him. More importantly, she realized that his kind of love was simply abusive. I loved seeing her close her flip phone, and the look on her face as she looked up at me right before she kissed me.

Kevin had called me up after a long period of silence. We had not spoken in a very long time. As soon as I heard his voice, I knew he was drunk.

"Hey, man," he slurred. "I got problems."

"You have problems? Alison left me," I said.

"Lea left me, too," he said.

"Damn." I said, "I'm sorry, man."

"Hey," Kevin said, "let's have a party."

Immediately "True Skool" by Roots Manuva played in my head. My house in Woodbridge was the perfect place for us to let off some steam and embrace our new beginnings. "Saturday night," I said. "My house. We'll have a divorce party."

As we spoke, we were transported back to the times we were teenagers. Every problem we had as adults was put on hold during that phone call. Our friendship was like a reflex.

The four of us were going to have a divorce party. Kristen, Kevin, Lynn and I planned a night for the four of us to get drunk and have some fun. Lynn stayed over the previous night to get everything ready. I gave her a wad of cash to get food and snacks. I left some Svedka for them to start. I had to run some errands, stop at my parents' house, and get more alcohol. The October wind was brisk. When I purchased the 1.75 liter bottle of clementine Svedka vodka, I noticed that the color on the bottle matched the Halloween decorations. As I looked at the orange color of the bottle and the orange and black decorations in the store, I realized that we were having a divorce party on the same date that I got married.

As I parked my car, I heard the noise coming from inside my house. I walked in wearing blue jeans, an untucked blue button-down Geoffrey Beene dress shirt, and aviator sunglasses. As I walked in, I felt magnificently welcome as everyone shouted, "Hey!"

I pulled the huge Svedka bottle out of the bag and asked, "Is this enough?"

"To kill us!?" Kevin asked.

Everyone laughed. The four of us drank, talked, and laughed as we watched parts of the stand-up special by Christopher Titus titled, "Love Is Evol." While I am not a huge fan of Christopher Titus, that special has important emotional elements about divorce, love, and moving on. We drank and laughed all evening. We walked to a 24 hour convenience store off of Main Street to get some more snacks. We had pictures taken of us standing with Mokey.

Alison called and she was not happy. I do not remember what she was complaining about. She started to ramble on about something that she hated about me. At this point, I had lost track of the details and did not care anymore.

While I was very drunk in front of my friends, I said, "Look. I'm busy right now. I have friends over. You left. Please just leave me alone and let me be."

"You do not have friends over!" she said. "Everyone hates you! My cousin drove by and no one was home."

"That's a lie," I said. "You are blatantly lying."

"Ugh," she said in a snobby guff.

"I don't have friends over?" I asked, slurring my words. I held the phone up and said in a loud voice, "Everybody! Tell Alison you are not here!"

The roar of the small crowd was so overwhelming to me that I almost was knocked down by their energy, laughs, and alcohol breath.

I heard the following lines, though I do not remember who said them:

"We do not exist!"

"We are not here!"

"We are all holograms!"

"Nicholas knows the 4 quadrants! The upper left!"

"The orgy started without you!"

"Get off the phone because every woman here worships your cock!"

"Alison is a fool!"

"Get off the phone with that tacky bimbo dingbat!"

"Come back to bed!"

"Is that the fat woman from the wedding photo you showed me?"

I laughed and said, "Look, I have to go. Take it easy. I have a busy night ahead of me."

As soon as I said that, I heard Kristen yell out, "Nicholas, get off the phone, you have pussies to suck!" I clicked the "end" button, looked at the three drunk friends on my couch, and smiled. We all burst out laughing.

I looked at Lynn and just extended my hand. Immediately, she got up off the couch and walked towards me. We kissed and walked up the stairs. As soon as the bedroom door closed behind us, we embraced and made love to each other. By this point, Lynn and I had evolved from the typical love-making episode. Basically, after an hour, she ended up blind-folded and tied down to my bed wearing a full French Maid outfit and my face between her legs.

Afterwards, as we rested in my bed, we heard Kevin and Kristen downstairs. Lynn was extremely nosey. She quietly opened the door and crept to the top of the stairs to listen. I was too tired and was content with the knowledge that we had brought two people together. I fell in and out of sleep as I laid in my bed. When she jumped into the bed and under the covers, her arms wrapped around my body as she hugged me with an intense appreciation.

"I think we connected two people," she said with pride.

"Tonight was fun," I said. "I knew it would be."

"Yes, it was, my love," she smiled. I could feel the curve of her cheek on my chest. "Yes it was…" We wrapped our arms around each other and fell asleep.

TELL ME EVERYTHING

Because of the circumstances that led to her losing custody of her daughter, Lynn was legally not supposed to live in the same house as Mia, so she had an apartment in Spotswood. Basically, the apartment was empty most of the time. Her friend Mischa lived there, but she traveled often. Lynn's friends would use the apartment for their sexual transgressions. Kristen used the empty apartment for meeting her lover. I nicknamed the apartment, "Caligula's Sex Pit."

Alison and her friends would sometimes stop by my house in Woodbridge unannounced to pick up Alison's things. Lynn and I both figured that we should take our love outside the place that I lived, so we often went to her apartment in order to not be disturbed.

Mischa's signature belongings were scattered throughout the empty apartment. Since Mischa was a seamstress and a costume mistress for Broadway plays, there was a sewing machine and various French burlesque items. Lynn's friend, Kristen, was a nurse, and she gave us hospital restraints. Lynn tied them to the legs of the couch.

Lynn and I loved being with each other in a place where no one would disturb us. Even though we were lovers before, we had the passion of new lovers. Lynn soon discovered that she loved to wear lingerie. She would wear thigh-high stockings, garters, a

French Maid outfit, high heels, and corsets. She began to embrace the sexual power she had over me. Whenever I saw her in lingerie, she wore it with confidence. She was not just a woman who wore it because I wanted her to. She wore it because she loved feeling sexy, and she loved my reaction. She walked around like she was a madam at a brothel. Eventually, the thigh high stockings, garter belts, slips, and corsets were standard attire. She wore lingerie by choice, not by request. I became mesmerized. She would smoke cigarettes in the bathroom while wearing lingerie. She would wear it under her very non-feminine clothing. She did this because she knew I loved it, and because she loved it, too.

One evening, we had just finished making love. Lynn was wearing black thigh-high stockings, a garter belt, and black corset. She said, "Thank you."

"Thank you for what?" I asked.

"Thank you for bringing this out in me," she said. "I always felt stupid in lingerie. The fact that you love me in lingerie gives me such an appreciation for it. I honestly feel transformed. I feel empowered."

In my cocky way, I said, "Anytime and every time, baby."

We made love again and took a shower together. We ordered dinner from the Italian restaurant down the street. As we ate dinner, we watched the very unsettling film, "Irreversible." In the film, the beautiful actress Monica Bellucci plays a woman who gets brutally raped in a subway walkway tunnel. The scene is 10 minutes long and it struck an emotional chord in Lynn. I had chosen that film as a fan of Monica Bellucci, and had not known about the rape scene.

When I saw that Lynn was upset, I grabbed the remote control to stop the movie. I accidently hit the button that switched it to the stereo, playing the song, "Bishonen" by Momus.

After I comforted her, she looked up at me. "I have to tell you something. Seriously, I have to tell you something extremely important," she said.

"Okay," I said. "Sure."

"No," Lynn said, tears falling from her watery eyes. "I have done bad things. I was a junkie. I did bad things for money and dope."

"I know," I said. "I've been there. I know you. I know that you had a husband who abused you. I know you were homeless. I know you lost your daughter."

"No, you do not know it all," Lynn said with more tears rolling down her cheeks.

"It's okay," I said.

"Seriously!" she said. "I did things for money… and for drugs."

"We both did things to make sure we would not go through withdrawal. I understand. I accept you," I said.

She looked away and put her hands over her face. She was so ashamed to tell me. She was afraid that I would leave her if I knew the truth about her. She reached her hand to mine and grasped my hand tight. Her hand started to shake. She took a very deep breath and finally picked her head up and looked me in the eye. "I was a whore," Lynn said.

There was a silence. I looked away and then took a deep breath. "So?" I said.

"No!" Lynn said. "You do not understand. I used to have sex and do sexual things for money. I used to stand on the corner and get married men to pay me to do disgusting things. I'm so fucking ashamed!" She started crying and I held her in my arms. Through the tears, she cried, "You are never going to want to be with me again!"

I pulled away from her and with my hand I lifted her chin so she could look me in my eyes. I saw a woman so terrified that she was going to be judged. I said, "You are with me now. You do not have to do that anymore." Lynn smiled. I continued, "Now, I am broke. I will get a job and pull my weight… You were once a drug addict, but you are not anymore. I am not a drug addict anymore. I do not care if you were a prostitute. You're not living that life anymore. You love me. Do you love me?"

"Yes, I love you! I have always loved you." Lynn said as she wrapped her arms around me. "I adore you. Please don't leave me!"

"Why would I leave you?" I asked. "You are the only woman who truly accepts me and loves me." Lynn was so gracious in her gratitude. She moved her fingers through my hair and moved her body closer to mine.

"Really?" Lynn asked. "You are alright with this?"

"I love you," I said. "I had this epiphany that I should love the people who love me. It sounds so simple, but it is truly not that simple. You have always loved me. I am sorry that you went through such a hard time, but let's make an agreement. How about you accept my past and I will accept yours?"

Lynn took another deep breath between tears. "Are you sure?" she asked.

"I am 100% sure," I replied. "You know, you may be looking at it the wrong way. In your heart, you are a true feminist. Did you ever hear of the pro-sex feminism movement? The book <u>Baise Moi</u> by Virginie Despentes? Some prostitutes actually love doing what they do. Seriously, there is a whole movement of sex workers and prostitutes who not only write about their experiences, but they are proud of their experiences. These women are taking back their sexuality."

There was a silence as Lynn thought about what I had said. "You know, I actually helped many men and women. For some, I was the only person they could talk to. I was the only person who knew their secrets."

"I have been in many sexual relationships that were kinky. Marriage killed that. Personally, I felt like one of those men who could not trust my own wife with my deepest and most secret fantasies. I refuse to live like that anymore."

"It is amazing that I feel like I can tell you anything or do anything with you," Lynn said.

"I am so thankful for that, too," I replied. "Honey, sexually, you are a different woman now. Your experiences have opened your mind and you have become an amazing lover. Now, since you do not have hang-ups about sex, you are magnificent. Feel the enlightenment! Prostitution should not be criminalized. Women have power with sex and I think they should embrace it. Some people think that men are so afraid of a woman's sexual power that they criminalized it. Do not be ashamed, baby."

"I would not do it again," Lynn replied. "I hated doing it because I had to. I needed dope."

"You do realize the power you have, don't you?" I continued. "I'm not suggesting that you do this but you do realize that you could make money over the internet just telling men what to do in chat rooms."

"I read about that," Lynn said with a deliciously sexy smile. "Money slaves."

"There are men who like to shower women with gifts and money," I said. "Some of these men are married and they aren't buying their wives crap."

"Probably because the wife does not do anything good sexually. You know, maybe we can have one of those cross-dressing sissy maids come over here and pay us to clean the apartment."

I smiled. "I love you."

Over time, Lynn told me countless stories of spousal abuse, drug abuse, prostitution, danger, and homelessness. By most people's standards, Lynn would be considered the kind of person who would be dismissed, tossed out of their catalog of people they should care about. I embraced her, even though I was disturbed and saddened by her stories. My heart was broken by every word. Maybe I was drunk on love, but I did not care. I just loved the fact that she loved me so much. Dear reader, do not think that I accepted her because I needed love. I accepted her because I saw the beautiful person inside of her, and I loved the way she loved me.

THE EGG

Sex toys are wonderful and should be appreciated. Lynn and I were in this delightful sexual frenzy. We were at Caligula's sex pit and could not keep our hands off each other. She whispered my name in my ear and said, "I want to wear new stockings for you." All of her stockings had ripped, so she needed a new pair.

I pulled away and I looked her in the eyes, and said, "I fucking love you."

The feeling of being sexy is a feeling only sexually enlightened people understand, accept, and appreciate. The feeling that you know when someone is sexually vulnerable in a beautiful and willing way is priceless. There are few people who are in our club. It starts with a look and ends with a kiss goodbye. Lynn and I were members of this beautiful, secret, and sensual club.

"I love making love to you while you wear black thigh high stockings," I said as we kissed.

"I do not have black thigh high stockings," she said as she quivered in my arms.

"You will," I said. I reached into my black bag of tricks. I pulled out a remote controlled black magic egg. The little black egg came with a small remote control that changed the vibration. I said, "I am going to slide this inside you." I put some Astroglide on the egg shaped device. I held her face in my hand and kissed her as

I slid the vibrating sex toy inside her. I slid her black silk panties back into place, and held the remote control in my hand. I moved the switch to "on" and I heard it vibrate.

Lynn jolted and said, "It works!"

"Shall we go to the mall?" I asked.

"We shall," Lynn replied. As she slowly walked down the stairs and held on to the railing, I flipped the switch. She stopped, turned her head to look at me, and smiled. I just laughed.

We drove 5 minutes to a mall in East Brunswick while listening to the song, "This Is Hardcore" by Pulp. The song has this magnificently sexy build up with thick, slow drums and a lush orchestration sample. The song is an erotically emotional soundscape that lasts for 6 minutes. The subject matter pertains to a hardcore sexual lifestyle and way of thinking.

I pulled into a parking space and asked her, "Is it inside?"

She smiled and said, "Oh, it is inside."

We got out of the car and walked into the mall's entrance. We walked along the lingerie section of a department store and I flicked the switch on the little black box. She paused once again. As we passed the shops in the mall, I quietly followed her, slowly turning the little black remote control box between my thumb and forefinger. We walked to a kiosk and I purchased a peach smoothie. As a half-joke, I said, "I can eat a peach for hours."

She smiled and said, "I'll make sure of that."

Lynn stopped in front of the mannequins wearing lingerie in the window of the lingerie store. She looked at me and I smiled my devilish smile.

As soon as we stepped inside, we went our separate ways. The lace and silk were mesmerizing. The outfits seemed sexier than usual. The women working there looked sexier, too. Lynn and I loved that no one knew what we were doing. We were not stealing from them, but we were secretly owning our eroticism. Lynn walked in front of the mannequin that had on a beautifully classic black corset, garters

THE COOLEST WAY TO KILL YOURSELF

and stockings. She looked up at the outfit and I switched the remote to the "on" position. Her knees went weak as she grabbed the counter. She closed her eyes for a moment. I smiled and left the remote on. I loved watching her quiver in public at my control. I asked myself how long I should keep it on. Her legs began to slightly shake as I left it vibrating longer. I imagined the egg vibrating inside her, simultaneously making her feel pleasure and nervousness. She continued to grab the counter and lifted her head back. I turned the remote off and Lynn let go of the counter and stood up straight. She walked up to the stockings section and found the correct size of black thigh-high stockings. Our eyes met and we walked up to the cashier.

As Lynn put the stockings on the counter, I took out my wallet. The cashier rang us up for $16.00. I gave her a $20 bill and took the change. As the cashier put the stockings in the bag, she said, "Thank you and please come again."

Lynn was about to speak. She said, "You're..." Then, I hit the switch and she stopped. She continued, "Thank you." Then, she grabbed the bag and we walked away. The device was left on for the walk from the register to the entrance of the store. Every step Lynn made appeared normal, but there were those little expressions in her face and subtle changes in her body movements. This was not like any other purchase. This was not like any other walk. As we exited the store, I shut the device off.

She turned to me and asked, "Did you have your fun?"

I smiled and said, "Oh, yes. I did."

"Good," Lynn said. "Because now, it's my turn." She leaned in closer to me and looked me in the eyes. "And I have not even started yet. I do not mean right now when get home. I mean that now it's my turn to have fun. We're just getting started, love." She gave me a quick kiss and walked towards the exit of the mall. The smile on my face could not be described. A feeling of pride engulfed me. I was proud that she was proud. "Come on, then!" she said. I could not stop from smiling as I put my hands in my jacket pockets and followed her.

MISCHA

Lynn and I started talking about the future. Every little aspect of our lives began to change. Lynn's apartment was no longer "Caligula's Sex Pit" for the women who wanted to cheat on their husbands.

Lynn, Mischa and I had sexual moments as a threesome, but they were light-hearted and fun. Mischa actually made a French maid outfit for Lynn. With the three of us, sex was not passion. Sex was just pleasure. Mischa was hardly around and constantly talked about moving to Europe. She was honest and direct. Although there were many threesomes with Mischa, my favorite episodes were when both of them took control of me. They would tie me to the bed and go down on each other and then take turns riding me. One time, they tied me face down on the bed and took turns having me lick their pussies as they straddled my face with their legs over my shoulders.

A beautiful woman in her early 30's, Mischa could have gotten any man or woman she wanted. She enjoyed sex, but was more like a sexual nomad, moving from person to person and town to town. She had thick black hair and a voluptuous body. She looked like Betty Page without the bangs. She always told us, "Darlings, do not fall in love with me because I will probably be gone in the morning." One morning, she was. We woke up after a night of

THE COOLEST WAY TO KILL YOURSELF

complete debauchery and saw a note. The note read, "I'm going to Europe. I love both of you!"

Lynn and I looked at each other and I said, "Can I move in here with you?"

Without hesitation, Lynn said, "Then, we have to be monogamous."

"What?" I asked, half hung-over and half asleep.

"If you are going to live here, with me, we have to be monogamous," she said.

"Babe, come on," I said. "We obviously have a good thing going. Let's not let labels break us down."

"Fuck that!" she said. "This is what I want. I'm worth it. I deserve it. We just had one of the three people in this relationship walk out that door. That was fun. I had my share of threesomes with Ron, but I do not want to do that anymore. I do not want to do that with us."

"Babe, I just woke up," I said. "Let's talk about this later."

"I will bring this up again," Lynn said.

"I'm sure you will," I said as I made her breakfast in my My Bloody Valentine t-shirt and gray sweat pants.

THE PLACE I ONCE LIVED

The relationship between Lynn and I was evolving and my lease in Woodbridge was about to end. Alison hated the fact that I still lived there. Lynn and I agreed that I would move into her apartment. The answer to the monogamy question was something I danced around. Lynn and I planned to go to my Woodbridge apartment to pick up some of my belongings.

As I pulled in front of the house with Lynn in my car, I did not notice Alison's friend's car on the street. Lynn and I got out of the car. As I popped the trunk, Lynn automatically grabbed the black duffle bag out of my trunk. Caligula's traveling sex kit was filled with sex toys, lube, DVDs, and lingerie. We had this sexual timing that we perfected. As I walked up to the front door, I heard Mokey scamper and bark. I put the key in the doorknob and as soon as I opened the door, I saw Alison's mousy little friend standing right in front of me. She was dating a guy who loved Nine Inch Nails and looked like a pathetic vampire with his creepy triangle beard, like Sardu from "Bloodsucking Freaks."

"What are you doing here?" I asked. Meanwhile, Lynn did her best to not be blatantly obvious as she threw our black bag of sex over the backyard fence. From past experiences, Alison would have known what was in the bag if she saw it.

Lynn walked into the house in jeans, sneakers, and one of my male button-down dress shirts. Underneath those boring clothes, she wore a white corset and thigh high stockings. I heard Alison's heels click from upstairs. She walked down the stairs wearing her business attire, a skirt suit. Mokey ran directly to Lynn. "Mokey!" Lynn exclaimed as she petted and kissed her. Mokey's tail waved in defiance of Alison. Lynn repeated the dog's name as Mokey panted, kissed, and jumped all over her. Of course, Lynn was more than willing to be engulfed by the loving, glorious nature of Mokey. "I love you! I love you! Mokey, I love you!" Lynn said.

"Do you think Mischa loves Mokey?" I asked.

Lynn looked at me as I looked at Alison. Lynn said, "Mokey and Mischa love each other. All four of us will make a very happy family," Lynn said. I could not have twisted the emotional knife in a more perfect way. We knew Mischa was gone, but Alison did not.

"What are you doing here?" I asked. "You told me you would let me know when you would come by."

"My shit is here!" Alison snapped. "I have to come and get it!"

"That was elegant," I said in a sarcastic tone. "Well, go and get it."

Lynn and Alison's mousy friend locked eyes. They shared one of those "what are you gonna do" awkward moments.

Alison started throwing DVDs down the stairs that she thought were hers. The uncomfortable feeling was too much for her friend to bear, so she walked up the stairs.

"They are probably talking shit about us," Lynn said.

"Good," I said. "Fuck them."

As I looked at the pile of DVDs, there were some that were rightfully Alison's but most were rightfully mine. I took "The Wicker Man" (original), "Gangs of New York," "Fight Club," "24 Hour Party People," "Control," and "Dr. Katz Professional Therapist." I started to hide the DVDs under the couch and the coffee table. Lynn immediately knew my intention. She started to hide the DVD cases, too. When we heard the heels, we immediately sat on the couch and Mokey jumped right on Lynn's lap. Mokey seemed to be in on the ruse.

"Some of these DVDs are mine," I said.

"I don't care!" Alison said as Lynn snuggled with Mokey. Alison and her friend walked to the front door. Usually, Mokey would go absolutely insane when Alison would open the front door. Mokey would bark and run around in circles. Lynn opened her arms so that Mokey could say goodbye to her "mommy." Mokey just sat in Lynn's lap and then licked her face.

"Do you have what you came for?" I asked.

Alison looked around in anger and said, "Yes. Come on!" She and her friend carried out Alison's stuff.

As the door closed behind them, Lynn and I looked at each other. Lynn said, "They are probably making fun of us right now."

We kissed and embraced as I said, "They are probably saying the meanest things about you and I right now as I kiss you." My hands danced over her clothed body. She was wearing a corset and thigh highs beneath my shirt and her jeans. I could feel the garters beneath her pants. "They are probably making fun of your appearance."

Lynn replied, "They are probably making fun of you. They are saying that you are not with some typical pretty girl. But, deep inside, they know. They know that you love how I please you. They wish they could feel the passion in the kisses that you are giving me right now."

I wrapped my arms around her and made love to her on the floor of the house that I was about to leave. All I cared about was the beautiful honesty that Lynn and I had for each other. We felt a freedom of sexual expression.

Many kinds of people in this world exist. There are people who are "down," and those who are not. There are people who get "it," and those who do not. Lynn was "down." Lynn got "it." Alison did not.

THE BALLET OF AN ARGUMENT

Alison was toxic, and seemed to have a need to argue. She was the type of person who would say any number of nasty things to me, but would consider herself harassed if I said something to her that was negative in response. Even though we had broken up and gone our separate ways, she continued to send me abusive text messages and hassle me with angry phone calls.

Alison's text messages just piled on top of one another. Most were meaningless insults and empty threats that her cousin would kick my ass. When she relocated for a new job, she sent me a photograph.

"I got a job in Puerto Rico and I am in paradise! I am sending this picture to remind you that you live in shitty New Jersey and I am in paradise."

I tried to ignore her, but I ended up writing, "Your idea of paradise is not mine."

"I am pretty. Your two girlfriends suck," Alison texted.

"I have two beautiful women who love me. You would not understand what I have going on. Send me the divorce papers and I will sign them," I texted.

One afternoon, when I had Mokey out for her walk, Alison

called me, going on about how I am a loser and how I am just plain wrong. I tried so hard not to reach that tipping point.

I told her, "Alison, seriously. You are just trying to hurt me. Please just stop. Send me the papers and I will sign them. I don't want to fight."

"Jackass!" Alison said. "You are a loser! Everyone hates you! My father almost did not give you permission to marry me! My mother hates you! You're ugly!"

I stopped the barrage of random insults by asking, "Then why did you ever want to marry me?" Right then and there, while Mokey was urinating on one of Alison's horrible CDs that had fallen out of my car, I realized the battle tactic that Alison was using. She just wanted to draw me into an argument.

"Alison," I said. "Please just stop. I am hanging up the phone. Your goal is to make me upset and I will say something that will make you upset. Then, you will yell at me for what I say and tell all of your friends and family."

"Fuck you!" Alison said. "You have a fucked up, snobby family. You and your family think that they are so high and mighty because they are educated. So what! I don't have a college education, but I have friends who love me! You are a fucking loser who cannot find monogamy, so you have to brag about living with two women. They are just disgusting loser whores!"

As I exhaled, I saw the air in front of me form a weird pointy figure in the cloud of my breath. I laughed as I thought of an animated version of this scene, where I exhaled on a winter evening, and my breath looked like a middle finger. "Do you really want me to respond to your comments?" I asked.

Alison yelled, "Say what you want, asshole. Come on! Say it!"

"I'm serious," I warned. "Do you really want to know what I think of you?" Though I knew what she was doing, I still let myself get drawn into her game. I couldn't hang up the phone.

"I hope you die alone," she sneered. "I hope that everyone who you love dies alone, too."

"Alison, you are a dirty slut who I never wanted to marry in the first place. All you have to offer is the opportunity of sex. Your sexuality is a lie. Do you know why it is a lie? It's a lie because you are not good at sex. You are just easy."

Alison tried to interrupt me and I said, "No! Zip it! Think about it. You fucked every guy you ever liked. You fucked them because you have low self-esteem. Why do you have low self-esteem? I will tell you. The reason is because you have nothing, absolutely nothing, to offer. You are not erotic. You are not a giving lover. You are not creative. You are just pretty. Guess what? Pretty gets old. You use sex to get something that you can brag about. You do not really enjoy it or put your heart into it. You are horrible at sex and I was never comfortable to be myself with you. When I first met you at that party, I felt an attraction to you, but as I lived with you, I realized that you are a terrible person in an epic sense. All you care about is yourself, and what your friends think about you. You want to make them jealous. You have no individuality. I may be flawed and fucked up, but I am myself. I called you beautiful every single time you walked down those steps before you went to work. I called you beautiful and meant it. Seriously, the way you act makes you ugly. You are ugly to the core of your being."

"Fuck you!" Alison said. "You are an asshole."

"Alison, I do not want to argue."

"Fuck you!" Alison said. "Also, guess what? Fuck your family!"

As I walked back up to the door, I continued, "The main problem with you is that you're shallow. All you care about is image."

"Yes, I do care about image!" Alison yelled.

"Then you should probably get those lesions on your lip checked out. You didn't get them from me."

As Alison growled on the other end of the line, I closed the door behind me and stopped dead in my tracks. I looked up the stairs and saw Lynn waiting for me in a corset and thigh high stockings, garter belt, and high heels. As I looked up at my goddess in silk and lace, I pressed the button to hang up on my screaming wife. It had felt good to stoop to Alison's level and tell her off, but I realized I was better than that. I realized what was truly important. I had a woman who loved and accepted me, and I loved her.

At any moment, the other people in that hallway could have opened up their front doors. At the top of the stairs, Lynn stood fearless and magnificently sexy. With every single step I took, I could only imagine being with her. Lynn smiled as I reached the last step, and put her arms around me.

"Come inside," Lynn said. I walked inside and the door closed behind me.

Like me, Lynn was plagued by unwelcome calls from her ex. She did not want to talk to Ron, and turned her phone off most of the time. Lynn had finally realized what a negative influence he was on her and her child, and she was completely done with him. One evening, she received a voicemail from Ron: "Call me back or I am calling social services, you cunt!"

It was obvious that I had to leave her alone to talk with him. She took Mokey outside for a walk and called him. She was outside for a solid 45 minutes. I started to get worried so I went downstairs. I saw her arguing with him on the phone as she paced around in the gazebo, holding Mokey's leash and smoking a cigarette. I walked up the stairs and got her a glass of wine.

Mokey's footsteps scampered up the stairs and I heard Lynn's steps slowly follow. As she opened the door, Lynn said, "Well, Ron and I are finally, officially getting divorced."

"Isn't that what you wanted?" I asked.

Lynn took her jacket off and said, "It is so what I wanted."

"How did everything happen?" I asked. "Tell me everything."

"He knew about you, and he was mad that I was proud that I was with you." Lynn said. "He saw some pictures that I posted on Facebook. He always was jealous of you. I hadn't talked to you in

THE COOLEST WAY TO KILL YOURSELF

15 years, but I talked about you sometimes."

Lynn's phone rang. She looked at it and saw that it was Ron again. Her shoulders immediately slumped and she had a look of dread. "I do not want to take his call," she said.

"It's alright, baby," I said. "I'll give you privacy."

Lynn answered the phone and walked into the bedroom. Her yelling turned into crying. After 10 minutes had passed, she walked out of the room with the phone on speaker phone. Ron's voice was slurred as if he was on serious anti-psychotic medication. "Well, if you did not want to trick, you did not have to," he said, barely completing the sentence.

Lynn looked at me, flabbergasted. She was embarrassed and amazed at how insane he sounded. She asked, "What about the abuse?"

"Pfftt," Ron said. "What abuse? Big deal! I hit you a couple of times. It's not the be all, end all."

Lynn's eyes lit up as she got truly angry. "Ron! You beat me with our child in my arms! You punched me in the face and made me clean my own blood off the walls of our house… the house that you blew up!" Lynn yelled. "You fucking asshole! This whole time, you did not even ask how Mia is doing!"

Ron let out a long moan and in a drugged up voice said, "You are my fucking wife. You tricked! You fucked other men."

Lynn placed the phone on the coffee table and yelled into it, "You fucking beat me! You fucking hit me! You abused me! You prostituted me! I did not start doing drugs again until you stole my Oxycontin! Fuck you!"

I grabbed the phone and said, "Ron, leave her alone." Then, I flipped the phone closed.

"He's fucking horrible!" Lynn said as her face fell into my chest. I wrapped my arms around her. She cried into my chest. "I'm so sorry!" she moaned. "I'm useless! I'm trash! I'm a piece of shit!"

"No! Baby, I love you!" I exclaimed as I held her tighter. She continued to cry into my chest. She let me hear that call for multiple reasons. First, she wanted me to hear how insane and abusive Ron was. Second, she wanted me to know that her pain was real.

We all get into those moments where we cannot take anymore and we become too vulnerable and too emotional, when we need a chest to bury our face in and cry into. This was a time where this woman needed me. Lynn needed loving arms around her. I saw the remote control and picked it up with one hand. As she cried, I put the Blu-Ray player on. Her favorite stand-up comedy concert, "Dressed to Kill" by Eddie Izzard, was in the player. I pressed play.

Those little moments where two people share an experience of intense emotion become lasting memories. As I held her in my arms and her tears began to slow down, I felt gratitude that I was there for her. I did not feel that she was lucky that she had me. I felt lucky that I was there for her.

EPILOGUE

Sitting on the couch with Lynn in my arms and Mokey at our feet, I truly appreciated the fact that Lynn and I had each other. Although we felt exhausted by the cruelty of my ex-wife and her ex-husband, Lynn and I felt thankful to have each other. The comfort was truly magical in the sense that we both felt that we would never be alone again. We felt that we would always feel the love of one another in our hearts. We were looking forward to our time together. We were looking forward to our lives together.

ACT THREE

With very little money and without a job, I started a new life with Lynn. We did not have cable television, but I had a plethora of DVDs that I received from publicists and television stations. The DVDs and CDs took up quite a bit of space in our small apartment. We ate very inexpensive meals. During the day, Lynn stayed at her mother's house and spent time with her daughter, while I looked for a job online.

We settled into the apartment complex in Spotswood. The next door neighbor across the hall was a stoner who probably sold weed. There were people coming in and out of his apartment at all hours of the day, and he always asked us to smoke with him. He was also blatantly cheating on his girlfriend. There was the white trash redneck who lived in the apartment underneath us. He was constantly drunk and played heavy metal music. At least once a week, the police would come to his apartment because of the noise. A masculine female body builder lived across from the white trash redneck. As soon as she moved in, she wanted to leave. All of us shared a building with four apartments.

As Lynn and I walked the dog, we became friends with many people. Bobbie was an older woman who was kind but appeared to be mentally ill. Marissa was a tough single woman in her 30's from Staten Island who lived alone. Luisa was a Puerto Rican woman who cursed and laughed all the time. A new family moved in who were white low-middle class. The mother would let her teenage children drink, as long as they did not drive. Lisa was a late 20's single mother who had left her baby's father. Lisa would groom Mokey for half the price of what a dog grooming salon would charge. There was a woman in a wheelchair with cerebral palsy who would always call out Mokey's name when she saw us walking. We settled in as part of the neighborhood.

Lynn and I would love to sit on the couch and watch films and television shows. Once, my soon-to-be ex-wife, Alison, texted me from Puerto Rico: "If I was still with you, I would just be sitting on the couch watching films and comedy."

When I showed Lynn the text, she laughed and said, "That sounds like heaven to me!"

We did more than sit on the couch and watch television. We would make love almost every single day. Our libidos never slowed down. There were times I woke up and she was going down on me. Other times, she woke up and I was going down on her. We continued to look at pornography and became kinkier as the days passed. Even though money was tight, I would order lingerie for her. When you have a fetish, buying lingerie becomes addictive. For us, lingerie websites were like casino card tables for someone with a gambling addiction.

We went to a shoe store to get her high heels. As I was at the cash register purchasing them for her, she laughed.

"What's so funny?" I asked.

"I never thought I would wear heels again," she said. "I'm glad that I can wear them for you. I'm glad I can wear them for myself."

When packages came in the mail, we would open them with great anticipation, like kids on Christmas morning. She would model the black corsets and attached garters. She would tell me to wait on the bed for her. Night after night, she would come out of the bathroom, wearing the beautifully sexy lingerie. At first, I only saw her silhouette, but then, she would walk in the room with the high heels. As I heard the heels click on the wooden floor in front of the bathroom and then soon silence as she walked into the carpeted bedroom, I would see her in the outfit. The blood red corset with the black thigh-high stockings was her favorite. "I feel powerful in this outfit!" she would often say.

We shunned the outside world and just hungered for each other. As I went on job interviews, she would send me text messages like, "IWYCIMMRN." It was a game that we played. I had to figure out that it stood for: "I Want Your Cock In My Mouth Right Now."

As a gentleman, I had to respond, so I texted her, "ICWTLYP." As time went on, the text acronyms became filthier and longer.

After an amazing evening of love making, the afterglow embraced us as we collapsed in the bed. "Do you think I am normal?" Lynn asked.

"No," I responded. "You are far from normal."

"Seriously," Lynn said with an adorable laugh. "When I was a child, we had this ottoman. I used to rub myself against the corners of it. My mother would get so mad at me. After many times being caught and being yelled at, I continued to do it. I did not care if I got in trouble and I did not care if anyone saw me. I knew it felt good to hump that piece of furniture. I did not even know that I was being sexual. Eventually, whenever they saw me doing this, they would say, 'Lynn is doing her thing again.' I was unapologetic about it."

I snickered a little, but held her in my arms. "We're sexual beings," I said. "It's okay."

"No, I mean we are different," Lynn said. "I think about sex all the time. I know very well that you think about sex all the time. Most couples would be past this by now. I like the power I have over you. I love the power I have over you. I crave the power I have over you. I have the kinkiest plans for you."

As I looked her in the eyes, I saw a mixture of love and worry. "Lynn," I said, "I love you. You are right. We are not normal. We are a hypersexual kind of people. I was not satisfied in my marriage because my wife did not understand that and I gave up on it. Still, I could not escape who I am. We cannot escape who we are."

"But is it healthy?" Lynn asked.

"Probably not," I said with a slight laugh. "No, I'm kidding. It can be healthy if we are smart about it and honest with each other. Are you happy?"

"Yes," she said.

"Please make me a promise. Please promise me that you will always express yourself sexually with me. Never be afraid to ask me, or even tell me to do something. I am open-minded. I love you. You love me. We were meant to explore life and explore our sexuality… together."

Lynn's arms held me closer to her. We kissed each other as we shared the small bed. "I love you so much!" Lynn said and I felt her cheek move as she smiled. "We are going to have some fun." As the moonlight shone throughout the room and Mokey slept in her little bed, I felt the garters on her legs. I looked down at her stocking-clad legs and smiled.

"Yes, my love," I said. "We will."

THE ONE WHO WILL NEVER BE

Lynn and I could not stop making love. When filled with passion, rational thought does not come into play. I knew the second I got her pregnant. We had just moved into the apartment in Spotswood. We had boxes to unpack and an apartment to decorate. We had lunch sitting on the dining room table. Nothing mattered but our arms around each other and our lips connected. We immediately went to the bedroom and made love. We used a condom, but when we were finished, we found it on the bed.

Days passed and we continued to make love as we settled into the apartment. I continued to look for work using her mother's Internet connection. The cash from my 401K began to dwindle as my unemployment ended. We began to be very cost efficient. I was a marketable person. I was applying to job openings and going on interviews. We were both broke, but hopeful because I was looking for work.

We tried to ignore the obvious question we had in our minds. Lynn's mood swings increased. I kept on looking for work, and an entire month passed. Doctors had told Lynn that her body could not handle a pregnancy. If she became pregnant, the baby would not be healthy. At that point, she did not even think that she could get pregnant. Although Lynn and I had our fun, she was not well. Years of illness, the chemotherapy, and hard living had taken its toll. She was simply not healthy.

As I went throughout my days, I had the idea in the back of my mind that I may be a father. I was living a delusional life. Every single morning, I would wake up and go to job interviews. I tried not to think about the possibilities in those 7 words Lynn said each morning: "I did not get my period yet."

Every day just rolled into the next. I remember walking into a pharmacy to get a pregnancy test. The pregnancy tests were locked behind glass. My first thought was, *Who the hell would steal a pregnancy test?* Then, my mind answered the question as if I should have known. I thought of every desperate teenage girl who got pregnant and could not go to anyone for help. I became forlorn looking at that glass case as some pimple-ridden teenage employee who reeked of marijuana walked by me. I asked him if I could get a pregnancy test.

"Sure thing, dude!" he said and laughed. "Good luck." As dumb as he sounded, I realized how that was a loaded statement. He unlocked the cabinet and gave me the pregnancy test. On the way to the cash register, I walked past the sexual lubricant. In one second, my mind began to race again. *Should I buy Astroglide? This is why I am worried in the first place! Either way, it's always good to have.*

I walked up to the counter with a pregnancy test, a 5 oz. bottle of Astroglide sexual lubricant, and a pack of Durex Extra Sensitive condoms. I did not realize the irony or the comedic element of the moment until I heard the beeping of the scanning. The woman at the cash register was taking a sexual inventory of my life.

I went home to our apartment and gave Lynn the pregnancy test. She told me that she had to take it in the morning. It seemed like every single film we watched reminded us of pregnancy. Every movie title I pulled out of the box of DVDs made fun of the situation. I do not even know how I ended up with this film, but "Baby Boom" with Diane Keaton was the first DVD I pulled out. Then, I found the Kevin Bacon film titled, "She's Having a Baby." There were others: "Parenthood," "Due Date," "Knocked Up," and "The Godfather Part II." The list did not seem to end. I collapsed on the bed after putting "Tim & Eric Awesome Show, Great Job" in the DVD player. Just like the show, the current situation was awkward.

The next morning, my life changed when I heard Lynn call my name after the toilet flushed. I had been sleeping in our bed and I saw Lynn's beautiful silhouette in the bedroom doorway. She called my name again and I could hear the tears in her voice. I knew she was going to say the two words I did not want to hear.

"I'm pregnant," she said.

I felt like a failure. I knew I was a failure. I got up out of the bed and embraced Lynn. I did not want her to feel alone. I did not want her to feel any kind of pain at all. I held her so tight that she had to gently push me away as I accepted the truth.

Lynn whimpered, "I used to have a bumper sticker on my wall that said, 'God Is Pro-Life.'" I just held her in my arms. "The doctors said my body cannot survive having a baby," she said as I felt the tears fall onto my neck.

As I moved her hair out of her face, I wiped her tears away. I kissed her and then looked her in the eyes. "We can get through this. We can get through this together."

"How?" she cried. "We have no money."

I stated, "We'll figure something out." We spent the rest of the night watching television in bed. Since we both loved to watch "Dr. Katz Professional Therapist," I changed the DVD hoping that Lynn may be able to have a laugh. We fell asleep in each other's arms.

When I woke up, I saw that she had opened a bottle of vodka. Usually, she stayed up, took a bath, smoked, played with her iPod, and talked on the phone. I realized that she drank herself to sleep. Seeing the open bottle of vodka was a reminder of what we were going to do.

In the middle of the night, I got the leash and took Mokey out for a walk. I walked around the condominium complex and had one of those deep conversations with myself within my mind. *Would she risk her life so she could give birth to a child? What kind of father would I be? Will I ever have a legacy? I would love the child, but is love enough? We cannot even take care of Mia. If we could not even afford an abortion, how could we afford to have a child? What kind of person am I?*

Days passed and we told only our closest friends. She even called Carmen for advice. Now older, and very compassionate, Carmen was helpful and kind. Although their friendship ended in an extremely harsh way, a mature reconciliation had been made.

We found out that the abortion would cost us $400. Lynn had a friend named Katy who was nice enough to drive up to Spotswood and meet Lynn in person to give her the money. Katy also told Lynn that she did not want the money back. That was a true sign of friendship.

Lynn and I were going through such an emotional time that there was nothing more important than her at that moment. Alison called me up and yelled at me because the credit card companies and the auto loan collectors were contacting her. I just said, "Alison, there are things that are so much more important right now."

"What?" she asked with anger and disgust. "What? Your two girlfriends?"

"Mischa is not even around anymore. Anyway, it's none of your business. Something extremely serious is going on in our lives right now. Just send me the divorce papers to sign and I will sign them."

Lynn and I made an appointment and drove to Woodbridge.

Driving through the town felt surreal, since I previously had a so-called normal and boring life there when I was with Alison. The clinic was on Main Street and I remembered driving on that road as I went to and from work every week day. On my commute, as I drove past the clinic, I always noticed an old man holding a large crucifix and wearing a sandwich board that said, "It's a baby, not a choice." I used to give him the middle finger every time I drove by. This time, I was not just passing through. When we pulled into the parking lot, we saw him. As we walked in, he shouted something, but we could not hear him. Angry, I thought to myself that he should have been aborted. Women walked into that clinic to make one of the most difficult decisions of their lives and this self-righteous religious zealot was making them feel worse.

Inside the clinic, I made sure Lynn was comfortable before I went back outside. As I walked towards the old man, I could tell that he thought I was going to hit him. I am not a large man. I am less than 200 pounds and I am more thin than muscular. I was dangerous because I had love and passion, not because of size or physical strength. I wanted to kick him in the knees, punch his face until blood poured out of his nose. He backed up as I approached. I looked this old miserable man in the eyes and said, "I do not care what you say or do, but if you yell at one woman who walks in or out this door while I am here, I will go to fucking jail because you will be beaten. I do not care that there will be witnesses. Do you fucking understand me?" He did not say anything and tried not to make eye contact. "That's right. Do not say anything!" I said and walked back into the clinic.

We waited for an hour and Lynn finally saw the nurse. When Lynn came back out, she stated, "I saw our child on the ultrasound."

I asked, "Are you sure you can go through with this?"

"Yes. I do not want to, but the baby cannot survive because of my health. I would not survive another pregnancy because of my health. We have to."

Lynn and I sat in the waiting room as they played some inappropriate Tyler Perry film on the television. Instead of watching the film, we played "Word Mole" on my Blackberry. I looked around the waiting room and saw the different types of women waiting for the doctor. There was a young teenage couple in hip-hop attire. I saw a young girl sitting in between two very angry blue collar parents. I saw a Black woman in her twenties who was completely alone. There was a middle aged white woman who was also by herself, and there was a couple with a very disobedient toddler.

We sat there for another two hours. I asked the nurse when we would be able to see the doctor and the nurse told me that the doctor had not arrived yet. I asked to speak with the nurse in a private room. We walked into a patient's conference room.

"So, wait. Are you telling me that the doctor is not here?"

The nurse answered, "Correct."

"How late is he?" I asked in astonishment.

"He's three hours late," the nurse said.

"Did you actually talk to the doctor?"

"No. He's not answering his phone."

"So, let me get this straight. You have a room full of patients. The doctor is late. The doctor has not called and you cannot get in touch with him. Is that correct?"

"Correct," the nurse said.

"So, there is a good possibility that the doctor may not show up, isn't there?" I asked.

"Correct," the nurse repeated.

When I left the private room, I almost punched the wall as I entered the waiting room. I looked around at the people waiting. These poor people, who were in emotional turmoil, blindly trusted these so-called medical professionals. Immediately, I told Lynn that we were leaving. She was confused, but she followed me. We walked out of the waiting room, out of the clinic, and into my car.

I told her the situation as I opened the car door for her.

Lynn stated, "If you hadn't asked, we would have stayed here all night."

As we started to leave, we saw the old guy with the sandwich board that said, "It's a baby, not a choice."

"Please get me away from that dreadful person. I do not want to hear him," Lynn said.

I rolled down the window as we approached the end of the driveway. I was waiting to make a right turn and I looked at him. He looked at me and I just tilted my head as if to say, "Say something… Come on, I want to see blood coming out of your mouth and your teeth on the concrete." He stood there silently as I drove away.

We had to wait until Thursday to go back to the clinic. Because of what happened the last time, they promised us that we would be the first patients they would attend to. I found out that the doctor never showed up the day of that first visit. Once again, I drove down that street in Woodbridge and felt that surreal feeling.

As I pulled into the parking lot, I saw the old man with the crucifix and the sign on his chest. I said as I held her hand, "Don't even look at that guy, baby."

Inside the clinic, Lynn did not even get a chance to sit down before they called her name. After I settled the paperwork, I watched as some of the same patients slowly entered the waiting room. Since the doctor had never arrived the other day, those of us who had waited together acknowledged each other. New patients arrived as well. There was a different young teenage couple that was dressed in hip-hop attire. There was another young Black woman who was alone. There was the same young white girl with working class parents. We sat in the waiting room sharing a slowly spiraling moment of despondency.

Lynn came out with a bag in her hand. We quickly gathered our belongings, signed the necessary papers, and walked to the car.

Lynn had chosen the non-surgical method.

I asked, "Are you okay?"

"Yes, baby," she said as she lit a cigarette, "I'm fine. We did the non-surgical method. The doctor basically put something inside me to terminate the fetus. I'm going to have to bleed for almost two weeks. I have to take some pills and stick these things inside me. So, you know what that means?"

"What?" I asked as I opened the passenger side door for her.

"That means no sex for a little while." She chuckled as she threw her cigarette on the concrete and sat down in the passenger seat of my car. "Don't worry. I'll still blow you."

As I closed the door, I was taken aback by her comment. I soon realized that it was one of those moments in life when you just have to laugh, because the alternative is breaking down in tears. I knew she was just trying to make me laugh, and I loved her for that. Even when we had nothing else but each other, we also had our sharp and dark sense of humor.

At the end of the driveway, once again, I was face to face with the self-righteous old man. I rolled the window down and tilted my head, challenging him to say something. He remained silent.

I said, "If there is a hell, you are the one who will burn. If there is a god, she is a god of compassion. You will burn in hell because you have no compassion." I made a right turn and drove Lynn home.

The next two weeks were arduous on many levels. I started interviewing for jobs almost every day while Lynn was having serious cramps and constantly bleeding. There were times where she would curl up in the fetal position (for lack of better words) as she sobbed for hours. Sometimes, she cried because of the pain. Other times, she cried because of the shame. Because she had chosen the non-surgical method, Lynn was constantly reminded that she aborted her baby because blood and tissue came out of her every single day for two weeks. The mental torture became unbearable and weighed on her conscience. The only thing I could do was support her and show her love. I made sure that she always had something to drink and something to eat. I tried to distract her by renting comedy DVDs. There were many evenings where she cried in my arms. She would cry and yell, "We killed our child! We killed our child!" Eventually, the emotional intensity ebbed.

I did have those feelings of regret and I asked myself those "what if" questions, but I did that in my head. All of those questions were answered when I walked inside the apartment after walking Mokey one evening. I saw Lynn on her knees with her head in the toilet, vomiting without pants on. There were bloody panties in the garbage. Immediately, I asked if she was alright and if she needed anything. I got her a glass of water and a paper towel to clean herself. She truly was a sick woman. There was no way that our baby could have survived. If Lynn had remained pregnant, there was a high probability that her body would have failed. Both Lynn and the baby would have died.

After I helped her clean herself up, I started a bath for her. She was so happy because it seemed like I read her mind.

She said, "Thank you, Darling."

"Baby," I said as I looked into her eyes. Her glasses rested low on her nose, and she peered over the top of the wire frames. "I love you. I absolutely love you with all of my heart," I said.

She looked at me, smiled, and used one finger to move her glasses to rest properly on her nose. "I know you love me."

"Do you need anything?" I asked.

She smiled as she took the rest of her clothes off and got into the warm bath. "I got everything I need, baby."

EVERY DAY I TAKE MY MEDICATION

Methadone is a double-edged sword that will simultaneously free you and own you. My situation was that I was clean, but dependent on methadone. Lynn and I did not need Narcotics Anonymous, Alcoholics Anonymous, or religion. We were completely finished with recreational drug use. Many couples have one person using or wanting to use while the other one does not. Lynn and I were the exception to the rule. I was on methadone and she had to take Oxycontin, but we did not abuse our prescriptions anymore. While at one time, I was still using dope on 100 mg of methadone, I had reduced my dosage to 30 mg and I was not using dope. I was sober, but tapering off of methadone to keep my normal life normal.

While the dose decrease is quite substantial for many people on the inside, withdrawal from long term use is torture. Withdrawal from the low doses is almost worse. Think if you were on 100 mg and they lowered you 2 mg every week. That is only a 2% drop. If you are on 10 mg, and they lower your dosage 2mg, that is 20% less methadone every week. That's 20% less of an addictive pseudo-opiate that you have been taking for years. Now, imagine you have no money to pay for the week and you cannot get dosed at all.

As the week passed, each day made me worry more. I refused

THE COOLEST WAY TO KILL YOURSELF

to go to my parents. I had shamed myself and disappointed them enough. They thought I at least had some money saved and hated that I was on the program even though it helped save my life. Lynn asked her mother, but there were certain complications. Her mother would have given it to me, but could not. As Friday arrived, I was sweating and shaking from withdrawals because I was only taking ¼ of each "take home" bottle.

"I got it!" Lynn said as she came out of the bathroom.

"What?"

"I asked Kevin," she said. "He'll give it to you but you have to drive us to where he lives in Wayne."

"You asked Kevin?"

"Yes, baby," she said. "He understands."

On Sunday, we drove up to Wayne, NJ. I put on "I Am I Be" from the "Buhloone Mind State" LP by De La Soul. In the song, Posdnuos raps a line about not using protection and getting a woman pregnant.

"This is really something I do not want to hear right now!" Lynn yelled. I immediately changed the song to "Paint a Vulgar Picture" by The Smiths. "Sorry," Lynn said. "It's frustrating. Our situation is frustrating sometimes."

"I know, baby. Trust me, I know. Please, let's just get through it. We can do it. We've been through worse. At least neither of us is using. I'm not beating you like Ron did. We are not homeless. We have each other."

"Yeah, baby," Lynn said, "You're right. We have each other. My daughter and you are the only things that get me through life."

As we drove down Route 46, the mood lightened. We started to talk more about us and of course, the topic of sex came into our conversations.

"You know what, baby?" Lynn asked.

"What, baby?" I asked

"We are going to have some fun. I have not forgotten my plans."

AN OLD LOVE IN A NEW LIGHT

In the years after our affair, Lianna quit drugs and started her own business. She and her husband became very successful. Although she could not give me a full-time job with benefits, she was kind enough to give me some part-time freelance work. Years had passed since I had done any kind of work with or for Lianna, and I was very thankful for the opportunity.

Lynn never had any jealousy issues with Lianna. In fact, Lynn used to say, "Lianna is the only woman that I do not mind you hanging out with." She always thought that Lianna was very cool, intelligent, and open-minded. While Alison hated whenever I did freelance work for Lianna, Lynn always supported our friendship.

Lianna and I met for lunch one afternoon at a café in New Brunswick. She looked beautiful and healthy. As always, her erotic bohemian gypsy style enchanted me. Her scarf flowed around her neck and her tasteful bracelets and earrings complemented her appearance. We shared a friendly hug and kiss before we sat down to eat.

We had a wonderful conversation as we sat outside in front of the café. We talked about the methadone clinic and how we had decreased our dosages and stayed clean. We discussed her marriage and how she had grown closer to her husband. We talked about how my marriage had fallen apart. Naturally, the subject of Lynn arose, and we discussed the unconventional and rewarding aspects of the relationship. Since I knew Lianna was a deeply sexual person, I mentioned how Lynn and I went beyond any previous kinky experiences I had in the past. A nostalgic and amiable honesty was shared between us. There was an atmosphere of tenderness since we both had a deep love for each other that allowed us to respect each other even though we were ex-lovers.

"You know, Nicholas, I knew Alison was toxic for you, and I knew I was not just thinking that out of jealousy," Lianna said. "I thought I was going crazy. It blew my mind that no one could see it and everyone seemed to love her. I know I hurt you, but I was in bad shape when you were not in my life anymore. I cried for days. I locked myself in my room. My husband had an idea of what was going on, but he never mentioned it."

"I know," I replied. "We had an absolutely beautiful love affair. I felt like we were in the film 'Henry & June.' You were Anais Nin and I was your Henry Miller. I always wonder how things could have been different. I will always have love for you. You know that, don't you?"

Lianna smiled. "You look well. I think Lynn was exactly what you needed in your life. I can tell that she loves you and you love her, even though she is not here. I think you two saved each other."

I loved flirting with her again and I loved how our friendship and love for each other had matured. Most people who knew our story and our situation would not have understood or accepted a friendship like ours. She gave me the details and the paperwork for the assignments, then we hugged and kissed goodbye. Her touch was comforting and familiar. Although much time had passed since we had seen each other and we were living different lives, we left the café that day with the knowledge that we were still the same people at heart, bonded by a unique love for each other.

I WON'T SHARE YOU

Monogamy is a concept that I thought was preposterous. After my marriage failed and I found the comfort of an open relationship, I truly thought monogamy was an idea that was from the dark ages. Why should one woman only live with and love one man for the rest of her life? Why should one man love and live with one woman for the rest of his life? Even if it was just for the course of the relationship, why should one person commit to *only* one other person? My philosophy was to follow the love.

When I was going through my divorce, I told Alison, "Well, we can have an open relationship." She hated that idea and took offense to that. I honestly did not see anything wrong with what I had suggested. I know the idea is not for everybody, but as long as people are honest, I do not see a problem.

Lynn did not want an open relationship anymore. After years of having her heart broken, Lynn wanted monogamy.

I specifically remember one argument while we drove Mokey to the dog park. "I don't see the big deal," I said. "We have a good thing going. Why do we have to put labels on it?"

"It's because I feel better if you are committed. It's like the song by The Smiths called 'I Won't Share You'!"

"We can just be together," I said. "Both of us have been through so much with marriage and monogamy. I seriously do not understand the reason why we have to label us. It just puts an unneeded pressure on us."

Lynn said my name. I loved it when she said my name. "Listen, I need this. I am worth it. Please. Make me feel worth it." I laughed it off and we went to the dog park.

One evening, Lynn came home crying and woke me up. Half asleep, I asked, "What's wrong?" Lynn went to the bathroom and immediately began to wash up.

She entered the bedroom and said, "I have something to say."

"Okay."

"Some guy tried to force himself on me and I kicked him in the balls."

Immediately, I sat up and asked, "What?!" I began to get dressed.

"No, baby!" Lynn said. "He's gone!"

"What happened?" I asked as I sat down on the bed next to her.

"You were asleep and I was not tired. I went to the party next door. I smoked. I got really high and everyone was drinking. There was this guy there. He was like a frat guy, a dumb jock type. He was drunk and he kept on trying to kiss me and touch me."

"Okay," I said. "I didn't think you liked dumb jock frat guys."

Lynn cried, "I fucking don't, and you don't care, do you? You don't care if I fuck someone else, do you?"

I shook my head in disgust. "No. I do care. I do not get jealous, but I would like to think you have some taste."

"Well, I was emotional! You don't know what it's like. I only have you, but you can, will, and do fuck other women. For the first time since you, someone wanted me. I did not like him. I did not know him. I did not want to be with him, but I hate the fact that you can and will fuck these women who are prettier than me. I did it because you do not want to be monogamous. I don't have it like you! I'm not lucky like you!"

"Baby, don't talk like that. You're beautiful. Tell me what happened," I said.

"I thought I left some clothes in the laundromat downstairs. I walked down there and he followed me. Before I walked in, he took my hand and took me behind the apartment, in the alley. Right away, he tried to put his fingers in my ass. I told him to stop, but he wouldn't. So, I kneed him in the balls. Then, I grabbed his balls and twisted them. He hit his head against the bricks and fell to the ground. As I ran back here, I saw him stumbling to his car. I heard his car speed away. I think he hit part of the dumpster."

"Lynn," I sighed. "What the fuck?"

"If you wanted to be monogamous, this would never have happened!" Lynn yelled, in tears.

"That's bullshit!" I stated. "You can fuck whoever you want and I can fuck whoever I want. The difference is that you would at least approve of the women I have sex with. I'm not having sex with them just to get back at you or make you jealous. I am having sex with them because they are attracted to me and I'm attracted to them."

"I'm sorry!" Lynn sobbed. "I'm sorry! I cannot stand it. I cannot stand knowing that you are with some other woman. What if you fall in love with her and you leave me? This would not have happened if I felt secure. This would not have happened if I knew you were monogamous! This would not have happened if I was not so fucking insecure that I had to feel what it was like to have your open relationship! Nicholas, we are not kids anymore. We're in our 30's! I can give you all the kinky sex you want and you know it! No one loves you like I do. No one will ever love you like I do! Am I not good enough? Why? Tell me!"

After a long pause, I sighed. "I'm disappointed. You know, having an open relationship does not mean that you get with someone to make me jealous or get back at me. If a man or a woman wants you, I would expect that you would be with them only because you truly want to be with them. Lynn, I thought you had more sense than this."

"Well, I guess I don't," Lynn whimpered. "Look, it happened and it's over. I know you want to kill this guy, but it's not worth it. He'll never show his face around here again. Mark from across the hall kicked him out of the party."

"You sure know how to pick them," I said with a sarcastic laugh.

"Fuck you," Lynn said. "I'm serious. We tried the open relationship thing. Loving both Mischa and you was wonderful, but that's over. I know who I am and I'm telling you that I want us to be just us and only us."

Lynn took a bath and then put on her black negligee. As she got into bed, she hugged and kissed me. "I love you," she said, "and I don't want anyone else but you."

We fell asleep in each other's arms. We went through our mornings and evenings as if the incident had not happened. Every once in a while, Lynn would mention monogamy and I would say two words that would drive her crazy. I would say, "Ass fingers," and she would cringe.

Through the next several days, I noticed a change in Lynn. She acted listless and could not look me in the eye. She was just going through the motions in love and life. We would hang out with her daughter and her parents. Afterwards, I would drive her back to our apartment when it was time for her daughter to go to bed. A bizarre staleness began that lasted for three days. We were not having those wonderful conversations anymore. We were not laughing as much anymore. She did not care what we watched on television.

Mark Rothko once wrote, "Silence is so accurate."

We were sitting on the couch watching the Japanese horror film "Audition" directed by Takashi Miike. The film is about a widower who holds fake auditions to meet women. He finally meets a woman who happens to be insane. The woman kidnaps the man, performs torturous acupuncture on his face and then uses a wire saw to cut off his feet. She saws off a foot, giggles, and says, "Even if you give your entire self, you will never give me yours." This was not the best film to be watching while we discussed monogamy.

Being the idiot I can be, I finally asked, "What is wrong?"

She said my name again. "I love you," she said, and started crying. "Our relationship is important to me. It has saved me and I think it has saved you. Don't you understand that? We are not like other people. It's a beautiful and monumental element in our lives that we found each other. We accept each other. I accept you for who you are and you accept me for who I am."

"I know," I said.

"No!" she said. "I do not want to be in a relationship with you unless we are monogamous. I do not want anyone else. I think you're a fool if you want someone else." Lynn got off the couch and walked into the bathroom to have a cigarette. "And I would be a fool if I wanted someone else," she said as she closed the bathroom door.

My selfish ego truly backfired on me. This woman loved me and I loved her. Everything I was looking for was right in front of me. I grabbed the leash and took Mokey out for a walk. As I walked Mokey behind the apartment complex through the area that Lynn and I called "Rape Alley," I realized that I was an idiot. I started talking to myself.

"This woman loves me! I am lucky to have a woman who loves me! This woman accepts me for who I am. She deserves loyalty, honesty, and monogamy!"

As I walked back inside, I let Mokey off her leash and she ran up the stairs. Lynn let her in and saw a very different look on my face as I went inside. I looked her directly in the eyes and told her, "I love you. I do not want anybody else."

Lynn wrapped her arms around me and I felt as if she melted

in my arms. I felt like the male movie lead who swept the woman off her feet. We started frantically kissing and we made love. I remember the moonlight shining on us through the window with the broken shade.

Her touch felt more comfortable. She giggled and I asked, "What is so funny?"

"You have no idea," Lynn said. "You were searching for something. You were not satisfied. I was not either. This decision you just made is important to you and important to me. Trust me, I've got you. I'm going to take good care of you. I know how to take care of my man. I love you."

We began to fall asleep in each other's arms and then Mokey jumped up in the bed to snuggle. Lynn and I laughed and cried a little bit. Lynn was magnificently affectionate, but would pull herself back every once in a while. "I know what you are," Lynn said. "You are a sex addict freak. I am, too. You have been in relationships for so long. I have been in the same place. Now, we can just be with each other and be honest. We can just be honest with other."

As the handsome leading male in our unconventional love story, I wanted to say something dashing. I wanted to say something beautifully poignant, but the only words that I could say were, "I love you."

We wrapped our arms around each other. The whole scene was so typically cinematic. We fell asleep kissing each other. A wave of comfort crashed over me. The woman who I held in my arms loved me. Maybe, she was right. The more I looked back on my life, the more I felt that I had been wrong.

Comfort engulfed my life in a magnificent way. The comfort of Lynn's love let me settle in. I loved the fact that she loved me. We were two people who some would have said the world may have been better without. Still, we loved each other.

PANTIES

The atmosphere changed. Lynn and I became closer than any couple I had ever known. Although we jumped into sex, I knew that Lynn was masking her pain with sex. She constantly wanted to have sex. I constantly wanted to have sex, too. There was a line that needed to be crossed.

While Lynn and I became accustomed to a "normal life," we were still kinky. There were times when I would come home from work and have groceries in my hand. When I walked in the apartment, she was there waiting for me dressed in lingerie. Many times, groceries went bad because I left them on the kitchen table overnight. When we woke up, I could only smile because of the reason why the groceries went bad.

Honesty was essential to our relationship, and sexual honesty prevailed. We talked more about our sex addiction. We were both sexually insane. We were both insanely sexual. There were countless times that we could not stop looking at pornography. The kinkier the pornography, the more we became turned on. Instead of chastising me, Lynn wanted to know what I liked. Lynn would tease me with text messages like, "You are going to cum so hard tonight." Other times, she would text me, "I want you to pull over and masturbate." When I was not with her, I heard Lynn's voice in my head. I constantly thought of her waiting for me in lingerie.

THE COOLEST WAY TO KILL YOURSELF

When I opened the apartment door, I loved when she was sitting there in her black slip. This woman knew me to my core. I could tell her the most shameful aspect of my life and she loved me for it. She had her faults and her past, but I accepted her.

There was one evening that changed everything. Lynn wanted to spice things up even more. She already knew that I loved women in lingerie. I had hinted several times about how I loved when women dominated men. Something clicked in her brain. Something clicked in her clitoris. Something changed and it was beautiful. The days of begging and desperation were over. For the first time in her life, she felt absolute power. She had become a woman who not only knew that she could sexually please a man, but that she could make that man beg for her. More importantly, she could own the man who she had loved since she was a teenager.

We were in our apartment in Spotswood. She had decided that she wanted to be in control this time. She told me, "Take off your clothes. Take off all of your clothes. I want you completely naked." Then, she went into the bedroom.

I felt weak in the knees, thinking: *Is this the time she takes control? Is this the time she crosses that line?*

I was under her spell. All of these pornographic scenes raced through my mind. I did not know what reality was and what fetish porn was. The line between fantasy and reality did not just blur, it disappeared. I took off all of my clothes and felt the coldness of being completely naked. I did not want my cock to look like a simple "penis." I was stripped down, emotionally and physically, and I covered my private parts with my hands.

She came out wearing thigh high stockings, a garter belt, and a beautiful black slip. She looked beautiful, but more importantly, she felt beautiful. She owned me. I would do anything for her. I wanted to touch her. I wanted to apologize for every selfish thing I ever did. She was a goddess. She was my Goddess. From that day on, I would worship her.

She commanded, "Lay down on the floor in front of the couch. Grab both of the front legs of the couch." Without question, I got on the floor, reaching for the legs of the couch. She straddled me. I felt her silk panties against my hard cock. This was not romance. This was not fucking. This was pure passion that somehow transcended all of these things. She grabbed my wrist and pulled it towards one of the couch legs and hospital restraints. She looked me in the eye and saw that I was completely terrified in an erotic way. She smiled a smile that was deliciously evil.

Then, I heard the *click*. She paused for just a couple of seconds to look at my face. She had such a joyful look as her smile lifted her cheeks. It was the look of victory. She reached over and grabbed my other wrist. The next thing I heard was *click*. I was her property. She lifted her back and just looked at her man lying on the floor of her small apartment. She was a silk, satin, and lace-clad Goddess straddling me as my wrists were tied to the legs of a small couch. I was lying on the floor, completely naked and at her mercy. She winked at me and then got up.

She walked into the bedroom and pulled out the panties that Kristen purchased for her. They were black with white trim. With the panties, her Newport cigarettes, lighter, and cell phone, she walked in the bathroom and sat on the toilet. She lit a cigarette and took a minute to collect her thoughts.

From the living room floor, I heard her make a phone call.

"Kristen? Hey, so I have Nick tied up to the couch. What should I do with him?" There was a pause, and I imagine that shy, conservative Kristen was speechless on the other end.

"Never mind… I know what I'm going to do," she said.

Lynn told me later that she took the panties and spread them out with two fingers from each hand holding each end, and thought, *"Am I really going to do this? Do I want this? Should I go through with this?"*

I could not see her. From where I was lying on the floor, tied to the couch with hospital restraints, I heard the words, "Fuck yes! I want to own him!"

She walked out of the bathroom and I was actually scared, but of course turned on. She knelt down by my feet and said, "I'm going to put these panties on you and from now on, you are going to be my sissy slut. I own you now."

My cock began to throb. At first, she slid them over my right leg, then, she got the left leg. When the panties covered my pulsating cock, I did not have any sense of space, time, or dimension.

"I own you now," she said and kissed me as she patted my panty-clad cock. "Now you are going to lick my pussy until I cum. If you do a good job, maybe, just maybe, I will let your panty clad cock have some kind of release. Maybe..."

She straddled my chest and moved her panties to expose her magnificent pussy. I craned my neck, wanting to taste her, but she said, "Uh-uh... No... You have to beg me. You want to lick my pussy, don't you?"

I could do nothing but nod, like I was degraded to some kind of animal who lacked the capacity for speech. The truth was that I *was* degraded to her animal.

"Please," I said. "May I lick your pussy?"

She raised her hand and slapped me in the face hard. "May I lick your pussy, what?"

"Please may I lick your pussy, Goddess?"

"That's better," she said as she held the lace underwear to the side. As I began to suck on her clitoris, she moved her hand to my cock, which was covered by women's silk panties.

"You like that don't you?" she asked.

I was shaking with excitement, but I kept on licking, and she came quickly. She got off of me and started stroking my cock through the panties that she had put on me.

"I see all that kinky porn you like," she said. "This is a whole new life for both of us. You wanted this all along, didn't you? You are so fucking hard! Things are going to be different now. Yes… Things are going to be different now. I like this. I really fucking like this."

She pulled my cock out of the black silk panties with the white laced trim and started sucking on it. I came instantly. This was an orgasm like no other. This was not me trying to please a woman. This was not me being handsome. This was not me trying to impress. This was me being owned by a woman who knew and loved that she sexually controlled me. After I came, her head fell onto my chest, and some of her hair fell onto my face. She patted my head and said, "Oh, the things that I have in store for you…"

I was terrified but so aroused. My new life had started…. I was breathing heavy and had that post-orgasmic come-down feeling. Lynn winked at me and blew me a kiss.

Dear reader, I am wearing black silk panties right now as I am writing this.

THE POWER OF WRITING

Writing is beautifully subjective yet can be intensely powerful. Writing is one of the most basic, precise, and important forms of communication. While it can be misinterpreted, misrepresented, and misunderstood, writing always made me feel important and alive. One poem by William Carlos Williams was just a note he left for his wife, and now it is taught in schools.

I am not saying that I am a great writer. I am writing about how important writing is to me and how much I enjoy it. Ever since I was a child, I would write stories and plays. In my mind, I would have these little movies in my head. I spent countless hours attempting to get those ideas on paper. When I was in 8th grade, I wrote three 80-page-long screenplays. Sure, they were horrible, but the effort was there.

Effort is beautiful when it comes to any form of art. I may not like a painting, film, or book, but at least that painter, director, or writer is creating something. A true artist creates whether it is brilliant or horrible. They are creating something out of nothing while most people just sit and wait to experience it. Before I became married, I was extremely prolific. Countless stories, unfinished novels, poems, reviews, and interviews were born in my mind and lived on the paper through my words. As soon as I was married, I felt my creativity crumble.

When I was with Lianna, I filled eight volumes of those handwritten journals that people buy at stationary stores. I called them <u>The Lianna Papers</u>. When I was with Alison, I started <u>The Alison Papers</u> but never completed a single book. Although I remember <u>The Alison Papers</u> book being very cool, I gave it to Alison at the time of our divorce. I blamed Alison for stifling my creativity because she wanted me to focus on making money and having a normal life. As a man, I own up to my shortcomings. When I was married, I felt no need or desire to write or create. When I saw hilarious stand-up from Eugene Mirman, the bold writing of Virginie Despentes, or the prolific artistic expressions of Momus (Nick Currie), I would feel a jealous melancholy. These people were creating. I was creating nothing.

Lynn became my muse. "Soon" by My Bloody Valentine became our theme to start writing and be creative. As months passed, we attempted to be creative and artistic. Some ideas were dumb and some were interesting. We thought of twisted animated television shows that were subversive Saturday morning television. We thought of children's books about Mokey. We thought of comedy routines that we actually practiced. Kevin joined in whenever he came over. Podcasts were becoming popular and we had multiple she said/he said ideas for shows.

Lynn once told me, "Nicholas! I love when you are like this. You are so happy and amped when you are being creative. I love this side of you."

We would tell each other stories about our lives and make up stories that we wished could have happened. With the pornography, drugs, and crime, we had an endless amount of ideas and material.

I said, "We could write a book. We can do something where one chapter is from my point of view and then, the second chapter is from your point of view."

"You would never write a book about me," Lynn said.

I replied, "You never know."

"All of the crazy stuff both of us have done in the past… what we do now. We would have to change our names."

"My name could be Todd. It sounds pretentious. Remember that George Carlin bit about that name?"

"I have an idea," Lynn said. "Fiction is beautiful. We could use real life but make it fiction, too. Let them wonder what is true and what is false. Let them wonder if we get crazy kinky in real life. Let them wonder if we did drugs and lived insane hedonistic lives. Let them try to figure it out."

"I like that. I always think of Nick Swardson. Because of his character on Reno 911, people come up to him and say he's gay and he responds, 'It's fiction. Tobey Mcguire is not really Spiderman.'"

Lynn said, "You are probably going to drop an endless amount of music references, aren't you?"

"Of course I will." I thought for a moment, then said, "I am mainly worried about the sex and drugs."

Lynn replied, "Sex sells. Drugs sell, too. People are sure buying."

"You know, I always thought that the best art represents the time and place it was made." I continued, "Shakespeare and Twain grew up with a different style and different surroundings, and their work reflects that. If we write anything, we have to write from this messed up New Jersey culture we live in, even if it is fiction."

"Babe, I think it is important that you write as yourself even though what you write is fiction. Too many writers are trying to write like other people."

"If we write about our lives, people would not understand. Everyone is so quick to judge."

"Fuck them," Lynn said. "It's the coolest way. All memorable writers stir emotion and break normality."

"I'm not a memorable writer. No one remembers me."

"So what? I remember everything you write. Anyway, at least you're creating something. So many people are quick to criticize writing when they have not written anything."

I laughed to myself and looked at her as she prepared one of her usual baths. "This is fun."

"Baby, I love doing this with you," Lynn smiled. "We are having a great time. We may not finish any of these little projects that we are working on. That's okay. The point is that we are being creative. Sure, some of it is absolute crap, but some of what we put onto paper is truly unique and interesting. Plus, I love the energy and the vibe. You become like an ultra-version of yourself. We get creative in that bedroom. Through our writing, we should put ourselves in every single kind of crazy fantasy that we talk about. You know how we tell stories to each other? We should write stories like that."

"Really?"

"Oh… the things my character is going to make your character do in the book…" Then, Lynn announced dramatically, "Get me the razor and shave my legs, my slave!"

After my typical moment of pause and trying to look cute, I obediently turned around and got the razor.

"And later," she added, "You will paint my nails."

Dear reader, I sent an extremely rough draft of my book to Alison by accident. She was far from pleased. Any negative reviews online were probably written by her or by someone she strong-armed into writing for her.

Alison texted me, "I do not care about Lynn or her daughter! I do not care if the proceeds go to Lynn's family! I know very important people! This book will never be published."

Alison's cousin texted me, "You are dead! Plain and simple."

As I sat back in my writing chair with a smile on my face and Mokey by my feet, I replied, "It's fiction."

HUMBLE LIFE

We were broke, and I was still trying to find a job. Sometimes, my Blackberry was shut off because of lack of payment. I could barely afford my car payments and car insurance. The repo men and the car company did not know where I was living because I never changed my address. I would get dozens of text messages from Alison that said, "Pay your bills!"

I would always respond, "I would love to pay them if I had the money. You can always give me the money from my 401K that I gave you for your car… right before you left."

When my brothers told me that the repo men actually visited their houses looking for me, I told Lynn how embarrassed and ashamed I was. Lynn was always sympathetic. She would hug me, kiss me, and say, "Baby, I love you. Don't worry. Just keep on, keeping on. Keep on doing what you're doing. I'm here for you." I was finally in a relationship with a woman who I could be completely honest with. She would know all of my faults. She would know my secrets. She would know when I was an idiot and when I was brilliant. She accepted me for who I was and she still truly loved me. Lynn knew what it was like to be poor and even homeless. She was instrumental in helping me save money by making do with little. We lived this way for almost 9 months.

In the beginning, Lynn wanted to give me a birthday present but did not have any money. She wrote me the following letter:

"August 2011

To the love of my life,
　Happy Birthday Baby! I love you so much and I wish I had more than this to give you to show it. I love how witty, clever, poetic, beautiful, and sexy you are. I love the trust we have in each other that lets us 'do our thing' – and, of course, how much fun it is!
　Thank you so much for making me feel like a woman again. Thank you for making me feel pretty even when I'm yellow. Thank you for sharing Mokey with me. Thank you for being so sweet and kind to Mia. Thank you for sitting on our little couch watching movies and for sleeping in our little bed with me. And, of course, thank you for literally saving my life.
　Thank you for loving me.
　I love you with all of my heart.

Love always,
Lynn"

This letter was the best birthday present I ever received from any lover I ever had.

From that summer to winter, I tried to find employment. I worked at Lianna's company part-time. Eventually, I found a full-time, extremely low-paying, unstable job at a company in Plainfield that was barely paying their own bills. I was back to the suit & tie office guy role. Even though the economy was in a horrible state and the unemployment rate in New Jersey was 10%, a feeling of failure haunted me like a ghost. I was thankful to have a job, but felt like I should have been doing better.

Bills began to be paid. The refrigerator began to be filled with food. I began to have a presence in her family's life. I would take Lynn's daughter, Mia, to the dog park every couple of days. I would go to work in my suit and tie. After work, I would pick up Lynn from her parents' house so we could be together for the evening.

After several months, I got a job interview at a well-known and prestigious company via a personal referral. I took the morning off from work to go to the interview. Lynn surprised me when she ironed my dress shirt and had my suit dry cleaned.

On the morning of the interview, I remember my alarm going off and not feeling Lynn in bed next to me. I figured that she was having a smoke in the bathroom. I hit the snooze button and thought of a line from the comedian, Jim Gaffigan: "Nothing like starting the day with a little procrastination." I always set my alarm early enough so I can hit the snooze button multiple times and still be early for wherever I have to go. I got out of bed feeling horrible and groggy. My messy brown hair was in my face. As I stood up, I looked around for Lynn and Mokey but did not see them. I shouted out Lynn's name and then, Mokey's name, but the apartment was quiet.

As I stumbled to the window and opened the shade, I rubbed the gunk out of my eyes. Suddenly, I was blinded by a white light. This white light was not actually a light. This white light was an apartment complex covered in snow.

"Fucking snow," I cursed. "I hate snow." As soon as I said this, I heard the downstairs vestibule door close and heard Mokey's little feet run up the stairway. Then, I heard Lynn slowly limp up the stairs with her bad hip. I walked to the front door of our apartment and opened it. Covered in snow, Mokey greeted me with a precious exuberance. As her paws made my sweatpants wet, I looked down the stairway. I saw Lynn limping up the stairs with her hand on the handrail. With a red face that was wet from melting snow and sweat, Lynn said, "I hate these stairs, but I love where they lead."

I smiled and said, "Mokey could have waited to go for a walk. I could have taken her. I have to brush my car off anyway."

"You don't have to brush off your car," Lynn said as she looked up at me over the rims of her glasses, which had slid slightly down her nose. "I brushed off your car. You're ready to go."

In a state of astonishment and gratitude, I said, "Oh my God! Baby! You did not have to do that!"

"I know. I wanted to."

My arms could not hug her fast or strong enough. The snow from her jacket made my t-shirt damp. "Thank you," I said. "Seriously, I truly appreciate what you just did. It was symbolic. I love you. I love you so much." My eyes began to get a little watery.

"You'll stain your t-shirt," she said as I hugged her.

"Forget it," I replied. "It's worth it."

"Now, shave, take a shower, and get dressed," Lynn commanded. "Get this job."

Immediately, I went into morning preparation mode. Lynn would always hang out with me and play on her iPod as I shaved, took a shower, and got dressed. Looking back, I cannot remember a time when I was getting ready to go somewhere and she did not hang out to talk with me. We talked about Kristen and how she got the hospital restraints. We talked about the band, The Smiths, and what songs we loved. Her favorite song by The Smiths was "Paint a Vulgar Picture." We talked about the shows and films we watched. We talked about her daughter and how much she loved her. We talked about Ron and how he was living with some prostitute in Atlantic City. We discussed how the sexual honesty and trust was lacking in my relationship with Alison. As we talked, we laughed with an intense connection and understanding.

She stated, "See, this is what it will be like every morning when you get this job."

"What if I don't get it?" I asked.

"Just think positive, baby. Look at me. Remember, I love you." With a smile and a kiss, I replied, "I love you, too."

After I finished getting ready for the job interview, I kissed Lynn goodbye and walked down the stairs with my jacket in my suit bag. As I opened up the outside door, I saw nothing but snow-covered branches and a barely shoveled sidewalk. I texted the person who was going to interview me and asked if the interview was still on. Immediately, he replied, "Yes."

Carefully, I walked down the icy sidewalk to my car with my pants pulled up to my knees. In a parking lot filled with snow-covered vehicles, my perfectly clean red Ford Focus stood out from all the other cars. It was as if every single snowflake missed my car and fell on the other automobiles. As I got into the driver's seat, I put in the CD "Dwight Spitz" by Count Bass D. This was my lucky CD for when I went on job interviews. I drove down to Princeton to a very respectable company. I took my jacket out of the bag and went to the bathroom to freshen up. I checked my hair, my tie, my teeth, and made sure my hands were not clammy. As I looked at myself in the mirror, I received a text from Lynn that simply said, "I love you. You looked beautiful, sexy, and handsome when you left our apartment this morning. Good luck!"

As I walked into the company's office space, I immediately thought that I would love to work there. I felt confident that the interview went well. They were a completely new office and the Division Director wanted to do something new and different for the company. The past colleague of mine who referred me, Jason, walked me out after an hour-long interview.

As he smoked a cigarette, Jason asked me, "So, how's married life treating you? I remember your bachelor party."

"I'm not married anymore. But... I am with a woman who loves me. Even with the economy the way it is, I have never been happier."

"Cool," Jason said. "Good for you. I hope things work out here."

I thanked him for the opportunity and left.

As I drove home, I just hoped for the best but was expecting the worst. As I returned to Spotswood and pulled inside the same parking space, I saw the other cars were cleaned off in a very half-assed way. Some cars had huge piles of snow on their roofs. There were a couple of cars that were now covered in ice. As soon as I turned the car off, my Blackberry rang. As I looked down, I saw that it was the man who had interviewed me. I answered the phone and he said, "We want to make you an offer." As he relayed the details, I just sat in my warm, clean, snow-free car and smiled. He talked about salary, commission, and a start date.

He asked, "What do you think?"

I paused to not seem so eager, then said, "I accept your offer and I look forward to working with you."

"Great," my new boss said. "Be here Monday at 9 AM. By the way, each new person has to buy a six pack of beer for the office for the late nights. No domestic. Take care. I will see you on Monday."

As I got out of the car, I almost slipped on the ice because I was so excited. I walked up the stairs and opened the door to our apartment. Mokey ran to me and I tried to stop her from messing up my nice suit.

"How did it go, baby?" Lynn asked. She wore a black and white French maid outfit with a black lace slip, panties, garters, thigh high stockings and black heels.

Once again, I paused to maintain anticipation.

"Well?" she asked.

I said with a huge smile, "I got the job."

Lynn jumped off the couch in her own way and hugged me. I could not hug her strong enough to show how much I appreciated her support.

"Time to pay some bills," I said. "Also, let's get you some new lingerie." We smiled and chuckled.

Lynn said, "I made lunch for us."

As I watched this woman slowly move about the apartment like a fetishistic angel, I felt a kind of gratitude that I had not felt in so long. The support that this woman had given me was unlike any woman I had ever loved. This woman truly accepted me for who I was. I broke her heart, we both became drug addicts, and then we both became ex-drug addicts. We both fell and fell hard, but we were picking ourselves up together. As she served lunch, she said, "Congratulations, baby! I knew you would get the job. Now, the real work begins."

"Yeah, right," I said. "Thank you, honey."

Lynn laughed, kissed me on the top of my head and said, "Well, I have a way we can celebrate tonight." As my mind wandered, I smiled and ate the cheese tortellini she made for me.

YOU CAN DO BETTER

Kevin would always call me while he was alone and drunk. Kevin had quite a bit of lonely time after his wife left and took the kids. He had always been a solid friend. Some evenings, after Lynn and I made love, she would fall asleep and I would take Mokey out for a walk. Kevin and I would talk on the phone. Sometimes, we would reminisce, while other times, we would think about creative projects or comedy routines.

One evening, while both of us were up late and I was walking the dog, Kevin was sloppy drunk. I walked around the apartment complex longer than usual. Eventually, the topic of Lynn came up.

"Hey man, hey brother," Kevin slurred. "What are you doing?"

"What do you mean?" I asked.

"Lynn," he said.

"What about her?"

"You can do better."

"Excuse me?"

"Okay. See, you are a little different than me. You always loved that kinky shit. When it came to women, you did alright. I didn't do bad myself. Now, you have a job. You're good looking. You're intelligent. You have a college degree. What are you doing with Lynn, man?" Kevin asked.

As I stopped dead in my tracks, Mokey pulled me towards

the gazebo. I almost was astonished by what I heard. "What do you mean by 'what am I doing with Lynn?'" I asked as I walked into the gazebo. Looking up at the stars, I wished Lynn was with me in the gazebo. Instead, I was talking to Kevin, who was bad-mouthing her.

"Look, man, I love Lynn. You know that I love her to death, but she's unhealthy," Kevin said. "Do you really just go from one woman to the next? First, it was Zia. Then, it was Lianna, who I loved. Then, you went out and got fucking married! Brother, I am alone. Do you even know what it's like to be alone?"

As I sat in the gazebo, Mokey jumped right up next to me on the bench while I looked at the moon and listened to my intoxicated friend ramble.

Kevin continued, "We have both surpassed heroin addiction! I have a shit job. You have a suit and tie corporate job. I have kids and you have no attachments. What I am asking is this: why are you truly with her? Is it just the kinky sex? Is it to bounce back from Alison? When Alison dumped you, man, you moved into that apartment with Lynn quicker than I can drink a shot of whiskey. Alison leaves and you get Lynn? It's like you ordered a pizza with half ego, half revenge. Even she was wondering why you moved in with her and that chick, Mischa. I mean, is kinky sex worth that much to you? Why do you do this? Man, I love you, and I love Lynn. I just do not understand why? Why are you with her?"

After a long and dramatic pause, I cracked a smile and said, "Because I love her. I love her. You wouldn't understand."

"Hey, man. I didn't mean anything," Kevin said, as though his words could have been misinterpreted as anything other than what they clearly meant.

"It's alright, man," I said. "I'm not mad. I still love you, bro. Drink some water. Get some sleep. Good night." As I hung up the phone, I looked up at our living room window that looked over the gazebo and saw Lynn's silhouette in the window looking down at me. Knowing that she was now awake, I waved to her and she waved back. I stood up but Mokey stayed sitting on the bench.

As I looked down at Mokey and she looked up at me, I asked, "Mokey! Do you want to see Mommy?" Immediately, she jumped off the bench and we both walked to our home.

HELP THE AGED

As I mentioned before, our apartment complex had an assorted cast of characters. There was the white trash unemployed wife abuser who constantly drank Coors Light and complained about the noise while he blasted low-rent hick metal music. We called him Squidbilly after the television show "Squidbillies" on Adult Swim. The woman with cerebral palsy would drive her electric wheelchair in the middle of Main Street hoping that a car would hit her. The handyman of the complex was actually killed on the same street, and some people gossiped that he had been trying to save the woman in the wheelchair. There was a crazy old man who threw bags of dog feces out of his 2nd floor window and onto his car's hood because he did not want to walk down the stairs. Overall, the level of quirky behavior became normal for us.

Out of the varied types of people, one person was a fixture who stood out. Bobbie was an elderly woman who lived alone with two dogs. Her son rarely came to visit or check up on her. On any given day, Bobbie could be seen walking around the apartment complex, her crazy hair, like frayed white insulation. Imagine Albert Einstein's hair on an elderly lady in a housecoat, walking down a semi-busy street, talking to herself. I would run into her almost every other day while walking Mokey. Since she lived near the main entrance, I would see her standing outside at least once a day. Even during bad weather, she would be outside asking passersby for cigarettes or change. Since Lynn was often alone in the apartment with only Mokey to keep her company, she would walk Mokey outside and see Bobbie. Of course, their love of smoking cigarettes was just a small link in the chain of their connection. They developed a quirky neighborly friendship, sharing stories of bad husbands, health problems, and people who gave up on them.

Every time Bobbie saw me with Mokey in the gazebo, she would come by to talk.

"Ohhh," Bobbie said, as if it were her signature saying.

"Hey, Bobbie. How you doing?"

"I'm good. I'm good. How's Lynn?" Bobbie would ask.

"She's well," I would always respond.

She would then ask, "Do you have a cigarette?"

My reply was always the same, "Bobbie, I don't smoke."

"Ohhh." Bobbie's head would wobble, and then she would get up and say, "Goodbye. Say hello to Lynn for me."

One Friday evening, Lynn and I did not have any plans but to walk Mokey, watch a film, and retire to the bedroom. In the middle of the Edith Piaf biopic, "La Vie En Rose," Lynn stood up and said, "Oh my God! I forgot. I have to do something."

I asked, frustrated yet curious, "What? What on earth do you possibly have to do right now?"

"You don't have to come with me if you don't want to. I have to see Bobbie. Her son was supposed to visit this morning, but she thought he was going to cancel. He drops off all of the food, money, and everything she needs." Lynn walked to the kitchen and got a brown paper grocery bag. She began putting food inside. She took a couple cans of soup and some of the leftovers from last night's dinner. "Do you have any cash?" Lynn asked. "Do you have any cash on you at all? She's going to need cigarettes."

With some hesitation, I said, "Yeah, baby."

"Thanks, babe," Lynn said as she smiled and kissed me on the cheek. I gave Lynn a $10 bill and she put it in her pocket. Lynn asked, "You coming?"

"Um, yeah," I replied as I switched gears and started to get ready to leave the apartment.

Lynn and I took Mokey to Bobbie's apartment, carrying a grocery bag filled with food and drinks. The windows did not have curtains and the screens were stained by a window fan from years ago. As soon as Lynn rang the doorbell, the two dogs inside let out extremely loud barks.

"I hope she's alright," Lynn said. "Seriously, she could be in trouble." Lynn rang the doorbell several more times. The image of Bobbie lying face down on the kitchen floor in her old lady house dress flashed in my mind. This made me knock on the front wooden door with force. All of the sudden, I heard rustling in the apartment and I heard her inside apartment door open. Then, she opened the vestibule door that led outside.

"Bobbie!" Lynn said, "I was so worried about you!"

"Ooh," Bobbie said as her head wobbled, "Come in, Lynn! Come on in." We followed this rickety elderly woman into her apartment that had one black & white television and two large brown basset hounds. The dogs were not fed and the television was broadcasting fuzz.

"We brought some food. I have a half a pack of Mavericks for you and $10 so you can get a new pack tomorrow," Lynn said.

Bobbie hugged Lynn. "Oooh! Thank you my sweet, sweet girl! I wish that you were my daughter."

Lynn replied, "Thank you, Bobbie." Lynn asked, "Nicholas, could you feed the dogs? They eat dry food."

I replied, "Sure." As I walked into the kitchen, I smelled rotting food. After I put the fresh food away, I took the rotting food and threw it in the grocery bag to take to the dumpster. I took the gigantic bag of dog food and filled two large metal dog bowls. As soon as I put the food in the bowls, the dogs began to eat as if they had not been fed in a long time.

I heard Lynn talk more with Bobbie. She asked, "Hey, what about your son? He did not come by this morning?"

"Ooh! He called and said he was sorry."

"That doesn't matter," Lynn argued. "He needs to come by and see you."

"Ooh, he told me that he will come by, not tomorrow, but the day after tomorrow," Bobbie replied in her scratchy smoker's voice.

"The day after tomorrow?" Lynn asked with skepticism.

"Yes, Lynn," Bobbie said. "Don't worry about little old Bobbie. You came and gave me enough food and cigarettes until then. My Lynn! Ooh! Give me a hug!" The two women, both frail despite the large age difference, hugged each other as they sat on the couch. They continued their conversation and I fixed the television set.

"Ooh! You fixed it!" Bobbie exclaimed. "Lynn, keep this one around!"

Lynn smiled, looked at me, and replied, "Yeah, I think I'll keep this one."

As Lynn and I said our farewells, Bobbie hugged Lynn one more time. This time, Bobbie did not want to let go of her. With watery eyes, Bobbie said, "Lynn, you are the only one who cares about little old Bobbie. Thank you, my sweet, sweet girl."

Lynn laughed and replied, "Well, we have to continue our conversation about bad husbands."

"Ooh! Yes! Those sons of bitches!" Bobbie agreed. "They don't know when they have a good thing."

As Lynn and I walked out with Mokey on the leash and a bag of garbage in my hand to take to the dumpster, I looked at Lynn and saw her, once again, in a different way. Lynn looked beautiful even though she was wearing an old My Bloody Valentine T-shirt, a ratty blue jacket, and poorly fitted jeans. Lynn's kindness enlightened me to see her other beautiful side. As we closed Bobbie's front door behind us and Lynn lit a cigarette, I looked up at the clear star-filled sky and thought of Mimi, my grandmother. Mimi was a kind woman who was physically weak but an emotional Hercules when it came to loving her family. As Mimi grew old, I was the grandchild who took care of her. As a teenager, I thought of taking care of Mimi as a burden. As I grew to my 20's, my love for my grandmother made taking care of her not feel like a chore. There is a nobility in helping the aged.

As I watched Lynn that evening, I was touched by the fact that this broken and beaten woman still had so much kindness for a woman she had only known for less than a year. Lynn did not have to learn to love and care for someone. Lynn was just a kind person. My thoughts raced in my head as we walked. I threw the garbage in the dumpster and Lynn extinguished her cigarette.

Lynn stated, "We did a good thing tonight, babe."

At that moment, I felt small beside such a genuinely kind heart. I looked at her face in the moonlight. She did not see it coming, so I lifted my hand to her face and gently rested it on the back of her neck. Slowly, I pulled her towards me and kissed her on the lips. She lifted her arm and ran her fingers through the hair on the back of my head. As we pulled away from the kiss, Lynn asked, "What was that for?"

After the usual pause and smile, I said, "That's for you being you, baby. That's for you being you." Lynn smiled and put her right arm through my left arm as we both put our hands in our jacket pockets and walked our adorable dog back to our apartment under the moonlight.

She asked, "Do you think anyone will care about me when I'm an old lady?"

FROM ONE WOMAN TO ANOTHER

Ron kept texting Lynn saying that he had moved in with a new girlfriend. She would often write back, "Does she know about you?" Ron wanted to make her jealous, but Lynn was past that point and honestly happy.

One day while I was at work, Lynn got a phone call from Ron's cell phone as she was listening to "The Queen Is Dead" album by The Smiths. She ignored the call twice. During the third call, she finally picked up and heard a woman crying. The woman quickly hung up. Lynn grabbed a cigarette, a lighter, a leash, and Mokey. As they went for a walk around the apartment building, Lynn called the number back. When the phone was answered, no one said anything.

"Hello?" Lynn said. "Is this Ron's girlfriend?" There was silence. "Come on. I can help you. What's going on?"

A scared voice whimpered, "Hey."

"What's your name, honey?" Lynn asked.

"Dana. I'm Ron's girlfriend. He's living with me."

"Okay," Lynn said. "I don't mean to be rude, but why are you calling me?"

"I don't know," she said.

"Yes, you do," Lynn responded.

"He talks of you a lot. I think he's trying to make me jealous."

"He does that. Girl, you have nothing to be jealous of," Lynn said. "I want nothing to do with him. I am in love with a wonderful man who does not do drugs, does not beat me, does not steal from me, and does not make me prostitute to pay for his drug habit."

"Oh, well, I was doing that before we met," Dana said.

Lynn's head shook sadly as she picked up after Mokey. She continued to walk and smoke her cigarette. "Dana, do you know what you are getting into?"

"Well, that's why I wanted to talk with you," Dana responded, the sniffling sound giving away her tears. "I don't know if I can trust him. Money is missing. Some of my stuff has gone missing."

"Listen to me very carefully," Lynn said. "Ron has psychological problems. He is a drug addict. He was a neglectful father and an abusive husband. He stole my painkillers when I was stuck in a wheelchair. There was a time when I had to protect my baby from him while he hit me with a plastic wiffle ball bat."

"Really?" Dana asked with disbelief.

"Yes, really!" Lynn exclaimed. "Do what you want. Live your life. I'm not telling you not to see him, but as a woman, I think you should know the truth. You should know all this about Ron. What's he doing?"

"Well, I think he's using me," Dana replied. "I can't find the cash that I put in my purse. He disappears for several days. When I have tricks over, he gets mad… like, real mad. Sometimes, I'm afraid."

"Dana!" Lynn yelled as she threw the bag of Mokey's excrement into the dumpster. "I suggest you get rid of him. Follow your heart. You were tricking already. Do you need a person like him in your life?"

"People do not fall in love with whores."

Lynn laughed. "I thought that I was not good enough for anybody. That just led to poor decisions. I was wrong. I realized that I am good enough, and someone does love me. Like I said, from one woman to another, you need to know that he is abusive. He made us homeless, and basically forced me into prostitution because of his drug addiction, which became our drug addiction. Do you understand that?"

"I think he's home now," Dana said in a terrified tone. Suddenly, Lynn heard a shuffle.

"What are you doing on my phone!?" she heard a voice exclaim from far away. There was more of a shuffle and then Lynn heard Ron's voice. "Who is this?" Ron asked.

"If you hurt her I will call the police right now," Lynn threatened.

"What?" Ron asked in a slurred voice. "What are you talking about, B?"

By this time, Lynn was on her way back up to our apartment, and I came home in the middle of her phone conversation.

"Listen to me, Ron!" Lynn said in a stern voice. "You texted me your address for some stupid reason. I know where you are living. I want her to call me tonight. I want to hear her voice. No, no, no. Shut up. If I do not hear her and if I do not know she's alright by 11 PM, I will call the police on you."

"Come on, B," Ron said, barely intelligible. "You wanted to trick."

"No, I fucking didn't! You asshole!" Lynn yelled.

"Well, it was a long time ago," Ron said. "What did you say to her? Did you like her?"

"Listen, Ron. Listen to me very carefully." Lynn enunciated every syllable slowly. "If she does not call me to say that she is alright tonight by 11 PM, and then call me in the morning, I will fucking call the police on you."

"I'll call the police on you, bitch!" Ron said. "I'll call DYFS

THE COOLEST WAY TO KILL YOURSELF

and say your parents are not taking care of Mia."

"Listen to me, you wife abusing junkie fuck!" Lynn yelled. "If they take one look at you, they will not believe you. They take one look at me, my daughter, my parents, and my better-than-you boyfriend, they will know the truth."

"You're still fucking that dude?" Ron asked.

As much as I had my flaws, she loved saying, "He's a better lover than you. He's a better partner than you. He's more of a father to your daughter than you will ever be. He does not hit me and he does not do drugs. Now, do you fucking understand?"

"Alright, shit!" Ron said. "Chill, B!"

"Do not call me 'B!'" Lynn snapped. "Let me talk to Dana."

"Fine!" Ron shouted.

As I changed out of my suit and tie, I was fascinated as I listened to the one-sided conversation.

After some indistinguishable yelling in the background, Dana picked up the phone. Lynn heard Ron say, "I'm fucking serious!"

"Hello?" Dana asked.

"Are you alright?" Lynn asked with genuine concern.

"Yes," Dana sniffed.

"Listen, if you need anything, give me a call. You know my opinion. You know about me. Call me tonight at 11 PM. Do not text me! I want to hear your voice. Then, I want you to call me in the morning. Sometimes, he would wake up in the middle of the night in a fit of anger and just hit me while I was sleeping."

"Okay," Dana said unconvincingly.

"No!" Lynn yelled. "I'm serious! There will be cops at your house if you do not do this!"

"Okay!" Dana said again. She paused and then said, "Thank you," right before she hung up the phone.

Lynn and I had dinner, watched some stand-up by Louis CK, and the film "Shortbus." There was a time when she looked at me and put her fingers to her lips. This always made me smile; it meant that she was waiting for a kiss. Of course, I felt foolish for not initiating a kiss sooner, so I immediately let my hand grace the back of her neck, pulled her towards me and kissed her. Afterwards, she checked her phone. Ron had texted her three words that had nothing to do with anything. She showed me the text from Ron, which read, "I hate niggers." We shared a sad laugh because Ron was just a horrible person, and he was out of his mind.

Eleven PM arrived and Lynn held her phone in her hand as she waited for the call. Five minutes passed and Lynn started to do her version of pacing. For Lynn, "pacing" was trying to get up and maybe having a cigarette in the bathroom.

"Should I call?" she asked. "Should I call them? Should I call the police? Am I doing the right thing?"

I interrupted, "Baby, you are doing a very loving and positive thing." Suddenly, Lynn's phone rang and she quickly answered.

"Here," Ron said as he passed the phone to Dana.

"Hi, Lynn," Dana said. "I'm fine. Seriously, I'm fine. He was upset but we worked it out."

"Are you sure you are alright?" Lynn asked.

"Yes!" Dana insisted.

When Lynn heard this, she covered the phone and looked at me as she whispered, "Ron is there, right next to her, and listening to this call." Lynn uncovered the phone. "Seriously, Dana, are you honestly okay? Hit a button on the phone if you are not okay."

"Yes, I'm fine," Dana said and hung up.

Lynn called her back, but it went to voicemail. She left a message and texted her to remind her to call in the morning.

Days went by. I went to work. We spent time with Mia, and took care of Mokey. Throughout our everyday routines, Dana was in the back of our minds. Lynn made several calls to check in, but there was no response. Eventually, Ron's temporary burner phone ran out of minutes.

After another wonderful night of kinky passion, the phone

rang while I was in the afterglow and Lynn smoked a cigarette. Half asleep, I heard Lynn exclaim, "Dana! Are you okay?" Interested, I woke myself up to listen.

Lynn wanted to make sure that a woman would never be taken advantage of or hurt by Ron again. In a way, Lynn was a complicated feminist. She loved being the stereotypical woman who was loyal by default, but she wanted every woman to have a good man.

As I lay there in bed, all I heard Lynn say was, "Okay, good luck." Then I heard her flip phone close. Like always, I watched her exit the bathroom and admired the beautiful outline of her body in a silk slip. Once she was beside me, she grabbed my head and kissed me.

"What goes on, baby?" I asked.

"She told me that he tried to hit her in front of one of her johns. Some guy literally threw him onto the concrete. She threw all of his shit onto the ghetto streets of Trenton." After a very short silence, we laughed. "I think I saved her from him," she said.

"You did, baby!" I kissed her. "You did. And…it was just honesty. You did not seek to mess up his relationship. You did great, baby! I'm proud of you."

"Let's fall asleep while we watch 'Seinfeld,'" Lynn said. She turned to me. "For a perverted freak, you are a good man," she said. "You are a good egg."

MOKEY LOVES GLASSES

After taking many pictures of Lynn, I realized that her wire-framed glasses helped to create this iconic image of her. While many women do not like wearing glasses, Lynn and I thought that her glasses made her look intelligent and sexy. Though her long black hair was thin, it framed her adorable face. And every time she looked up at me with her glasses sliding down her nose, it was as if she were saying, "I got you. You love me and I know it." I have many pictures of her looking up at me over the top of the wire frames.

One morning, I woke up and went through my morning routine as usual. I fed Mokey, took her for a walk, shaved my face, showered, and got dressed. I kissed Lynn goodbye and drove to work. Usually, I would talk to Lynn while I drove to work, but for some reason she slept in late. While I was at my desk in my office, on the phone with a client, Lynn called three times. As soon as I was able to call Lynn back, she yelled four words that coworkers near my desk could clearly hear through my phone: "Mokey ate my glasses!!!" I could not help but giggle, but then I stopped myself.

"Hold on," I said as I walked out of the office with my Blackberry to take the personal call. Once in the parking lot, I said, "Okay. What about Mokey and your glasses?"

"Mokey ate my glasses!" Lynn yelled. "I cannot see! I love this dog but I found my wire frames chewed up on the floor. I found the lenses on the bathroom floor, after I stepped on them. I cannot see!"

"Okay, calm down. We can handle this. Let me finish the day at work and we will work something out."

A few hours later, Lynn called to tell me that she could get new glasses for free but had to wait an entire week because that was when the insurance would be able to pay for the new glasses. When I arrived to pick her up from her parents' house, after Mia was asleep, I noticed a change in Lynn. She was agitated, nervous, and could not wait to get into my car and go home.

"What's wrong?" I asked, realizing it was a stupid question as soon as it came out of my mouth.

"I feel isolated and handicapped!" Lynn yelled. She took a deep breath and said, "Listen, it is very stressful when I do not have my glasses. You are lucky you have good vision. Seriously, you are lucky. You have no idea what it is like to not have sight. Let's just go home."

As the week went on, little aspects of regular life started driving Lynn insane. She accidentally confused spray deodorant with hair spray. She was tripping over Mokey. She could not see the screen on her iPod clearly. Instead of The Smiths, she would hit The The. Instead of the song "Laid" by James, she would accidently pick The Primitives.

When I was as work, I was inundated by her phone calls. She kept on calling about problems that were easily solved, and I found myself constantly having to calm her down. Every single time she answered the phone when I called her, she would bark, "What!? What do you fucking want!?"

Once, Kevin called me and said, "There is something wrong with Lynn. She's not herself. What's going on?"

"Mokey ate her glasses," I said.

"You know those artists that think they are cool and put out music and all the typography is all messed up?" Kevin said. "They are assholes. I will tell you why. People want to see. Words are meant to be read. Understand that. Being blind is lonely."

When I arrived home, I heard Lynn crashing the pots and pans in the kitchen as I walked up the stairs. As I opened the door, I saw her crying.

"Baby!" Lynn exclaimed. "I feel like I am going insane! I cannot see!"

In the beginning, I had thought she was being overly dramatic, but I realized that her poor eyesight was frustrating her to the point of genuine distress.

I held her and tried to calm her down. "It's okay, baby. Let me help you out." I felt like a helpless fool. I wanted to give her a new pair of prescription glasses right then and there, but I could not materialize these glasses for her, no matter how badly I wanted to. Kevin was right and I had not realized how difficult it was for her. Lynn and I went to the store that evening and ordered a pair of glasses that made her look beautiful.

A week went by, and Lynn finally got the insurance paperwork right. She had gone from feeling isolated and handicapped, to feeling so frustrated and aggravated because she simply could not see. When she woke up in the morning, she dreaded the morning rituals. When she put the toothpaste on her toothbrush, she would miss and the toothpaste would fall into the sink. She would button her shirt wrong.

I remember falling asleep one night and hearing her say, "I am giving up on make-up right now! If you want me to have sexy lips and eyeliner, you have to wait until I get glasses."

My bank account started to grow and I offered to buy her glasses, but she refused. "No!" Lynn said. "I can get them for free!"

I replied, "But you will probably kill me before you get them."

"Yeah, I will probably put something poisonous in your drink by accident." She laughed and said, "Oh, I made you coffee." It was not poison, but it was better described as milk with a hint coffee.

Finally, we pulled into the mall in East Brunswick so that we could pick up her glasses. As I parked the car, she said, "Can you imagine if we did the vibrating egg thing while I did not have glasses?" I looked at her and she could not see me looking at her, but I thought that it would have been one of those very funny moments where you connect with the person you are talking to and laugh out loud. Unfortunately, she could not see me looking at her.

Once we were in the eyeglasses store, Lynn commented, "You are lucky that I cannot see you flirting with her." The lady behind the counter laughed and as soon as Lynn put on those new glasses and looked at the beautiful woman behind the counter, she winked at her and said, "You had your chance." She turned to me. "Let's go home so I can punish you. I have quite a bit of pent up aggression to get out on your sexy ass." She slapped my ass as if I was some sex object. She looked back at the girl behind the counter and said, "Girl, everyone should have a Nicholas." Lynn walked out with a confidence and rock star quality.

Lynn's face lit up and she smiled. "I can see!" Her voice echoed through the mall. "I can feel my sanity returning to me as I speak." As I walked out of the mall with her hand in mine, I thought to myself that it was good to have her back.

SOMETIMES PEOPLE JUST DO STUPID THINGS

One evening, Kevin came over, and by the time I arrived home from work, he and Lynn were drunk. Lynn and I were not drinking anymore, but she decided to indulge since we had company. They were watching the "Jackass" collection, which featured the entire MTV series. After many drinks, we walked down to the gazebo with Mokey.

Dumb. Dumb. Dumb. For some reason, we started slapping and hitting each other… for fun. Although I had never hit a woman in my entire life, I slapped Lynn in the back of the head and she hysterically laughed. With a huge smile, she slapped me across the face, and we both erupted in a fit of laughter. A passerby saw the three of us in the gazebo, grown adults in their 30's smacking each other and laughing. The man shook his head and walked on.

The night went on and we invited our neighbor, Denise, to hang out with us. Of course, Lynn and I thought that maybe Kevin and Denise could get together for a fling like Kevin did with Kristen a while back. Kevin was far too drunk and Denise was far too sober. Lynn and I had no problem retiring to the bedroom. We locked the door behind us and "did our thing" very quietly. Our whole episode only lasted around 20 minutes, and we heard Kevin and Denise speak as Lynn and I collapsed on our backs. Of course, Lynn went to eavesdrop at the bedroom door, and motioned for me to come over. Even though I wanted Kevin and Denise to have privacy, I stumbled over and felt a sense of déjà vu.

"Well, you don't have to leave," Kevin said. "I mean you live just a couple of apartments over."

"Yeah, I know," Denise said, "but I have to get up for work really early in the morning. Ask Lynn, she sees me leave before the sun is even up."

"Oh, yeah?" Kevin slurred. "What do you do?"

"I have a government job."

"Wow! So do I. What do you do?" Kevin was trying so hard to keep the conversation going and convince her to stay.

"Well, it's a utilities position," she said.

"Why don't you just stay for a little bit and we could watch TV, have a couple of drinks. I'm tired. I think you are beautiful, but I won't try anything."

Denise laughed and said, "Thank you, Kevin. You take care of yourself. Drink some water."

Lynn and I heard the door gently close as Denise left our apartment. Lynn and I each had an arm around each other's waist. She was wearing one of her legendary black silk slips. We looked at each other and turned around to go to bed.

"I'm glad I have you, baby," Lynn said.

"Baby, I am so thankful that we have each other."

The day after, Kevin called me up from his house in northern NJ. As soon as I saw his name on my phone, I grabbed Mokey's leash and a plastic bag. As I attached the leash to Mokey's collar, I heard him crying on the other line.

"Kevin?" I asked. "Are you alright?"

"Yeah, man," he said. "It just fucking sucks."

"What does?" I asked.

"Dude, I'm fucking alone. I had a wife, two kids… well, I still have two kids, but they don't live with me. Last night, I had a blast!"

"Yes, it was crazy," I laughed. I bent down to pick a flower for Lynn.

"Seriously, man. I saw a different side of you two last night. Hey, I'm sorry I said that a long time ago."

"What do you mean?" I asked, knowing exactly what he was talking about.

"You know," Kevin said. "All those things I said about Lynn. I'm sorry. I was wrong, man. I was drunk. You two truly love each other. You two are very and truly happy together. I wish I had that."

A smile of redemption covered my face as I replied, "Hey, man. Don't worry about it. I'm glad you see it now."

"I do, man. I do. She's just cool, loving, and accepting."

"I know. We really get each other. She does not care about money, or what her friends think. When it comes to our relationship, all she wants is my love, lingerie, cigarettes, a lot of kinky sex... and me."

"Wow," Kevin said. "That sounds like a prostitute... a prostitute you don't have to pay for. That's awesome."

I laughed, and asked, "So, when are you coming back down?"

"Shit! I don't know if my liver can take it. We're getting older now. I cannot believe we are in our mid 30's."

"Time waits for no one."

We continued to talk through the night with a friendly honesty. As I strolled down the sidewalk, I saw Lynn's silhouette in the bedroom window as she put on one of her negligees. As Mokey bopped down the sidewalk, I continued to talk to Kevin with that smile stuck to my face the entire time.

KINKY LOVE

As lovers, one of our many theme songs was "Kinky Love" by Pale Saints. The song is a cover version of a Nancy Sinatra track. The song has a gentle wah-wah guitar and an elegant bass line. Whenever the song came on the iPod or CD player, we would just look at each other. We would smile as if we were lovers who were enlightened. We had a love like no other. Some other songs that made us feel that way were "This is Hardcore" by Pulp, "Laid" by James, "Gravitate to Me" by The The, and, of course, "Mother of Pearl" by Roxy Music.

We played our wonderful games. The complete trust and sexual honesty was something I had always strived for, but never felt I completely reached with anyone else. Lynn was willing to go there with me. We both looked at pornography and talked openly about sex. We just wanted to please each other. We felt that we reached the connection of the passionate couple from the film, "In the Realm of the Senses." If the world crumbled around us, we would feel joy because we had each other. Although I thought I felt this before, this was deeper and much more intense. The absolute honesty we shared made us both realize that most people say they feel this way in a relationship, but do not live that way. We lived that way.

We began to look at everything in a different light. As couples argued in public, we just looked at each other and knew that they were not kinky. Marriages of friends failed while we were still acting like horny teenagers. The beauty of kinky sex is that it is not only therapeutic, but empowering. It was ours. We shared this secret that brought us closer together. When Ron and Alison would call us, we both felt like they no longer had the power to draw us into their negativity. Lynn would respond with comments like, "You only wish you could do with me the things I am doing now." At the office, when I saw a strong-willed woman in heels walk into the conference room with confidence, I thought, "I wonder if this person is kinky?" Seeing confident women made me think of Lynn, and the way that kink had freed her.

Putting me in women's panties was only the beginning. She would shop online and buy corsets, garter belts, and dresses for both of us. She would make me wear panties to work under my suit and tie. On some nights, she would just say four words and the whole episode would start.

"Get dressed for me."

I would have to go into the bedroom and bring her lingerie. She loved to wear black, but one of her favorites was this magnificently sexy, deep red corset with garters. There was a little skirt on the bottom that had black lace over the red silk. She would wear black stockings and heels. Every time she put on that red and black corset, she would say, "I love the red one. It makes me feel powerful." This became her mantra.

We constantly discussed sex and sexuality. We understood each other. "I do not want you to be a woman," Lynn would say. "I want a man in woman's lingerie, who is owned by me. I think you love women so much, that this is a way you can be closer to women. Plus, you have a lingerie fetish. I love owning you."

When I was being sexually submissive, she was not my mistress. She was my Goddess. I answered everything she said with either, "Yes, Goddess" or "No, Goddess." We established safe words. "Moonlight" meant "stop." If we did not want to stop, just slow down or change, we could say "moonbeam."

After all of our kinky times, Lynn once told me, "I love how you never had to moonlight or moonbeam me."

When your lover calls you "Goddess" and truly worships you, your confidence will rise. Lynn completely managed her Oxycontin prescription. We both became more responsible. Bills were paid. Lynn and I grew to be healthier and our only addiction was kink. We did not drink anymore. We did not need the night life. We did not need drugs. There was no need for fancy things. We just needed each other. Our lives began to fall into place.

Creativity and sexuality rushed through us. We discussed writing a blog and doing a podcast. One of my favorite things that we did was tell each other fantasy stories. As we "did our thing," she would talk to me. She would say things like, "I have two other women with me and they are all wearing strap-ons. They look at you, a man in a dress. They see a chastity device on your cock and the key around my neck. They pay me money so they can fuck you. They take turns fucking you in the ass. Then, you serve us dinner. Afterwards, I make you go down on all of them. I'm so proud that you know how to make my friends cum."

Usually, after my Goddess gave me permission and I reached orgasm, the dynamic changed. She would say, "Tell me a story. You know, one of those different ones."

Back in my regular clothing, I would tell a very different kind of sex tale as I used a vibrator on her. "We go to an exclusive party we were invited to and I see this beautiful woman wearing lingerie. She's gorgeous. She's tall, thin, and powerful. Her breasts look magnificent in her black corset. I cannot keep my attention away from her. She wonders why I am with you. She knows that you are powerless. She knows that she has control and that she will own me."

"But, you do not want to hurt me, right?" she would ask between heavy breaths. "But… but you cannot stop yourself."

"Yes," I would say in my deep voice. "Our mouths just cannot stay away from each other. We kiss and she goes down on me in front of you. She knows you're upset and she laughs at you. She whispers in my ear and she points my cock towards your face. She strokes my hard throbbing cock, which is hard because of her. She points my cock towards you and makes me cum all over your face while she laughs at you. My cum drips all over your face and then she makes you clean my cock." Lynn would orgasm while listening to my voice, and we would collapse into each other's arms.

Both of us knew we were very different from typical lovers. Most people have wild fantasies and strange kinks, but keep them private from everyone, including their own lovers. We not only talked about our fantasies, but created these stories for each other that became more intense each time. We also ended up making some of our fantasies reality. We tried to top each other with ideas and stories. We had regular, "normal" sex often, too, but the control of forced feminization and female domination was the aspect she loved most. She would say things like, "You can only cum when I give you permission." She began talking about ordering a male chastity device online. As we continued to explore on the internet, she looked at strap-on dildos, cat of nine tails, and other toys.

The phallic aspect of a dildo is symbolic not just as a toy for orgasm, but power. Lynn wanted to make our sessions more intense. Over the course of our relationship, I had purchased several new dildos for her. They were kept in pristine condition and placed in a special drawer. There was one that we used to use on her in a time when we could barely afford the batteries to make it vibrate. This dildo was my ex-wife's. Lynn had found it in the house in Woodbridge when Alison left it behind. I like to think that it was inside my ex-wife out of sad desperation and inside of Lynn as a tribute to the beauty of erotica.

One night, we were watching a DVD of "Preaching to the Perverted" and Lynn and I began talking like we always did. The film is a very humorous tale of an American dominatrix and a very conservative young English male. There are many different kinky scenes, but it is more of a comedy than a film to get you aroused. The beauty of the film is how it portrays people in the kink culture. They talk about dildos, anal beads, clit piercing, and whipping with such comfort and ease because that is part of their everyday life and conversation. Lynn and I became like this. We could say, watch, or do anything with each other without censoring ourselves.

"I'm going to fuck you tonight," she said as she sipped her drink.

I smiled and looked at her with my usual quirky smirk, so proud of my lover. I said, "Cool." I thought we were going have another kinky evening of forced feminization, bondage, teasing, and my face between her legs.

"No," she said. "I am going to love watching myself own you. I know that you're thinking that it will just be another night of forced feminization, bondage, teasing, and your face between my legs. I am going to slide that dildo up your ass tonight and I am going to love, and I repeat, love watching you. You're a virgin. You never had anything inside you." She turned her head to look me in the eyes, and said, "Tonight, I'm taking your virginity."

I remained silent and tried not to let her see that I was terrified. I shrugged and just said, "Uh… Okay." I tried to keep my cool, hoping that my deep, fortifying breath was not obvious.

While she kept watching the film, she said, "Get dressed for me."

I slowly got up and walked into the bedroom. From the living room, I heard her say, "Get me my red corset and stockings!"

I went through the closet and drawers and got everything she asked for. I walked into the living room.

"Collar!" she reminded me. "Get Alison's pink dildo that she purchased because it's the one that bimbo uses on 'Sex & the City.'

Get the Astroglide. I want you wearing thigh high stockings, black panties, and the old… no, get the new French maid outfit. Go!" she ordered.

Immediately, I went back into the bedroom. Then, I heard her say, "Oh, and you better have fucking heels on!" My eyes closed the minute I heard those words. I was terrified, yet turned on.

I got dressed. I could see the hair on my legs through the nylon thigh highs. I was wearing a black and white French maid outfit, white petticoat, and my feet were crammed into women's size 11 high heeled shoes. I looked ridiculous.

Lynn was in the bathroom, smoking a cigarette. The fear and anticipation was driving me insane. I felt vulnerable and I was scared, but I trusted her. As a million thoughts and worries raced through my mind, I could hear small noises coming from the bathroom as Lynn got ready. Lipsticks and nail polish bottles fell on the floor. I could hear her pick them up and put them in her make-up bag.

"Lights!" she commanded. I turned down the lights and left the hallway light on and the bedroom door open.

"Have your collar ready," she said.

Shit! I thought to myself. *Where did I put the black collar?* I fumbled around the room in my heels and French maid outfit, looking for the leash and collar. I actually heard my petticoat swish as I moved around the room and my black high heels clicked when I was not walking on the carpeted floor. I found the collar the moment she walked in.

Her silhouette was awe-inspiring. She stood in the doorway in her blood red corset with black thigh high stockings attached to its garters. Her heels made her look powerful. She knew the supremacy she had over me. She was no longer the woman who begged a man to come back. She was no longer a battered wife. She was no longer a prostitute. She was no longer a drug addict. She was a Goddess. She was my Goddess.

That night, we crossed a line. At one point, I almost said the safe word. I trusted her, and I let her have something I had never given anyone else before.

Whenever someone said something negative about Lynn, or told me that I could do better, I was proud to say, "She loves me. I love her. No one accepts me or understands me like she does. No one knows me like she does." We were not only a couple, but we were a happy couple. Finally, we could face the world. Finally, we could face the future. Finally, there was not fear because we had each other.

THE COOLEST WAY

Conversation is an art that Lynn and I had perfected. We knew when to make each other laugh. We knew when to be poignant. We knew when to comfort each other. Sometimes, we would finish each other's jokes. Those days of passing the phone around while she talked were over. We never got sick of hearing each other's voices.

One conversation sticks out in my memory. Lynn and I began talking about death and suicide in a laid back manner. She was taking a bath and smoking a cigarette. The warm bath always made her feel better. I loved how her cute little stomach would pop through the top of the water and her small breasts would gently float.

"Damn," Lynn said. "I've been through hell. All the sickness, the abuse, and the hard times. I mean it. I don't want to die, because of Mia, and because of you, but sometimes I feel like I am ready. I've done it. I've found happiness. My body is just in pain so much of the time... I am ready to die."

"Don't say that," I said as I sat on the toilet wearing my My Bloody Valentine shirt and sweatpants. "I tried to commit suicide twice."

"I remember you telling me that," Lynn said. "It is sad that you tried to use drugs, but I get terrified when I think of you putting

THE COOLEST WAY TO KILL YOURSELF

a gun to your mouth."

"It always seemed like the easy way. Plus, I was always fascinated by Anne Sexton, Sylvia Plath, and Hunter S. Thompson."

"They killed themselves, right?"

"Yes," I said. "That is why their writing is the way it is. Passion and pain."

"Well, you are filled with passion," Lynn said with a wicked smile.

I smiled at her, then said, "You know, some people think suicide is cool because when they see artists who have done it, they feel a connection and this justifies their own sadness and depression." I paused. "I realized something since you came into my life."

"What's that?"

"Instead of blowing my brains out or hanging myself, I will just do what I want to do. I was in a marriage where I was afraid to talk to my wife about kink. Not only would she not understand, but I would never have been able to trust her with that part of myself. She would actually use it against me."

"That's why I love what we do. It's ours. It's private. It's secret. That makes it so special to me."

"Personally, I cannot believe that we have come this far," I said. "Lynn, I have been with many women, but you are truly the first lover that I could be completely honest with, and completely trust. I am talking emotionally, spiritually, physically, sexually…"

Lynn took a puff from her cigarette. "Now that we do our thing, both of us see life in a different way. We are enlightened."

"All those fantasies that I have had, I never thought I would live them out. It's not exactly the ones we do when we do our thing, but the beauty of it is that both of us are completely open and willing to try anything with each other."

"You know, we still have to be careful," Lynn said. "You are not gay. I know this. You are the farthest thing from gay and when I put you in women's clothing, it's a femdom thing. It's not a transgender thing. I want you, a man, owned by me."

"I fucking love how kinky we are," I said with a devilish laugh.

"Still, we have to keep this quiet," Lynn said. "For as long as I am alive, this is ours. It's private. Do you know what would happen if some of these ignorant people knew that I put a collar and a leash on you and made you wear silk panties and stockings... made you be my footstool... kept you in state of sexual frenzy and had you constantly lick my clitoris? You know they would not see past the forced feminization or a dildo in your ass. And you are not gay! You're just kinky. Some of these homophobic assholes find out about this, they will fucking kill you. I'm not talking about having a couple of assholes beat you up, but people have been murdered for this."

"That's what's crazy. I lived in fear of being shunned for so long. My marriage did not work out. I was miserable with Alison when I realized that she would never accept me for who I was. I cannot fit into that normal mode. You and I are not normal. Now, with you, I do not care if I die as long as I am with you. We're not hurting anyone. We're just living life without caring what anyone thinks about us, without caring about the consequences."

"It's the coolest way to kill ourselves," Lynn said.

"Yes, you're right, baby," I replied. "I guess that attitude also stems from my childhood. When I was a kid, the only sport I enjoyed was skateboarding."

"I saw pictures. You were a skater boy. I loved early 90's skater boys."

After a modest laugh, I said, "I was never good, but that's what was cool about the culture of skateboarding. Sure, people like Tony Hawk and Rodney Mullen were praised for being excellent, but the energy and individualism was most important. I remember my first time being on a half-pipe. I was not scared. I had a Steve Caballero board by Powell Peralta and I just went for it. I dropped in and went up the pipe and tried to do a simple 180. I fell on my

THE COOLEST WAY TO KILL YOURSELF

face. It could have been worse. I could have broken something or had some teeth knocked out. The point was, I did not care about getting hurt. I just wanted to experience something. Until I became sexual, until I discovered my love for the arts and writing, skating and that feeling was what I was passionate about. I did not care if I died as long as I felt that feeling with 100% truth and honesty."

"Like I said, it's the coolest way to kill yourself."

"It's curious to me," I said. "Living a normal life with you outside these walls and a kinky life within these walls has made me the most fulfilled and happiest that I can remember."

"Get me a towel. Tonight, I'll give you something to be passionate about." Lynn smiled at me as she stood up in the bathtub. The water from her naked, wet body dripped into the full bathtub and the sound of the droplets echoed throughout the tiny bathroom. As I got her a towel, she put her glasses on. She pointed at her lips and I gave her a kiss. "I have something special planned for tonight."

"Oh, yeah?" I asked.

"Oh, yes!" Lynn stated. "You are going to make me cum. If you're lucky, maybe, just maybe, I will let you cum, too."

With both of us smiling at each other, I left the bathroom and walked into the bedroom, waiting eagerly to find out what my Goddess had in mind.

REALITY BREAK

My dear friend who is reading this… I told you this was going to get a little weird, maybe a lot weird. Stay with me though, because I think that it's worth the journey. I would be very surprised if you had ever read a love story with prostitution, angel dust, and male chastity devices. Even if you have, this story is unique because it is ours.

Right now, I am sitting in my parents' basement in Edison, NJ, during the aftermath of Hurricane Sandy. I have reached out to many of my ex-lovers and other people in my life. I have realized who the people are who truly love me. On Christmas, I told my family that I was writing a book for Lynn, and that some of them may be included. Dear reader, if you want to know what your family and friends really think, tell them the same thing. The reactions are priceless.

So here I am, writing about a woman who I loved, and telling the world every intimate detail. I talk to my friend, Melissa, who is helping me edit this work. I talk to Kevin, and other friends who have been involved in the things I am writing about. I talk to anyone who will listen. I realize that I have to write about Lynn, and I have to finish. If a day goes by that I do not write about her, I feel empty. If I do not write her story, I have failed her. There is a reason I am writing her story.

THE COOLEST WAY TO KILL YOURSELF

Dear reader, you have stayed with me this far. I beg you to stay until the end. Loving someone means not only that you stay with them, but they have the beautiful heart to stay with you. I do not know if you have grown to love me and Lynn, but I know that I love Lynn and always will.

THE MAIL CAME

As we continued to try new things, Lynn found something where her fetishes for control, dominance, and jealousy overlapped: male chastity. She found several male chastity devices on the internet. She was not someone who did not want me to have an orgasm; she just loved controlling my orgasms.

At first, I was absolutely terrified by the idea of not having control. After Lynn ordered the device, she posted on Facebook, "Just waiting for the mail to come." She used one of those winking smiley icons. Several days later, we found a package in our apartment mailbox. As we stared at the box, the smile on her face was gorgeous, though scary because of what it meant for me.

A typical male chastity device is fairly simple. First, there is a part that goes under and around the testicles. Second, the penis goes into either a tube or set of rings. The plastic or metal device forces the penis into a downward position, though the ones that are made of metal rings and leather are flexible. The ring or strap that goes around the testicles is locked with a padlock to the tube or metal rings that hold the penis. A man in chastity can urinate, but cannot have a complete erection. Depending on the device, this can either be painful or overwhelmingly tantalizing. It is still possible to have an orgasm while in chastity, though this can be very uncomfortable depending on the device. That is called a ruined orgasm, which is another fetish.

When I was in chastity and we were together in public, she would act normal until she was very close. I could hear her lips part and the saliva break between those lips as she put her mouth to my ear. She would say things like, "I own you. You know that, right? Just nod. Just nod because you agree with me. Let everyone think we are talking about something else." As I nodded my head in the affirmative motion, she looked me dead in the eyes and smiled. I never felt so comfortable and uncomfortable at the same time. My erection felt like it was going to poke through my pants, but because I was wearing a chastity device, it was not so obvious. Every single time I walked out of the apartment, she looked at me with a deliciously evil look on her face, leaving me to imagine what she had in store.

My behavior began to change. I became extremely polite and attentive. I listened to everything she said. Not once did I tune her out while she spoke (and I know that I have mentioned how much Lynn loved to talk). She had my complete attention. I would cook her dinner and end up doing the dishes. The house was cleaner. Sometimes, I painted her fingernails and toenails. Other times, I gave her full body massages. She would wear lingerie and order me to perform oral sex on her every evening as she constantly teased me with sexual stories. Day after day, she promised to eventually unlock me and let me have an orgasm.

As we explored chastity, Lynn continued to look at new ways to use her power over me.

"Hey, baby," Lynn said while she was sitting in front of the computer in the office room at her parents' house. "Can you give me your credit card for a second?"

"Why?" I asked.

She replied, "It's a surprise. I want to buy something for us. It's not expensive."

"Come on. What is it?" I asked.

"Seriously, I want this, but I want it to be a surprise. I can give you a clue. It has to do with kinky sex." Without hesitation, I gave her the credit card and she placed the order.

The next evening, we had the kind of sex where she wanted me to be the dominant one. I made love to her from behind, pulled her hair, kissed her earlobes and neck, and told her a story about having sex with a beautiful woman in front of her without remorse.

Afterwards, while lying in our very small bed, Lynn said, "I want you to do something for me tomorrow."

"What?" I asked.

Lynn got up and walked out of the bedroom. The sound of her rifling around quietly echoed throughout the cozy apartment. Lynn walked in the room with a turquoise, hand-made bracelet, and a necklace with a tiny metal key attached. She sat on the bed with her back to me. She handed me the necklace and said, "Put this on me." I sat up and laid the necklace around her neck so the key fell in the middle, above her breasts. "Tomorrow morning, I am going to put that chastity device on you."

"Wait…"

"No, you wait," Lynn stated with authority. She put the bracelet on my left wrist. "This bracelet means that I own you. I want you to go to work wearing panties underneath your manly work clothes. Every single time you sit down, you will feel that chastity device on you. You will feel the silk feminine panties on your skin. I want you to be constantly reminded that I own you. Now, go to sleep and do not disappoint me in the morning."

Speechless, I fell asleep while we watched "Fetishes," a documentary about the New York City house of domination called Pandora's Box. Before I drifted off, Lynn whispered in my ear, "I want you all riled up. I want you horny as can be. I want you to beg me for freedom. I will not give it to you until I decide. The male doesn't cum until the mail comes."

The next morning, I woke up and saw Lynn had everything

prepared. She had even picked out lingerie for us both and laid it out on the ottoman. After shaving and taking a shower, I got dressed.

"Don't forget." Lynn threw me a pair of black silk panties and watched as I obediently put them on. Then, she said, "Come here."

After I walked over to her, she pulled down the front of my panties. I could not look away as she wrapped the bottom strap under my testicles and slid my cock through the three rings. She took a little lock and slid it through the base. Then, she grabbed the little metal ring at the end and connected them with lock. As the lock clicked, Lynn smiled.

"Click!" Lynn laughed. "I love that sound. You are mine now. It's time to go to work." She slapped me on the ass and let out a sensuous, sinister laugh. I finished dressing and went to work... wearing a male chastity device on my manhood.

With every movement of my body, I felt the device. As I walked, I was aware of the feminine panties on my hips and behind. When I sat down in the driver's seat of my car, I had to adjust myself. My mind began to race. *What if I get into a car accident and have to be rushed to the hospital? They will not only see the chastity device, but they will see a middle-aged heterosexual male wearing black silk panties. What if I get pulled over and arrested for some reason?*

Even though I had no warrants and did not break the law anymore, the fear of being in jail like that was terrifying. An entire day of work was ahead of me and I did not think I could survive. Up until that point, the longest period of chastity I had experienced was several days, over the weekend.

As the day progressed, I actually got used to the feeling of both the chastity device and the panties. Sometimes, I forgot they were even there. As a reminder, my Blackberry was constantly receiving text messages from Lynn.

"Send me pictures!"

"How is my little slave doing?"

"I have tons of porn to send you."

Pornographic images and links flooded my personal emails and text messages. Lynn's final text message that day read, "The package did not come in the mail today. You know what that means. You have one more day like this. You will not 'moonlight' me, will you?"

That evening, I contemplated if I should ask to take the chastity device off but I thought that would disappoint her. Throughout the evening, neither of us discussed the situation. Right before we got ready for bed, we began talking about our kinky little game.

"So, my love, how was your day at work with all those filthy thoughts in your head and all those pretty women you work with?"

"It was fine," I said in an eye-rolling tone.

"I'm sure it was… fine." Lynn played with the key around her neck. "Let me see it. Come on, let me see it." I took off my pants and got my sweatpants. "No, my darling," Lynn said. "I want you to sleep in that black silk slip. I want to feel your body next to me, holding me. I want to feel those manly arms you have but I also want to feel that silk at my fingertips. Every time I do that, I am reminded that I own you. It turns me on. I am so serious."

Silently, I took the larger black silk slip out of the drawer and put it on.

"Get me my vibrator," Lynn commanded. I went to the side table drawer, pulled out the Rabbit vibrator, and put Astroglide on it. Lynn pushed back the hair that fell in front of my face and said, "I get to cum tonight… and you don't." She looked at me with a kind of sympathetic pride. "Now, my love, tell me a story, but go down on me first. Then, I want you to use the vibrator on me and worship my neck, my breasts, and of course, my lips." Without hesitation, I did exactly as she ordered. After she reached orgasm, she told me to put the pink vibrator away. "You have an amazing voice," Lynn moaned in her sexual comedown. "I love the way you kiss me. I love hearing your voice when I cum. Never forget how thankful you should be that I am so sexual."

"My Goddess," I said, "I am thankful. I am very thankful."

"You would love it if I unlocked that chastity device and let you cum, wouldn't you?" Lynn asked.

I replied, "Yes."

"Yes, what?" Lynn asked.

"Yes, Goddess," I replied.

"I prefer the term 'Goddess' to 'mistress.' 'Mistress' has a classless feel to it. I don't want to be someone's mistress. I don't want to be your mistress. I prefer to be your Goddess."

I replied, "You are my Goddess."

"I know," Lynn said with a naughty smile. "Get some sleep. You will need it for tomorrow." Once again, we fell asleep with the television on in the background. This time, we had the Greek black & white film, "Singapore Sling." Lynn commented, "This film is insane, but for some reason, I get turned on by it."

"That's because we are weird people," I replied.

"Oh, yeah," Lynn agreed. "We are… we are weird people."

Morning arrived and we went through our normal morning rituals. I fed and walked Mokey. I shaved, showered, and got dressed in my business clothes. This time, Lynn picked out a different pair of black silk panties for me to wear along with thigh high stockings and a garter belt. She actually checked to see if I was still securely locked. As she played with the little metal key on her necklace, she looked up at me and smiled through those thin wire framed glasses. She said with a devilish smile, "Have a good day at work, my love."

My work day was unusually hectic but I was reminded of my kinky contract at various times. Every time I had to go to the bathroom, or if I sat down quickly, I was reminded that there was a woman in a small apartment in Spotswood who sexually owned me. My Blackberry alerted me while I was in a meeting with a client. When I looked at the phone, I saw Lynn's text saying, "The mail came." Dismissive of the text after reading it, I went about my business. The next text message said, "The male came." Realizing what this meant, my aroused state made me aware of the device I wore beneath my suit. Thoughts of what Lynn had in store for us raced through my mind.

While driving home from work, Lynn called me and said, "I am not at my parents' house. I am at our place tonight. Come straight home. Tonight you are mine. Trust me when I tell you this... Tonight, you are mine."

As I pulled into the apartment complex, I noticed the lights were off in our apartment but the shade of darkness was somewhat lighter than the other apartments without lights on. As I walked up the stairs, I heard the song "This is Hardcore" by Pulp through the walls. As I opened the door, I saw that our apartment was lit by candlelight. Slowly, I walked in and called, "Lynn? Mokey?"

"I told you, tonight you are mine," Lynn stated with authority. I could not see her, but I heard her voice. "Well, you have been mine. Don't worry. Mokey is at my parents' house. It's just us tonight."

"Oh, okay," I replied, following the sound of her voice into the bedroom.

"Stand in the middle of the bedroom," Lynn said through the closed bathroom door. With a slight laugh, I decided to play her game. One part of me thought it was funny while another part of me loved every second. The bathroom door opened and my goddess in lingerie came into view. She wore high heels and thigh-high stockings. I could tell because the skin of her thigh was slightly lighter than the rest of her long legs. The tight, black corset gave her an hourglass figure and lifted her breasts. In the past, she was a woman with low self-esteem and devastating issues about the small size of her breasts. At that moment, she was a goddess with breasts that deserved to be worshipped.

As she came closer to me, I could see that her eyeliner was

applied to perfection and the red lipstick made her thin lips look full, as if it were an honor to think of kissing them. "My darling, the mail came today," Lynn said. "You have been locked up for quite a while now. I'm not ready to let you out yet." She picked up a brown cardboard box from the side table and pulled out a pink strap-on dildo. "Take off that corporate uniform you wear," Lynn laughed. "You are not there anymore. You are in here. In here, the world is different for us, isn't it?" After a little pause, Lynn asked again, "Isn't it?"

"Yes," I replied.

With one motion, she grabbed the leather paddle on the side table and smacked my ass. "Yes, what?" Lynn yelled.

"Yes, Goddess," I replied, recovering from an unexpected paddling.

"Do you see what I got in the mail today, my love?" Lynn asked. "Do you know what you are in for tonight?"

After a gulp, I replied, "I think I know."

Lynn grabbed my cock through my pants and felt the chastity device still locked in place. "Oh, you are locked up," Lynn stated. "I hold the key. I love that. I am the one who tells you who to fuck, when to fuck, how to fuck, and when to cum. I own you. Tell me. Reassure me. Tell me that I own you."

I took a deep breath and looked down at the floor. Without looking her in the eyes, I said, "You own me."

"What?" Lynn said in jest, just to hear me say it again. "What was that? Say it again, please."

"You own me, Goddess," I stated without lifting my head.

"Yes, I do," Lynn stated as if it were the only absolute truth.

My body began to slightly tremble in a mix of fear and excitement. With one finger under my chin, Lynn lifted my head so that I was eye to eye with her. She had a delectable mischievous grin as she looked at me. With a wink and a smile, she said, "I love owning you. I love the power I have taken from you. Now, I am going to have a cigarette and you are going to get dressed."

In her glorious sexual empowerment, she seemed to glide away on high heels. The anticipation and the dark kinky sexuality was overwhelming. Drunk off of the freedom of not making decisions and not being in control, I felt absolute trust and love.

That evening, like many evenings, I did not have to think of ideas or even try to be romantic. The trust became the romance.

THANKSGIVING

Family holidays always had mixed emotions for Lynn. On Thanksgiving, the plan was to have an early dinner with Lynn's family, and then I would meet up with my own family in Monroe.

The difference between the two Thanksgiving dinners was almost astounding, but in the past, both dinners had always been pleasant. Lynn's family gathering was very intimate and subtle, while my brother's Thanksgiving dinner was filled with children, dogs, and a magnificent variety of food. Both styles are important and should be appreciated.

Recently, my dog, Mokey, had taken up peeing on the carpet more often than usual. Although I planned to take Mokey with me to both dinners, I was worried that she would ruin carpets all over central New Jersey that day.

When Lynn, Mokey and I arrived at Lynn's parents' house, everyone seemed on edge. The atmosphere suggested that someone would become upset. Someone was going to yell or cry. Which person would it be?

Mokey and Mia played with her toys as Lynn and I helped set the table. Lynn's father carved the turkey. Once the dinner table was set and the feast was ready, we all sat down. The table consisted of Lynn, Mia, Lynn's mother, and her father. Mia said grace. Adorable as always, I could not pay attention to the prayer because she was so cute and innocent. As the portions of the food were distributed, Mia complained that she did not want certain vegetables and that certain portions were too much. Frustrated, Lynn's mother commanded, "Just eat it."

Lynn played the "good guy" and said, "It's okay, baby. Just eat a little bit."

The argument began. Rightfully so, Lynn's mother was upset because she always had to play the "bad guy." The role reversal was frustrating, because Grandma was the disciplinarian instead of being the typical grandparent who got to spoil the child. After several argumentative statements were thrown against each other, everyone around the table became silent, except one person.

Mia sat at the dining room table crying. Her bottom lip was quivering.

"Oh, come on!" Lynn's mother said. "Don't ruin my Thanksgiving."

"Jeeze, Mom!" Lynn exclaimed.

Lynn's mother argued, "I'm just trying to have a nice Thanksgiving. Things should have been different."

Mia became that stubborn 9 year old girl, crying about what she wanted and did not want to eat. All kids cry at the dinner table sometimes. In reality, she cried because she hated when her mother and her grandmother argued. Lynn's parents were good people, and had the right to express their frustration. Just when I thought the situation could not get more awkward, Mokey urinated on the kitchen floor.

"Mokey!" Lynn's mother yelled. Mokey absolutely adored Lynn's mother, and she adored Mokey. Often, I used Mokey to break up the tension, but the fact that Mokey began urinating in the house was not helping the current situation.

Obviously, my time to go to my brother's house soon arrived. I invited everyone to come with me, but no one wanted to go. After a quick dessert, I kissed everyone goodbye and took Mokey to my brother's. The atmosphere at Lynn's parents' house was still a little tense, but was calmer when I left.

As I drove to my brother's house, I listened to "A Prophecy" by Close Lobsters. The feeling of melancholia was soon shattered as I pulled onto the street where my brother and his family lived. The entire cul-de-sac was filled with cars. I found a place to park only when someone was leaving. As I walked up to the gigantic house, I heard laughing and music. One of the two garage doors was open and three guys were drinking beer around a hot oil fryer that cooked one of several turkeys.

As I opened the front door, I saw a huge crowd of family and friends of all ages and several dogs running around. I let Mokey loose and she instantly ran to play with the other dogs. My brother put a beer in my hand before he even greeted me. Suddenly, nephews and nieces surrounded me and hugged me. As I walked into the kitchen, I saw a myriad of food and felt drunk off the atmosphere.

I felt welcomed by my huge family and the only thing I could think of was that I wished Lynn, Mia, and the rest of her family were there. I wished that they could experience the abundant amount of food, games, and laughter. My nephews and nieces are awesome. They are not only smart and beautiful kids, but they are truly good-hearted young people. As I watched them play their video games, I actually asked myself, "How did the asshole gene skip a generation?" These children were well-balanced, intelligent, fun, tolerant, and accepting of others. Immediately, I texted Lynn, "Why don't I come pick you and your family up and bring them here? Everyone will have a great time!" I knew my attempts were futile, but I had to ask.

"Mokey peed on the floor!" my niece said. We took Mokey out to the back and tied her leash to the deck.

During dinner every year, my mother demands that we go around the table and say what we are thankful for. Everyone usually says, "I'm thankful for my family." My nephew, a big Star Wars fan, once said he was thankful for George Lucas. When my turn came, I always got a little choked up like a sentimental fool. That evening, I said, "I am thankful for my family and everyone sitting at this table. I am also thankful that I have a woman who loves me, and she has a daughter who loves me. I am thankful for my little dog, Mokey. Honestly, I am thankful that we are all alive here and now to experience this… very… moment."

"Here! Here!" the family at the table said before sipping their wine and beer.

After a lovely meal and even lovelier dessert, my brother came to me and said, "Mokey peed on the carpet. We have to keep her outside."

"Shit!" I cursed as I got up and took Mokey back out. As I was outside on the deck, tying Mokey to the wire again, my cousin was having a cigarette.

"I love that dog!" she said. "You know, she's probably diabetic."

"You think so?" I asked.

"I work with a veterinarian. I know a diabetic dog when I see one." I closed my eyes and sighed. She said, "Don't be upset. This is fixable. She probably just needs insulin. Take her to your vet. She'll be alright."

I left my family's Thanksgiving dinner with a gigantic bag of food, filled with trays of sweet potatoes, two types of turkey, two types of stuffing, broccoli, perogies, carrots, spinach, cranberry sauce, macaroni, cookies, and two types of pie.

As I pulled up to Lynn's parents' house, I saw Lynn smoking a cigarette on the front steps. As I got out of the car, I let Mokey out and she ran right into Lynn's arms. Slightly upset, but resigned to her situation, Lynn looked up at me with her glasses falling down her nose in their signature way.

"How did everything work out?" I asked.

"It is what it is. We're all good. Everyone is better now. I love that little girl."

"You know, you and your family were welcome to come. We had food, dogs, games, and there were many kids that Mia could have played with."

"It's not our scene, babe," Lynn said. "Thank you for the invite though."

Suddenly, Mia peeked her head out of the screen door. She was wearing pajamas. Mokey went right to her and licked her face.

"Mokey!" Mia said as she kissed the little dog. "Happy Thanksgiving!"

"Give me a hug and kiss, Mia," I said as I opened my arms. Mia's little arms wrapped around me.

"Happy Thanksgiving," Mia said. I watched her do an adorable little dance with Mokey's paws in her hands.

"Come on, jellybean!" Lynn said as she took her daughter in her arms. "I love you!"

"I love you too, Mommy," Mia said. "We're going to the dog park soon, right?"

Lynn replied, "You got it baby!" Mia went back into the house. Lynn, Mokey and I walked to my car. I put Mokey in the backseat but she immediately stuck her brown and white fuzzy head between the front seats. I opened the door for Lynn as she slowly walked to the passenger side door.

"Did you have a good time at your family's Thanksgiving party?" Lynn asked.

"Yes," I said. "All of you were invited. You should have come." I paused, and added, "Mokey pissed everywhere. My cousin said that she probably has diabetes."

"I thought so," Lynn said. "We'll have to take her to the vet. Let's go home, baby. I'm exhausted."

As I drove home, I put on "Blue Flower" by Pale Saints (a cover version of a song by Opal). "I love this song," Lynn said. "It reminds me of you... us. I love this song."

"What if Mokey is diabetic? I'm worried."

"Don't worry," Lynn said. "We'll take her to the vet and everything will be okay. Worse comes to worst, she may need insulin."

"You're right. So, how was your Thanksgiving after I left?"

Lynn smiled. "I love my daughter. She's so smart. She's so cool. She's everything I wish I could be. She's good at everything that I am not. Did you see her cry at the dining room table? That broke my heart."

That evening, we watched a South Korean film titled, "Sympathy for Lady Vengeance," directed by Park Chan-wook. Without going into too much detail regarding the beautiful yet brutally violent film, the theme of a daughter forgiving her mother is powerful.

After the melancholy Thanksgiving dinner where Mia cried at the table, Lynn was quiet the entire evening. Throughout the cathartic ending of "Sympathy for Lady Vengeance," the reunited mother and daughter relationship struck a deep emotional chord in Lynn. After asking what was wrong multiple times, Lynn just brushed off the question. Knowing Lynn the way I knew her, I knew that she would tell me in her own time. Still, I knew what was breaking her heart.

At 3 AM, I woke up to the sounds of sobbing. I saw the bathroom light on. My first instinct was to get out of bed and comfort her. I paused, thinking that maybe she would rather be alone. Maybe, it was just a quick and intense emotional outburst. As I listened to Lynn continue to loudly sob, I got out of bed and walked to the bathroom in my boxer shorts.

As I turned the corner and walked into the bathroom, I saw Lynn lying naked in the filled bathtub, crying her eyes out. Her bottom lip was quivering just like Mia's bottom lip quivered at Thanksgiving dinner. She did not see me standing there. For a moment, I felt that she did not want me to see her like that. Regardless, I had to comfort her.

"Baby, what's wrong? Tell me. Tell me everything," I said as I rushed to her and got on my knees beside the bathtub. The cold porcelain tiles hurt my knees but I did not care. I put one hand on her cheek, moving the hair out of her face, and I wiped the tears away from her eyes with my other hand.

"I failed her. I failed her," Lynn cried. "She's never going to forgive me. I don't deserve to be forgiven. I'm horrible. I'm a horrible mother. I'm a horrible person. God, will she ever forgive me?"

"Oh, baby," I said, comforting her and kissing her on the cheek as I held her hand. "She will."

"Mia is everything to me. I failed her. She'll never forgive me."

"Look, life is complicated. She knows that already. She loves you," I said. "She loves you. She hangs all over you. She loves being around you. She even loves me. She never wants you to leave."

"I failed her. I'm horrible. She'll never forgive me. Why? Why did I have to fuck up so hard?" Lynn cried.

"Hey, you were not well," I declared. "Years of abuse led to a relapse of your drug addiction. I'm not saying that you are without fault, but you would not have been in those situations if it weren't for Ron fucking up your life and her life. He does not even call to see how she is. You are with her every single day. She will always remember that."

"I fucked up so hard," Lynn sobbed. "My little baby! My little girl does not deserve this! She does not deserve this much… this much… sadness. Every time I see tears in her eyes, I feel as if I am dying. I feel that I caused those tears. Those tears are my fault." Lynn had a picture of Mia on the side of the bathtub. She picked it up, looked at the photo and cried, "Baby, I'm so sorry!"

"Lynn, you have to look at this with some perspective. Yes, you fucked up, but Ron fucked up far worse. You and your parents at least made sure that she was safe with your parents."

"But I put myself first. I put Ron first!" Lynn wept. "It was like he was pulling the strings and I was a puppet. I don't think he ever cared about her and here I am a fucking weak idiot, thinking that no one would ever love me! I'm so sorry. I'm so sorry. I'm so sorry. You don't understand. My heart is broken. Not romantic heart break. It was only a couple of years, but I missed out on times when I should have been there. I am her mother!"

"You have been given a second chance, though. Not many women who have been in your situation have been this lucky."

"Lucky?"

"Yes, lucky. You forget that I was an addict, too. At the clinic, we had to go to group meetings. Do you know how many women that I have met who have lost their children due to the abusive man that they were with? You are not alone in your suffering, baby. You are lucky that you were given a second chance and that you can be in her life. I have met women, broken women, who will never see their children again. If they did see their children, those children would hate them. Mia loves you."

"I am so scared." Lynn stared into space, as if she was looking through another dimension that only she could see. "I am terrified that she will never understand. I am terrified that she will never forgive me. I love her so much!" Lynn reached over and I held her in my arms as she sobbed in my chest.

"Hey, the situation is busted up, but it is not broken," I stated. "You are her mother and you see her every day. Be with her. You know me. I never get jealous of your relationship with her. I want you to be with her as much as possible. Do what you have been doing. Stay with her all the time and when she goes to sleep, we can be together. I'll hang out with you two like always. Sleep over there, if you want to. Be with her. Be her mother."

After she wiped her eyes, I saw that she had calmed down. Lynn looked at me with red-rimmed eyes and asked, "Do you think she will ever understand? Do you think she will ever forgive me?"

I replied, "Do you want the truth or do you want the 'calm

down, it'll be okay' answer?"

"I want the 'calm down, it'll be okay' answer," Lynn said.

"Yes," I said. "She will."

After a deep breath, Lynn said, "No, I want the truth."

After wiping away my own tears, I said, "I believe she will forgive you. She has a beautiful, beautiful heart. She may not understand, and it won't be easy, but I believe she will forgive you."

At this time, Mokey got out of her little bed and walked into the bathroom. She laid down on the tiles and closed her eyes.

Lynn took another deep breath as she closed her eyes. As soon as she opened her eyes, she asked, "Why are you with me? I'm a fuck up. My past is all fucked up. I'm a mess."

I looked Lynn directly in her eyes and gently put my hand on her face. "You have to ask me that?" Lynn nodded her head. After a soft smile, I said, "I love you. You love me. That's why I am with you."

Lynn wiped more tears from her eyes and gave me the International Lynn Sign for a kiss by putting a fingertip at her lips. I wrapped my arms around her wet, naked body and kissed her. She held me so tight that I fell into the bath. The water splashed out of the bathtub and made Mokey jump up and run out of the bathroom. As we embraced in the warm bathwater, we kissed.

"I'm so thankful for you," Lynn said as the bath water created these little waves that splashed on our faces and our hair. "Thank you for loving me. Thank you for loving Mia. Thank you for being in my life."

"Thank you!" I said. "We saved each other." I loved the way her face looked, covered with drops of water as her wet hair stuck to her face. "We saved each other."

Miraculously, despite all of the commotion, the wallet-sized photo of Mia did not get a drop of water on it, nor did it fall off the side of the bathtub.

The next morning, I woke up and could not find Lynn. Mokey was not in the apartment either. As I looked out the front window,

I saw her outside in the gazebo with her head in her hands while Mokey sat next to her. I put on shoes and a jacket, and walked down the stairs and outside. The early morning fog in the apartment complex was dreamlike. As I walked towards her, I noticed that she was sitting up straight and just staring into the light fog as Mokey snuggled next to her.

"Lynn?" I asked. "What's up? Are you okay?"

Lynn shook her head back and forth and stared as if she had been traumatized. "I am a bad person," she said slowly, with a tear coming out of her right eye. "I used to be a good person. I have caused so much pain for the people who love me. I stole so much money from my parents. My baby, my little girl, cannot be raised by her own mother. I- I- I used to be a good person. I truly used to be. I do not know when it happened exactly. This tidal wave of selfishness just came over me. I did not even notice… because I was so selfish."

The sobbing of the night before was nothing compared to the harsh emotional reality that engulfed her broken heart. This was a different side of shame and remorse.

Lynn spoke softly. "I don't know what to do to make things right. There's no way I can make things right. Where do I even begin?"

As I sat down next to her and held her hand, I said, "Hey, you can. You may not be able to make everything right. You can't change the pain you have caused, but you can show them that you have changed. Be a kind and loving person to your family."

"They will never forgive me. I don't deserve to be forgiven."

"You can only do what you can. After all of the shit you did, they let you back in their lives."

Lynn quickly replied, "They let me back because of Mia. They don't want me. They shouldn't want me."

"The fact that they let you back is important. Your family is filled with loving people. Good people. Ron's family wrote him off… as they should have."

"I want to make it up to my mother, my father, my sister, and most of all, Mia," Lynn said. "I do not know where to begin. I can never pay back the money I stole from them. Do you realize that they could have had me arrested for that?"

"That shows that there is still love for you, right there. Look, I drove my family crazy. I put them through hell, too."

"Not like the way I put my family through hell," Lynn replied.

"Everyone is different," I continued. "The point is that I am sober except for the occasional drink. I am attempting to get my life together. I am no longer a threat to them. It took years, but they love me and they trust me now. Of course, I'll get comments sometimes, and my mom will constantly worry. Still, I know that I did some fucked up stuff in my past, but I am trying to be positive and I feel that I am a good person. I'm a good person who did bad things in the past. My family knows that I'm a fuck up, but they also know that I will be there for them if they need me. They know that I can be a shoulder to cry on. I can be their ride to the hospital. My parents know that if it snows, I'll shovel the driveway if they need me to. You have to start with small steps."

"I have dug such a hole for myself and I have caused so much pain to them," Lynn stated. "Any effort is just… futile."

"No, it isn't. Be with Mia as much as possible. Help your mother and father out when they need it."

"I can't fucking do anything," Lynn cried. "Physically, I can barely play with Mia. My mom's disappointment of me just washes over me every single time I see her. I am so ashamed. For some reason, my dad and I get along great, and I am seriously wondering why I deserve kindness from my parents."

"Well, would you still love Mia if she did to you what you did to your parents?" I asked.

"I will always love Mia no matter what."

"Well, there's your answer," I said. "Look, be kind to them.

Even if your mom or sister make some comments, take them. With all of the pain you caused, they truly didn't stop loving you. So, don't stop loving them."

"I do love them," Lynn said. "I love them very much. That is why I feel this way now."

"It's never too late. It's never too late to at least attempt to make amends. You see them pretty much every single day. You don't always fight."

"I have to do something, though. I have to take some extra step."

"Start off slow," I said. "Right now, just love them. Respect them."

Lynn wiped her eyes. "You know, ever since we got back together, my life has been better. At first, everyone thought that you were a bad influence. Now, you helped me fix my problem with Oxy. Now, I have some hope. It's not much hope, but it's some. I'll take it."

"It's us, baby," I said. "It's us. I said it before and I'll say it again. We're two fuck ups who fell in love and truly saved each other. I don't want to get high, I don't want to steal or break the law. I just want love. I want you in my arms, with Mokey and Mia by our side."

Lynn took a deep breath and gave me a quick kiss. "The fog is getting thicker. Let's walk across Main Street and take Mokey for a morning walk in the fog."

"Okay, baby." Together, all three of us walked out of the gazebo and into the fog.

Later that evening, when I went to pick Lynn up, I walked into her parents' house to the sound of laughter. As Lynn's father read his spy novel, Lynn, Lynn's mother, and Mia were playing a dance videogame. As I looked at the scene, I was so pleased to see smiles on everyone's faces.

"You have to go to bed, peanut!" Lynn said to Mia.

"Nick!" Mia shouted as she ran and jumped into my arms. I

spun her around as if she could fly. She started to play with my hair.

"Come on, kiddo," Lynn said. "Let me read you some of the owl book, but you have to be in bed." The two of them went off to the bedroom.

As I sat on the couch next to Lynn's father, Lynn's mother asked, "How are you doing?"

"I'm well," I said. "Everything is alright. How are you?"

"Oh, I'm tired," Lynn's mother said as Mokey sat in her lap. "We all had so much fun tonight. We were all dancing and playing videogames after Mia did her homework. You know, she made the honor roll."

I replied, "Well, that's because she's smart." As we watched The Discovery Channel, we talked more until Lynn emerged from Mia's dark bedroom.

Lynn asked, "Ready to go, baby?" After getting Mokey on the leash, we said our farewells and walked out the front door.

After Lynn lit her cigarette, she stated, "That dancing, ugh! That game made my hip hurt." Once we were all in the car, Lynn said, "Nicholas, I want to thank you."

"Thank me? For what?"

"For what you said to me this morning. You were right. I took your advice. All of us had such a good time today. We all got along great. I feel that… even if sometimes, we do not get along, my heart is in the right place and that means that it will all be okay." She took her index finger and pointed to her lips. I leaned over and kissed her. As I sat back, we both smiled.

"Look at you… all proud of yourself," Lynn said. "Just because you give good advice, don't think that I do not own your ass. I'm going to make you paint my toenails and fingernails tonight."

"Oh, yeah?" I asked.

"Oh, yeah," Lynn responded. "Let's go home."

STILL ILL

"Everyone is sick!" I shouted in frustration. Recently, I had taken a day off of work because of my stomach and liver issues. While I was not vomiting like when I lived in Woodbridge, I needed a day off. Lynn was still sick to the point that she was on Medicare. Her health problems were a constant battle. The final patient was my adorable little Mokey. Our carpet had so many urine stains that it looked like a 1970's children's water color book. When Mokey and Lynn stayed at her parents' house while I was at work, Mokey would urinate in every single room. The dog even pooped on her parents' bed. Luckily, Lynn's mother loved Mokey, so she was forgiving.

Lynn and I made a veterinarian appointment and the doctor confirmed that Mokey was diabetic. After blood tests were run, we ended up having to give her 5 units of insulin twice a day, and had to purchase special food. Before Mokey was regulated, the question of putting her to sleep was brought up by several people who I will leave unnamed. Lynn and I had a discussion.

"I'm not killing that dog!" Lynn said. "She's my shadow. She follows me everywhere. She sleeps in the bed with me when you are not here. She has brought joy to my daughter, and even my mother."

"There's no way in hell I'm putting her to sleep," I replied.

"Mokey's staying with us."

"Good!" Lynn said. "That's the way it should be and that's the way it is."

Lynn, Mia, and I would take her to the East Brunswick Dog Park often. Mokey was a regular. Lovable and free-willed, Mokey would walk around and win over every single person she encountered. Even my friend Kevin, a mailman who hated dogs, loved her.

Mokey soon became regulated with insulin and proper diet. Just like her parents (Lynn and I), Mokey was ill but she got through it. With all the illness in my life and in the lives of the ones I loved, I looked at Mokey as a furry beacon of hope. She was such a lovable dog who could cheer anyone up. The idea of putting her to sleep because she had diabetes was completely preposterous.

As I am writing this now, Mokey is by my feet, looking up at me. With everything that I have been through, be it health-wise or emotionally, I look at Mokey as not only a survivor, but a survivor with grace, charm, and lovability.

Even though she pees on the carpet sometimes.

SEX THERAPY

Addiction had plagued my life for as long as I could remember. When I liked a band, I wanted every single album they released. I remember bicycling my way to Vintage Vinyl in Fords for the new singles by Pixies, The House of Love, Close Lobsters, and Trisomie 21. When I first did anything sexual with a woman, I wanted nothing more than to be with that woman again. Drugs almost killed me and everything I loved. Hedonism made me out of control.

Lynn and I admitted to ourselves that we were both sex addicts. We understood and accepted our situation. After addiction to drugs, alcohol, and stealing, we had to face our addiction to sex. Although we loved the fact that we were comfortable enough with each other to give into our sexual urges, we wanted to make sure it would not affect our lives together in a negative way.

I actually visited a therapist. The doctor was a very sexy, erudite woman in professional attire. She was tall and thin, with straight, long blond hair. For a second, I felt like Thomas Crown from "The Thomas Crown Affair."

"So, what is troubling you?" the doctor asked.

"I constantly think about sex."

"I see," the doctor said. "How often is constant?"

"I think about it every second. I have sex almost every other day." I added, "With my girlfriend."

"Does she enjoy it?" she asked.

"She usually initiates it. Sometimes, I do. I mean, we are both sex addicts. We love sex. Now that we crossed the line and became so honestly kinky, we constantly talk about, think about, and have sex."

"That could be healthy," the doctor said. "Is it getting in the way of other things in your life?"

"It has in the past. It isn't now. But sometimes I feel like a freak. Everyone says I talk about sex constantly."

"Do you?" the doctor asked.

"Yes. I do. We were watching this film called 'Shame' about a middle aged professional man in New York who is a sex addict. He was successful, good looking, and had no problem meeting women. At the same time, there was this sadness in him. There was this emptiness in him. I do not want that in me."

"Do you feel that emptiness and sadness is inside you?" the doctor asked.

"No. That's the weird thing," I replied. "If most people knew about my current relationship, they would think that we are mistaking sex for love. That's not true. We both have our own sordid pasts. This is different. At the same time, we have this need… this compulsion to have sex with each other. It's not that cheap, dirty, shallow sex. Sometimes, we cry when we make love because the moment is so precious."

"So, what is your concern?" the doctor asked.

"I don't know. Maybe, it's because I have been in many relationships that have been so sexual that if we were not having sex, we did not know what to do. It took a while. I broke this woman's heart a long time ago, and we found each other again. We both come from failed marriages. Personally, I think we used sex and our complete honesty with each other to transcend what is typical for a couple. I can safely say that I do not want to be with anyone else and she does not want to be with anyone else. I think... I hope that it was that honesty in the bedroom that made us so comfortable around each other. I mean, we do not hide anything from each other... at all. She has seen me at my weakest and she still embraces me. We have seen each other at our ugliest and we still want to embrace each other."

"Well, it seems that you two have a healthy relationship. Unless your sexual urges get in the way of everyday life or stifle you, there is nothing to worry about."

"I think about sex all the time, though," I stated. "I love pornography! I support the pro-feminist porn movement. Everyone thinks that I am a sex-starved pervert. Lynn tells me that I am the 'good kind of pervert.' She says that she is one, too. She told me that she used to hump the corner of her ottoman when she was a kid."

"Hmmm."

"Hmmm is right," I said. "I do not think we are normal people, but I like it and I am not ashamed of it."

"Well, normal is subjective."

"Sometimes, not all the time, but sometimes, she puts me in women's lingerie and locks a chastity device on my cock. Sometimes, she fucks me with a strap on dildo." Okay, I'll admit that I was trying to shake her calm demeanor.

"Oh." The doctor paused. "Do you enjoy this?"

"I cum." I paused. "For years, all I wanted was for my ex-wife to wear a sexy French Maid outfit. Now, my girlfriend wears one all the time. She constantly wears lingerie."

The doctor asked, "So, you have a fetish?"

"Well, I lost my virginity when I was thirteen years old. I think it changed my life forever. She was a sixteen year old punk/goth girl who was very dominant. I was completely in love with her and she knew it. Right from the start, she told me, 'I will never have a boyfriend. You will never be my boyfriend. I will never be totally yours.' Then, she would just play these dominant games with me where she would tie me up or make me do things."

"How did that make you feel then?"

"I was just so excited that a girl wanted me, and wanted to take charge of me," I said. "She was so cool, so free. She did not have a care in the world what anyone thought of her. I was in awe of that."

"How does it make you feel now?" the doctor asked.

"For a long time, I was afraid to truly express myself to my lovers. I tried, but they did not understand my fetishes for lingerie and female dominance. Now, what I have found with Lynn... Well, there is no going back. When I see a woman in a corset and thigh high stockings..."

"How does that make you feel?"

I replied, "I feel like I should worship her. I feel like the female body should be worshiped on every level."

"So, you enjoy giving women orgasms?" the doctor asked.

"I feel like it's a privilege. You know how they say that driving is a privilege? Well, I feel like I just turned 17 and can drive a car. I feel that youthful excitement every time I think of licking a woman's clitoris."

"Any woman's clitoris?"

"Honestly? Yes. Kind of. But I absolutely love licking Lynn. I love giving her an orgasm. I love how I can feel it in her thighs, and the rush of fluid. I love how she almost passes out afterwards. I'm not just doing it for my own sexual thrill. I do it because I want her to feel worshiped and pleased. Actually, I think I have grown quite a bit from the days of licking pussy to satisfy my ego."

The doctor asked, "Giving a woman an orgasm to satisfy your ego?"

"Yes. As a younger man, I wanted to walk away from every sexual encounter as if I sexually conquered. As I got older, I became someone who worships women. Honestly, I thought of sex when I saw you."

"When you look at me?" the doctor asked.

I laughed. "The things that I... You have no idea... You are beautiful. This is not helping."

After a slight pause and a quick note in her pad, the doctor asked, "So, what are you trying to accomplish?"

"I don't know," I shrugged. "I am an addict. We do not abuse drugs or alcohol anymore. We do not steal anymore. We do not hustle. We are law-abiding, moral, good people who just happen to love sex. I personally think we are happy. Maybe, I do not want it to end. It's like I want to be normal but I don't."

"There are other things besides sex. Have you tried exploring that? Honestly, it seems like you have a very healthy relationship, especially considering everything both of you have been through. Do not make it a point to not have sex, but make a point to do other things as well. You seem happy. It is my diagnosis that you two are in a happy, healthy relationship."

The smile on my face could not have been bigger. I walked out of the doctor's office with the proud knowledge that my kinky love life had a medical seal of approval. I left happy that Lynn and I were deemed to be in a normal, healthy relationship, but I also could not help but imagine the psychiatrist masturbating after I left. Sure, I know that is just perverted wishful thinking, but old habits die hard.

Lynn and I continued to have wonderful sex, flirtatious moments, and affectionate times. Within those times, I began to write more. I wrote reviews again and conducted interviews. Lynn was an amazing editor. She told me when my writing was poor and when it was a piece of work that I could be proud of. Together, we were building our lives together. We were still sexual, but we were also creative.

One evening while in bed, we began having one of our before-sleep conversations.

THE COOLEST WAY TO KILL YOURSELF

Lynn said, "You know, baby, I love you. Thank you for being with me."

As always, I paused and closed my eyes to be dramatic. Then, I said, "I never thought I could be so happy being wrong."

"What do you mean?"

"I fought it," I said. "I fought loving you. These days, I cannot wait to talk to you. I cannot wait to see you. I cannot wait to hold you. When I drive to work, I only want to talk with you. I get disappointed when I get to work and have to end our conversation. I am so thankful that you love me."

"Come here, my love." Lynn pulled me close and wrapped her arms around me. Never did I appreciate such an embrace. At that moment, Lynn read my mind.

She said, "Never did I appreciate such an embrace."

THE COMMITMENT CEREMONY

Love engulfed us like a warm blanket. Lynn and I were in sync. We put the "bond" in bondage. After a wonderful evening of love making, I held her in my arms and asked her, "Will you unmarry me?"

"What do you mean?" Lynn asked.

"We live our lives in a very different way. We are very unconventional."

"That's true."

Mokey chose that moment to jump onto the bed with her pink rope toy and drop it in front of me, like a little ring bearer. There was a 3-inch long piece of string that was falling off the toy. I pulled on the piece of rope and asked for Lynn's hand. I tied the rope around her ring finger as if it were an engagement ring.

"We can have a commitment ceremony," I said. "We can have a huge party and everyone will come."

"Really?" Lynn said with a teary eyed smile, and some skepticism. "You would do that?"

"Of course, baby. I love you and I want everyone to know that I love you."

"You said that you would never get married again," Lynn said.

"This is not like you."

"It is me," I responded. "It's an unmarriage. It's a non-wedding. We can have both families there. Everyone can bring food. No money. No gifts. Just everyone together. We can have bands and DJs play. Our un-wedding song would be 'Mother of Pearl' by Roxy Music."

"That is our song," Lynn said. "You know, I would love to do this. I have not been to a party in ages. The last time I did anything social was that gathering after my high school reunion. I was showing you off that night. I knew the girls thought that I looked horrible, and they were thinking 'How did you get a guy like him?'"

"If they only knew the things we have done… and do now!" I said. "You know that I think you're beautiful, even when you're sick. Still, that's sweet. I'm happy you feel proud to have me. So, what's your answer?"

"My answer?" Lynn paused and looked up at me, glasses resting low on her nose. "My answer is 'yes.'" We embraced and kissed.

"I love you, Lynn. I love you so much that I have never felt this kind of love before. No one has ever accepted me for who I am and loved me for who I am."

"I know, baby. I have never loved or felt love like this, either."

We spent the rest of the night and some of the following days talking about and planning our unique commitment ceremony. We told our friends and family members. Some of them did not understand. Others had very interesting ideas. Even though I was once married, I never had that feeling of zeal in planning a romantic ceremony. When I was getting legally married, I had no interest at all in the planning. With Lynn, I felt the excitement of what the bride-to-be feels. Lynn was just as excited. She started to look at dresses and places to get her hair and make-up done.

One evening, when we had just gotten into bed, we began talking. The film "Personal Services" was playing on the television set.

"You know what, baby?" I said. "Life is good."

"I know," Lynn said. "I never thought I would feel a kind of happiness… not like this."

"You're getting healthier. I have a job. Bills are being paid. I always felt like I was a fuck-up. I know I'm a fuck-up and I have fucked up. But, I feel we can live a normal life and still be weird, still be eccentric. I am actually looking forward to the future."

Lynn laughed as she put her glasses in her case and placed them on the side table. She gave me a little goodnight kiss and said, "I was always terrified of the future. This is probably the first time I am looking forward to the future. I am so grateful that I can have that future with you."

HURRICANE SANDY

Hurricane Sandy devastated New Jersey during the end of October 2012. Using the generator to power my laptop, I stayed up each night writing this book in my parents' basement, while all I wanted was to move into my new apartment. Although we had a shed full of filled gas cans, we needed more gasoline for the generator to keep the heat, refrigerators, and my laptop running. My father asked me to take a ride to see if there were any open gas stations. Most stations were without power, or had run out of fuel. At 4 AM, we placed several empty gasoline cans in back of my mother's small SUV and drove off.

It felt like we were in a dream; the streets were desolate as though there had been an apocalypse. Trees were down all over the streets and some even fell on some houses and cars. Branches and dirt were scattered everywhere. The street lights and traffic lights were not working. We drove from North Edison to St. George Avenue in Woodbridge. We passed empty gas station after empty gas station. As I listened to "Herculean" by The Good, The Bad & The Queen, that sense of surrealism set in again. This time, the feeling was filled with a tender sadness. The temperature was cold and the storm had passed, leaving behind devastation from an unapologetic and emotionless attacker.

My father drove past familiar sights in Woodbridge. "Extra

Ordinary" by Ultra Vivid Scene played on my new iPhone as I looked out the window with a melancholic nostalgia. We passed the pharmacy that Lynn, Kevin, Kristen, and I went to on the evening of the divorce party. We passed the liquor store that I used to frequent. We passed my old house that I had lived in with Alison. I noticed the brand new fence that Alison and I put in just for Mokey, before we broke up and moved away. I began thinking of my marriage to Alison and the completely different life I had lived. It felt as if it were a lifetime ago, when in reality, it was only a couple of years before.

I began to remember the times Lynn and I had in Woodbridge. I had vivid memories of watching films and television on that comfortable green couch with Lynn in my arms and Mokey sitting behind us, looking out the window. Memories of the divorce party and our long talks danced through my mind. I remembered the French Maid outfit she would wear for me as she cut fruit and served me wine. I smiled as I remembered the kinky sex where I was the dominant one who tied her up and blindfolded her in that same French Maid outfit and slid a vibrator inside her, leaving her to reach orgasm as she wondered when I would untie her. My head was filled with the awkward moments of Lynn and Alison meeting in the house. One time, Lynn and I bumped into Alison's mother in the liquor store. Like little films, memories played in my mind of our wonderful walks throughout the streets of Woodbridge. I thought of the neighbors, who were so used to seeing me with Alison, seeing me with Lynn. As my father and I drove past the train station, I smiled as I remembered seeing Lynn for the first time in 15 years when she walked down those steps at the Woodbridge Train Station.

As my father drove onto Route 1 South, I had to wipe my teary eyes. Route 1 South was a wasteland, too. Usually busy and well-lit, the highway was dark and empty. The Costco gas station was closed, but the lines of cars went out of the massive parking lot and down Route 1 South. We slowly made our way to Route 18 South. By this time, "The Last Beat of My Heart" by Siouxsie & The Banshees was playing on my iPhone. The song has a dreamy rolling drum rhythm and an atmospheric melancholy. The nostalgia hit ever so harder as Route 18 had two layers of memories for me.

The first layer of memories was when I first met and dated Lynn when I was 16 and 17 years old. I remembered how she would drive from Spotswood to Edison and drive me back to Spotswood just to be with me. The little ice cream shop we used to go to was still there after more than two decades.

The second layer of memories was from more recent years. I noticed the Halloween store where we purchased French Maid outfits and petticoats. Just by coincidence, my father turned onto Summerhill Road. All of the gas stations were closed. For the past two years, I drove on Summerhill Road almost every single day. We passed the kiosk where I rented DVDs because we did not have cable television. Then, we passed the street near the bank. My eyes became teary again as I looked down this dark street without street lights. It was the street where I would pull over and kiss Lynn goodbye before dropping her off at her parents' house. We always listened to the second section of "Mother Of Pearl" by Roxy Music and shared a kiss that felt beautifully endless. In my headphones, I heard Siouxsie sing, "The Last Beat Of My Heart."

Within a little more than an hour, I experienced a tour of the past two decades of my life. I relived a failed marriage and a renewed love with Lynn on the streets of Woodbridge, and our magnificent, passionate romance in Spotswood.

"There's nothing out here that's open. We have enough gas for a while." My father took a U-turn. "Let's go home."

A moment of clarity occurred within me. I thought, "Everything is dead. Every place I lived in is dead. The memories must be preserved somehow." This epiphany was clear and true. As we drove home on Route 18 North, I thought, "I must finish this. I must finish this book for Lynn. I'm going to write a book for the woman who thought that no one would ever write for her." At that moment, I could not wait to get back to my computer. Ideas about structure filled my mind, but most of all, the truth embraced my creative spirit. Memories shot through my mind from every direction. Inside my mind and at light speed, I re-experienced every time we made love, every time we were kinky, every time we argued, every time we cried, and every single time we laughed. Right then and there, I was filled with a purpose.

At one point, I thought that living a kinky and unconventional life was "the coolest way to kill myself," as Lynn would say. Well, writing a complete and honest tribute to Lynn would be the coolest way to kill myself now. I decided to throw caution to the wind. I did not care what my family or friends would think of me. I did not care what anyone thought of me or if anyone would harm me for what I wrote. I had a story to tell. I was not doing this for money or fame. I decided to do this for love. It may have been an unconventional love, but it was our love.

Hurricane Sandy may have devastated New Jersey, but it could not defeat the memory of the love of my life. While it was an event that Lynn missed, it was an event that would inspire me to complete my tribute. Now, I was truly awake and my spirit was open. A sense of enlightenment glowed within me. A focused sense of determination overwhelmed me like a beautiful warm bath of passion and creativity. My work may never be read, but it would be written. It would be written for the woman I love.

When my father and I arrived at the house in Edison, I was experiencing a welcome nervousness and creative impatience. Quickly, I put the empty gas cans in the shed and then went into the house. In a frustrated hurry, I took my jacket and shoes off. As Mokey ate, I prepared her insulin shot while thinking of writing the book. In my mind, an outline formed. Between every single

THE COOLEST WAY TO KILL YOURSELF

entry to this mental outline, I thought of how Lynn would love how much I was obsessing over a work of art that was for her. By this time, it was 7:30 AM and the sound of the generators was echoing throughout the streets of suburban Edison. With a suburban James Bond-like style, I injected Mokey with her morning insulin shot and discarded the needle in the plastic medical sharps container. My morning responsibility with Mokey was completed. In one quick motion, I took my morning vitamins, got myself a seltzer, and quickly ran down the stairs to my basement bedroom. As soon as I walked in, I saw my laptop waiting for me. I made sure that it was plugged into the generator and then, turned it on.

Once again, the 26 letters sat at my fingertips. Although I had started the book already, there was more white on the screen than black. I said to myself, "I need music." I chose CDs with the precision of a super spy. Soon, I had a pile of CDs that included Roxy Music, My Bloody Valentine, Siouxie & The Banshees, The Smiths, The The, Cinerama, The Stone Roses, Ultra Vivid Scene, Television Personalities, Massive Attack, The Verve, Felt, Momus, and PAS/CAL. I was ready without a sentence in my head. I just let my fingers dance over the keyboard, knowing that this was the only way I could ever make love to Lynn again.

NOT QUITE LIKE ALL THE REST

One summer evening, Lynn and I were setting the dining room table as we got ready to sit down to our homemade pasta dinner with salad.

"You know what I love about you, baby?" she asked as we placed dishes down and walked around the table.

"What, baby? You think that I am good looking?" I let out a chuckle that I tried to make sound sweet and endearing as I walked around the other side.

She smiled and replied, "Oh, you know I do. You are good looking. Sexy, handsome, and very unique. I love it when I walk Mokey with you around the apartment complex and meet couples and other women. The women ask me, 'Who is that?' When I reply, 'Oh, he's with me,' they act as if they were surprised. I feel proud."

"Why would they be surprised?"

"Oh, you know, baby." She placed a fork down next to a plate. "My hair has become stringy. My clothes are not nice. They wonder why someone like you would be with someone like me. When they see how much you love me, they tell me 'Good job. He's a catch.'" A couple of tears rolled down her cheeks.

"Baby, I love you. I have never been with another woman who has loved and accepted me for who I am like you have."

"I know," she said with a teary smile. We both stood up straight as she continued. "No one else has ever accepted and loved me for who I truly am. Especially, after the life I have led and the things that I have been through. I love you so much."

The table was set, complete with a centerpiece of lilies. We just stood there facing each other in our everyday clothes. A silence hung in the air. As soon as our eyes caught, we fell into each other's arms. When I held her, I felt her body melt into mine. We kissed with an intense hunger. As we gradually slowed to a more tender pace, I realized we both were crying. Gently, I held her face in my hands and felt her tears on my fingers. I moved my lips down her neck as she breathed heavily. "Oh, my God! I love you!" she said in between breaths.

"I love you so much, baby," I replied as we began to undress each other. Gently, I laid her body down on the carpeted floor next to the table we had just set. We made love under the delicious dinner that we had made together.

LADIES AND GENTLEMEN, WE ARE FLOATING IN SPACE

Several weeks later, Lynn began to act in a very peculiar manner. I first noticed when she woke me up because I heard her talking to herself. She was slowly walking back and forth from the bathroom to the bedroom. As the days passed, she started to make less sense in between lucid conversations. As she sat on the couch watching one of our DVDs, she rocked back and forth in her seat.

She began visiting her daughter and mother less. One day, I arrived home from work and I saw her get off the phone with her daughter. She was trembling in her black slip. I noticed her skin looked yellow.

"So what did your daughter say to you over the phone?" I asked.

She looked down at the floor. "Ron said that he has hepatitis."

"What?" I asked.

"I don't know the cubes."

"What? Baby, just sit down." I guided her over to the couch. "Look me in the eyes," I said as I held her face up. Her eyes did not seem able to focus, and she looked rapidly all over the room. "Baby, I'm going to take you to the hospital."

"No! No! No!" she yelled, shaking frantically.

"Okay! Just be calm," I pleaded. "Let's just sit down, relax and watch a movie." I stood up to take my dress shirt and tie off.

"Where are you going?!" she screamed.

"I'm just going to change, baby. I'm just changing my clothes."

"I need a cigarette." She stood up, walked to her purse, got her cigarettes, and her lighter. "Not allowed to drink, but I can fucking smoke!" she said to some imaginary person in the kitchen.

"Lynn?" I asked. "Who are you talking to?"

She slowly turned her head to face me. "I'm talking to you! Who the hell do you think I'm talking to?" She stormed into the bathroom and sat on the toilet to smoke her cigarette. She dropped her ashes straight into the sink. Usually, she would ash in a small cup filled with water. I noticed that her hand and arm were shaking. Her chin and lips trembled when she inhaled but were perfectly calm when she exhaled.

While standing above her, I looked down at her and said, "Seriously, I can take you to the hospital right now. I want to take you. Please let me take you to the hospital!"

Her head rose up and her eyes were piercing as she looked at me above the wire rims of her glasses, which had slid down her nose. She pushed her glasses up the bridge of her nose, and with dramatic authority, she said, "No."

"Okay," I said, giving in. "But I will if you want."

She stood up and walked to the couch. "I want to finish the movie."

I washed my hands and asked, "What movie?"

"Irreversible," she said as she sat on the couch. The film "Irreversible," directed by Gaspar Noe and starring Monica Belluci, is a film that is a part of the French extremity movement. The film follows a couple through a horrifically violent evening in Paris, France. The film is known for its brutal and very realistic 10 minute long anal rape scene. While I brushed my teeth, I realized that Lynn was not in a good frame-of-mind to be watching something like that. As soon as I spit the toothpaste out of my mouth, I ran out of the bathroom. Lynn cringed and yelled into the pillow as the rapist forced himself on Monica Belluci's character. Every single time Monica Belluci wailed in muffled agony, Lynn cried, moaned, and whimpered. I stopped in my tracks as the gravity of her past rape hit me.

"Let me shut this off," I said as I went for the eject button.

"No! Don't stop it! Why? Why would someone do that to someone? Why would someone do that to a woman? Why?" I went to the couch and consoled her. She cried in my arms and soon fell asleep.

Later that night, noises of dishes being broken and Mokey running around barking woke me up. I heard the front door open and close, then footsteps going down then back up the stairs. As she walked back in the apartment, I heard her mutter, "No… no… no. The court does not know. I have warrants. I cannot get caught. No! No! No!"

As I became completely awake, Lynn came into the bedroom and I saw that she was in an absolutely psychotic state.

"Babe! Lynn! Babe, are you okay?"

She looked at me and just turned around as she mumbled, "I have to find it! I have to find it!" She started rummaging through the closets, pulling out her jewelry making kit, old books from her stay in the hospital, and crafts that her daughter gave her. She stumbled from room to room mumbling and searching for something.

"I'm taking you to the hospital," I said as I quickly threw some clothes on and packed a bag for her. I took Mokey and the bags out to the car, then ran back up to the apartment, taking several stairs with each step. I left the door propped open.

Lynn was shaking and crying as she tried to put her shirt on. She could barely move, let alone walk.

"Come on, baby." I helped her get dressed. As I held her in my arms, I said, "It's going to be alright." I put one arm around her back and looked her in in the eyes. I asked, "Do you love me? I love you." She nodded. With my left arm, I swept her legs up and lifted her so that I was actually carrying her in my arms.

Damn, I thought to myself. *I usually do not carry women like this. You're skinny, but you're heavy. I have to get in shape.*

As I straightened my back, I exited the apartment and used my foot to close the door behind me. Luckily, the bottom lock always locked by itself. As I looked down the narrow stairway, there seemed to be more stairs than usual. The long, dark stairway looked as if it was in a Tim Burton film. I took a deep breath and then, I took my first step. By accident, Lynn's head hit the wall and the sound echoed throughout the narrow stairway.

"Thanks," Lynn said, her weird psychotic state not getting in the way of her sarcasm. "You know how to treat a lady."

"Are you alright? I'm sorry, baby," I apologized as I lifted her head and shoulders with my shoulder. Slowly, I made it down the stairs with Lynn in my arms. As I got to the bottom, I let her feet on the ground. She did not seem to know what was going on. I took her hand and led her to my car. I had to put her seatbelt on for her.

I called Lynn's mother. As soon as I pulled up in front of their house, Lynn's mother was out front waiting for us. I got out of the car, took Mokey out of the car, and handed the leash to Lynn's mother. She took one look at Lynn and said, "Oh, dear God."

I ran to the driver's side of the car and got in. As I sped off to the hospital, Lynn insisted, "I have to call Dr. Danielle!"

"It's too late for that! We have to get you to the hospital!"

Lynn took out her phone, found the number, hit the button, and for some reason, gave the phone to me. As soon as the phone was answered, I gave the phone back to Lynn.

"Dr. Danielle?" Lynn said, slurring her words. "I'm going. I'm going. I'm going to the hospital. I don't know. I – I – I cannot. I need my prescription and I cannot get it with you!" Lynn started crying. "Please, please, please. I don't know. I'm going."

Lynn gave me the phone and wept beside me.

I asked, "Dr. Danielle?"

"Yes?"

"I'm taking Lynn to the hospital. This is an emergency. She is acting completely irrational. She's not making sense."

"Yes, I can hear that. Just be with her. I will call the hospital."

We drove on Route 18 North to New Brunswick, cutting off cars and trucks while I tried not to get into an accident. I couldn't help taking my eyes off the road to check on her. A mixture of sadness, worry, anger, and heartbreak filled me.

We pulled into the Robert Wood Johnson University Medical Hospital and parked. We left her belongings inside the car and walked straight to the emergency room. The instant the nurses saw her, they told me to move aside. Lynn looked like a helpless human being dragged away by ravenous zombies in "Day of the Dead." They strapped her to a gurney and took her away.

"Are you the husband?" a nurse asked.

"I'm her fiancé," I said.

"Well, we have some questions for you, sir." The nurse asked, "Has she been here before?"

"Yes."

"Does she have any medical issues?"

"She had ovarian cancer and had an ovary removed. She is allergic to penicillin. She used to be a drug addict but is not anymore. She sometimes drinks alcohol. She is on Medicare…"

A million and one questions were asked and I tried to answer every one of them. A whirlwind of emotions and confusion increased the stress of the situation. After many questions, I did not realize that 40 minutes passed.

"Just stay here, sir," the nurse said.

"Wait!" I asked, "What's wrong with her?"

"That's what we are trying to figure out, sir," the nurse said and walked away. The hallway seemed to get longer as she walked away from where I sat in the waiting room chair. I decided to go out to the car to get her bag. The thankful feeling that I got her to the emergency room in time was a small comfort. As I slowly trudged my way to the car, the realization that she may just die hit me with a brutal force. My eyes began to fill with tears, and everything was blurry. It felt like slow-motion. Slowly, as my mouth cracked open, the tears began to gush down my face. Eventually, my breathing became normal and I wiped my eyes. I brought the bags inside and took a seat in the waiting room.

As I sat back, I realized that there was no way that I could read a book or magazine. I could not watch the television that was hanging in the corner. I could not even look around the waiting room at the other people waiting. All I could do was stare into space and think. At that moment, I could not remember feeling more alone.

My next memory was being awakened by Lynn's mother. Hours had passed and I attempted to quickly adjust to the present. Lynn's mother said, "She's going to be in overnight. Go home." I stopped and picked up Mokey on my way back.

Saturday morning arrived and I woke up in the small bed with only Mokey by my side. Our tiny bed felt endlessly vast without Lynn. Mokey missed Lynn and she made it very clear by the look on her face and the way she slowly walked through the apartment. There was a text message from Lynn's mother that just said, "No word yet." I figured that I would walk Mokey, take a shower, get breakfast, and then go visit Lynn.

As I walked into Lynn's parents' house, I felt the uneasy atmosphere of unspoken fear and worry. Lynn's daughter was playing a videogame in her pajamas. She knew something was wrong with her mother, but no one had told her how serious the situation was. She just knew that her mother was in the hospital again. As

I watched her play, I just wanted to hug her and cry into her arms. She looked like a little version of Lynn. She even had Lynn's same glasses.

Lynn's father said, "Grandma is shopping for things Lynn may need. She said that she will meet you at Robert Wood Johnson. Leave Mokey here." Mokey jumped right up on the couch and cuddled next to Mia.

I said to Mia, "Give me a hug." She climbed off the couch and gave me a hug.

"Are you coming back?" she asked. "Maybe we can go to the dog park again."

As I hugged her, I replied, "Maybe, kiddo. Take care of Mokey for me, okay?"

"Okay," she said in her adorable little voice, as she sat back down next to Mokey.

At the hospital, I checked myself in and was directed to the ICU wing. As the elevator opened, I saw doctors and nurses huddled by her door. Before I went into her room, I was stopped by one of the nurses. "Are you her husband or relation?"

"I'm her boyfriend," I said. "I mean, I'm her fiancé."

"Stay here just a moment." The nurse went to speak with the doctors. Suddenly, a female Indian doctor and a man in pastel colored scrubs walked towards me.

"Sir, we have an issue," the female doctor said. "Her liver is failing, and there is a major problem with her intestinal tract. There is severe scar tissue in her rectum."

In a panic, I asked, "Is she going to be alright?"

"Sir, please. Let me explain," the doctor said as several people went into Lynn's room.

"What's going on?" I asked, watching the medical staff work on her as if they were preparing for war and her body was their main weapon.

The doctor said, "She is going to need surgery. The scar tissue is so thick that it is causing major problems within her digestive system. Think of a hose that is attached to a faucet. The water is running, but someone stepped on the hose. When the hose is blocked, the hose begins to expand. That is what is happening to her colon, intestines, and her stomach. Everything is backed up. The build-up of toxins in her system is what was making her behave irrationally. On top of all of that, she has severe liver and heart problems."

"So, you are going to fix it?" I asked.

"She is being prepped for surgery now. Normally, this surgery is very effective and safe."

"What do you mean normally?" I asked. "What is not normal about this?"

"This is different," the anesthesiologist stated. "It's her heart. Her heart is incredibly weak. The surgery is not the problem. The issue is if she can survive the anesthesia."

A wave of fear crashed over my body and my eyes immediately began to tear up. "Well... well... well..." I stammered. "What are the chances?"

"Not good," the anesthesiologist said.

"What are they?" I asked.

"We truly cannot say," the doctor said.

"Percentage-wise? What is it?" I pleaded, "I will not hold you to it. I swear. I just need to know."

The doctor and the anesthesiologist looked at each other with concern, then the anesthesiologist looked me dead in the eye and said, "Fifty percent."

I felt as if I was in a movie where the shot just pulls back at my sheer amazement of the situation. "Fifty percent?" I asked. "So, you are telling me that there is only a fifty percent chance that she will survive this operation?"

Both nodded their heads and said, "Yes."

"Do it," I begged. "Please... please... please save her. I love her."

The doctor said, "We could not do it until we talked to her parents. Actually, we just got off the phone with her mother before you arrived."

As though on cue, the elevator doors opened and Lynn's mother rushed out from the elevator, sobbing. She fell into my arms weeping, "Oh my God! My baby!" I held her and we both cried into each other's arms.

As I backed up, I told her to speak to the doctor. Between tears and sniffles, I overheard them tell her what they told me. The only difference was that they told her mother that there was a seventy-five percent chance of survival.

My own mother knew the situation from previous texts and phone calls. When my mother called me back, I answered the phone by saying, "Lynn only has a fifty percent chance to live." I began sobbing on the phone as I told her the situation.

"Oh my God, honey," my mother said. "Just pray."

"Fuck praying! There is no God. What God lets this happen to someone who is only 37!"

"Don't say that, sweetie. You do not know what is going to happen."

"She is going to die," I cried. "This woman has dodged every bullet and survived hell, but the odds are against her. Mom, I think this is it."

"Listen to me!" my mother demanded. "Listen to me! I'm older than you. I've experienced this. You do not know. You do not know. You're not God. What you are is the love of her life. You have a responsibility. Be there for her mother. Be there for her father. Most importantly, be there for the little girl. Be there for Mia."

A wave of reality washed over me this time. "I know. I will. I have to go."

As I walked into Lynn's room, I saw her lying there with tubes coming out of her mouth, her nose, her arms, and between her legs. She looked lifeless even though her chest was moving up and

THE COOLEST WAY TO KILL YOURSELF

down with each breath. The machine in the room made a constant beeping sound.

"Baby." I could not speak without crying as I held her cold, limp hand. "Please don't die. Please don't die. Please don't die. I love you so much. I'm sorry. I'm sorry. I'm sorry for breaking your heart so long ago. Get through this. You can do this. Stay strong for me, baby. You have been to hell and back. You survived so much. Please do not leave me! Please don't leave me! Please do not die! I love you. I love you so much. I promise. I promise that I will be here when you wake up. Please… please wake up."

Lynn's mother walked in and started crying again as soon as she saw her 37 year old daughter laying on a gurney, looking lifeless. "Mothers are supposed to die before their children. It should not be the other way around," she said sadly.

The hospital Chaplain entered the room and asked, "Would you like me to give a blessing?"

"Yes," Lynn's mother stated.

The Chaplain said, "Let's join hands." After we joined hands over Lynn, the Chaplain started her prayer. "Dear Lord, please help Lynn survive this operation. Please accept her as one of your flock and let her stay on this Earth and continue to be the loving and beautiful person she is. If you must take her, please accept her into Heaven for eternal peace and happiness. Please, give her one more chance so she can be with us. This is your child. Please give her strength. Please give her peace. To the father, the son, and the Holy Ghost. Amen."

As the Chaplain left the room, Lynn's mother stated, "I'm glad the Chaplain blessed her. I would hate it if she died and she was not blessed, because she had an abortion. I don't want her burning in Hell." I was speechless when I heard that comment, but thought it best to just move on.

When the nurses came in to take Lynn to surgery, the reality of the situation hit again.

Lynn's mother wailed, "Oh my God, my baby!" I held her back and she collapsed in my arms. She just kept on crying, "My baby! My little baby girl." All I could do was stand and hold her. We stood there in an empty, bed-less hospital room. The tubes were on the floor and the machines were not attached to anything. Lynn had left us there alone.

Lynn's mother and I made our way to the hospital lobby. We sat in the black leather chairs and got ourselves together. We made phone calls to our loved ones to let them know what was happening. Lynn's mother even called Ron and told him the news. He was sad, but only asked to be informed of what happened.

We returned to Lynn's parents' house. As soon as I walked in, Mokey ran to greet me, though she was not her usual energetic and bouncy self. She seemed to know we were all worried. We were numb, going through the motions like robots, trying not to show our emotions because we did not want to worry Mia.

Mia continued to go about her playtime. There was concern behind her eyes, but she truly thought that everything would be fine. As I watched her play with such innocence, I almost started crying again. At first, I thought to myself that I had been crying too much. After I had that thought, I realized that Lynn was worth crying for.

Lynn's mother asked, "You staying for dinner?"

I replied, "Of course."

Mia ran up to me and did a karate chop. I pretended that she hurt me. Even though the act was extremely half-assed compared to the usual, I felt she deserved a performance. "Can we go to the dog park?" Mia asked.

"Sure, kiddo," I said. "Ask Grandpa."

Mokey, Mia, and I packed into Lynn's father's car. Grandpa drove all of us to the East Brunswick Dog Park. There was a bizarre feeling in the air. The only word I can use to describe it is "unfun." We could not have had fun if we wanted to.

When we arrived at the dog park, Mia jumped out of the car with Mokey and ran into the small dog section of the park. Mia loved playing with the other little dogs and would talk about how she wanted to become a veterinarian when she grew up. As I watched her play and socialize, I was envious of her childhood. I wished I could not have a care in the world. I wished I had the whole world in front of me. Then, a realization hit me. Mia was a very intelligent 9 year old girl. She knew that something was very wrong. She knew that her mother could die. She knew that there was absolutely nothing she could do but be herself and wish for the best. Soon, I was not jealous of her. A feeling of brutal heartbreak washed over me. If Lynn died, Mia would grow up without parents.

Stoic in nature, Lynn's father just stood there watching the dogs and their owners. Outwardly, he appeared calm, but I felt that he deserved a loving shoulder to cry on. Lynn's father always was, and still is, a man of decency. He loves his family and has provided for them. He did not deserve the pain, and certainly did not deserve the anxiety. As I approached him, I tried to distract our thoughts with a different subject but realized that I was just replacing one bad thing with another.

"We called Ron," I said. "He really did not react."

"Yeah, well, Ron is a very selfish man," Lynn's father said. "This one time, of many times, he hit her, and Lynn ran to us. We took her in and told her that she did not have to go back to him. By this time, they were in deep. It was after many calls, arguments, and conversations... See, it's the conversations. The conversations are the things you have to look out for when you have a daughter who is with someone abusive. An argument is one thing, but those conversations... they lead to things. So, one day, she says she wants to go home. We beg her not to go, but she's an adult. One thing about Lynn, when she loves, she loves."

After a small pause, I looked him in the eyes and said, "I love your daughter very much."

"I know you do," he said. "I know you do." We stayed at the park for about an hour, then headed back to the house.

During dinner, the gravity of the situation made us all uneasy, but we tried to keep calm. Even Mia felt that she should not be picky about the chicken nuggets or the rice. Throughout dinner, we kept to safe, mundane topics like The Jets (which I knew nothing about) and Mia's schoolwork. The dinner was long and empty, but not because of the family. The dinner was empty for the sadness and disquiet of the situation. The dinner was empty because we all felt Lynn's absence.

After Mokey had eaten and had her insulin, I said, "Mia! Do you want to take Mokey for a walk with me?"

"Sure," Mia said.

Before I even got out of the chair, Mia was ready with the plastic bag, Mokey's harness, and the leash. Outside, Mia bopped along the sidewalk with Mokey. "If dogs could be astronauts, do you think Mokey would go on the space shuttle?" Mia asked.

I replied, "Of course. Mokey can do anything."

Mia laughed and said, "I think that Mokey communicates with other dogs."

"Are you excited to go back to school?"

"Yes. I am," Mia replied. "My friend, Robert. You met him. He lives down the street. He said that he would protect me if anyone messes with me."

"Do people mess with you?" I asked.

"No. But he told me that he would protect me. I guess it's always good to have someone looking out for you."

I responded, "That's the truth." After a quick laugh, I could not help but be serious. I knew I should not burden this beautiful little child with emotional anguish about her mother, but I could not stop myself. "Mia? You know your mother is in the hospital, right?"

"Yes, I know. What about it?"

"Well, we are worried about her. You know I love your mother very much," I said. What the hell was I thinking? What was wrong with me? Why was I doing this to her?

"I know," she said. "I love you, too."

"I love you, too. Are you worried?" I asked.

"You worry too much. I do hope she's alright. Either way, we can't do anything about it. Come on, let's keep walking." There I was, getting emotionally and spiritually educated by a 9 year old girl. She was the one with the most to lose, yet somehow she remained centered, faithful that she would see her mother again. There was a very real possibility that her mother may have been dead at that very moment, but I could not tell that to a little girl.

Mia, Mokey and I went around the corner and up to the house. As soon as we walked in and I let Mokey off the leash, I saw Lynn's mother answer the phone. She quickly walked into their master bedroom. I looked at Lynn's father and he shrugged as if he did not know what was going on. Every minute felt like several hours. I started pacing, but I did not want to make Mia nervous. I laid on the carpet and played with Mia and her toys. We made up some weird game where we sat on the floor with our feet touching and threw tennis balls at each other. From far away, I heard Lynn's mother crying. My eyelids became heavy and closed in sadness.

"Did you hear that?" I asked Lynn's father.

"Yes, I did," he said. "Yes, I did. Stay here." Lynn's father stood up off of the couch, put his spy novel on the coffee table and walked towards the bedroom. Within 30 seconds, he walked back and commented, "She was crying but closed the door."

The family room was silent. This was once a room that was filled with the sound of a family laughing. Mia and I were silently playing on the floor with the tennis balls and dog toys. I heard the bedroom door open and heard Lynn's mother walk through the hallway, through the kitchen, and into the family room. She stood there with tears in her eyes.

"Well?"

Lynn's mother stated, "She made it." There was a collective sigh of relief.

"Lynn!" I exclaimed. "You got us again!"

"Well, we're not out of the woods yet," Lynn's mother said. "There's going to be a pretty intense recovery. Still, she made it. She made it." We all gave these appreciative hugs to each other. Once again, we got on our phones, this time to let everyone know that she was okay.

As the night ended, I packed up my stuff and took Mokey back to the apartment. In the car, I listened to "Blue Flower" by Pale Saints (a cover of a song by "Opal"). At a stoplight, Mokey popped her head from between the back seats and kissed me on my mouth. I looked at her and she looked at me with that adorable face, seeming to say, "Mommy's coming home?"

There I was at a light, on the corner of Summerhill Avenue and Main Street in Spotswood, talking to my dog. I said out loud, "Yes, Mokey. Mommy's coming home. Mommy's coming home soon." As I made my turn toward the apartment, I could not remember feeling such a sense of relief and such a deep appreciation for the people who love me. Tears of joy were in my eyes and a smile was on my face. At that moment, I realized that I would have given my own life if it meant that she would live.

After the devastating weekend, I returned to work on Monday without a clue to what the immediate future held for us. When my boss walked into his office, I immediately knocked on the door and asked to talk to him.

"I had a brutal weekend," I said.

"What happened?" he asked.

"Lynn almost died. I had to rush her to the hospital. She had to get emergency surgery and the doctors said there was only a fifty percent chance she would make it."

"Wow, oh my God!" my boss said. "Is she okay?"

"She made it, but the recovery is going to be intense. It's going to be hard. I would not ask you if I did not need it, but I may have to leave at a moment's notice."

"Yeah, man," my boss said. "Just let me know. You can make up some of the time you take off later. I understand, man. Seriously, are you okay?"

My eyes became slightly teary and I said, "I've never been in a situation like this. Words cannot describe the fear and anxiety I felt… that I still feel."

"Take it easy. Do your thing. She's in recovery now, right? You cannot do anything. Try to work and get your mind off it and go see her later."

I replied, "Thanks." As I left his office, my mind was divided. At one side, any job is not worth keeping if I could not be there for the woman I love. I had a small feeling of resentment when he talked about making up the hours. On the other hand, I understood that he was running a business and his manager was a cold hearted miserable human being who constantly yelled at him.

During the next several days, I worked but left early to go and see Lynn at the hospital. She was in a chemically-induced coma. Every time I walked in the hospital room, I saw her lying there, asleep. Though she looked lifeless, the color in her skin was back and she was less yellow. Her heart rate was normal and she was being fed through a tube. There were still tubes everywhere. I would sit next to her in a chair and hold her hand until visiting hours were over. I paid for the crappy television set with 15 channels. Each time I went to visit her, I wrote her a little letter that told her how much I loved and missed her. After each visit, I would pick up Mokey from Lynn's parents' house. Mia was acting normal and happy. She took Mokey for walks with me, and played with Stevie, her hamster. Her mother never came up in conversation and it was decided that we would not take her to see Lynn because she may be scared if she saw her the way she was.

One day while I was at work, my Blackberry rang. When I saw Lynn's name on the screen, I immediately picked up the phone. "Baby!?" I asked with anticipation.

A gravelly voice whispered, "Hey baby." Lynn's voice was strained and barely audible, irritated from the breathing tube from the surgery.

"You're awake!" I said with a huge smile as I jumped out of my desk chair and walked out of the office into the hallway. "Are you okay? How do you feel?"

"What happened?" she asked.

"You had major surgery. You almost died."

"Really?" Lynn said in her raspy, laryngitic voice. "Wow. I lived?"

I laughed at the absurdity of her question. "Yes, you lived!"

I went to see her every day, but she was in and out of consciousness. Every day, she became a little more awake and easier to understand. Still, she had a long recovery ahead.

While I was at work, she called again.

"Baby?" Lynn asked.

"Yes?"

"I need you to bring me cigarettes," she said.

"What?"

"Cigarettes."

"Yes, I heard you," I said. "They will not let you smoke in ICU."

"Bring me cigarettes!" she coughed.

"Don't worry about that. They will not let you smoke in ICU," I repeated.

"There's a balcony! Bring me cigarettes!" Lynn moaned as she coughed more. "Baby! Baby!"

"Yes, baby, what is it?"

"There's a robot in my room."

THE COOLEST WAY TO KILL YOURSELF

"What?"

"There's a robot in my room and it talks to me. I don't know its name but it watches me and I'm scared." Lynn began crying. I realized that she was not yet back to herself.

"Baby, go back to sleep. Rest. I will be there soon, okay?"

"Okay," she said, and fell asleep while on the phone.

After I went back to work for a couple of hours, my phone rang again. I answered as soon as I saw that Lynn was calling. "Baby?"

"How did I get in space?" Lynn cried into the phone.

"You are not in space."

"I can see planet Earth out the window!" Lynn started weeping. "I want to go home!"

"You are not in space. You'll be home soon, baby! I'll come over after work."

"Bring me cigarettes," she said as she hung up. I thought to myself, *If she is in space, will she be back in the hospital by 6:30 PM when I go to visit?*

A couple more hours of work passed and Lynn called me again. As soon as I answered, she yelled with her scratchy, barely audible voice, "They are doing experiments on me!"

"Baby, please. You must calm down and get some rest."

"Time travel! This fucking robot! You don't believe me! The army is here! The government is here! I heard them! I need to get out of here, baby! I can't take it! I can't take it!" Then, she whispered into the phone as if she was telling me government secrets. "You have to get me out of here. I cannot stay here. This robot is recording everything. They're going to kill me. I'm taking my tubes out of me."

"No! Baby!" I yelled, "Don't do that! Don't do that! Stay in the bed." I heard a rustling and then I heard the nurses come in and scold her. Then, the call ended.

After work, I drove over to New Brunswick to visit Lynn. I

purchased a stuffed dog puppet. Before I walked into the room, I talked to the nurse, who told me, "I must warn you, she is hallucinating. She's extremely agitated. She tried to take her IV out and we cannot have that. We had to restrain her."

As I walked into the hospital room, Lynn immediately started crying as she laid there in restraints. My heart broke as her bottom lip trembled and she could not wipe her own tears. I wiped the tears from her cheeks and gave her some water through a straw. There was a computer monitor next to her bed with a screensaver of the planet Earth as viewed from space. As I looked at it, I realized how someone who was drugged up could think that they were in a spaceship.

"I don't want to be here!" Lynn cried. "I don't want you to see me like this. I'm so scared. Please undo these. Please!"

I said, "Baby, I can't."

Lynn started sobbing and I thought that I could undo them just for a little while. The second I leaned towards the restraints, I heard the nurse's voice, "Don't you dare do that."

Lynn's whole body shook, which made the hospital bed shake. "You fucking don't know what it's like! You don't fucking know!" The nurses came in and gave her some medication. Not long afterwards, Lynn passed out. I kissed her goodbye and left.

When I picked up Mokey, I told Lynn's parents about my visit. Lynn's mother said, "We have a long road to travel. We have a long way to go."

Day after day, I visited her as she was in restraints. Lynn was completely out of her mind. She was either passed out or not making any sense. Finally, I received a phone call from Lynn while I was at work. "How are you talking on the phone? Are you out of the restraints?"

"Yes," Lynn said, her voice still scratchy. "They have a nurse who sits here and watches me. She does not fucking leave."

"Oh, okay."

"Don't you fucking 'okay' me!" Lynn said with a laryngitic fury. "I heard everything."

"What are you talking about?" I asked.

"I heard you," Lynn yelled. "I heard her. I heard you and her in the other room. Your fucking girlfriend is lying in a hospital bed and you have to fuck a nurse in the other room? What the fuck is wrong with you?"

"Baby," I pleaded. "I did no such thing. I did not have sex with a nurse in the ICU. I have not had sex with anyone since I was with you."

"I fucking heard you!" Lynn cried.

"Baby, you are hallucinating. Please believe me. You told me you were flying in space a couple of days ago. I will be there after work. I'm glad that you are not in the hospital restraints anymore. I love you."

"Get me cigarettes!" Lynn said quickly, trying to get the sentence in before I hung up.

Emotionally and mentally exhausted, I left work and visited Lynn at the hospital again. As I walked in the room, I saw her standing up and holding on to the sliver tower which held her IV bag and the heart monitor machine. As soon as she saw me, she asked, "Did you bring cigarettes?"

"No, baby," I replied.

Once again, Lynn's whole body began to shake and she started sobbing. "Why?" Lynn yelled. "I asked you for one fucking thing, just one fucking thing!"

"They will not let you smoke here! Even if there was some kind of balcony, they will not let you leave this room!" I turned to the nurse sitting in the chair reading her magazine. "Aren't I right? If I had cigarettes for her, would she be allowed to smoke?"

"Nope," the nurse said, with a fed up look on her face. "There is no way we would allow her to smoke now."

"See, baby?" I tucked her into the bed and showed her the dog puppet I bought for her. "Look at this. I bought this for you. What do you think?"

"He's cute," Lynn said with a hesitancy to actually like it. She took the fuzzy brown and beige dog puppet from me and held it close to her heart.

"What are you going to name it?" I asked.

"Puppety," she said. "His name is Puppety. Can I make a little video for Mokey? I want to make one for Mia, but she should not see me like this."

"Sure thing," I said as I put the video camera on my phone.

Lynn looked into the phone camera and said, "Mokey, I love you. I'll be home soon. Be good." She made another video for Mia, but then told me that she did not want me to show it to her daughter. Lynn started playing with her hair. "My hair is so thin. My mother was here and said the back of my head had this gigantic knot the size of a Cinnabon. She cut it all out and now my hair is all thin. I look disgusting."

"No, baby," I said. "You are alive. That's what matters."

"I'm ugly!" she cried.

"No, you're not. You are always beautiful to me."

With a deep breath, she looked up at me without her signature glasses. "I love you. Thank you for being here for me."

"Anytime and every time," I said as I kissed her goodbye.

As I walked out of the hospital room, down the cold, clinical hallways, I felt thankful that her status was improving. She was not completely sane, but she was on her way to the city of sanity. A feeling of gratitude filled me. I decided to clean the apartment, stock the refrigerator, and get her a present. Lynn always liked a gift certificate to iTunes.

When Lynn was released two weeks after the operation, I was thrilled yet exhausted when I picked her up. She was ready to go when I arrived at her room. She had her jacket on and her bags packed. Before we left the room, she said, "This is one room that

I won't miss." As the orderly pushed her in a wheelchair, she said goodbye to the nurses as we passed.

As soon as we got outside, she said, "Please tell me that you brought cigarettes." After a quick laugh, I gave her the pack of Mavericks and a lighter. She lit a cigarette and inhaled with an extreme appreciation. As she exhaled and looked at the cigarette, she said, "Hello, my old friend." We walked to the car and I opened the passenger's door so she could get in. Lynn said with a wicked smile, "By the way, I stole the hospital restraints."

As soon as we arrived at Lynn's parents' house, Mia ran out the front door with Mokey on a leash. "Mommy!" Mia said as she ran to hug her.

"Oh, baby!" Lynn said as she squeezed Mia. "I missed you so much." Lynn held Mia in her arms as if they had not seen each other in years.

"Mommy! I'm so glad you're back. Grandma made dinner! Let's eat." Lynn, Mia, Mokey, and I walked into the house for an old fashioned family dinner. Two weeks earlier, this was a dinner we thought we may never have again.

DRY

Slowly, our lives returned to normal. While I was at work, Lynn and Mokey spent time with Mia. After Mia went to bed, Lynn and I would return to our apartment. Sometimes, we would watch films and television. Other times, we would take Mokey for long walks and just talk. Even the most mundane topics were interesting because of our flow and connection. We continued to have our kinky episodes as we "did our thing." Normal life with an unconventional kinky touch was a life we both appreciated. Outwardly, everyone who knew us saw a normal, happy couple.

As time passed, I became a much closer element in Mia's life. I would stay for dinner and help her with her homework. Sometimes it seemed like some of the unstable emotional elements from her parents had been passed on to her. Sometimes, she would throw a fit when she had to do her homework or when she had to eat something she did not want to. This poor little girl did not deserve her situation. Most of the time, she was an intelligent and loving little girl. I was actually surprised that she was as stable as she was, considering all that Lynn and Ron had put her through.

Just when we had gotten settled in, my job in Princeton ended. The company completely dissolved the Princeton office. I got a job in Parsippany, but the commute was over 90 minutes long. The second night, I was feverishly worried about Lynn and upset about

THE COOLEST WAY TO KILL YOURSELF

the commute. I could not bear to be so far away from her in case there was another medical emergency. We were in bed, watching the film, "Maitresse," but I could not concentrate. Lynn held me. With sympathy, but most of all, love, she went down on me to calm me down. This was not a blow job to tease and turn me on. She understood the pressure I was under, and this was her way of trying to help me feel better. Within one week, I found a job with a new company in New Brunswick. I felt as if I were a big fish in a small pond. Oral sex can do wonders for the male ego. It seemed like the more Lynn went down on me, the more confidence I had, and the more job offers I received. (Note: Lovers, keep this mind!)

Months passed and one time, I found an empty bottle of vodka in the apartment. When I heard Lynn vomiting in the toilet, I said, "Lynn, you know that you cannot drink! Where did you get this?"

"I found some money," she said in between wretches. "I could not sleep when you were at work. It was only a small bottle."

"How old is it?" I asked.

"A good week old," she said.

"Dammit, baby!" I yelled. "You know that you cannot drink anymore! The doctors said it will kill you!"

"I'm dying anyway," Lynn said into the toilet.

The vomiting episodes became worse and I eventually took her to the hospital. This time, there was not a sense of emergency. The doctors admitted her and she stayed for two days to go through alcohol withdrawal. She was not given a room, just a section that had a curtain. When I visited after the first night, the doctor walked in and checked up on her. I got the feeling that Lynn did not want me to talk to the doctor or hear what he had to say.

"Feeling better?" the doctor asked.

"Yes," Lynn said. "The pills and the hydration help."

"Listen, Lynn," the doctor said. "You cannot have any alcohol at all. You cannot have Ibuprofen or Acetaminophen. Basically, the only thing you can have is Tums."

"Come on, doc, I cannot even have an occasional glass of wine?"

"A glass of wine will kill you. Look at it this way. You had your fun. The party is over, my friend. The years of drugs and hard living combined with chemotherapy and all your other health problems have practically destroyed your liver and your kidneys. Listen to me. I am extremely serious when I say that you cannot drink alcohol anymore. You cannot have even a single drink. That one drink can lead to many drinks. Now, I talked to your primary doctor. I suggest that you get off the Oxycontin." The doctor looked at me and asked, "Are you her boyfriend?"

"Yes. I will make sure she doesn't drink. I will make sure that there is no alcohol in the house."

"Good," the doctor said. "I must be honest with you. We may be too late. It is not as simple as taking away the alcohol. It's a dietary issue, too. Alcohol is not the only problem. She is unhealthy. It's also the heart, lungs, kidneys, everything."

"I know!" Lynn said with frustration. "It's not like I can get a liver transplant."

"That's not necessarily true. You can try. It will take a long time and you may not get approved, but try. Most importantly, you have to change your diet and stop putting anything in your body that can hurt the liver or your heart." The doctor checked her pulse and blood pressure. "You should be able to go home by tomorrow."

As I kissed Lynn goodbye, I said, "I'm making sure all the alchohol is out of the apartment." Lynn rolled her eyes before kissing me goodbye.

At the apartment, I found half-empty vodka bottles everywhere. Mokey was sniffing around, too. I found a bottle under the couch. As I looked through her old purses and personal things, I found a Vitamin Water bottle filled with vodka. Mokey was burying a bully stick in a pile of clothes in the bottom of the closet and I heard the clanking of glass. There was an empty bottle in the clothes. When I went to the kitchen to feed Mokey, I used the last of the kibble. When I picked up the bag, I found an empty vodka bottle underneath. Some of the partially-filled bottles were bottles that I drank from a year ago, before I stopped drinking. I didn't always finish them, and I realized that Lynn had saved them because she knew that I would not give her money to get alcohol by herself. When Lynn went into the hospital for the operation, I completely stopped drinking. Being around all of these bottles was tempting me, but I thought of Lynn and decided that they must immediately be removed from the apartment. The kitchen garbage bag was half full and the glass clanked while I walked down the steps and to the recycling bin. When I threw the bag in the dumpster, the loud crashing of the glass echoed throughout the apartment complex.

The next day, Lynn returned home to an alcohol-free apartment. Although she did not look very healthy, she looked better than she did when she went to the hospital. We agreed not to drink and that she would not take any unnecessary medication. That evening, we sat and watched one of her favorite stand-up comedy concerts, "Glorious" by Eddie Izzard.

After a month without alcohol or harmful medications, I wanted to give her a little gift. During lunch, I went to the store and purchased all of the Harry Potter films, including the final film in the series. When I picked her up from her parents' house, I gave her the bag and she was thrilled.

"Thank you, baby!" Lynn said. "I have not seen the final film yet."

"I know," I said. "I know how much you love the books, so I thought you should have all of the movies."

"I'm such a nerd. I love it. Don't get me wrong. You know I like cool shit, too. I read the Harry Potter books to Mia all the time.

You know, my whole family does not call Ron by his name. They call him Voldemort. I wish that I could read Stephen King to Mia. When she's older, I will read her The Dark Tower series."

"It's funny that you should mention that," I said. "I have something else for you since you have not touched a drop of alcohol for a whole month." I reached in the back seat and pulled out another bag and gave it to her. When she opened it, she pulled out the brand new hardcover edition of The Dark Tower: The Wind Through the Keyhole by Stephen King.

"Oh, I love you! I cannot wait to read this!"

I smiled. "I'm so glad you like it. See, I listen when you tell me what you like."

"Oh, I know you know what I like," Lynn said with a satisfying laugh. "It's funny. I like all this crazy and so-called 'alternative' stuff. I have these crazy tastes. Recently, many of them are influenced by your kinky mind. Still, I am a self-confessed nerd. I'm proud of it. I got straight A's. I like Harry Potter. I like Lord of the Rings, especially that guy who plays that elf. I don't know. There's something about that man who plays that elf. I do not like him in any other film unless he's playing an elf. Is that weird?"

After a slight pause, I said, "Yes. It is."

"Well, I'm weird," Lynn said with a smile. "You're weird, too."

"We're both weird."

"I know," Lynn said with a bigger smile. "Isn't it wonderful?"

Lynn and I went home with Mokey to relax. We watched the new film and she read her new book. Although we knew anything could happen, we continued to take one day at a time.

PERFECT WEATHER TO FLY

While I was at work one day, my Blackberry would not stop ringing. I called Lynn after she sent a text message that said, "Call me! Urgent!"

"We have to move!" Lynn cried when she answered the phone.

"Wait!" I said. "Calm down. What are you talking about?"

"Someone ratted us out!" Lynn said. "Some snitch in the apartment complex told the landlord that we had a dog."

"Dogs are allowed in the apartment complex," I replied.

"I know, but when I got this apartment, my landlord thought I did not have a dog… because I did not have a dog! He did not know that I had a Nicholas either. My landlord came here and looked at the place. He was pissed. His wife was worse. She's a bitch! She told him what to do and kept on saying that we should pay extra. You should have seen her. She makes the girls on the 'Jersey Shore' television show look classy. Didn't Alison watch that show?"

"Yeah, she did watch that show," I laughed. "Listen, the lease is up this month anyway. We'll get a new place. I saved up some money. We can do this. We'll get a nice place, a bigger place."

Lynn asked, "Are you sure?"

"Yes!" I stated. "We deserve it."

"I'm not getting rid of that dog!" Lynn exclaimed. "Mokey stays with us. I don't care."

"Oh, I know," I said. "It's you, Mia, Mokey and me till the wheels fall off."

"Okay, baby," Lynn said and hung up the phone.

Throughout the next several days, I looked at apartments around Spotswood and East Brunswick. We needed to be close to Mia and we needed a place that was pet friendly. I took Mokey to look at an apartment that was within walking distance of our current residence. It was a two bedroom apartment on the first floor. The kitchen had brand new stainless steel appliances. The place was perfect. I knew that Mokey would love the extra space and Lynn would love the fact that she would not have to walk up the stairs.

Giving me more information than I needed, the landlord told me, "I'm getting a divorce. My soon to be ex-husband is an asshole. So, I'm leaving." The one relevant piece of information she gave was almost an afterthought. "We have 8 different parties interested."

I asked, "How much?"

"We would need a $1,500 deposit," Jamie said as she twisted her long blonde hair. She wore an East Brunswick T-shirt that she probably purchased at the local pharmacy. She also wore black, skin tight cotton pants that hugged her legs and ended at her ankle, and her feet were bare. Feeling like I did not have much choice, I wrote her a check for $1,500.

"The apartment is yours," she said.

After I shook her hand and took one last glance at my future apartment, I took Mokey and left. The song "Weather To Fly" by Elbow was instantly in my mind. As I walked Mokey behind the apartment complex into the grass field, I thought of the lyrics to the song. Thoughts of a positive future raced through my mind. I felt that Lynn and I actually had a wonderful future ahead of us. Finally, everything was falling into place. We would have an extra room for Mia to sleep over and hopefully, eventually live with us. We would actually live in a respectable place where we could have people over. We were at the point where our plans were not just talk, but becoming reality.

At that moment, I felt a foolish sense of positivity. I think positive things happen to positive people. Lynn was unhealthy, but I could not help thinking of the future that we could have together. I knew it was ambitious to an almost naive degree, but I thought that this was a place where all of us could be healthy and happy. A large chunk of my savings was given away in a signature on a rectangular piece of paper to some blonde woman.

As Mokey and I walked home, I felt a childish glee because I imagined our life in that beautiful new apartment. I saw Mia waking up and coming out of her bedroom as I made breakfast for her. In my mind, I saw Mokey following behind Mia as she came into the kitchen in her favorite cartoon character pajamas, rubbing her tired eyes. For the first time in my life, I thought that I could be a father. I imagined my two beautiful, intelligent, loving girls with glasses eating breakfast while Mokey stood on her hind legs and begged for food. I imagined them making fun of me for being so happy that they were happy.

"We can do this," I said to myself aloud as if it were a mantra. Maybe I was delusional. I was hopeful. I was in love. All I knew was that I was happy and had positive thoughts in my head. Sometimes, that is all we need to get out of bed in the morning.

NEW BRUNSWICK Rx

As always, our past came to haunt us. When I say the past, I mean drugs. Even though Lynn was not abusing Oxycontin, her past abuse raised red flags. In order to originally get the prescription, she had to sign a narcotics contract. She needed to see Dr. Danielle once a month to get the prescription. If one illegal drug was found in her blood or urine when they drug tested her every month, the doctor could legally take away her prescription. The doctor could take away her prescription even if she only suspected illicit behavior. Lynn lived in fear of losing that prescription. When we got the prescription, we had to find a place to fill it. Oxycontin is one of the most well-known and abused pharmaceutical drugs in the country. Most pharmacies do not carry the drug anymore. Every single month, we had to go to a different pharmacy because they did not have enough Oxycontin in stock. Since it was a narcotic, we could not get a partial refill. Every single month, Lynn would be haunted with the horror of her Oxycontin prescription. She was not abusing the prescription or illegal drugs anymore, but she was at the drug's mercy.

Even though I just started a new job, I took one half day every single month to drive her to Dr. Danielle's office in New Brunswick to make sure her prescription was refilled. As Lynn and I waited, we always joked around and played "Word Mole" on my

THE COOLEST WAY TO KILL YOURSELF

Blackberry. We flipped through old copies of magazines.

When Lynn was called into the doctor's office, I left the building to walk around New Brunswick. A feeling of nostalgia slowly overwhelmed me. For me, New Brunswick had been a city that was filled with wonderful high times and sexy women. Now in my mid-30's, I was there for Lynn's melancholic, middle-aged health reasons. I walked around George Street and saw new stores that replaced some of my favorite old stores. The poetic coffee shop, Indigo Jones, was now a sub sandwich shop. The old record store that I used to work at, Cheap Thrills, was now a bank. The only storefront that remained unchanged was the theater where I took acting classes.

While looking for a place to get a falafel sandwich, I heard someone call my name. As I turned around, I saw a Black man who looked like he was homeless. I recognized Reggie, who I knew from the methadone clinic. I was wearing my suit and tie and polished black shoes. Reggie was wearing ripped jeans, Converse sneakers with holes in the side, and a dirty, beige Carhart jacket.

"Hey, my man!" Reggie said as he smiled a toothless smile. "Looking good, nigga." I always thought it was funny that he called me that.

"Reggie!" I said as I shook his hand and gave him a pound. "How have you been?"

"I'm alright," Reggie replied in his raspy voice. "I'm doing what I'm doing, hanging in there. Can't complain."

"It doesn't do any good anyway," I said.

"That's right!"

Suddenly, memories of him and his wife talking in group therapy came to mind. Reggie had been trying so hard not to use dope while his wife continued prostituting herself and robbing every customer. "You still with your lady?" I asked.

"Nah," Reggie said. "She got beat up real bad. She's in the hospital. She's trouble anyway. I'm living with my moms. I help her."

"Nothing wrong with that." I asked, "How are you holding up? You staying clean?"

"Shit, I'm trying," Reggie said. "It's bad out there. I don't want anything to do with it, but it's everywhere. I live in the ghetto. It's right at my front steps sometimes. You know John, the guy with the beard who talked funny because some dealers beat him with a bat?"

"Yeah, I remember him."

"He's dead. They found him dead on the street, face down in the snow."

"Damn, that's horrible. He had a rough life."

"You know Katrina?"

"Yeah, I remember her. She was crazy."

"She's dead. She fell out of a 5 story window trying to climb down the building on a rope made out of bed sheets. The cops came to her door. The crazy thing is that they weren't going to arrest her. They were looking for her boyfriend."

"Damn," I replied again.

"You remember that real big, big girl, Margaret?"

"Yes," I replied. "Wasn't she going to prison because she gave someone else her methadone and they died?"

"Yes," Reggie said. "She's dead. She swallowed all these drugs in a balloon the day she went into prison. I guess everything exploded in her stomach."

"Wow!" I said as I looked at him with sympathy. "Hey, Reggie, did you eat today?"

He said, "A little bit."

"Hey, here's a couple of bucks. Go get a couple of slices, okay?" I said as I gave him a $5 bill.

"Aw, you don't have to do that, man," Reggie said, but took the money anyway. His skinny fingers were ashy and wrinkled. "God bless you. What are you doing here anyway?"

"My girl is at the doctor's," I said. "After she's done, I have to get back to work."

Looking sad, he said, "Alright, my man. Stay cool." Reggie shook my hand, gave me a pound, and walked off. As I saw this old, broken little man who would have been shunned by everyone I knew, I could not help thinking that I could have turned out that way. At that moment, I was grateful that I had survived drug addiction. Completely sober, with a job and a woman I loved, I vowed never to be that sad. Sure, in my early 20's, I was a dumb white boy who was fascinated with the ghetto and drug culture. In 2011, the come down was officially over and I was proud of my sober life.

Back at the doctor's office, Lynn came out of the examination room as soon as I walked in. She had the prescription in her hand and made a new appointment.

"How did everything go?" I asked.

Lynn replied, "I got the prescription. My blood pressure is high again. She told me that the psychiatrist that I have been seeing is excellent. She is glad that I am seeing her. They will help with getting me off Oxycontin."

"That's good."

Lynn lit a cigarette the second she walked outside through the revolving doors. "It's messed up," Lynn said. "I'm not abusing the pills anymore. It's been so long, but they always think I am going to mess up again. It sucks being known as a junkie. Wait. Let me rephrase that. It sucks when you need a person to trust you when that person saw you be a junkie."

"That's the truth," I said. "Hey. I wanted to get a falafel, but could not find any around here."

"Let's go to Evelyn's!" Lynn said with a childlike excitement.

"Nice!" I replied with a smile, and drove us to Evelyn's Lebanese Restaurant.

"Remember when that place used to be real small and inexpensive?" Lynn asked. "We used to get falafel there after raves. We spent so much time there. It was like the epicenter for the scene in New Brunswick. Café News was across the street. I always liked that poem you wrote, making fun of pretentious poets. 'The Cool Poet.' I remember when that one got published."

In less than 3 minutes, we arrived at Evelyn's and Lynn was shocked to see how much the place had changed. The restaurant used to be an all-night paper napkin Lebanese diner. Now, it was an elegant restaurant and bar. "Wow!" Lynn said with astonishment. "I cannot go in there. The waitresses are too pretty. Even though they will not remember me, I cannot go in there looking like this. Can you run in? I don't want to embarrass you."

I replied, "Lynn, I will never be embarrassed by you."

After I parked the car on the street, I ran inside Evelyn's and ordered two falafel sandwiches and some drinks. The owner and I talked for a bit about how New Brunswick had changed. He told me that the people in the 90's were much more kind and everyone had felt like family. When the sandwiches were done, I went back out to the car.

As I drove Lynn to her parents' house before returning to work, we ate the falafel sandwiches and listened to podcasts of "The Best Show on WFMU with Tom Scharpling." We laughed as a caller told an amusing anecdote about seeing a monkey in a diaper.

"You know, time and age is a mind-blowing concept," Lynn said. "Forget about the science of it all. Think about the effect it has on the psyche. My memory of Evelyn's Restaurant is nowhere near what it became. Sometimes, I feel like time has passed me by."

"I know," I said. "Sometimes, it feels like we were at a different party and we're late for the reality."

"Now we have to put back the pieces and make sense of everything," Lynn said. "Thank you. Seriously, thank you for taking me. Thank you for being there for me."

"Well, baby, we'll put the pieces to this puzzle back together."

THE BEST SHOW ON WFMU WITH TOM SCHARPLING

WFMU or 91.1 FM is one of the most unique and diverse radio stations in the world. The radio station is free-form and listener-supported. When it comes to types of people, New Jersey has the entire spectrum and WFMU provides a forum for New Jersey natives to be uniquely creative. There are music shows that vary almost every hour. A listener can tune in and hear electronic trance music, then hear British independent rock the next hour. Some shows mix almost every genre of music. WFMU is a radio station that is like an old friend who will always accept me as my quirky self.

WMFU has brought a peculiar type of humor into many lives. My friend and colleague Phil (from the band ex wife) introduced me to "The Best Show on WFMU with Tom Scharpling" because we share an intelligent wit and love of music. We started downloading and burning the show on CD-Rs so we could listen to them when the show was not on. While Lynn stayed at home, I would drive back and forth to work listening to podcasts of "The Best Show." I became addicted, and I still listen to the station regularly. The show has created a community that understands people like me.

"The Best Show on WFMU with Tom Scharpling" is a call-in

radio show that is on every Tuesday evening at 9 PM. For more than a decade, the list of guests and phone callers has included names like Jon Wurster, Patton Oswalt, Zach Galifinakis, Tim Heidecker, Marc Maron, H. Jon Benjamin, Aimee Mann, Ted Leo & The Pharmacists, Kurt Vile, Chris Elliot, Jim Gaffigan, Paul F. Tomkins, John Hodgman, Aziz Anzari, and Andrew Daly. Although there have been many famous guests and callers, each 3 hour show has a humble yet quirky New Jersey charm.

Scharpling & Wurster are the indie New Jersey equivalent of Andy Kaufman and Peter Sellers teaming up on the radio. Some people need a punch line, while guys like Tom and Jon are witty enough to stretch the joke out in a conversational style that makes for a unique and witty radio show. Jon is a drummer of the band Superchunk and also a band member of The Mountain Goats. Tom Scharpling was an executive producer and writer of the show "Monk" and is now the host of "The Best Show on WFMU." I always thought it was funny that they met at the My Bloody Valentine show at the New York City Ritz, because I was also at that Superchunk, Pavement, and My Bloody Valentine show.

One evening, I wanted Lynn to hear this comedic, staged radio phone call that I thought she would love. In the 80's and 90's, Lynn was a punk rock girl. Before Lynn and I had met, we both went to hardcore shows at Middlesex County College and saw The Ramones at City Gardens in Trenton. By the early 2000's, most of The Ramones had died. Basically, Jon Wurster called in as Marky Ramone from the legendary punk band, The Ramones, pretending to propose a reunion.

After work, I picked up Lynn from her mother's house at around 9 PM. Her daughter should have been getting ready for bed. I heard the arguing from the front steps. I walked into a maelstrom of anger and sadness. Lynn was arguing with her mother. I heard them yelling at each other as Mia cried. Lynn was not well. Her hair was thin and her skin was yellow. They were having another one of those arguments where her mother had accused Lynn of not taking care of herself. She was fed up with Lynn constantly being in and out of the hospital. Lynn did put her parents through a unique kind of hell with her past. Some of the damage done to their relationship would never heal. While it should have been a discussion, it turned into a shouting match between Lynn and her mother.

I was a silent witness to the argument, but I offered comfort with my adorable pom-poo, Mokey. I cheered up Mia by playing with Mokey as Lynn went outside for a cigarette. I got Mia laughing again by making Mokey dance around on her hind legs. When Lynn came back inside, the emotional atmosphere was restored to normal. There was no yelling or crying as everyone cooled down.

When Lynn walked in the door, I could see the tired frustration in her face from arguing with her mother. Her eyes were red. She felt like a disappointment as a daughter and mother. "We have to get home," she said. "I need to get into the bath and get in bed."

"I've got something to play for you in the car," I said, with a clever looking smile.

"Okay, sure." She brushed off my comments. She had worries and sadness in her mind and a tiring pain in her body.

As Lynn got her jacket and purse, I talked to Lynn's mother. "She knows how frustrated I get," Lynn's mother sighed. "We're trying to raise Mia right. I'm her grandmother, not her mother. Lynn is going to end up in the hospital again if she doesn't take better care of herself. She looks horrible. Her hair is thin, her skin is yellow, her liver and kidneys are failing because of all the surgeries and drugs from the treatment… not to mention the lifestyle she lived before she left Ron."

"I know. You have been amazing through all of this, and you have so much to deal with. She's trying. It's hard for her. It's overwhelming. Does Ron even call to ask about Mia?"

"No," she replied. "He's probably dead somewhere. He

probably overdosed on the streets of Atlantic City. I hate to say it and I am not the kind of person who wishes it, but he deserves it."

I looked at little Mia playing with Mokey. "He is a bastard for what he did to her." I got the leash and clipped it to Mokey's collar.

Lynn and I kissed her daughter goodbye. We walked out of the house to my car. I always made it to my car first. I loved how Mokey would always jump right into my back seat and look at the world with naïve anticipation. I waited for Lynn to slowly limp to the passenger's seat. I always hated myself when I would feel the tiniest bit impatient for her bad hip and the way she slowly walked. I always thought that I should know better because I used to take care of my grandmother who used a walker at one time. I opened the door for Lynn and she slowly got in the car. She was breathing heavily. She was physically and emotionally exhausted. I closed her door and walked around to the other side of the car with anticipation.

It was a five minute long drive between Lynn's mother's house and ours, but I could not wait to play her the WFMU clip. I knew this would cheer her up. I hit the play button with a mischievous smile. Basically, the segment began with Marky Ramone calling in to promote his trashy romance novel. I skipped to the second half of the call, when he announced that he was reforming The Ramones. Although Jon Wurster was pretending to be Marky Ramone, Lynn did not know this was a fake call.

NOTE: This is a transcript from "The Best Show on WFMU." Dear reader, I cannot capture the truly hilarious nature of the entire phone call. I suggest you go to www.wfmu.org and look the show up.

"It's not possible!" Tom Scharpling said.

"What ain't possible?" Marky Ramone (Jon Wurster) said in his illiterate-sounding New York accent.

"Getting The Ramones back together!" Scharpling exclaimed.

"Sure it is," Marky Ramone said.

"You're getting them back together? Who's in it, then?" Tom

THE COOLEST WAY TO KILL YOURSELF

asked with astonishment. "Joey passed away. Johnny passed away. Dee Dee passed away."

"It's me, Richie, Tommy, and CJ... The Ramones," Marky Ramone replied.

"Hold on," Tom said. "You? Marky Ramone, drummer."

"That's me, second drummer, kind of the definitive drummer."

"Okay. Who else?"

"Richie Ramone, the guy who replaced me, briefly, for about 3 records."

"Also a drummer..."

"Tommy Ramone, he's the founding member, kind of the brain of the band early on and I kind of replaced him," Marky Ramone continued.

"Also a drummer..."

"Yea, and then CJ Ramone."

"Bass player."

"Final bassist in the band, replaced Dee Dee when Dee Dee didn't want to be in the band no more."

"So, basically, this line up you are talking about is... three drummers and a bass player," Tom said in summary.

"Yeah, sounds good. Don't it?"

"You must be switching off. Like, who's switching off on other instruments, then?"

"Nobody! It's the three of us playing drums and then, CJ playing bass. We just kind of hammer out the songs. The set goes for two and a half hours."

"Two and a half hours!?"

"We play just about every song."

"Every Ramones song?"

"Pretty much, yeah."

"So who's playing guitar and who's singing?"

"Nobody! That would be disrespectful to the guys who have departed."

Lynn and I began laughing so incredibly hard that I had to pull over. I stopped near the spot where I would always kiss her goodbye before I dropped her at her parents' house as "Mother Of Pearl" by Roxy Music played. This time, we were facing the opposite direction. As we listened to this call, I wondered if she thought it was truly Marky Ramone. I saw a tear roll down her cheek as she could not control her laughter.

When we heard Jon Wurster (as Marky Ramone) say, "It's great. It's real percussive," we broke out in a burst of uncontrollable laughter. It was that kind of hysterical laughter where you have to make an effort to calm down. You feel as if you are coming down from some kind of high, but in a beautiful and rewarding way.

As the call went on, we kept on laughing. Lynn started to actually slap the dashboard of my car when Jon Wurster said, "That ain't not no funny to no one else neither."

As I looked at Lynn, I could almost see past her jaundiced face, her thin hair, and her tired eyes. I saw her truly laughing for the first time in so very long. She had been so sick for so long that I felt like she forgot how to laugh, or that she was almost afraid to. We had endured several hospital ordeals. She suffered physical and emotional pain. She had just left a horrible fight with her mother and experienced the sadness of having her own child cry. For the first time in a long time, she found humor in life again. She was always a woman with a sharp wit. We had some laughs together, but it seemed like ages had passed since we shared a laugh like that. I was so grateful to share this beautiful moment of carefree laughter with the woman I loved. The radio show transformed her mood when I had not been able to cheer her up on my own.

I had that beautiful feeling of hope inside of me. Although I knew in my heart that it was fleeting, I wanted to cherish that feeling. It was the feeling when I find a new band or a new record. I want someone to hear it and I revel in the fact that they like it. When I love artistic work, whether it is comedy, film, television, or music, I want the people I love to experience that art, too. I love introducing cool things to the people I love. I felt so amazing and proud that I found something that made her laugh so magnificently deep. For a very brief moment, I did not worry. When I saw her smile and laugh so hard, I thought that we could both get through this ordeal. Her laughter gave me this tiny feeling of hope. The feeling was tiny, but I was thankful for it. Her wit had returned. Her laughter was back. For that one, fleeting moment, I had the old Lynn back.

"This isn't the real Marky Ramone," she said. "Is it?"

"No, of course not," I said.

"Oh my God! This is hilarious. I remember seeing them at that dump, City Gardens, in Trenton," she said as she came down from her laughter high. "I'm feeling good. Let's go home."

"You got it, baby," I said as I put the car in drive and headed home.

PARADISE IS FOR THE BLESSED, NOT FOR THE SEX-OBSESSED

Although Lynn's skin was yellow tinged and her liver was enlarged, she was not vomiting and was actually a little more energetic. There were times we even did various sexual things, but they were always initiated by her. Of course, she was slow moving and gentle. She always slept in her favorite black slip. We tried to go about our normal lives, but I saw her becoming sicker every day.

One morning, before I went to work, she began to vomit. I was immediately concerned and asked her, "Have you been drinking? I stopped drinking and I made sure there was not any liquor in the house!"

"I have not been drinking!" Lynn yelled. "I'm fine now. It's okay, just go to work."

"Baby?" I said as I stood over her in the bathroom, dressed in my suit and tie. "You want me to take you the hospital?"

"No! I'm fine. Seriously, go to work." She stood up with a profound stance and smiled at me. "Have a good day, baby." She grabbed her toothbrush and began brushing her teeth.

I looked at her with concern and worry. After I kissed her goodbye, I left for work. While I walked down the steps, I called

THE COOLEST WAY TO KILL YOURSELF

her mother and told her that Lynn vomited. Her mother sensed my worry and asked more questions.

She finally said, "Give it the day, but I will still have her father check on her."

An entire week passed without incident, but then the vomiting episodes started again. Every time, I would say, "I'm taking you to the hospital."

"No!" she said. "I'm fine!"

Once again, I called her mother and told her the situation. That morning, I had my monthly review at work. Lynn's mother said that they would check in on her in one hour. I told her that if she got worse, to interrupt my meeting. While I was in the middle of my review, one of the receptionists interrupted and told me that there was an important call.

I jumped up from the chair and took the phone. "How is she?" I asked.

Her father was at the apartment and said, "I think she should go to the hospital. She was fine in the morning when I checked in on her, but now she is in bad shape."

I cringed and said, "I wanted to take her this morning!"

"I'm calling an ambulance," he said.

I ran out of the office and drove to Spotswood to get Lynn's medicine. As soon as I got into the apartment, I got a phone call from Lynn's mother. As I answered, she said, "They are not taking her to Robert Wood."

"Why?" I yelled.

"They said it is not close enough," she said. She continued to tell me which hospital the ambulance took her to. As I drove to this other hospital, I cursed the EMTs for not taking her to her regular hospital.

In the emergency room, I saw her father and ran towards him. I saw Lynn lying on a gurney behind the blue curtain as several nurses struggled to find a vein.

I called a nurse towards me and gave her the medicine bag. "Here is a bag of all the medicine she takes." I felt fear growing in the pit of my stomach as I watched the nurses working on Lynn.

"Are you her husband?"

"Her fiancé. Can she die?" I asked.

A nurse said, "We are doing everything that we can."

One of the other nurses said, "Yes! She could die."

"Her reports are at Robert Wood Johnson! They saved her life several times!" I felt so frustrated that Lynn had not let me take her there that morning.

Lynn's father stayed until she was stable. By that time, she was sleeping.

THE PHONE

I was worried, and I visited her after work every single night. I would always write a letter to her and leave it for her. She was extremely weak and her thighs and ankles were retaining water.

One evening at work, I called Lynn, but she did not answer. I called her mother and father and they had spent a couple of hours with her earlier that day. Afraid that something was wrong, I raced to the hospital and as I walked into the room, the curtain was drawn because the nurses were bathing her. I dialed her phone but did not hear it ring. Had her battery died? She had the charger. Did she turn off the ringer? I talked to her every evening. Why would she turn the ringer off?

The nurses opened the curtain and in a weak voice, she said, "Hey baby." I was elated to hear her voice regardless of how weak she sounded. I leaned in to kiss her, fix her hair, and give her the letter I wrote to her. She smiled and touched my face.

"I've been calling!" I said. "Your phone is not ringing."

"I don't know," she said.

I looked in her purse. I looked in her sheets. I looked in the drawers and the medicine bag. Then, I realized what must have happened. I ran to the nurses' station and asked, "Nurse! Where do you put the soiled sheets?"

"In the soiled linen room, sir," the nurse answered with a

confused look on her face.

"I think the nurses wrapped my girlfriend's phone in the sheets by accident. Please show me that linen room." We hurriedly walked to this tiny room of white cases and clear bags that were filled with soiled bed sheets. Even though my phone's battery was dying, I called the number over and over again. Another woman in scrubs walked in and was surprised to see me in there.

"My fiancée is a patient here. An orderly accidentally wrapped up her phone in the bed sheets. Can you help us look?"

I looked at my phone and saw the battery was in the red. *Why did I not make sure my phone was charged?* I kept calling Lynn's phone as the nurses lifted up huge bags of soiled linen. Finally, we heard a faint ring of Lynn's phone.

One of the nurses held up a bag and yelled, "The phone is in this bag!"

"Thank you!" I yelled and as I looked at my phone, the battery died and the screen went black.

"We will clean this up for you, sir. Please wait in the room."

As we waited for her phone, I told Lynn the entire story. "You did that for me?" she asked.

"Of course I did!" I looked at her frail body while she lay in her bed in her hospital gown. We talked for a while and made a list of things that she needed. When the nurse came in the room with the phone, I thanked her once again. Before I left, I made sure Lynn's phone was plugged in and not in the bed.

Later that evening, we were on the phone as I laid in bed with Mokey. Lynn seemed so far away from me and I felt so alone. She always ended the evening calls by saying, "I love you and say hello to Mokey for me." This time she added, "Thank you for finding my phone. You know that I always love talking on the phone with you."

"I DECREE THERE IS A HIGHER PLAIN, SOME PLACE OF LITTLE CONSEQUENCE, THAT I MIGHT SEE YOUR FACE AGAIN BEFORE THE LIVING AND THE DEAD ARE REUNITED"
- *Withered Hand*

I have a fool's heart. I always think that the best will happen. Maybe it is a defense mechanism. Without caution, without coolness, without acknowledging deceit, I automatically think that everything will be fine. I always think the pain of time will never catch up to me. Still, I would rather be a fool who has felt love than the most intelligent man who has never known true love.

My Saturday night plans consisted of visiting Lynn in the hospital. Running late from work, I drove to the hospital, trying to keep my spirits up. Once again, I saw her lying in bed with an assorted amount of tubes going in and out of her. Her legs were puffy again and her lips were chapped. Her phone was by her side and she held Puppety in her arms. I saw the letters I had written her on the side table.

"Hey, baby," I smiled.

"Hey, babe." She sounded exhausted, her voice raspy. "Thanks for coming." This woman, who was once filled with opinions and talked nonstop, could barely speak.

"Baby, I have the new season of 'Californication' from Netflix. I know you wanted to see that."

"Yes, I do," Lynn said. "I'm a little busy now, but save it for me. When I get home, I want to watch it. You wish you were Hank Moody, don't you?"

After a mutual laugh, I could only say the words, "I love you."

"I love you, baby," Lynn said. As soon as she finished the sentence, a nurse came in and told me that visiting hours were over.

"Did you get in touch with Robert Wood Johnson?" I asked. "Do you have her medical records? Are you taking care of her? Please… Are you taking care of her?" She had already been there for several days, and I had been trying to get them to transfer her to Robert Wood. The doctors said that Lynn was improving and I believed them.

I walked down those empty, sterile hallways and drove home. Purposely, I made myself think that everything was normal. This was just another part of our life. This had become a regular part of our relationship. I thought that Lynn was in the hospital again, but she would be home soon.

On a Sunday morning in July 2012, the sun woke me up because the blinds had fallen off the window. The sun hit me directly in my face. After taking care of Mokey's food and insulin shot, I dropped Mokey off at Lynn's parents' house and went to the hospital to see Lynn.

For the ride, I took too many comedy CDs. I had a variety including Patton Oswalt, Marc Maron, Eugene Mirman, David

Cross, Mitch Hedberg, and Scharpling & Wurster. Not even the intelligent and honest monologues of George Carlin and Richard Pryor could change the atmosphere. I listened to 30 seconds of each CD and kept on changing them. The funniest routines and bits that had always made me laugh made me feel nothing. Like a zombie, I drove to the hospital.

When I walked into the hospital room, Lynn was unconscious. She was lying on the gurney, completely alone, and I pulled a chair up next to her. I sat down and held her hand. I could feel the life in her fingers. I was overwhelmed by a sense of absolute sadness and the fear of loss.

"Baby, please," I cried as I held her hand. "Please stay with us. Please don't leave us. Please don't leave me. Mia needs you. Mokey needs you. I need you. Please... please... please... just come home. I love you. I love you so much."

As I looked at Lynn in her unconscious state, I tried to deny the gravity of the situation. Lynn's mother walked in the room. We hugged each other. Both of us were crying. The nurses walked in and asked us to leave the room. Once we left the room, we began the usual conversation as we waited for them to tell us when we could go back inside.

Almost immediately, a nurse walked out and stated, "She's gone."

Lynn's mother and I looked at each other and collapsed into each other's arms. I wanted to sob and wail. I wanted to yell and scream. I wanted to curse God and be dramatic. I wanted her mother to know peace. I wanted Lynn's daughter to have a mother. I held Lynn's mother in my arms and she embraced me. The comfort of Lynn's mother's arms was beyond description or comprehension. My pain and loss was nothing compared to hers. I felt ashamed to cry because I had lost the love of my life, but I did not lose my daughter. I thought of Mia, and I felt selfish, because I did not lose a mother.

As I looked at Lynn's still, frail body in the hospital bed, I asked,

"Can I have a moment alone?" Once the nurses stepped out, I left Lynn's mother in the hall with them and went to the hospital bed. Lynn's hand felt lifeless in my grasp. "I'm sorry!" I wept. "I'm sorry! I'm sorry I didn't love you enough. I'm sorry I broke your heart so long ago! You deserved more. You deserved to be loved! You deserved to know how much I love you! What am I going to do without you? I love you! I love you so much! I'm sorry!" I paused and looked down at her for the very last time. "I wish that I had loved you more."

Lynn's mother and I walked out of the hospital knowing that there was a storm that we had to endure. There were phone calls to be made. There were arrangements to make. There were tears to cry. There was a child to comfort.

Feeling numb, I drove home. Everything I passed triggered a memory. There were the restaurants we stopped in to get take out. I passed the stores we always talked about shopping in. As I drove across the railroad tracks in Spotswood, I remembered when I got pulled over by the police when it was snowing and Lynn talked us out of a ticket. I realized that I would never have new memories again with Lynn. My life with Lynn was over. She was gone. There was no dramatic or cinematic scene that I could relive. It was just over.

As I walked up the stairs to our apartment, I thought that Lynn would never walk up those stairs again. As I walked inside, I saw the empty couch. I saw the empty chairs. I saw the empty bathtub. As soon as I saw the empty bed, I collapsed against the closet and just wept. Mokey was not even in the apartment because she was at Lynn's parents' house.

My life was nothing to me. After years of throwing around the concept of death in a literary way, it caught up to me. There I was, lying on the carpeted floor in between the bedroom and the bathroom, sobbing, curled up in the fetal position. As I looked at her black silk negligee on the floor, I wept because I yearned to hold her body next to mine. I wanted to feel her hands on my body. I wanted to kiss her lips. I wanted to make her feel beautiful. I

THE COOLEST WAY TO KILL YOURSELF

wanted her to melt in my arms. Out loud, I pleaded, "Please, God! Please let me hold her in my arms one last time." Heartbroken by the silence that answered me, I grabbed that silk negligee, held it in my hands, and fell asleep on the floor of my empty apartment.

The next morning, I woke up with bloodshot eyes and puffy eyelids. In that zombie-like state, I went through the motions. I told my family and I told the people at my job. I told the woman who Lynn and I were going to rent the new apartment from. The landlord refused to give the money back for the security deposit. I was mortified that someone could be so cruel, but I did not have the strength to argue.

The days were a blur. As I lived alone in our apartment, I kept having that feeling that Lynn would come home. I wanted to make the apartment somewhat decent before Lynn's parents saw the remains of her lifestyle. I found a vast amount of lingerie and wonderful sex toys. Papers were hidden in pockets and crevices.

I found this letter Lynn had written to our unborn child:

To the one who will never be,
  You will always be in my heart.
  I have never seen you, but I don't have to in order to know how beautiful you are.
  We loved you enough to not let you suffer the pain and confusion of not knowing who you clearly are.
  You would have been born of love –but you would have suffered. Suffered more than I can bear a child of mine to suffer. I wanted you, and, in his own way, so did Nicholas. But I am the one who is about to feel you leave this earth. Please know that we did what is best. I love you.
  Please FORGIVE ME… US.
  We wish it could it be different
  Love,
  Us.

As I began to pack up my personal belongings, I felt overwhelmed. How could I pack up a history of someone who loved me? There was the Astroglide, French Maid outftits, and her red corset. There were the beautiful poems and jewelry she made. In her drawer, I found a little box that said, "For Nicholas." As I opened it up, I saw the turquoise bracelet that she made for me. Right next to it, I saw the necklace that she made for herself; a silver necklace with a little key. That key opened the lock that locked up what she owned... me.

The day of the wake and funeral arrived too soon. Every funeral arrives too soon. I prepared my best black suit. I ironed my best white dress shirt. I polished my black dress shoes. As I got ready, I thought of Lynn helping me get that job when we were living that humble life.

On autopilot, I went through the motions of the funeral. The blonde funeral director was very professional and gave the family her condolences. When the family was not in listening distance, I asked the young lady, "Can I speak to you?"

"Of course," the lady said. "I'm so sorry for your loss."

"Please, I want to give you something." I handed her the necklace with a single key attached to it. "Please.... Please... Please make sure this is around her neck. This is a necklace she made. This is important."

The woman looked at me and said, "I promise. I promise that Lynn will be buried with this necklace and this key will be with her... always." As soon as the key and the necklace left my hand, I began to shake.

As the funeral proceeded, I felt thankful that I was blessed to have been loved by such a woman. "Non Je Regretten Rien" by Edith Piaf played in my head. Then, I thought of kissing Lynn to "Mother Of Pearl" by Roxy Music.

I found myself in a funeral pew surrounded by Lynn's family and my parents. Lynn was a woman who my family did not truly know but my parents and my aunt arrived for support.

I was a broken man. Still, I felt some comfort knowing that I had felt a love like Lynn's love for me. In a silent church, the coffin was carried to the front of the altar.

"Mommy!" Mia cried. "My Mommy! Mommy!" There was not a dry eye in the room as that little girl cried. As I sat in the wooden pew, I held Mia in my arms. She cried into my suit and I could not do anything but hold her. I tried not to cry. I tried to hold myself together. I tried not to cry as I held her in my arms, and I promised myself that I would stay in her life.

Soon, the time when I had to leave our apartment arrived. I had packed up the letters, the poems, the evidence of kinky sex, and discarded the lighters, and unfinished cigarette packs. Lynn's father and I took the bed apart. Lynn's mother helped me clean the apartment.

Honestly, I did not want to leave. I wanted to have Lynn hold me while we slept in our little bed. I wanted something to fall back on. Most of all, I wanted her to be known. I wanted people to know how loving she was.

Eventually, I packed everything into my car. I had no choice but to move on with my life. With tears in my eyes and a melancholy feeling in my heart, my mind raced through thoughts of our past…

SHE WROTE ME
A POEM

When I was a high school senior, Lynn began her freshman year of college in Trenton. We were no longer a monogamous couple. Lynn knew that I was infatuated with Zia, but she did not want to let me go. Lynn always seemed to know when I was not with Zia. Lynn would call me as soon as I was alone. The mysterious coincidence was worth investigation, but I honestly just enjoyed the fact that there were women who wanted to talk to me.

"You know, some of the people in my dorm hate you," Lynn said over the phone.

"Why would they hate me?" I asked. "They don't even know me."

She said, "They think you're a fool."

"Well, that remains to be seen. That's no reason to hate someone they do not know."

"They hate you because they see me cry," she said.

"Is that him?" someone yelled in the background. "Tell him to get his act together."

"Great!" I said sarcastically. "Hey, I have been honest with you since day one. I did not cheat on you. I did not lie."

THE COOLEST WAY TO KILL YOURSELF

"Forget all that," Lynn said. "Are you coming down to Trenton this weekend?"

I paused and then replied, "I don't know, maybe."

"Come on!" Lynn demanded. "All of the people from the New York scene are traveling to Baltimore."

I replied, "They have good parties down there."

"I know they have good parties down there, but I have a Lit final on Monday morning. I cannot be all strung out on E and get a perfect score. Come on, I know you are not doing anything but failing to get in Zia's panties. Why don't you come down? Don't make me have to come up there and pick you up."

After a pause, I paused again just to stretch the anticipation out. (Yes, I can be like that sometimes.)

"What's your answer?" she asked.

"Okay."

"Yes!" Lynn said.

"I can hear your smile over the phone," I said.

"Oh, I know you can," Lynn laughed. "I have a surprise for you."

"Really?" I had a huge smile, thinking that finally, it would be lingerie for her to wear for me. "What is it?"

"It's a poem." The smile dropped off my face. Lynn said, "Trust me. This is a poem that you will remember. You never know, if you ever write something about me, you may mention it."

Previously, my typical weekends included going to New York City, taking ecstasy, dancing till 9 AM, and having sex until the afternoon. This weekend included me abandoning that whole hedonistic plan and traveling to South Jersey to hang out with my crazy ex-girlfriend. Since variety is important when making weekend plans, I was persuaded to drive down to Trenton.

For some reason, the snow felt colder and dirtier in Trenton. After getting lost on the campus (which I have been told is mandatory for any first time visitors), I eventually found her building.

As I walked into the dormitory, the security guard and R.A. asked me, "Name?"

After I told them my name, they looked at each other and one of them said, "Oh, you're him... hmm." The R.A. led me through the dormitory hallway. As I arrived at Lynn's door, the R.A. said, "We like Lynn. Be nice to her." Then, she walked away.

Before I had the chance to knock, Lynn opened the door and jumped on me. I stood there in the hallway with Lynn's legs around my waist and her arms around my neck. Carrying her body (while carrying an overnight bag over my shoulder), I stumbled into her dorm room. Her roommate said, "Hello," but immediately left the dorm. As her roommate shut the door, Lynn and I fell onto the bed.

Consumed with excitement, Lynn gave me a kiss and jumped up. She grabbed a piece of paper from her corkboard and put it in her pocket. "I'm so glad you're here!" she said, bouncing up and down on her toes. "Come on!" She grabbed my hand and pulled me out of the room.

"Wait! My stuff!" I said as I tried to drop it, because it was still around my shoulder.

"Leave it!" she said and pulled harder. My bag fell on the floor.

She held my hand as she led me down the halls and greeted everybody by name.

A young lady by the name of Cindy stopped us and asked, "Is this him? Is this the legendary young man you speak about?"

"Yes, it is," Lynn said with youthful enthusiasm.

The blonde, blue-eyed cheerleader-type looked me up and down. After a dramatic pause, she stated, "Nice. You two have fun."

Lynn led me to a dorm room that was packed to full capacity. There was not a place to sit in sight. With a warm, quirky elegance, Lynn stated, "Good evening, everybody!"

"Lynn!" the crowd shouted with the love of a hippie commune.

"Ladies and gentlemen and those who are undecided, this is

him. May I introduce to you... Nicholas." Lynn winked at me.

As I went around the room shaking hands and greeting everybody, I noticed a mixture of emotions. Some people accepted me. Some seemed to disapprove of me.

We had been there for about 20 minutes when Lynn announced, "Everybody! Can I have your attention?"

Some stoned out hippie couple leaned in front of my field of vision. I could have sworn they just appeared out of nowhere. The white male stoned out hippie with dreadlocks said, "Lynn is our resident poet."

The stoned female white hippie with dreadlocks stated, "We love her poetry." I knew things were getting weird but I truly did not have a clue as to just how weird they would get.

"Ladies and gentlemen, I have a poem!" Lynn declared as she stood in the middle of the crowd. Everyone in the room let out an appreciative, yet stoned out, applause. Lynn looked at me from across the room with this deliciously evil smile.

Lynn said, "The title of this poem is, 'Dedicated to My Lover's Penis.'" For a second, I felt time stop and I did not know what to do. A shocking feeling of pride and embarrassment washed over me.

Someone shouted, "I love this one!"

Lynn went on reciting, in detail, descriptions of my private parts. She described the shaft, the testicles, the pubic hair, and even the wrinkles in the scrotum. Smiling throughout the entire ordeal and pointing directly at me, she proudly recited lines like:

"I would like to detach it and take it for walks with me."

"We would go to the beach, but I would make sure I would not get sand in it."

"Sometimes, I would rub it on my face and kiss it good night. It likes that. I can tell."

"I not only love his penis, but I think I love the man who it is attached to."

As the crowd clapped and I stood there with a red face, Lynn looked at me with one of those, "Gotcha, muthafucka!" faces.

All I could think was, "Touché."

Lynn quickly grabbed my hand took me out for a wild night in the dorms. From room to room, we drank a variety of alcohol and smoked a variety of marijuana. One of her friends needed to jump start his truck. Always being a helpful kind of person, I found myself standing in the snowy parking lot with jumper cables. As Lynn smoked a cigarette, she asked, "Hey, Moe. I wrote a poem. Do you want to hear it?" My head hit the hood as I heard Lynn recite, "Dedicated to My Lover's Penis." When she was finishing reading the poem, she giggled. Then, with an almost vengeful and sarcastic wit, she said, "Moe, guess who the poem is about?" With both pointer fingers aimed at me, Lynn said, "This guy right here!" I walked through the night with Lynn holding the reins of the evening.

Walking back into the dorms, Lynn joked, "See, this is proof that the pen is mightier than the sword."

I replied, "Especially when your pen is writing about my sword."

We partied through the evening. From dorm room to dorm room, I smoked more weed and drank more alcohol. The students listened to a variety of music ranging from Violent Femmes, Bob Marley, The Cure, New Order, A Tribe Called Quest, Faith No More, Nirvana, Beastie Boys, Echo & the Bunnymen, Guns & Roses, Roxy Music, Led Zeppelin, and others. Although I do not like all of those bands, they seem tolerable when you are 17 and the drugs and alcohol are free. At least I did not have to listen to New Kids on the Block. Walking down the halls, I heard a drunken guy say, "Hey! You're the man with the penis!"

"Yes," I said. "I am the man with the penis. Thank you very much."

"I have to go to the bathroom!" Lynn said and disappeared.

Suddenly, the blonde cheerleader from earlier came walking

THE COOLEST WAY TO KILL YOURSELF

down the hallway with one of her cheerleader-esque friends. "Hey," she said with a slightly drunk way about her. "You."

"Me," I said.

"Is your penis that great?" she asked.

"I don't know. I guess it's good enough for someone to write a poem about it and share it with an entire college."

She smiled and gave me a flirtatious slap on my ass. Before she walked on, she commented, "If you break her heart, we will break that penis of yours." Some football player came by and grabbed her ass in the most unromantic and garish way possible. There I was with someone walking around reciting a poem about my private parts while this meathead was one date rape away from getting expelled from college.

Drunk and stoned, I closed my eyes for one second. As soon as I opened my eyes, I saw the white hippie guy with dreadlocks in my face.

"Hi," he said in a smoky and somewhat psychotic voice.

"Hello," I said with freshly wide-open eyes.

"Lynn really likes you," he said.

"Yes, she does," I responded.

"She wrote a poem about your penis."

"Yes, she did." I slowly tried to move away by sliding my back against the wall.

"You must have a real nice penis," he commented as he nodded up and down.

Suddenly, Lynn reappeared, grabbed my hand and yelled, "He's mine! Shoo! Go away!"

We stumbled back to her dorm room. As soon as we closed the door behind us, she locked it. In my astonishment, I asked, "Lynn, what the fuck?"

"You like that?" she said, laughing as she looked into my eyes with a hunger.

Out of all the jokes I played on her and all the times I made fun of her, she ended up being the winner.

"You wrote a poem about my cock and recited it to everyone!" I exclaimed.

"I know!" she laughed. We looked right into each other's eyes like warriors with a mutual respect. "I knew you would get a kick out of it. Your ego will not let you hate it."

"Wait," I said. "That's not what I mean…"

"Shut up and kiss me!" she demanded and pulled me close to her. Our bodies became a sexual tornado and clothes flew across the room landing on desks, the small refrigerator, and a television set. She had me completely figured out. The combination had been cracked, but I was more than willing to let this robbery take place. I enjoyed it. My crafty ways of practical jokes and clever antics were checkmated by Lynn. There was absolutely nothing I could do. There was nothing astute I could say. She did it. She absolutely won. She got me and she knew it. I did not know if I should be embarrassed or proud of her technique. During that evening, Lynn was perfect. She was in her element. She was strong. She was beautiful, witty, intelligent, sexy, poetic, and victorious.

EPILOGUE

My dear friend who has come all this way with me, please stop reading this and tell the person you love that you love them. Let me know when you return.

You're back? Seriously, did you really do it? I would rather you threw this in the ocean if it meant that you had loving arms around you. I know what I'm talking about. I miss her so much it hurts. Tears are falling down my cheeks while I write this sentence that you read.

Here is the end scene:

I packed my bag, my car, and said my goodbyes. I was heartbroken, but so thankful that I had been given the opportunity to love and be loved so much that my heart could break. I was thankful someone loved me. As I left Spotswood, I realized that we are all in need of love. We are all equal in this way. We are all people who just need some kind, any kind of love in our lives and we should be thankful when it is there.

I found love and I lost love, but made sure we both experienced our love for each other. I found love in every sense of the word. We would have done anything for each other, and we did. Lynn and I shared a level of trust that no other couple we knew had. We did crazy, wonderful, kinky and creative things. Our love made us better people. My old self is dead. I am a new person. I am no longer that selfish man who just wanted to have sex with women, get high, and be cool. I want love and I want to love. Lynn made many mistakes. We both did.

This is for love. I will find love again, but never like the love I found with her. I do not care what your opinion is of me. You can call me a drug addict. You can call me a sex addict. You can call me a pervert. You can call me a bad writer. You can call me a hack. You can call me corny. You can call me crazy. You can call me nostalgic, sentimental, and melancholy. Still, I am going to publish this book even if it kills me.

If the person you love is in the other room, go to them and hold them in your arms. Kiss the person you love and make them feel loved. It does not matter if you come across corny, weird, or insecure. You will miss the people who love you when they are gone. Be with them – honestly and completely – while they are still here.

The coolest way to kill yourself is to love.

THANK YOU:

My Goddess, D. I will always love you.
Thank you to the K. family, my family, Mokey, Melissa Blair, Arianna Astuni, Kevin Mallon, Rajvi P., Jessica Caine, Denise Sante, Phil Connor, Harsh Sharma, Tom Scharpling, Jon Wurster, WFMU, Dr. Danielle, Carley Castille, Rita Srenker, Mischa Sloan, Whitney Urheim Leon, Michelle Rodriguez, James Lockwood, Brian Roll, Jason Johnson, Withered Hand, Gary from The Lavender Pill Mob, Herve Lomprez of Trisomie 21, Andrew Burnett of Close Lobsters, Walter "Wattie" Mink of The Jasmine Minks, Momus, Cristina Monet Zilkha, Quinton from Woodbridge, Bridgette Laureux, Sean Kazelesky, Adam Hreha, Dan Cody, Kim Midlany, and you… the people with love in your heart.

Edited by Melissa Blair
Front cover by Melissa Blair

NICHOLAS TANEK

If there were a soundtrack for this book, it would be the following:

1) "Soon" by My Bloody Valentine
2) "Something's Burning" by The Stone Roses
3) "Loose Fit (Remix)" by Happy Mondays
4) "Plastic Dreams" by Jay Dee
5) "Paint A Vulgar Picture" by The Smiths
6) "Gravitate To Me" by The The
7) "Kinky Love" by Pale Saints
8) "Dry The Rain" by The Beta Band
9) "Mambo Sun" by T-Rex
10) "Cat Vs. Mouse" by Marxy
11) "Protection" by Massive Attack
12) "This Is Why You Love Me" by The Brian Jonestown Massacre
13) "A Prophecy" by Close Lobsters
14) "Lovelife" by Lush
15) "Laid" by James
16) "Bishonen" by Momus
17) "This Is Hardcore" by Pulp
18) "Tie Me Up" by Cinerama
19) "Believer" by Low Low Low La La La Love Love Love
20) "Herculeon" by The Good, The Bad, & The Queen
21) "Oxycontin" by El-P (f/ Central Services)
22) "Love Song" by Bongwater
23) "Duchess" by PAS/CAL
24) "Love In The Time Of Ecstasy" by Withered Hand
25) "You Are The Way" by The Primitives
26) "Weather To Fly" by Elbow
27) "Extra Ordinary" by Ultra Vivid Scene
28) "The Last Beat Of My Heart" by Siouxsie & The Banshees
29) "Mother Of Pearl" by Roxy Music